ROUGH

DIAMOND

a DANNY LANCASTER investigation

By BILL TODD

GOT A PROBLEM?

INVESTIGATOR FOR HIRE
EX-MILITARY NO JOB TOO SMALL
VERY FLEXIBLE RATES
Call DANNY on 07748 053 889
Email Dannylancaster1@gmail.com
or leave a message behind
the bar at The Bellerophon

ROUGH DIAMOND

First published in 2013 by DLE Publications - www.billtodd.co.uk

ISBN-13: 978-0-9575243-2-3

The Danny Lancaster crime thriller novels are available as paperbacks and ebooks.

THE WRECK OF THE MARGHERITA
DEATH SQUAD
ROUGH DIAMOND
ROCK HARD (Published winter 2013)

Find out more about the Danny Lancaster crime thriller series at

www.billtodd.co.uk

FOREWORD

NAMIBIA, EIGHT YEARS AGO

"Time to say goodbye to our passenger," said De Ruyter. And Steele felt sick again. He unclipped his safety harness and pulled himself to his feet, bracing against the juddering of the aircraft in the rising air currents.

He made his way along the narrow aisle. Half way down, the aircraft lurched and he had to grab for a seat back. Steele glanced at the cockpit. De Ruyter was grinning.

At the rear, the big black case was waiting for him. De Ruyter's instructions had been clear. He snapped open the catches and lifted the lid. The zip on the body bag inside was stiff at first, then it opened with a rush. Steele lurched backwards. The gutted corpse was staring at him, wide dull eyes, their blood-shot whites yellowing. Deeper in the bag he could see dismembered organs slithering about as the aircraft rose and fell.

One of his bullets had hit just below the man's nose. The other had struck the lower left side of his face, ripped away part of the jaw, exposed broken teeth embedded in dull raw meat. The head was an odd shape, like a punctured football. Steele tried not to picture the exit wound at the back.

He braced himself against a seat and pushed the case towards the door. When he popped the latch the wind howled. He gave another heave. The case teetered on the edge. Then the wind took it and it toppled out into the air.

Gripping the edge of the door, Steele peered out. The open case turned over and over as it fell. Then the body bag fell out. The two objects dropped in close formation, tumbling as they plunged. Steele couldn't tear his eyes away.

He stopped breathing when an arm flopped out of the body bag. It was the courier's final farewell as the case and body bag smacked into the water, disappearing under flumes of spray.

Back in the cockpit, Steele strapped himself in, put his headphones on and lit a cigarette. Inland, purple and ochre desert was mottled by fuzzy puffs of cloud shadow. To the west, rows of long Atlantic breakers rolled in to pound the coast.

Steele looked across at De Ruyter. The man seemed to be whistling silently. He was enjoying himself. He caught Steele's eye, grinned, jerked his head.

Steele turned to see gigantic orange dunes a thousand feet high marching down to the waterline where banks of fog born from the icy Benguela Current rolled inland.

"The Langewand," said De Ruyter. "One of the driest places on earth. Oldest desert in the world, so they say."

Steele gripped his harness as the aircraft dipped sharply. Just when he thought they were going into the fog De Ruyter swooped under it and suddenly they were 40 feet above the beach, skimming sand ridges in a world of desolation stripped of its colour by the sinister light.

After cruising at 4,000 feet the aircraft seemed to Steele to be flying at a suicidal speed, streaking along with dark green waves boiling into white foam to their left, dull yellow dunes striped with 4x4 tracks rising above them on the left under a canopy of gloomily luminous fog.

"For Christ's sake…"

The 690 pulled up hard, instantly disappearing into the fog, climbing hard until it burst into clear sky. Steele saw a strange halo effect chasing them on the cloud below and realised it was the aircraft's shadow with the sun prisming through the Perspex.

"What the fuck do you…"

He looked across at De Ruyter. He was laughing.

"Relax, man. We've done it. Kaapse Kobra, we've really bloody done it. Have a little fun."

He wriggled in his seat, dug in his pocket, threw a small black cotton bag to Steele. It felt damp in his hand.

He opened the drawstring, tipped the contents into the palm of his hand. His face cracked into a grin, the scare of the beach minutes ago forgotten.

"Not bad, eh?" said De Ruyter. "What do you say, eh?"

Steele felt the aircraft manoeuvre but he couldn't take his eyes away from the contents of his hand. They didn't look like much, not what most people would imagine. And they were tinged red in places. But there were a lot of them, more than they had expected.

Steele heard his headphones hiss as De Ruyter clicked to transmit.

"Marine One, Marine One, this is Airborne One. We're passing Sandwich Harbour, turning for Walvis Bay now."

Steele vaguely heard a crackling acknowledgement but he was too absorbed teasing the stones in the palm of his hand with a finger.

De Ruyter returned the radio to 122.5 and called Walvis Bay control for permission to land on Runway 27 into the prevailing southwester. He looked down to check his position, saw the remains of the old American whaling station, began a belated climb to clear the salt pans and lagoons of the wetland bird sanctuary.

Steele wasn't listening, all his attention focussed on the stones that rested so lightly on his hand.

He felt the aircraft begin to turn as De Ruyter lined up his approach to the airport ten miles inland.

Steele stirred the stones until his eye caught something. He picked one out and held it up between his thumb and forefinger.

De Ruyter saw the gesture, looked across, saw the size and the pink patina. He whistled.

"Wow, that's what you call a blood diamond. Look at the shape, and that pattern. It looks like a demon's eye." He was laughing again.

De Ruyter looked back towards the airport. "We're really going to . . . *FUCK!*"

Steele saw the man's head mutate into some cheap horror movie monster.

The cockpit was a blizzard of blood and feathers. They coated his face, filled his eyes and mouth, hot and thick.

The slipstream howled through the shattered windscreen.

The aircraft jerked as the pilot's hands spasmed on the controls.

Steele struggled to understand what he was seeing.

The mangled carcass of the flamingo sat where De Ruyter's head should have been.

Its long neck flopped about like some alien probe.

The 690 lurched, whining into a dive.

"Fuck, we're going down."

Steele gripped the dual control but he couldn't fight the dead man's rigid grip on the pilot's yoke.

Looking ahead, his whole world was filled with glowing orange sand.

Steele started to scream.

HERTFORDSHIRE, SEVEN YEARS AGO

She burst through the door and stopped as she saw herself in the mirror. The image took her breath away. Weird, looking at yourself like that, but it was true.

She'd always known she was a good-looking woman. Had no time for those who spent their lives torturing themselves over big bums or droopy tits.

No one's perfect. She'd always thought her jaw was a bit too big, a bit manish. And the pounds would pile on her hips if she got careless. Maybe her feet would be better a size smaller. It didn't matter. The basics were fine – good tits, good legs - and she had the confidence and personality to capitalise on that.

But today was different. The wedding dress looked fantastic, a great waterfall of white satin tumbling to the floor, the veil cascading down over her long chestnut hair. It felt sexy against her skin, stroked her as she walked.

It was the best she had ever looked. She looked hot. She looked powerful. She was loving it.

"You look bloody fantastic."

Startled, she turned. He wasn't looking too shabby either. Morning suit, immaculate creases, shimmering waistcoat.

"Not looking too bad yourself."

He moved to her, tried to kiss her. She ducked away.

"Not the make-up."

"Come on, babe, you look amazing."

He nuzzled her neck. She purred.

"Somehow I never really thought you'd go through with this."

His hand cupped her breast.

She let out a long sigh.

"I had my reasons."

"You always do, babe."

His hand clawed up an armful of dress and she made a low growling noise. His fast breathing dampened her neck. The hand became frantic.

"Steady."

"Can't help it, babe. You just look too good."

She kissed him on the mouth, careful not to smudge her lipstick.

"You're crazy, we've got guests downstairs."

"They're all propping up the free bar. They'll never miss us. Five minutes, babe, just five minutes."

She kissed him again.

"You really are mad. That's probably why I love you."

He stood, lips parted, watching her face, high colour in his cheeks, eyes wide and bright, breathing hard.

She made him wait just too long, just to the point where desperation was taking over. Then she turned, bent over the dressing table and lifted the tumbling folds of her white dress.

She smiled when she heard the intake of his breath, knew he was drinking in the long legs, the white stocking, the garter, the flash of white silk thong between tanned buttocks.

He ripped the thong down her thighs with one swipe. Went at her like a farmyard animal. She had driven him to the boil and now he was whistling like a kettle.

He gripped her hips, pounded into her without control. Perfume bottles and jars of cream rattled and clattered on the dressing table.

She could see him in the make-up mirror, face red, mouth open, eyes distant. For all their flash clothes, their fast cars and their swagger, you could control them like puppies if you played it right, suck their spine out through their dick.

He thought he was a big man, a player. He thought he was smart, ahead of the game. Now he looked like a character in one of those old cartoons, when they stick their finger in an electric socket, hair on end, tongue hanging out, eyes on stalks.

Then his breath became short and rasping. This was the bit she always liked. When they were desperate, trapped, helpless. Total control.

Play that right and you could mould their entire lives for a few minutes of frenzy.

His gasps came closer and closer. Then she heard the grunt, felt the grip on her waist slacken.

She felt him take a step back and knew what he was about to do.

"Not on the dress! Use a tissue. They're on the dresser."

He wiped himself and smoothed his hair down.

She turned, pulling up the thong, saw the sloppy schoolboy smile.

"You really are something else, babe."

They both heard Bill's voice call up the stairs.

He shovelled himself back into the trousers of his morning suit. The creases weren't so crisp now.

He grinned. "Better get a move on. Your new hubby's coming."

They looked at each other and laughed.

CHAPTER 1

DEVIL'S DYKE, BRIGHTON, TUESDAY

Amazing thing, the human body. An intricate framework of linked bones powered by a complicated lattice of muscles, fuelled by a maze of tubes carrying oxygenated blood.

Fair enough, it's not indestructible. But it can flex and move in many ways, carry loads, withstand extremes of temperature.

You can even chop bits off and it'll carry on pretty much as before.

Danny zoomed the telephoto lens of his old digital camera. An attractive brunette wearing tight jeans tucked into brown boots snapped into focus. He smiled at the tick, tick, tick of multiple exposures.

He refocused on the hill opposite and snapped a few more. Digital was wonderful. You could bang away to your heart's content and delete the rubbish later. A lot easier than picking them up from Boots a week after you'd taken them.

And there was nothing wrong with enjoying a clear day at a local beauty spot, fill your lungs, get a bit of exercise, have a go at your hobby of photography. Nice and relaxed, just snapping anything of interest. An ordinary punter.

A movement caught the corner of his eye. Danny squinted against the brightness of the sky as the paraglider banked round to the west, the dot of a man swinging out like a pendulum under his narrow parafoil.

He swung the camera up, focussed, tracking the fluid movement as the bright red canopy rode the air.

As he came out of his turn the paraglider hung in the air for a few seconds, then began a gentle spiral down towards the crest of the hill.

Danny tracked his progress, snapping away as his target grew bigger.

Fifteen feet from the ground the man pulled his toggles to spill air and braced his bent legs. The canopy flared, his feet touched the grass and he walked half a dozen paces to a stop.

Danny took more bursts of pictures as the man turned and began to gather his collapsing chute.

As Michael Onslow, a graphic designer from Tunbridge Wells, looked towards the car park, Danny snapped another picture of him, helmet on, bulging folds of synthetic red OLKS fabric in his arms, a clear full-face image. The money shot.

As Onslow began folding his canopy into his stuff bag Danny flipped the camera to video and filmed him tidying up his equipment.

As a former paratrooper, Danny had to admire the man's skill and lightness of touch. It had been a textbook landing, gliding to touchdown with the delicacy of a dancer.

Onslow would need a bit of fancy footwork on Monday when his boss asked just how bad was the back injury that had kept him off work for so long.

Danny looked at the Bremont watch on his wrist. Just time for a spot of lunch before his next appointment. Business was on the up.

***

"Steak knife, pencil, two biros - one red, one black - box of matches." Danny sat back, head tilted to the ceiling, eyes screwed shut, concentrating.

"Kitkat, banana, five tea bags ... no ... six, corkscrew, phone charger, 50p piece - an Olympics one - two 2p pieces, screwdriver, condom - strawberry flavour."

Sitting cross-legged on the living room carpet, he opened his eyes, looked at the ceiling, studied the nicotine stains. Observation, reasoning, keeping the mind flexible, they were tools of his trade, skills he needed to sharpen. Sudoku Wally down the Bellerophon might be a grumpy old sod but he had all his marbles. In combat, miss a movement, or a lack of movement, something out of the ordinary, and it could kill you.

In this detecting business, tiny details counted. Looking was no good. You had to see, really see what was in front of you.

A muffled voice came down the hallway.

"Was your lunch ok?"

Danny looked at the last bite of his tuna sandwich on a plate by his knee. He still had his Kitkat to look forward to.

"Fine, thanks."

"I've sorted your mum. She was a bit restless but I think she'll settle now she's clean. I've got to get off. See you later."

He heard the front door close behind Emma, part-time carer, part-time girlfriend, as she headed home to her waste-of-space husband Benny.

Danny ran through his list again until he was satisfied, then whipped the tea towel from the tray. His eyes ranged over its contents.

"Sod, I missed the door key... and it was five tea bags."

If he could field strip, clean and reassemble an L85 assault rifle blindfold this shouldn't be so hard. It was always the same, practise, practise, practise.

He checked his watch, picked up his jacket. Time for a new client. On the way out he slipped quietly into his mother's room. Emma's clean up and the nappy change had freshened the place up a bit but you could never get rid of that bitter tang of ammonia.

His mother lay still, on her back, between the raised sides of the hospital bed just as she did every day.

Danny watched the metronome rise and fall of her shallow breathing, wondered what, if anything, was going on in her head.

He stepped silently forward, leaned and kissed her lightly on the forehead. Her skin was cold and salty. He paused at the door, looked back, left.

***

ST ANN'S WELL GARDENS, HOVE

Big dark eyes and a cute nose, shy nature but a sharp brain. No doubting, it was picture postcard pretty.

But beneath the cuddly exterior was a nature that could shred wiring, chew through pipes and play havoc in your garden with its frantic digging up and burying.

Danny looked at the squirrels. He had read about them in Jubilee Library, how the American greys had driven out the reds. They looked good, had the kids and grannies in the park pointing and cooing, but he was never sure whether they were cuddly story book creatures or acrobatic rats, probably both. Nothing's ever quite what it seems.

"Sure you wouldn't like a slice of cake with that?"

The woman with her handbag on her lap, neatly folded Daily Mail peeking through the open zip, looked up at Danny, startled.

"Oh, er, no thank you."

Danny put down two cups of tea and a slice of bread pudding on the cafe terrace table. The fresh air up on Devil's Dyke had given him an appetite.

"Hope you don't mind, had to skip breakfast."

She shook her head. They sat in silence, surrounded by yummy mummies sipping lattes and picking at salads.

A toddler, thrilled to discover his legs could be used for walking, tottered after a pigeon that stayed just ahead of his unsteady steps.

Two shrieking seagulls battled for a discarded pastry on a nearby table.

Danny sat back and smiled up at the sunshine, a brief window of good weather as the damp of autumn crept in. It was a beautiful spot, a little hidden oasis in the middle of the city, a stone's throw from the water.

He had come across St Ann's Well Gardens by accident when out running and had been back several times. Now he had his library on one side of town and this on the other when he fancied a bit of peace and quiet.

And he valued a bit of time on his own. Business was picking up. He was starting to get established, starting to earn. He reckoned that made him a professional in the detecting lark.

True, the money was all peaks and troughs but the peaks had paid pretty well, enough to cover the troughs. Just.

Danny sipped his tea, lit a cigarette, looked across at the woman.

He put her at mid-forties, give or take. Fit for her age with just a hint of fat gathering at the hips. She was fashionably turned out in a blue coat, blouse and skirt, restrained in an M&S sort of way, smart but safe.

Her highlighted blonde hair was immaculate. Minimal make-up had been applied with care. Both hands gripped the bag as if she needed something to hide behind.

"So how did you find me? Was it the website?"

Marion Carter shook her head. "No, I'm not very good with computers. I saw your card in a newsagent's window."

Danny looked faintly disappointed. Maybe he could get Karol to pep up the site a bit. He sipped his tea.

"You're very young, younger than I expected," said Mrs Carter.

"Older than I look," said Danny.

He drank his tea, lit another cigarette, watched the toddler chasing the pigeon, legs wobbling as he tired.

"In your own time, Mrs Carter."

She nodded, lifted her tea cup, sniffed to test the temperature.

"You said something on the phone about your husband being missing."

"Yes," said Mrs Carter.

"I know it's difficult. Just take your time and tell me what happened."

Marion Carter sipped her tea, gathered her thoughts. The cup clattered against the saucer as she put it down. She dabbed at the corner of her mouth with a manicured finger.

"There is one thing I want to make perfectly clear from the start, Mr Lancaster."

"Sure."

"I'm not some sort of tart."

Danny looked at Mrs Carter.

"Just begin at the beginning and we'll see how we go, eh?"

Her fingers gripped the bag a little tighter. She nodded sharply once.

"My husband won the lottery, then he disappeared."

Danny nodded and wrote something in his notebook.

"Big win, was it?"

"I don't know."

"Millions?"

"It must have been, what with all the big plans he suddenly came out with. But he didn't say how much. I can't find any record of it at home and there's no sign of it in our bank account."

"So he's taken the money and run. Do you think he went alone or is there someone else involved?"

The fingers gripped the bag even tighter. "No, no, nothing like that. We had a little… misunderstanding."

Danny looked up from his notes, "Oh?"

"When it happened, his win, Bill was so excited. He said we would be set up for life. He said we were moving to Thailand. We've been on holiday there a few times and both love the place. The people are so kind. Bill said we could live like royalty there on the money he'd won."

"But you weren't so keen?"

"We'll, no, not really. A holiday's one thing but moving permanently, away from family and all our friends, it's a very big step."

"And did you tell him this?"

"I tried but he was mad keen. He wouldn't stop talking about it, making lists, looking at property websites. You know what men are like when they get an idea in their heads."

Danny shrugged, kept writing in his notebook.

"Still, I would have gone with him. I wasn't against the idea. It was just such a rush, such a shock. I needed some time. I told you I wasn't good with computers. Well, a friend helped me get on to Facebook, you know, so I could keep in contact with everyone."

"And did you?"

"Yes, I signed up most of our friends and even found a few people from school I haven't seen in I don't know how long."

Her head dropped and she stared intently into her lap.

"And?"

The fingers danced along the top of the bag as if they were playing some dramatic piano passage. The long pause was broken by the squeals of the toddler who had his second wind and was chasing pigeons again.

"A long time ago, Bill and I, well, we hit a bit of a rough patch, if you know what I mean. He was working very hard, always tired, often moody. It all got a bit on top of me. My nerves were bad. I didn't know what to do. I was at my wits end. Then I met Ron."

The hands were still again now, clamping the bag shut, bending the protruding Daily Mail.

"Take your time, Mrs Carter. I know this is hard."

"I told you, Mr Lancaster, I'm not some sort of tart. But everyone makes mistakes, everyone has their weak moments and Ron was mine. He was a friend, fun, he made me laugh, made me feel young again, wanted. Being with him made my problems feel smaller, like I could cope. Does that sound stupid?"

"No, Mrs Carter, not at all."

"I'm not proud of what I did, Mr Lancaster, But I don't regret it either. Does that make sense?"

"Perfect sense, Mrs Carter. And did your husband find out?"

"The day before yesterday."

Danny looked up from his notepad, stubby bookie's biro in mid-air.

"The day before yesterday?"

Mrs Carter shuffled in her seat, avoiding Danny's eyes.

"I told you I was trying to keep in touch with friends on Facebook, for when we moved."

"And Ron was one of them?"

Mrs Carter nodded.

"What happened?" asked Danny.

"I was using Bill's laptop, just checking if anyone new had accepted my friend invitations. Then the smoke alarm went. I was so distracted I'd left dinner up a bit high. I went to sort it out and when I came back Bill was coming out of the lounge looking like he'd seen a ghost. He just pushed past me and went running upstairs.

"When I looked at the computer I realised I'd left Ron up on the screen. There was nothing, you know, explicit, just affection really. But it was enough for Bill to put two and two together."

"And then he disappeared?"

"He spent about half an hour upstairs, then came down, put on his jacket and said he was going to the pub. I said what about dinner and he was very rude to me. He slammed the front door and I haven't seen him since."

Danny nodded, tapping his upper lip with his pen.

"So he just dashed out? Spur of the moment. Nothing planned?"

Mrs Carter nodded.

"Does he know where Ron lives?"

Mrs Carter shook her head. "No, he's in Essex, Basildon, but that wasn't on his Facebook page."

"Is Bill's passport still in the house?"

She thought for a moment. "I haven't checked. No, wait a minute, we sent them away through the Post Office to be renewed. The new ones haven't come back yet."

Danny made more notes. "So, chances are, he hasn't left the country. When you made contact with … Ron?"

"Yes, Ron Hedges."

"When you made contact with Ron was that the first time since you …"

"Yes, it was amicable when we parted. We were good friends. But I wanted a complete break, a start afresh."

"And you haven't had any contact since?"

"No, Ron said he'd being trying to find me, just to keep in touch, as a friend."

"Have you any idea where your husband might have gone? Does he have any favourite places to visit or any hobbies, fishing, walking?"

Marion Carter shook her head. "No, nothing like that. His only interest is his garden and his tropical fish and they're at home with me."

"Mrs Carter, I have to ask this. Is there anyone he might go to, maybe another woman?"

"Bill? No! He was devoted to me. He wouldn't dare."

"Are you sure? I mean, you had your secret, maybe Bill had his. Guys get to an age and, you know, they try to live their youth again, bikes, girls, that sort of thing."

Marion Carter gave Danny a look that would wither flowers. Danny looked down at his notepad.

"Have you reported him missing to the police?"

"No, I… I didn't want them asking question, you know, about why he went. Then this arrived."

Marion Carter looked left and right, then drew an envelope from her bag and slid it across to Danny.

He picked it up, turned it over in his hands. White letter envelope, no address, no markings.

"It came through the letterbox yesterday."

Danny opened it and unfolded a sheet of A4 white paper. The message was written in untidy rows of type but from newspaper headlines. WE HAVE BILL. WAIT FOR PHONE CALL. NO POLICE

Marion Carter looked nervously around to make sure no one was looking as Danny studied the note, tilting it against the light. The roughly cut rectangles of newspaper headline were each held by a dab of Pritt Stick at their centre.

He folded each section over to study the back, careful not to tear the note. When he was satisfied, Danny folded the letter, put it back in the envelope.

"Can I hang on to that?"

"Must you?"

"I'd like to take a closer look later."

She gave him a reluctant half nod.

"Have you heard from them?"

Marion Carter shook her head.

"So, let me run through this," said Danny. "Just so I've got it straight. Bill says he's won the lottery and wants to move abroad. He finds out about your ex-boyfriend..."

Danny saw Mrs Carter wince.

"Bill found about your former friend and stormed out. Then you get a note that says someone's holding him."

Mrs Carter nodded.

"Did he tell anyone about the win?"

"I don't think so. I don't know."

"Fair enough," said Danny. "It would be helpful if I could visit the house, just to get some idea about the guy, and I'll need a recent photo. I'll call you tomorrow if that's ok."

"That's fine. I have some albums." Marion Carter opened her bag and took out another white envelope. It looked reassuringly thick.

"As discussed on the phone, Mr Lancaster."

Danny slipped the envelope into his pocket.

"Thank you, Mrs Carter. I shall do my very best for you."

"Thank you, Mr Lancaster."

Marion Carter seemed relieved her ordeal was over as she pulled the strap of her bag over her shoulder and stood up.

"I'll wait to hear."

Danny watched her go, long strides across the grass as if she were trying to increase the distance as fast as she decently could without breaking into a run.

School was out and the park was filling quickly with mums, their kids and the odd father or grandfather. Pigeons gathered for the expected crumbs.

Danny looked up, caught the eye of a young mum sitting at a bench on the grass as she studied him. She looked sharply away which sent her friend into a fit of giggles.

He looked down at his notes and tidied up a few scribbled words so he would be able to decipher them later. When he looked up the toddling pigeon fancier was being scooped up by his mother and walked towards his buggy. He protested, wriggled in her arms, pointing back at the birds.

Danny turned slightly and saw Mrs Carter as she started up the sloping path. Then he noticed that a young guy sitting on a bench at the top of the embankment was watching her. As she reached the trees the watcher stubbed out his cigarette on the arm of the bench, jumped up, stuffed a newspaper into his pocket and went after her.

Danny slotted his stubby biro down the spiral binding of his notebook, drained his tea and went after them.

CHAPTER 2

Danny walked through a grove of gnarled old trees, up the crumbling tarmac path past St Ann's Well. As he emerged from the park, he had no view of the junction downhill. He had no sight of Mrs Carter but the watcher was passing the bus stop, crossing over.

Danny went after him, saw him cut left at the junction through the driveway of a posh block of flats. By the time he was heading east along Lansdowne Road he could see the watcher passing the Buddhist centre opposite Winston Churchill's old school.

Parked cars along the north kerb offered good cover. Danny sped up so he didn't lose them beyond the rise in the road as Lansdowne turned into Montpelier Place.

When Mrs Carter reached the traffic lights Danny saw her turn right into Montpelier Road. The guy was still fifty yards behind his target. Danny crossed the road to get an oblique view of the watcher and then watched. He could see the traffic of Western Road zipping back and forth and, beyond that, the grey green of the sea.

At the bottom of the hill she stopped, took out her mobile. Danny watched but couldn't make out what Marion Carter was doing as she turned her head from side to side.

When she'd finished whatever it was she turned left into Western Road, her tail following. Danny sprinted to the corner to avoid losing them in the crowds of the shopping street. Had to keep eyes on. He took a peek, then waited a few seconds until the gap between them was wide enough.

Marion Carter was obviously a walker, keeping up a brisk pace in her flat, sensible shoes.

They both saw her pass Waitrose and McDonald's. As they approached Churchill Square she slowed, glancing in shop windows, pausing outside Primark. Danny thought she seemed to turn up her nose but it was hard to be sure at that range.

The watcher had closed up to keep her in sight amid the knots of shoppers. Danny narrowed the distance.

Marion Carter dodged across the busy road and used the ATM outside Santander before window shopping a little further along at Ann Summers.

Danny and the watcher hovered in doorways and were caught by surprise when she checked the traffic and darted between two buses to the opposite pavement.

The watcher kept with her but Danny was blocked by another bus. Just as he reached the other side he spotted her blue coat disappearing into Marks & Spencer.

Danny tried to blend, stopping to listen to a young busker with an acoustic guitar, head back, eyes closed, make a passable shot at the climax of Stairway To Heaven before strumming seamlessly into the opening bars of All Along The Watch Tower. He lobbed a pound coin into the guy's open guitar case.

Danny glanced across at a bunch of schoolgirls playing hooky. They were laughing wildly, dancing, acting out something they'd seen on a TV talent show. One threw her head back and started to sing. More laughter.

Danny envied their simple joy, moved closer to the door of M&S, wishing he knew how many exits the place had.

And there were other questions. If your husband stomped off in a huff, why do you get a ransom note? If he's vanished suddenly, would your first reaction be to go shopping? Maybe she just wanted to do something familiar, comforting. But it jarred with Danny.

As he looked in a shop window he saw the reflection of the watcher waiting at a bus stop ten feet behind him.

Danny sauntered on, hands in pockets, trying to look like just another shopper. When he was clear of the bus stop he took out his phone and snapped the watcher. But the guy was side on, his features screened by the hood of his fleece.

Danny considered manoeuvring to the opposite side of the bus stop when a patch of blue caught his eye in the crowd.

Danny looked at the watcher but the guy didn't react. Something didn't feel right. He started after Marion Carter, back along Western Road, then he realised. The coat was similar but it wasn't her.

He wheeled round and ran back to the store, bumping into two chattering girls. He apologised and swung back to see Mrs Carter board a single-decker No81 bus. As the queue shuffled on board he could see the watcher two people behind her.

He was running hard now, 20 feet from the bus when the doors hissed shut and it pulled away from the kerb.

He ran. Knew it was pointless. But Danny was angry with himself and he ran, all the time watching the bus pull further away.

He was 200 yards down Western Road and attracting attention when he gave up and watched the bus disappear into traffic.

***

Bradley Wilkins was having a good day. The contract to do the graphics for that new fusion food restaurant was a life-saver.

Business had been tough, setting up and getting established in the current economic climate. And you could travel the world for the cost of a MacBook Pro.

Then there was the competition. It seemed as if every third person in Brighton was a graphic designer. It had all seemed so simple at college.

But things were looking good now. He and Garry had nearly finished decorating the flat. Money was tight but it had been worth the effort.

All he needed now were a few bits and bobs from the Apple Store in the Churchill Square mall, then pick up some fresh aubergines and ricotta for tonight's pasta extravaganza and he'd be off home to Garry.

Bradley's day was ruined seconds later when an angry man burst through the crowd and grabbed his bike. It was out of his hands before he could react. The man swung into the saddle and was gone.

Bradley pointed to where his bike had vanished but the wall of shoppers had closed behind the thief.

"My Claud Butler," he muttered.

Stunned and disbelieving, Bradley, a splash of Lycra misery amid the bargain hunters, watched his helmet roll away down the pavement.

***

The watcher on the No81 sat three rows behind Marion Carter, hands in pockets, gazing out of the window. The bus was busy, one bored face among many.

He felt his phone vibrate, pulled it from inside his fleece, read the text message.

The aisle was crowded but he leaned sideways to look back towards the rear window. He couldn't see anything. It didn't matter. He already knew.

***

The bus was out of sight beyond Waitrose by the time Danny had mounted, wobbled, then gathered enough speed to keep stable.

As he racked his brains for the route of the No81 he almost hit two chatting girls as they stepped off the pavement.

Then it came to him. The 81 went down Western Road, kept going when it changed into Church Road in Hove before hanging a right inland up Tisbury Road. Then it dog-legged around Blatchington Road and Goldstone Villas to Hove Station before carrying on to the top of the town at King George VI Avenue.

Danny knew Hove, the city's other half, from his minicabbing days and wet afternoons studying street maps in Jubilee Library. The place was very different from Brighton. The residents made a point of it, said they lived in "Hove, actually." Lots of money there. Big double-fronted villas, ornate red stone houses that looked like Scottish castles.

Danny knew Marion Carter lived in the Wilbury area so it was a fair bet she'd get off the 81 at the railway station and use the footbridge. He knew the bus was somewhere ahead but it was starting to get dark now and he could waste valuable time trying to find it along the main road. He had a corner to cut.

But first he needed to make some distance. Danny leaned into it, powering down Western Road so fast with no lights that pedestrians stopped to watch.

As he raced past City Books a police car flashed its headlamps but it was travelling the other way and Danny was gone before it could react. He heard its siren whoop whoop a warning as he overtook a people carrier and a Toyota hatchback.

He streaked past St John's Church and out of Palmeira Square into Church Road, slicing over the zebra crossing as an elderly couple stepped off the pavement. Just beyond, he moved out to pass a bus. As he drew level it indicated and began to pull away.

Danny threw the bike to the right and stared straight into the headlights of an oncoming van. With no time to cross back he passed the front of the van with feet to spare and managed to straighten up just before he hit the opposite kerb.

Traffic was heavy and he pedalled against the flow until he spotting a gap and cut back across to the westbound lane.

The lights at the junction with Grand Avenue and The Drive were against him but he took a chance and swung right. Danny was lucky that the Skoda driver had good reactions.

The guy slammed on his brakes and swerved as soon as Danny cut across in front of him, managed to hit his horn as he went into a slide, skidding to a stop an arm's length from the Smart car waiting to turn right across the junction.

It was too late by the time Danny realised he was going too fast. At the apex of his turn the slender road race tyres lost it. The bike went from under him and Catherine-wheeled onto the pavement. Danny hit the tarmac and rolled, narrowly missing the street sign by the kerb, grateful for the dumpster that stopped him slamming into the wall of Caffè Nero on the corner.

Panting and sweaty, he checked himself and the bike. A few dents and scratches. Nothing Serious. Danny had felt the frame crack against his left shin as it went over. He grinned. No chance of a break or bruising. One advantage of a prosthetic leg.

He mounted up and began pumping up the gentle incline of the broad tree-lined avenue of villas and flats that was The Drive.

The lights at the Eaton Road junction were green and he powered straight across. He heard a siren, ignored it. An ambulance nosed out of a side street just ahead.

The lights at Cromwell Road were red. He took a quick look, left and right, and kept going.

Beyond the junction the big old period houses gave way to small blocks of modern flats.

The Drive narrowed with heavy parking along both sides but it was a short sprint to where it crossed the railway line. Danny powered on, breathing hard now. As the road dipped beyond the bridge Danny coasted down and freewheeled in a wide right turn into Wilbury Avenue.

***

Danny skidded to a halt opposite Marion Carter's home and dropped the bike against a hedge. Cloud masked the last of the daylight and the shadows were deepening. The street was deserted.

He studied the house. Discreetly expensive, a carefully trimmed front lawn and razor-edge flower beds with plants in regimented rows. Blue Toyota Prius on the drive.

The paintwork on the walls and frames was perfect. Net curtains hung in the ground floor windows, all identical. There was a light in the porch and another upstairs.

Danny crossed the road and down the front path. All was quiet. The immaculate gloss of the front door gleamed under the porch light. A coconut mat bore the greeting "welcome".

He guessed the path at the side of the house led to the rear garden. Bill Carter's pride and joy.

There was a gate. It was slightly open.

Danny gave it a gentle push and it swung wide, silent on freshly-oiled hinges. The side passage was in darkness but he could see flower beds beyond and a shed at the end of the garden.

He padded silently along the side of the house, ducking to slide below the sill of a kitchen window, watching the garden ahead and listening. He stopped at the end of the path and braced himself to peer round.

It was like being hit by a falling wardrobe. The guy must have weighed 15 stone, slammed Danny against the fence with the full force of his body.

The breath punched out of him, Danny sagged. Big hands grabbed the collar of his jacket. Danny brought his arms up in front of his face, snapping them apart to break the man's grip.

It spoiled the watcher's balance, caused him to topple which saved him from the full force of Danny's punch. Danny's momentum carried him forward and he took a counter-punch in the side, costing him the lost breath he'd just recovered.

Danny put out an arm against the kitchen wall to save himself from falling into it. As he hauled himself upright he turned to see the reflective strips on the watcher's trainers flashing in the light from the kitchen as he legged it out of the gate.

Danny put his hand to his side as he breathed. No damage done but he was too surprised to give chase.

After a minute doubled up, regulating his breathing, he pulled himself upright and walked towards the gate.

The big knife missed his face by four inches.

CHAPTER 3

"I'm so sorry, Mr Lancaster. I don't know what to say. I am so, so sorry."

Danny sipped his tea and smiled.

"Don't worry about it. No harm done."

"I heard a noise. I suppose I panicked. We're in the Neighbourhood Watch. You hear things, read things in the local paper. There have been quite a few break-ins around here."

Danny drank more of his tea, weaker than he'd have liked but anything was ok in the circumstances. He looked up at Marion Carter wringing her hands as she sat on the sofa opposite.

"I heard noises, saw a shadow pass the kitchen window and thought it might be the kidnappers come back. I panicked. The knife was in the block on the work surface just underneath."

"Like I said, no harm done."

Danny put the cup on the table, took a dark chocolate Hobnob from the neatly-arranged pile on the delicate China plate. He considered telling Marion Carter she had been tailed but decided not to, didn't know quite why.

"You said you wanted to see the house but I wasn't expecting you so soon."

Danny finished his biscuit, picked up another.

"Don't upset yourself. Look, why not show me round now so I can get a feel for Bill?"

Mrs Carter rose, then stared strangely at Danny. At first he didn't take the hint. Then he did, finished his biscuit and dusted his fingers lightly over the plate. She nodded and led them out into the hall.

The Carter house didn't reveal much. Everything, furniture, fittings, decoration, was quality without being flashy. And ruthlessly neat.

Bill Carter's treasured tropical fish lived in a large tank in the breakfast room next to the kitchen and overlooking the garden. Danny leaned closer to watch slivers of brilliant colour weaving among the fronds and bubbles.

The garden was in total darkness now. Danny peered through the double glazing and could make out precise flowerbeds and perfect lawns. The centrepiece was a large ornate fountain, a girl sliding out of her robe as she rose from among the rocks.

Behind him, Mrs Carter flicked a switch and the garden was bathed in light. Floodlights illuminated the grass while small coloured lights picked out details of the flowerbeds and the trees at the far end by the fence.

"Very impressive," said Danny.

"The lights cost a fortune in electricity but Bill insists. There's a security light as well. It's more of a nuisance really. The foxes keep setting it off. Bill spends ages out there. And in all weathers. It really is the love of his life, that and his fish."

He turned to look at her face, see if she was telling him something. Impossible to tell from her expression. Maybe she was a good poker player.

Danny made a mental note of the security light. The garden had been in darkness when he'd been in the side passage so the watcher couldn't have got as far as the back of the house or he'd have triggered it.

"Do you have Ron's address?"

Mrs Carter stiffened. "Well... do you really need it?"

"I'd like to check if he's heard anything."

"But Bill couldn't know where Ron lives."

"Just being thorough," said Danny.

She nodded reluctantly, picked up a leather-bound address book, wrote the details on a small notepad.

"There you are. Well, I think that's everything, Mr Lancaster."

"The photo?"

"Oh, yes."

She picked up one she had selected earlier from the sideboard. "Will this do?"

Danny took the photo. It could have been the invisible man, nondescript face, small mouth, thinning hair. Reluctant eyes too close together. No distinguishing features. You could bump into him ten times in a day and never remember. Made you wonder why Marion Carter had.

"That's fine, thank you. Anyway, I'd better get going."

"Do you think I'll be safe here?"

"Don't worry. It was probably just some random prowler. Just be sure to lock up after me."

***

Danny was aware of Mrs Carter watching him from her front door as he walked away. He mounted the bike and waved as he rode away. Heard the door click shut. Saw a net curtain flutter across the road.

The visit hadn't produced much but he had a lot to think about. And he felt sorry for the bike guy. It had been an unavoidable emergency, but nonetheless.

No way was he taking it to a police station. After some thought he decided to drop it back close to where he'd taken it and hope no one else nicked it before it was found.

Satisfied with his solution, he increased his pace.

Danny never noticed the moped tailing him.

***

Just down the road from M&S in Churchill Square Danny swung his leg off the bike and coasted to the kerb. As he came to a stop he saw the police community support officer. The guy saw Danny at the same moment and changed direction towards him.

"I was looking for you," said Danny. "Guy dumped this and ran off just up the road."

He pointed back the way he had come.

The PCSO studied Danny.

"A bike was reported stolen near here earlier. Did you get a look at him?"

Danny shrugged. "Not really, about my height, similar jacket, never seen him before."

He looked over his shoulder and let the bike go at the same time. Instinctively, the PCSO stepped forward to take it.

"Here, grab this would you. There's my bus."

"Hey!"

Danny sprinted across the road and jumped onto a bus, didn't even notice what number.

As he settled in his seat he saw the PSCO still holding the bike. Danny waved.

***

As the bus turned towards Brighton Station Danny looked at his ringing phone. He didn't recognise the number.

"Hello?"

"Is that Mr Lancaster?"

Woman's voice. Well spoken. Accent he couldn't place.

"Yes, what can I do for you?"

"I would like to hire you to find out some information. I have..."

"Let me stop you there. I'd love to help but I'm really tied up right now. I wouldn't want to take your money if I couldn't deliver."

"It is very urgent, Mr Lancaster."

"Yes, I'm sure it is. But like I said, I couldn't give it the time it deserves. Maybe next week."

"No, it is too important to wait."

"I'm sorry."

"Thank you for your time, Mr Lancaster."

The woman rang off. Danny looked at his phone. He didn't like turning away work. But it would be wrong to take something on, get their expectations up, then stick it on the back burner while he was busy with other jobs. He wanted a reputation as an investigator. You couldn't put a price on that.

Danny's seat gave him a clear view of the nearside pavement and shops. He couldn't see the moped behind the bus.

***

BRIGHTON STATION, TUESDAY

Crowds poured from the train. They bunched up as they shuffled to the exit barriers, jockeying to be first away to the buses or taxis.

Some were set up for a night on the town, cheap drinks already downed at home to get the evening going and keep the budget down. Others were hunched, weary, glad to get back after a long day's work in London and another signalling delay.

A handful popped into WH Smith for copies of the Argus. A few others shopped for snacks or something from the M&S Simply Food.

One guy was so keen for that first taste from a six-pack he sprinted to the cheap booze outlet down the hill. Half a dozen girls by the barrier began jumping up and down, screaming and waving when they spotted their friend emerging from the crowd.

When the train's passengers had scattered through the city, only a handful of people were left on the concourse.

No one noticed the skinny girl in the dark green Rasta tam. She wore a long parka over ripped jeans and scuffed trainers. As passengers began to board the newly arrived train for its return journey, she looked around, pale face blank and apprehensive.

Long thin fingers rummaged in her big shoulder bag until they closed on the comforting shape of her iPhone.

She checked her messages, her Facebook, then her fingers started to fly. Blind to the swirl of the station around her she tapped away frantically for ten minutes.

When she dropped the phone back into her bag the worried expression lined her face again.

She saw a sign for a toilet and began to walk that way, then paused, checking her pockets.

She didn't have 30p in change.

Lost and unsure, she weighed her options, fiddling with a long strand of red auburn hair that had escaped the tam.

Then she walked outside and set off down Queens Road into the heart of the city.

***

MAIN BAR, THE BELLEROPHON, BRIGHTON, TUESDAY
As Danny placed the drinks carefully on the table Bob Lovejoy emerged from the gents, fiddling with his trousers.

"I wouldn't go in there wearing sandals if I were you."

Danny looked across at Karol Jachowicz who pulled a sour face and shrugged.

"We're cheerful tonight," said Danny

"Just one of those days. Ignore me," said Bob.

He plonked himself in his chair. A knee clipped a table leg. The drinks spilled. Bob sighed and picked up his pint, held it out, studied it through narrowed eyes.

"Who poured this, Mr Whippy?"

"New barrel," said Danny. "Not the quiz again, is it?"

Bob growled.

"So why the long faces? What's up?"

"Scotch Jack's been taken into hospital so I've got to sort the pub quiz. He always has a themed bit. The next one's Greece."

"Oh, right. And you're looking for questions?"

Bob, staring at the papers in his hand, nodded absently.

"What are you working on?"

Before Bob could answer, Karol snorted a laugh. "Greek love."

"What?"

Bob dived in again. "Turns out they have four sorts."

"They would," said Danny.

"Makes things complicated," said Bob. "Philia is serious friendship, Storge's for the wife and kids, Agape... I forget that one, and Eros, well, that's the shagging one."

Danny looked thoughtfully at his pint.

"Clever, really. Avoids misunderstandings."

"You reckon?" said Bob, puzzled.

"Well, you wouldn't fall down the old 'I love you/I'm in love with you' bear pit for a start."

"'spose."

They drank.

"What about the Greeks inventing GPS then?" said Danny.

Irritated, Bob looked up. "What?"

"The Antikythera mechanism."

Bob's jaw dropped. Karol's puzzled face surfaced from behind his laptop.

"What?" asked Bob.

"The Antikythera mechanism."

"*What?*" asked Bob.

"The Antikythera mechanism."

"And where did you get that one from?"

"Read about it in Jubilee Library, amazing box of cogs and gears that fixes your position with the sun and stars, about 3,000 years old. And it's a calendar for sporting events, Olympic games, that sort of thing. Handy piece of kit. They found what's left in an old shipwreck. It's in a museum in Athens."

Bob did goldfish mouths for a moment, then shrugged. "Why not? Karol, can you see what you can find?"

Just as the skinny carpenter's fingers began to fly, Danny chipped in. "Before you do that, I could do with some help."

"We've got to get this quiz sorted, Danny."

"Yeah, I know that. But this gizmo's been around for 3,000 years. It'll keep. I've got a case on the go."

The skinny Pole rolled his eyes theatrically.

"Always, it is the same. The big businessman must have help from Karol. Now the big detective wants my help. And I am just a poor immigrant worker."

"Is everyone in a funny mood today?" said Danny.

"When I help you, Danny, people beat me up, shoot at me. You are a dangerous man to know."

"I bought you a beer."

Karol shrugged, "Ok." He took Danny's notepad and studied the names. "Marion Carter, Bill Carter, Ron Hedges, these are not unusual names."

"Do your best."

Karol's manic fingers blurred across the keyboard. Bob had his nose in his pub quiz notes, muttering.

Danny sipped his Stella and looked around. The Bellerophon seemed unusually busy.

Emily the barmaid was in her usual spot. It gave a clear view all around the bar and the chance to keep a sisterly eye on the new Bulgarian barmaid.

Gavin the easyJet steward was perched on a bar stool, sipping his red wine. Slate, the pub's rangy mongrel guardian, watched the comings and goings with lazy interest from a blanket-lined basket by the fire place.

Danny continued to scan the room. It was good training, observe and remember, an essential skill for his new trade.

Near the window a striking young woman sat reading a book, sipping white wine. She reminded him of someone, a singer, no, actress... pirate film... and the new Bond... funny spelling. Naomie ... Harris, that was it, Naomie Harris.

At the next table was a big guy with a black eye patch. He was sitting in a wheelchair parked beside a young girl. The guy would have made a great Bond villain. The girl looked bored.

Sudoku Wally sat hunched in his favourite chair, arms curled on the table to protect his puzzle book, a pack of pork scratchings and the last of a pint of Guinness.

A bunch of young guys, faces pink with drink, were debating football and breasts. Nearby, a noisy crowd of girls talked bastard boyfriends.

Danny loved the Bellerophon. Its burble of conversation and familiar face were an oasis in a crazy city.

"Not much," said Karol, a shaking head rising from behind his laptop screen. "Marion Carter, nothing, Bill Carter, nothing. But Ron hedges, this."

He swung the laptop. Danny leaned forward to look at an advert, plumbing and central heating installation and repairs, "Don't hedge your bets, call the best for all your plumbing needs!" 24-hour emergency call-out, Basildon and beyond.

"Interesting," said Danny.

Karol tabbed to another screen.

"And this."

It was a newspaper report of a court case. Ronald Edward Hedges was sentenced to six months for common assault. The court heard he had impressive form including conviction for armed robbery and possession of firearms.

"Very interesting," said Danny, writing the details in his note book. Something bumped his chair.

"Sorry."

He turned to see the young girl trying to manoeuvre round their table. The guy with the eye patch glowered at him. The girl gave him a sweet smile, looked about 14 but can't have been. He'd noticed earlier, she was downing vodka Red Bull.

"Well," said Bob, looking at his watch, draining his pint. "I've got to collect Wanda."

"Another of her classes?" asked Danny.

"She's upstairs."

"What is it this time? Pilates? Zumba?"

"Something like that."

"I'll come with you, say hello."

Bob looked doubtful, then hauled himself off his seat. Danny, carrying his pint, followed him through a door by the fire place and up the stairs.

At the top of the creaking steps was a dark door. Bob opened it. Danny was so surprised his pint almost slipped through his fingers.

A mass of frothing red hair over pale shoulders. Large breasts capped by big, oval speckled nipples. Strong thighs meeting at a bubbling triangle of red pubic curls.

"Woops!" Wanda swept the dressing gown closed and looped the belt, laughing. Bob made a choking noise.

"The look on your faces!" Wanda was still laughing and Danny couldn't help notice the way the stretched towelling shimmied.

"Any funny remarks and I'll have you in here posing. It's not as if there's anything you two haven't seen before."

The two men tried to think of something to say, failed, kept quiet.

"We're running late. I'll only be a minute," said Wanda. "See you downstairs."

They plodded thoughtfully back down to the bar.

"What...?" said Danny, slowly.

"Life drawing classes," said Bob. "You know Wanda, can't resist a challenge. She went along to draw a few times, then one week the model didn't turn up so off came the kit. Pays a tenner an hour."

"And you're all right with that?"

Bob shrugged. "Bit iffy at first but, you know, if people think your other half's fit enough they'll pay to draw her, who am I to argue? And it does pay a tenner an hour. We've got pictures all over the house now, in clip frames, Blu-Tacked to the fridge. It's funny how people see the same thing differently."

Danny shook his head. "So if you're ok with this drawing business why have you got a face like a bulldog licking piss off a thistle?"

Bob Shrugged.

"Got to find a birthday present for Wanda."

"You have my sympathies, Bob. Presents for women is a bloody minefield, and I've been in a few of those." He thought for a moment. "She tried drawing you?"

"You want another pint while we're waiting?" asked Bob.

"You know Kipling?" asked Danny.

"The cake bloke?"

"No, you silly sod, the poet."

"What about him?"

"He said, 'A man can never have too much red wine, too many books or too much ammunition'."

"You're turning into a bit of a scholar in your old age."

"Nah, just sitting in the library out of the rain."

"I take it that means you want that pint."

"Silly question."

***

NEAR EASTBOURNE, EAST SUSSEX, TUESDAY

He couldn't comprehend it. Even with an IQ of 138 he could not get his mind to identify the facts, analyse them and arrange them into an explanation.

His arms wouldn't move. His legs wouldn't move. He'd seen lights a few minutes ago, probably a four-wheel drive on a track, but it hadn't come close.

He couldn't control his limbs and his mind was racing like a runaway train.

Chalk formed in the Late Cretaceous period, more than 65 million years ago. It rose during the Cenozoic Era. The end of the Ice Age and rising sea levels carved them.

This was insane. His life had gone crazy and all his brain could do was spouting gibberish. It wasn't helping.

The chill wind made his trousers ice cold and clammy where he'd wet himself.

He wished he'd never got involved, never agreed to Clive's wild scheme, never had anything to do with any of them. It had seemed so easy. They had admired his expertise, massaged his ego. And the money, well, that was brilliant.

Solved all his problems at a stroke.

And created new ones.

Another miscarriage of his talent, another failure to identify the facts, analyse them and come up with an explanation.

If only he had known. But how could he? It was beyond his experience, beyond all parameters. He knew where he was and what was going to happen but he was beyond fear because it was all just too fantastic.

Weight didn't really matter. All objects falling in Earth's atmosphere accelerated at 32 feet per second per second. Maximum speed achievable would be 120mph due to air resistance.

It was hard to be exact, didn't know the precise height, hard to concentrate, but his best guess was five and a half seconds.

The iron grip on his ankles slackened, then on his wrists. He whimpered as the tape was ripped from his mouth.

This was happening. This was really happening. His bowels emptied into his damp trousers.

Then he was free, arms and legs flailing through nothing. He couldn't breathe, still could not believe that this was really happening to him.

He thought of school and Scouts and mum and dad opening their front door to find a policeman in the porch.

Damian Hitch was still trying to believe when he slammed into the shingle at the bottom of the chalk cliffs 5.6 seconds after he'd gone over the edge.

CHAPTER 4

The three of them were sitting in friendly silence at their usual table, nursing their drinks, when the street door of the Bellerophon opened.

Emily the barmaid broke off from a game of Angry Birds to serve the new arrival.

Karol was weighing up the options to upgrade his laptop, better speed, better memory stacked against what it was going to cost him.

Bob was still fretting over Wanda's present, colours and cup sizes, wondering if he could chance Ann Summers in Western Road again without getting tongue-tied.

Danny was crouched in filthy water up to chest in an irrigation canal, listening, watching foliage move, trying to spot a patch that didn't move in time with the breeze.

The sixth sense that made him glance up into the eyes of people standing in high windows made him look over at the bar.

Emily flicked her long lashes at the new arrival and mouthed to Danny that he had a visitor. Karol and Bob turned to look as a skinny kid thanked Emily and walked self-consciously over to their table.

"Hello," said Danny.

The girl's eyes flick up from the floor to his face, looked away, flicked back.

"Hello."

The voice was a whisper, eyes like dark moist chocolate.

"You're looking for me?"

The girl nodded.

"Take a pew."

She dropped into the fourth seat and waited, sitting with her hands crunched between her thin thighs, eyes flickering around the bar.

The skinny kid looked pale and nervous. Danny took in the ripped jeans, curls of dark hair escaping from a bulging Rasta tam. A parka with a fur hood hanging from her slim frame. Long fingers gripping an iPhone.

Danny couldn't put an age on the half-child half-woman whose scuffed trainers were tapping madly under the table.

The girl slipped something from the sleeve of her hoodie, let it drop on the table. It was one of Danny's business cards.

"Got it from a newsagent by the station. Says to leave a message behind the bar here."

"Fair enough," said Danny. "But are you old enough to be in here?"

"I'm eighteen."

"In that case, can I buy you a drink?"

"JD and Coke."

He raised an eyebrow, nodded.

When he returned Danny sat looking at his visitor. The girl looked at Bob and Karol, then at Danny. When Bob heard Wanda's voice coming down the stairs he rose to meet her. Karol looked up from his laptop, shut the lid and went with him.

Danny sipped his Stella, ran a finger round his lip to remove the foam.

"So, what can I do for you?"

"I can't find my boyfriend."

She had an accent he couldn't quite place, something northern.

"Look, I don't mean to be rude but shouldn't you be at home with your mum and dad?"

"Fuck off, I'm eighteen. I'm not a kid."

"Ok, calm down. Sorry if I was rude. It's just, well, I don't normally do matrimonial."

"What?"

"Domestics."

The girl looked blank.

"Look, if he's your age, a young guy, he's probably just off with his mates, lost track of time."

"I haven't spoken to him for six months."

"Six months? Don't you think maybe he's trying to tell you something?"

"I can pay you."

"It's not the money."

"We love each other. It's special."

"Look, love, it's always special till the wheels come off."

"I've got money. How much do you want?"

The thin pale fingers dived into her big bag, rummaging. Danny was sipping his Stella again when a wad of £20 notes spilled across the table. He almost choked for the second time that evening.

"For chrissake, are you crazy? Put that away."

He grabbed the notes, handfuls, and stuffed them back in her bag. There must have been a grand there.

"Look, what's your name?"

"Jessie."

"Just the one, is it?"

"It's Shafto, Jessie Shafto."

"Well, Jessie, maybe you are a grown-up but don't do that again or you'll end up face down on a pavement somewhere."

The girl nodded, started fiddling with her phone again.

"Look," said Danny. "Have you got somewhere to stay?"

Jessie shook her head.

"Have you eaten?"

Another shake.

"Well we'd better get that sorted first."

***

He fixed for Bob and Wanda to give them a lift. Wanda, who hadn't been drinking, took the keys to Bob's Range Rover. Danny and Jessie sat in the back.

As they drove Danny noticed Wanda's eyes flicking repeatedly to the rear view mirror.

"Been to Brighton before?" she asked.

Jessie shook her head.

"Staying long?"

Jessie shrugged.

Wanda slowed at traffic lights, glanced back again.

"You know, you're a very pretty girl under that hat. Have you ever thought about modelling for a life drawing class. It pays a tenner an hour."

Jessie didn't seem to hear.

They were dropped in Bedford Square and Danny fixed up a B&B for Jessie. No luggage, just the big shoulder bag.

That done, they walked in silence along the front to Buddies. Danny stopped at a newsagent and bought their last copy of that day's Argus.

While they waited for their food Jessie was head down, fingers flying, on her iPhone again.

"You're glued to that thing."

She said nothing.

"Half the time you look like that bunch in Star Trek, the ones that are half machine, what are they called? ...the Borg, that's it."

"What's Star Trek?"

Danny sighed. "Here's the food."

He was pleased to see the girl wasn't a picky eater. She attacked a large cheeseburger as if she hadn't eaten for days.

"Look, Jessie, I can't promise anything," said Danny. "I'm turning away work. But while we're here you might as well tell me what's happened."

Jessie nodded, wiped her mouth on a paper napkin.

"His name's Jason, Jason Knight."

Danny thought the name rang a vague bell but he couldn't place it.

"He's from Brighton. We were, really, you know, close. It was special, really special."

"Ok, so what happened?"

"I had to go away. We had an argument. It was stupid. I was wound up. I said stuff. We didn't talk for ages. Then when I tried to find him he'd gone. He didn't answer my texts, unfriended me on Facebook. I don't know what happened."

"What does this Jason guy do, then?"

"He was a footballer."

Then Danny remembered, a promising young talent, rising star with a bit of a wild reputation. Got injured, hadn't played since.

"So what you're telling me, Jessie, is that you had a thing with a teenage footballer and now he's blanking you."

"No! It's not like that. It was something special, really special."

"What is it you want, Jessie?"

"I want to talk to Jason, just talk to him."

Danny sat back in his seat, folded his arms, stared up at the ceiling.

"Like I said, I can't promise anything. I've got a lot on my plate and if he doesn't want to talk to you he doesn't have to."

"Please."

"I'll try. Just promise me you'll stay at the B&B till I get in touch. And don't go round flashing that wedge. What's your phone number?"

"I'll send you a contact card."

Jessie reached out with her iPhone, saw Danny's ageing dumb phone, wrote her number on a napkin.

"I'll walk you back."

***

ESSEX, WEDNESDAY MORNING

Danny smiled at the waitress who brought his breakfast. She wore faded low-slung jeans, the fat brown belt with the big buckle sitting on her hips drawing the eye to the tight Y of denim at her crotch.

She smiled at Danny, turned, then took a second look over her shoulder as she walked away.

There hadn't been time for a run. He had been up before it got light so he'd settled for one of his mini-workouts in the flat, running on the spot, a few press-ups and pull-ups, working weights using ten-litre plastic vegetable oil containers he'd got from a restaurant in Western Road. He'd filled them with water. Ten litres was about twenty two pounds. He'd looked it up.

Danny had set off early, made good time. He'd taken the A23 north from Brighton, east round the M25, then off just north of the Dartford Tunnel onto the A127. Next stop, Basildon.

He spread his newspaper on the table and stirred his mug of tea, good and dark, bubbles pirouetting in the middle.

He looked at his breakfast. An egg and bacon sandwich, one of Britain's great gifts to the world. He picked it up with both hands and bit, savouring the tang of bacon, then the rich goo of liquid yolk rolling across his tongue.

Danny put the sandwich down and turned a page. Nahr-e Saraj, some mother's son shot dead by a guy in the uniform of an Afghan policeman. A 20-year-old lad from the West Midlands who looked 14 in the photo.

Danny's pulse surged as he smelled hot dust.

Maybe a disgruntled cop. Maybe Taliban in disguise. A quote from the kid's CO saying how he was a popular guy and a thorough professional who would have had a great career ahead of him. Danny turned the page.

Hordes of tearful teens were holding vigil outside a pair of big iron gates. Talent consultant Herbie Fielder said in a statement that his client was responding well in rehab. He couldn't say how long Scheri would be in the clinic but the stress of winning the TV talent show Gonna Be A Star followed by three No1 hit singles had left her physically and emotionally drained.

He thanked her army of devoted fans for their continued love and support and appealed for his client to be given the time and space to heal.

The picture was a publicity shot of a pretty girl with dark eyes looking soulfully up at the camera. Danny shook his head, turned the page.

Dead frog found in bag of supermarket salad veg. Danny turned the page.

Two soap stars confess how love blossomed behind the scene. He turned another page.

Some ageing actor was demanding strict laws to keep the gutter press under control. Danny looked at the smiling face in the mugshot. In a world run by jobsworths reading stuff off clipboards that was going to be a big help when the next body armour or Snatch Land Rover cock-up happened. Danny turned the page.

Charred food can kill you. He chuckled. If that was the case his mum's toast would have done for him years ago. Danny turned over.

Some politician, sharp suit, immaculate grey hair, perma-tan, was struggling to defend himself against accusations of calling a policewoman 'a peasant'.

Danny gave up on the world, flipped over to the sports pages and went back to his sandwich.

***

"I'm in the middle of something. Come on through."

Danny closed the front door behind him and followed the man down the hallway and out onto the patio beyond the back door.

Along one fence was a row of wooden sheds, each one divided rows of cages. Ron Hedges opened a wire mesh hatch, reached in and brought out a pigeon. It rested unafraid in the cradle of his fingers.

"Come on, my lovely, come on."

He lifted one wing and examined it, then the other, peered into the bird's eyes.

"You're doing very nicely, aren't you, yes you are?"

He slipped the bird back into the cage, dusted his hands and held one out to Danny.

"Ron Hedges, sorry about that. He had a run in with next door's cat. Gave him a fright but no damage done."

Danny looked along the line of sheds.

"You've got quite a collection."

"Yes, I used to race them but I can't manage the travelling, what with all the work I get, so I just fly them here now, swapped over to fancy pigeons, Macedonian Doneks, rollers, that sort of thing. You don't get the rush of racing but they're pretty to watch."

Hedges pointed skyward, indicating a tight cluster of birds circling above them. As they watched one bird broke away and fell from the sky, twirling down in a spiral dive. A second followed. A third peeled from the other side of the circling group and did the same.

"Anyway, they'll be off enjoying themselves for a while. Come on inside. I've just brewed up."

Danny followed Hedges into the house. They collected tea and biscuits in the kitchen and went through to the sitting room. The mantelpiece over the marble fireplace was crowded with ornaments and knickknacks. Above it hung a large painting that kept drawing Danny's eye.

A naked woman sat astride a straight-backed chair in the style of the iconic 1960s Christine Keeler Profumo Scandal portrait.

She was naked, looking over a bare shoulder at the viewer. Her back was smooth and arched, a ripple of spine drawing the eye down over the golden skin to the flare of hips and buttocks. A tangle of blonde hair fell across her features. All that was visible of her face was one bright eye and a curl of amusement at the edge of red lips.

The woman seemed to be biting on something. A long loop of gold pendant chain sparkled across her shoulder and she held something between white teeth, something shiny and curled, maybe a snake.

Even when Danny moved the one eye seemed to follow him, a slight crinkling at the edge where her black eyeliner curled upward as if she was enjoying a private joke.

Danny tore his eyes away from the picture and looked around. The place looked expensive, big TV, big sound system, plush furniture. But despite the money spent something jarred.

The room was untidy, magazines and newspaper stacked on the floor, empty foil takeaway trays still on the coffee table.

Hedges settled himself in a worn armchair.

"You married?" asked Danny.

"Was, way back. On my own now and I like it that way. Got a woman who comes in to clean, the laundry gets collected and there's a few friends with benefits when the nights turn chilly. Confirmed bachelor, me."

Hedges looked hard at Danny.

"So you're a freelance journalist writing something about crime, that right?"

"Yes," said Danny.

"And you thought you'd come and have chat with me, right?"

"Well, you've had some experience in the past, robbery, that sort of thing. It's a matter of public record."

Hedges tapped a digestive biscuit on his saucer as he studied Danny.

"That's true. I've done my time, paid my debt to society, as they say. It was in all the papers. But that was ancient history. Why you interested now?"

"Well..." Danny fiddled with his notebook.

"Look, Danny isn't it? before you go on, let's stop wasting each other's time. If you're a journalist I'm Alex Crawford. God knows, I've seen enough of the scrumbags in my time to know one when I see one. So what's your game then?"

"Fair enough, I'm a private investigator working for Marion Carter. Her husband's gone walkabout."

"Bill? Whoa, you're going back a bit, aren't you? Us lot were knocking about, what, coming on fifteen odd years ago."

"Until you and Marion renewed your friendship on Facebook."

"Oh, you know about that?"

Danny nodded.

"Ok, so what's happened now then? They must have been married, what, seven years now? If I live to be a hundred I'll never know why she wed that useless wanker. Attractive woman, Marion. Could have had any bloke. Often did. And she goes and picks that spineless piece of shit."

"You two don't get on then?"

"As it happens, no. We've got a bit of history. Look, what's all this about? Why me?"

"Like I said, Bill did a runner, just after you and Marion made contact again."

Hedges threw his head back, laughed out loud.

"If I'd known that was all it took to get rid of that tosser I'd've done it years ago."

"How well did you know Marion and Bill?"

"We used to hang around, back in the day."

"The armed robbery day?"

"Yeah, for about ten years or so, long time ago. If I'd known then what plumbing pays I'd've given robbery a miss. It was the planning I enjoyed. Making connections, cogs and wheels. The way it all comes together - precision, symmetry, a cascade of options from Plan A downward, fallback positions, failsafes, like water running down hill, always finding the easy logical way, never defeated. A good plan is half art, half science, functional and a thing of beauty."

"Only it didn't always work out like that, did it?"

The smile fell off Hedges's face.

"You can plan all you want, down to the tiniest detail. It's the unforeseen that'll get you every time. Like a burst pipe you can't get at."

"So what happened?"

"Well, our own stupid fault, really. Got over-ambitious, off our manor, way out of our comfort zone."

Danny looked at the mantelpiece. A giant egg stood vertical on a wooden stand. Hedges followed his gaze.

"Abroad, was it?" asked Danny.

"Yes, a very long way abroad."

"It went wrong?"

"Bigtime, all that talk about the big score, stars in our eyes, got carried away. Afterwards, you get angry. Then you buck yourself up. Life moves on."

"It's not in the newspaper cuttings," said Danny.

"And it's staying that way, enough said."

"Was Bill involved?"

Hedges let out a harsh laugh.

"In a manner of speaking. But he's not your typical Guy Ritchie gangster, more of a bookkeeper. We did what we did for the adrenalin, the rush. But Bill, he's the nervous type. Sort of bloke who wears a helmet on an exercise bike. Half the time it was all he could do to stop wetting himself."

"And Mrs Carter, was she part of it?"

Hedges shook his head.

"Mrs Carter, the name just doesn't sound right. Yes, she was around all right. There was a lot of skirt. You'd be surprised how many women get turned on by guns and money. But Marion was in a class of her own. She had a way of walking, a way of carrying herself, like she was different and she knew it. Liked to play the ice maiden a lot of the time but she was a bit of an animal with her kit off."

"But it didn't last," said Danny.

"We had words. She went away for a while. I heard she had a kiddie but it was probably just a rumour. I used to wonder if it was mine but she never let on. Always played her cards close did our Marion. Then she goes on to marry that twat Carter. Women, eh."

"Your... um, activities. Successful, was it?"

Hedges shrugged.

"The blagging? We did all right. It was ticking along nicely until the foreign job."

"Whose idea was that?"

"Guy called Jim Steele."

"He the boss?"

Hedges laughed again.

"Thought he was, that's for sure. It all got a bit competitive, if you know what I mean. Professional jealousies, I suppose you'd call it."

"And personal ones? Over Marion Carter?"

"Look, I've been polite but all this is ancient history. I don't give a toss about Bill Carter and I don't like people coming round my house pretending to be people they're not so I think it's time you went."

Hedges cocked his head. Suddenly he was up out of his armchair.

"That bloody cat again."

Hedges ran from the room. Alone, Danny's eyes were drawn again to the naked woman on the wall. He took out his phone and snapped two quick shots of the painting. There was a distant banging, then Hedges was back clutching a big pump-action water pistol.

"That'll teach that little flea bag. Anyway, like I said, thanks for calling and don't bother again."

He pointed towards the door with the water pistol. Drips ran off the barrel onto the carpet.

As Danny moved towards the hall he stopped and looked at the desk in the alcove. It was half hidden my mounds of untidy paper, plumbing invoices and estimates. A modern fax-copier-laser print stood to one side. At the centre was a battered old PC that even Danny, who knew next to nothing about computers, could tell had seen better days.

"You could get a few bob from a collector for that thing. It's an antique."

"Not that it's any of your business but some little scrote broke in. Made a hell of a mess. Nicked my laptop. I haven't had a chance to replace it. Fucking kids."

Hedges jerked the water pistol towards the hall. Danny walked to the front door and stepped outside. Hedges filled the doorway, glowering.

"For your information, I haven't seen Bill Carter in years and I'm not interested. If you see Marion, give her my love. Now piss off."

The door slammed.

CHAPTER 5

Bloody traffic. Some halfwit had shed his load and the M25 was backed up halfway to Clacket Lane services.

Danny had things to be getting on with. He hadn't sorted the pictures from the sick-note paraglider job yet. And when he'd checked his message Mrs Packham had rung twice, asking about progress, sniffling down the phone.

Lots to do.

But if Danny had to be stuck in a tailback at least it gave him time to think. There was something he didn't like about this Bill Carter business.

The guy wins big bucks, so he says. Then he walks out of his own home, apparently after discovering his wife is in contact with an old lover. She gets what looks like a ransom note. There was obviously no love lost between Bill Carter and Ron Hedges but why snatch the guy? And why do it after so long? Where's the advantage? Who profits?

Something felt very dodgy about this job. Danny grinned. He liked a challenge.

Then there was that moody love-struck waif he'd got stashed in a B&B. Busy, busy, busy.

It was all going to need a lot of thinking about.

***

BRIGHTON, WEDNESDAY

They had been waiting for twenty minutes, trading reassuring half-smiles, when the door finally opened. Vic and JJ had been through this more times than they could remember but somehow it never got any easier.

"You two look well. Good to know I'm not working you too hard."

You could never be sure but it sounded like a positive greeting. They both chanced a hesitant smile.

"Nice job with Hedges's laptop, Vic. If it hadn't been for that photo of the Carter woman on the beach we'd never have found her. The chimney of Shoreham power station, eh? It's what I've always said, haven't I? Attention to detail. Well spotted."

Vic and JJ relaxed, just a little.

"You're sure Hedges won't be suspicious?"

"No," said Vic. "I made a sloppy entry, messed the place up a bit. It'll look like an opportunist break-in, kids."

"Good, good, excellent. Now, this Lancaster character, what's your take on him?"

"We've done a bit of digging," said JJ. "He's ex-army, works as a low-rent private investigator, bit of form with the Law. We spotted him the first time we tailed Mrs Carter. They met in a park in Hove. He spotted me tailing her but he didn't see Vic following him."

"So, this guy may be low-rent but he's on the ball. Is he going to be a problem?"

JJ shook his head. "I think he might be a bit of a bonus. Mrs Carter has him trying to find Bill. If we keep tabs on Lancaster we'll know everything he knows."

"Excellent, excellent, you've both done very well."

Vic and JJ waited, watching, half-smiling, while all their information was digested. Vic's vision was fused on the two big hands, long dry fingers locking and interlocking as the man thought through what he had heard.

It might have been their imagination but it seemed as if the scaly fingers rasped, like a snake hissing, as they intertwined.

"I don't like loose ends."

Vic and JJ stiffened as the voice broke the silence.

"No, no point taking risks." The man paused, coughed. The fingers turned pale with the pressure as they popped two tablets from a bubble pack. He swallowed them dry. "Go and see Hedges, make sure we know everything he knows."

"And then?" asked JJ.

"Oh, the usual, I think."

Vic was still focused on the fingers, remembered their harsh touch on skin, the scratching of the curved yellow nails.

The half-smile was almost impossible to maintain.

***

When the motorway blockage cleared Danny made good time back down the M23 to Brighton just ahead of the evening rush.

He stopped at the B&B near the front to check on Jessie. Her room was clean but basic with little natural light. He found her sitting on the edge of her bed, a bottle of WKD Blue on the carpet by her feet, texting.

"Take it easy with that stuff."

"The drink or the phone?"

She didn't even look up from the screen.

"Both," said Danny.

"You're not my dad."

"You eaten?"

A shake of the head.

Danny returned twenty minutes later with a burger, fries and a bunch of bananas.

"You found Jason yet?" She still hadn't looked up from her iPhone.

"Not yet, I'm working on it."

"It's urgent."

"Everything's urgent. Look, I will find him. You just wait here till I come back. Get some food inside you. And give your thumbs a break."

She was still tapping away as he closed the door behind him.

***

BASILDON, WEDNESDAY

Ron Hedges could feel the tiny heartbeat against his hand, delicate and fast, so fragile. Hard to believe what it could power that small body to achieve.

He held the bird close to his face, looking into her eyes. They were alert, head always turning. Carefully, he stretched out a wing, admiring the delicate framework of bone, muscle and feather capable of gobsmacking aerobatics.

He whispered, watching the bird watching him. She was relaxed, trusting. Then he heard the muffled sound of the doorbell and swore.

The bird began to flutter in his hand. He slipped it back into its cage, secured the latch, kicked open the back door, stomped down the hall, threw open the front door.

"Look, I don't need religion, I don't need..."

Then he registered his visitors, tall, beefy guy and another who looked like a pixie.

"Who the hell are you?"

***

BRIGHTON, WEDNESDAY AFTERNOON

It was a tricky question when you thought about it. Relationships were all about committing to someone, signing up for a whole load of stuff.

But what if some of the stuff didn't work out? Do you walk away and ditch the lot? Or maybe you could quietly try to fix the bits that were broken while hanging on to the things that still worked?

Tricky. There were lots of helpful suggestions, right from old philosophers to newspaper agony aunts. No one had cracked it yet.

Ok, so cheating was pretty low, has to be said. But if you're young and fit and have nowhere to put it... it's like flood water, it'll find a way sooner or later.

Danny didn't know the background, the whys and wherefores. Didn't need to. Didn't want to.

Mrs Packham had been in tears, gutted, fighting to get the words out between the sobs. World falling apart.

He'd been moody, Mr Packham. Then there were the absences, late home from the office, called in at weekends. He said he had no choice. Times were hard. If you didn't go the extra mile you didn't keep your job, let alone get the bonuses.

Mrs Packham tried to believe but something nagged at her. Danny hadn't been surprised. It had all sounded pretty thin to him too.

Then she'd found the photo. Fuzzy, badly lit, it had downloaded from his phone to their PC at home. An accident, maybe. It didn't prove anything. But it raised questions. And they were questions Mrs Packham had to have answered.

Danny had a stroke of luck when he left Jessie at the B&B. The timing was about right and his camera kit was in the back of the van. Traffic wasn't too bad. Well, not too bad for Brighton, and he made good time across the city to the university complex at Falmer.

Danny waited until Packham emerged from the office block where he worked near the university, followed him when he drove out of the car park.

The traffic was getting heavy now as the rush hour clogged the city's narrow arteries but he'd managed to follow Packham's Toyota to Kemp Town, saw him pick up his passenger, a slim shadow waiting in a doorway.

When they reached the car park Danny had taken care where he positioned the van. Directly beyond Packham's car, along Danny's sight line, was a street lamp, lighting up the vehicle's windows like a TV screen and silhouetting those inside.

He could see two sets of shoulders, two heads, slightly inclined towards each other. The heads met, merged, then parted. Danny took pictures, some zoomed it tight so the car window filled the viewfinder, others pulled back to include the car and its number plate.

Mrs Packham's suspicions weren't suspicions any more. No doubt Mr Packham had his reasons. Nobody's perfect. There would be pain, more tears. He'd only met Mrs Packham for twenty minutes, thirtysomething, attractive in a mumsy sort of way, two kids, a home-maker, liked baking. Danny didn't know why she'd mentioned that.

The heads melded together again. When they parted they stayed six inches apart, sharing something.

Danny looked at his watch. He didn't judge. Wasn't his business. Couldn't say he enjoyed it either but it came with the job if you wanted to be an investigator.

The head in the passenger seat leaned forward, downward. The head in the driver's seat, Packham's, tilted back. In the light from the street lamp he could see the Toyota's suspension rocking. It bounced gently for about three minutes, then stopped.

The bit Danny didn't fancy was breaking the glad tidings to Mrs Packham. She wasn't going to take it well. He wondered whether they'd have some dramatic rediscovery of whatever had brought them together and start afresh or if she'd take him for everything and move on.

Not Danny's problem. He was just there to record the facts. It was the job.

The front passenger door opened. The slight figure slipped out of the car, gave a little wave, then ducked down to say something to the driver.

Mr Packham's mystery friend turned away and as the orange of a street light washed over them Danny pressed the shutter.

He held it, listening again to the rattle of multiple exposures, until the slim figure turned a corner. Danny had taken maybe twenty pictures in that sequence but he knew he'd cracked it in the first few, when the streetlight had lit the face of Mr Packham's friend.

Good looking lad, thought Danny.

***

Marion Carter stood by the lounge door, hand pressed to her chest, fingers splayed, breathing hard.

"Whatever possessed you? Who... who gave you permission?"

"You asked me to investigate, I investigated."

"But Ron, why did you go to see Ron? I never asked... never expected."

"Calm down, Mrs Carter. He was a possible witness. He might have known something, heard something."

"But I..."

"You hired me to do a job. You didn't lay down any ground rules."

"But..."

"Look, Mrs Carter, if you're that upset I'd be more than happy to refund your money and call it quits. Maybe Bill doesn't want to be found."

She flapped her hand in front of her face, eyes jerking from side to side.

"No, no, I have to find Bill. You have to find Bill. It's just... I don't know what to do... what to think. This sort of thing doesn't happen to people like us."

"Well, I'm sorry Mrs Carter, but it has. What do you want me to do?"

She walked to the sofa, perched on an arm.

"No, I'm sorry, you're right. You must carry on, please. It's so important to me."

"Fair enough. Any other no-nos I should know about?"

She shook her head.

"No, do what you think best. Just, please, find my husband. Money is to object, Mr Lancaster. I have some more cash in the kitchen. I'll give it to you before you go. Just find him and bring him home safe to me. And please do keep me informed."

***

EASTBOURNE, WEDNESDAY AFTERNOON

Fitness and flexibility were the key. Nothing was more important than your health. Your lungs, your whole body, were the tools of your trade.

After a long and satisfying career as a dance and drama teacher, Penelope Blessington had no intention of ignoring the golden rules she had drummed into her thousands of students now that she was enjoying a well-deserved retirement.

She was so absorbed in enjoying her daily walk that she would have missed it if it wasn't for Gandalf.

He was a very naughty boy, very mischievous, but Penelope could forgive him anything. He was only a puppy when she'd got him, a big-footed, clumsy soppy thing. But for all his little pranks he had been such a tremendous comfort since Glenda had been taken. Losing a partner after 34 years had been so painful. But Gandalf, with his big soft eyes and that floppy pink tongue, had brought joy back into her life.

Penelope had walked down onto the shingle by the stairs at Birling Gap. Gandalf skittered off, tongue bouncing, to explore the chalk rock pools. The crabs, sea anemones and occasional blenny always got him excited.

A few hundred yards on Penelope was admiring the striped lighthouse when she noticed Gandalf prancing by the water's edge. At first she had thought he was playing another of his games until she became aware of his agitated barking.

By then they were closer to Cow Gap so she had jogged there gently on replacement knees, Gandalf dancing excitedly around her, as she kept checking her mobile phone in search of a signal.

Her 999 call had been directed to Dover Coastguard who had alerted the local coastguard team and Eastbourne lifeboat station. The officer who was the duty lifeboat launching authority decided the weather called for both the station's boats and he summoned their crews by pager.

Soon the inshore lifeboat Laurence And Percy Hobbs, a 16-foot inflatable with a four-man crew, was slicing through the choppy waters at 25knots.

She was followed by Diamond Jubilee, the all-weather Tamar-class boat that took a wider course in deeper water.

The two lifeboats made the journey in just over ten minutes, arriving in sector D6 near Beachy Head lighthouse and the Devil's Chimney where the cliffs soared to more than 500 feet. The chalk stack that gave the chimney its name was long gone but that's how everyone still knew it. This section of cliff was just inside the Eastbourne lifeboats' territory. Beyond Birling Gap was Newhaven's turf.

The Lifeboat Medical Advisor, a crewmember and local GP, transferred from the all-weather boat to the inshore. The inflatable began to approach the awesome wall of rock while Diamond Jubilee stood off to relay radio communications which could be difficult in the shadow of the cliffs.

The inshore lifeboat nudged towards the shingle, the helmsman holding it steady with shorts bursts of its fifty horsepower Mariner outboard.

The heavy swells of the night, driven by winds running up the Channel, were still rocking them hard. The water slapped wearily against the land, hissing into froth where the waves broke on the beach close to the famous lighthouse that had sparked a campaign to save its distinctive red and white stripes.

The body was only a dozen feet from the waterline. The helmsman put the big inflatable between the wind and the victim as two crewmen hauled the limp dark shape aboard.

The doc took a look and confirmed what they already knew.

"Young guy," said the taller of the two in the bow. "Teenager."

"Must have been determined if he avoided the patrols up top."

They eased the body gently into an ambulance pouch. As the taller man looked up his eyes followed the massive 500-foot wall of chalk that claimed dozens of lives a year. Beachy Head was Europe's most infamous suicide spot, third in the world after San Francisco's Golden Gate Bridge and the Sea Of Trees forest near Mount Fuji in Japan.

At the top he could see a cluster of a dozen heads peering down over the edge. Some were police and Coastguard. The others were members of the Beachy Head Chaplaincy Team, Christian volunteers who patrolled the cliffs to find and comfort those hell bent on ending their lives, carrying out hundreds of searches and rescues each year.

He saw an arm waving and signalled an acknowledgement. The lifeboat crew secured the body gently but firmly in the bottom of the inflatable. The taller one looked down into the broken face.

"Poor sod."

He sealed the ambulance pouch, looked back at the cliffs. They were rich in fossils and history, a magnet for tourists and a danger to shipping. As he studied their coarse white folds, a gap in the cloud lit the pale chalk. After all the years he had worked these waters the cliffs still gave him a thrill and a chill in equal measure.

He signalled the helmsman who began to ease the boat out into deeper water where they turned towards Eastbourne.

As the two boats approached the harbour they could see the coroner's officer and two policemen waiting by the lifeboat station. When the sealed pouch was safely loaded the helmsman watched the ambulance drive away, heading for the mortuary at Eastbourne District General Hospital.

When the helmsman looked back his eye was caught by the new guy, Dennis. Death and the fearsome mass of the cliffs could hit new crew members hard. He'd have a quiet word before Dennis went home.

The crews set about the job of decontaminating and washing the boats and equipment, ready for the next shout.

***

BRIGHTON, WEDNESDAY EVENING
The pub was empty apart from two young guys playing pool and an old fella feeding the slot machine in the corner.

Danny wasn't surprised. The flock wallpaper was stained and crisscrossed with yellow tape where posters for events long since forgotten had been stuck up and ripped down.

The only things left up there were a few faded flyers, some dog-eared postcards and a cluster of fuzzy photos, regulars mugging for the camera on their holidays.

The lino flooring was cracked. The bar hadn't seen a lick of paint since the Sixties, probably hadn't seen many punters either. The whole place smelled of piss and frying.

The juke box was set to automatic, pumping out country music Danny didn't recognised, a crackling dirge of poverty and damaged relationships.

The floor creaked under Danny's boots. The sound made the barman drag his head up from the sports pages of his newspaper spread across the bar top.

"Yeah?"

"Kronenbourg."

He poured, bumped the pint down. A spill trickled off across the surface of the bar until it found a row of scratches to hide in.

"Anything else?"

"Packet of crisps."

"Cheese and onion or salt and vinegar?"

"That all you got?"

"Yeah."

"Make it cheese and onion."

The barman dropped the packet into the wet patch on the bar top.

"That'll be £4.80."

Danny handed over the money. The change went into the wet patch. The barman went back to his paper.

Danny sipped his pint. It was flat. This was the third dump of a boozer he'd tried around the estate without luck. Not somewhere you'd want to be at chucking out time on a Friday.

He took another sip, couldn't waste beer at Brighton prices, and listened to the tales of misery from the juke box, the crack and clack of the pool balls. The old boy gave a grunt of joy as the slot machine spat out a few coins. Danny looked at the barman.

"I'm looking for Jason Knight."

"Never heard of him."

"Used to live round here, used to play football."

"You Old Bill?"

"Do I look like a copper?"

"Hard to tell. They're tricky fuckers."

"So what about Jason?"

"Why do you want to know?"

"A friend asked me to get in touch."

"What friend?"

"An old girlfriend."

The barman laughed, an ugly noise framed by teeth that matched the sound.

"Tubbed her up, did he? You could start your own football team with the sprogs that character's fathered."

"Nope, she's fine, just wants to contact an old friend."

The two guys playing pool had stopped to listen. One took a step forward.

"This is a local boozer, you know, for locals. We don't like strangers coming in here."

Danny looked around the dingy room.

"You surprise me, looking at the state of this place I'd've thought you'd be gagging for some new trade."

The guy raised his pool cue, pointed.

"You being funny?"

"I try."

The man gripped his cue like a rifle and thrust. But his grip was careless. Danny grabbed the end with both hands, jerked it free and upwards. The butt hit the man under the chin. He made a gargling noise and tottered back against the table.

The second guy took a step forward. Danny twirled the cue and held the chalked point forward, a foot from the man's face.

"Want me to go for the splash shot?"

The man backed away, turned, walked to his pint resting on a window ledge beyond the pool table. Coins tinkled from the slot machine. Everyone turned at the sound of the old guy laughing.

"You dozy bunch of bastards."

They waited while he scooped up his winning.

"Jason's after all the publicity he can get. And he never says no to crumpet."

The old man's wheezy laugh turned into a cough. He muffled it with the sleeve of his coat as he shuffled to the notice board. Nicotine-stained fingers shuffled through a cluster of wilting flyers until he found what he was looking for. He tore it down, beckoned to Danny.

"There you go, son. Whole new career for our Jason now. I saw him play, you know. Talented lad, could have gone a long way, been another Rooney. Tough luck, still, he's bouncing back. Here you go."

He pushed the stained flyer into Danny's hand.

The pool players were both nursing their pints on the far side of the table. The barman was watching through slitted eye. Danny reckoned he had something solid stashed under the counter in case of trouble. He headed for the door.

"What about your pint?"

"It tastes like the bogs smell."

"Don't forget your crisps."

Danny heard movement, turned half-way to the door, caught them one-handed.

"And you're barred, don't come back."

"Best news I've had all evening," said Danny as he stepped out into the damp night.

***

It was going to be bad, that much was obvious. It was going to be very bad. They didn't string you up in the buff, your tackle swinging in the breeze, just for a chat, not even for a serious talking-to. No, it was going to be a beating.

Still, it wouldn't be the first time. It wasn't as if he enjoyed this sort of thing but it came with the territory, had happened a couple of times before, way back, when he'd upset someone or got careless. It was just business as usual, a bad day at the office.

But why now? He'd given up all that lark years ago. Maybe it was a mistake. If it wasn't, someone had a long memory.

The handcuffs holding his wrists together above his head were cutting into the skin but it didn't matter. It was only pain.

He'd been beaten by experts, some of them vicious bastards and some with real imagination. He bore the scars, hazard of the job. The old one, anyway.

You just take what they dish out, say as little as possible to make them happy and treat yourself to a bottle of Bells and a kebab on the way home if they left you your wallet. And your teeth.

When he heard the door open he tried to turn but it was hard to get a clear view with his head squeezed between his vertical arms.

He waited as the sound of trainers squeaking on wet concrete grew closer. When he walked into view the guy looked the part, shaven head, solid muscles bulging from a stained white vest, tracksuit bottoms stretching over big thighs. The kid obviously worked out hard, impressive.

Still, he looked a bit young, confident but clueless. Maybe it wouldn't be so bad after all.

"You all right, mate?"

The young guy didn't reply. His eyes were dark and his jaw set as he paced back and forth in front of his prisoner.

"Look, we don't have to get nasty about this. Just tell me what you're after and we can sort it out civilised."

No reply.

"I'm telling you, I don't know anything."

"Anything about what?" said the young guy. The hanging man stifled a smile. They were talking, making contact. Result.

"Whatever it is you think I'm here for."

"And what might that be then?"

"Like I said, I don't know."

The punch was hard. His head snapped back and pain flashed down his arms as his wrists jerked against the handcuffs.

The hanging man shook his head, tried to focus, bare feet skittering for a grip on the wet concrete.

The coppery taste of blood filled his mouth. He spat and when he smiled his teeth were outlined in red.

"Come on, son. I've been down this road before and I'm not talking so why waste your time and mine."

It was a good thing the young guy was wearing trainers or the kick to the groin would have been worse.

The hanging man vomited, dinner slithering down his chest, the tang of stomach acids. He spat to clear his throat, breath rattling through the juices that flooded his mouth. He waited until his heart rate calmed before he spoke. When this had happened in the past, twice, he'd kept quiet, kept his head down and waited for it to be over.

But this young guy, he didn't look as if he knew what he was about. It was almost embarrassing. It was a risk winding people up in circumstances like this but he couldn't help himself.

"Look, son, giving me a slapping isn't going to work. You won't break me, you know."

The young guy smiled and that bothered the hanging man.

"No, you're right. I won't break you." He stood back, arms folded, careful to keep his trainers away from the fluids on the floor.

"So let's talk this over. If I can help, I will. There's no need for unpleasantness. What's this all about?"

"Volstruis."

The hanging man's eyes widened, his sphincter twitched.

"Volstruis? What's that when it's at home."

The young guy slipped a cigarette between his lips and lit it with a red disposable lighter, shaking his head. "We think you do know."

The hanging man jerked his head quickly. "No, no you've got the wrong guy."

"So who's the right guy?"

"I told you, I don't know anything about this Volstruis, never met him."

The young guy pulled on his cigarette, blew smoke over his prisoner.

"What about Kaapse Kobra?"

This wasn't going right. The hanging man felt a sick fist of snakes wriggling in his stomach. This wasn't like the other times. Got to keep calm. If they see you're scared... Got to keep calm. He ran the words through his head like a mantra but he was having trouble believing it.

"Kaapse what? What is this? Countdown? I'm shit at anagrams."

"We'll see."

They both turned as the door opened. The new arrival seemed tiny in the echoing space of the garage, small feet making the faintest tapping across the concrete. The new arrival looked at the big guy.

"How's it going, JJ?"

"Not so good, Vic. He doesn't know anything."

They looked at the hanging man. They weren't hiding their faces and didn't care that he knew their names. That was bad, very bad. His balls shrivelled as a shiver ran through him.

"Hey, look. I'm strung up here like a Christmas turkey. I can't think straight. Just give me a minute, will you?"

The smaller of the two placed a small shoulder bag on a work bench, took out a pocket tape recorder, placed it on the wood beside the bag, pressed record. A red light came on.

"Will someone tell me what this is about?"

Vic pulled a pair of disposable rubber gloves from the bag and pulled them carefully over delicate pale hands.

"This isn't going to work, you know."

Vic opened a small container the size of a matchbox and carefully fitted the two earplugs they contained.

"Hey, hey, come on you guys, this isn't funny."

Vic took a yellow tin from the bag and adjusted its red nozzle.

"Look, Volstruis, it's ancient history. I was hardly involved. I don't know anything."

Vic was so small, not much over five feet. The hanging man could see cheeks and forehead so pale they were almost blue, as if the skin was translucent.

He tried to speak but his eyes bulged as tiny, rubber-clad fingers lifted his shrivelled penis.

"What the…"

He felt a cold liquid drizzle over his genitals and streak down his legs. Vic turned away and offered earplugs to the young guy who took them with a smile.

When they were comfortable in his ears he passed back the box and something else, something red.

Vic stepped towards their prisoner again. He looked down at the tiny white hand and saw the red thing. It was the young guy's disposable lighter.

Then Ron Hedges smelled the rising fumes of lighter fluid.

"No, fuck no, fuck no, for fuck's sake *NO*."

CHAPTER 6

Danny took a long pull of his Stella and sighed, relieved to be back in the Bellerophon to enjoy a pint that didn't taste as if it had passed through the bar staff first.

"You think I am some peasant who waits to serve. I am carpenter, skilled man. I don't have to come here to be waiting on you."

"Steady on, Karol. I only asked you to do a bit of research."

"Always it is research, research, research. And only because you are Luddite who cannot tell computer from sideboard."

"Look, if it's money, I can bung you a few bob."

"Is not money, is respect. I have talents. I have skills. I am not your lackey."

Danny looked across at Bob who sat, head down, trying to work out his new smart phone.

"Is it me or is this national misery week?"

"Ok, ok," said Karol. "I will help but you must understand I am not your peasant."

"Fair enough," said Danny, smoothing the pub flyer out on the table. "What can you tell me about a young footballer, Jason Knight. Had a promising career till he got injured."

Muttering as he surfed, Karol's fingers skittered across the keyboard of his laptop.

"Here, Jason Knight, born in Brighton. A child star, played for England under-18s, courted by Premier League clubs. Newspaper say he is the new Rooney."

"So what happened?"

Karol scrolled. "Clubbing late night. Arguments with manager. Accusation about girl in hotel room. Is not proved but some people say money is paid. He is in trouble again for rude words on Twitter about black guy he plays. Then compression injury to left ankle. Pilon fracture, very bad."

Danny looked puzzled. "I thought with the big bucks those clubs had they could fix a broken ankle."

Karol shook his head. "No, Pilon is very bad, comes French word for hammer. This man was unlucky. Damaged to joint surface gives him problem always, career is over."

Danny pointed at the flyer. "So what about this?"

"That is old, when he is DJ for hire, weddings, parties. Now Jason Knight is Jas K. Hosts music events in Brighton and London. Very showbiz, expensive, with guest DJs, soap actors, model girls."

"Interesting," said Danny. "Any gossip? Anything dodgy?"

Karol shook his head. "Nothing in newspapers or blogs. He looks a big success."

"Ok, how about this?" Danny took out his phone and pulled up the photo of the painting on Ron Hedges's wall. Karol squinted at it, grimacing.

"Is naked woman. Always with you it is naked woman."

"Very funny, Karol. Can you blow it up?"

"Is postage stamp. Your mobile is rubbish."

"Try."

Karol rattled his empty Zywiec bottle on the table.

"Buy peasant a beer."

Danny went for another round.

***

He had a cold coming on, knew it, could feel his throat tickling. He'd have to throw a sickie. You can't take any chances with your health.

It was drizzling and the wind off the mercury sea was finding gaps in his waterproofs. Shit day, shit job. Life wouldn't be worth living if it wasn't for the few perks.

Even when the weather was crap, people were still drawn to Brighton beach. Raw nature or raw sex, there was always someone down there.

He looked into his barrow as he wheeled it along. The usual collection of crap dumped by people who should know better. Still, if they tidied up after themselves he'd be out of a job. And then there were the perks.

Tucked to one side of the cart, beside the rubbish he'd collected, the food cartons and the needles, was the morning's haul, a bottle of Diesel eau de toilette – whatever that meant – a half-full bottle of Smirnoff Blue, half a pack of Superkings – damp, but they'd dry off – two unopened bottles of Desperados tequila beer, seven condoms – unused – one small plastic wallet of white powder, another of blue pills, half a dozen disposable lighters and £18.35 in cash.

Not brilliant but not bad.

Still, look on the bright side, he was nearly finished. Then it was off home to the wife. Be nice if she was a bit more cheerful this evening but he wasn't getting his hopes up.

Losing the baby had really hit her. They didn't talk about it but the whole thing sort of loomed over them as they sat in the living room.

The sprog might have died in the hit-and-run before it was born but most of the time he felt like it was still there, in the room with them. Creepy.

Maybe a nice tea would jolly her up a bit. He'd said to get them some chops, a treat. Pity you can't get those ones with a kidney in any more. Bloody Common Market. He'd told her, just make sure they're sheep, not some dodgy foreign meat. Horses were for betting on, not eating.

They couldn't afford it, not really, but it might bring a smile to her face. And anyway, he'd heard about some copper cable that needed recycling. Just had to dig it up.

He looked across the shingle and noticed someone among the rusting iron pillars of the burned-out West Pier. Looked like a kid. There was something he didn't like about them, shifty.

He pushed his cart, shivering as the wind penetrated his waterproofs again. That squeaky wheel would drive him crazy.

Definitely something shifty. They were up close to one of the pillars, reaching for the ironwork. If they were nicking his precious perks he'd go ballistic.

He speeded up, cursing the squeaky wheel. When he drew level with the old pier the figure was still hunched against the pillar.

"Oi!"

Whoever it was jerked like a startled deer and sprinted off across the shingle.

He watched them go, then trudged wearily to the pillar. He couldn't see it at first against the crusty surface of the old rusted ironwork, didn't realise what it was when he did.

Peering closer, he saw it was a small padlock secured to the pillar with a chain. As he squinted he spotted something scratched into the red coating, "Jessie luvs Jason xxx" with a heart carved around it.

"We'll need specialist equipment to cut that thing off."

Benny Driscoll swore under his breath.

***

It was a mystery to Danny, art. Women, kit off, he could see the attraction. But dead sharks and sticky knickers were a joke. That said, the people who did that stuff were minted so either it really was good or there were a lot of mug punters about with more money than sense.

The fuzzy photo on Danny's mobile had given Karol nothing to work with. But the stroppy Pole did not give up easily. He had taken the phone home, downloaded the low-res image and enhanced it as best he could.

Now Danny had spent a frustrating morning touring the city's art dealers. Most had looked him up and down, been unhelpful. Some watched his every move, worried he might pocket something. Others peered reluctantly at the picture, clearly convinced he was trying to fence an item he didn't own.

He was on the verge of giving up when his eighth call came up trumps. It was a small gallery buried away in The Lanes that stocked an odd assortment of landscapes and portraits.

Antony Seward didn't seem to have had any trade for a while, was keen for a little human contact. He studied the picture, tapped it thoughtfully against his chin, looked again.

"Can't be sure, the quality's frightful, but it does ring a rather vague bell."

He studied some online catalogues at the computer on his desk, making quiet humming noises as he thoughts organised themselves into line.

"As I say, I can't be absolutely certain, but it might be by Sean Collins."

Danny looked blank.

"A promising watercolourist, had a couple of exhibitions, attracted some very favourable reviews, as I recall. But I haven't heard anything of him for a few years. Hardly surprising, I suppose."

"Why's that?"

"He took up painting in prison, part of some well-meaning scheme to introduce culture to recidivists. After his release he was all the rage briefly but, as I say, he hasn't shown anything new for quite a while."

"And you think he might be back inside?"

"Well, I don't know but it's quite likely, don't you think?"

Danny shrugged. "So, no news about him for a few years."

"Afraid not."

Seward tapped the picture against his chin again as he stared at the ceiling.

"Wait a mo. I've had a sudden thought."

He went back to his computer, mumbling to himself as he surfed.

"Yes... yes... I thought I was right."

He beckoned Danny over to the desk, slid his chair back to make room, coloured as Danny leaned in close.

"You see these?"

Seward indicated half a dozen images on the screen. Danny looked at them and nodded.

"These are the last of Collins's work that was shown, a few years back now."

"What about them?"

"What about them? Why, they're frightful. His early work showed some promise, some sense of subject and composition. These, well they're dreadful. A gallery would be embarrassed."

Danny looked closer.

"Windmills and canals."

"Quite, quite, they're not really proper paintings at all, just tourist tat."

"Amsterdam tourist tat," said Danny.

"Well, yes, I suppose they are."

"That's a big help, Antony, thanks."

The art dealer looked him up and down. He seemed to be blinking a lot.

"My pleasure. If I can be of any further service, er, Danny, wasn't it? Do call again."

***

Helen Spencer would have burst into tears if she wasn't so bloody angry. It wasn't fair, it really wasn't.

She had put a lot of time and effort into this, planned everything. She's spent an age chasing people to chip into the whip for beer and shots. She'd spent hours working out the perfect playlist on her MacBook.

Her course work was starting to get behind because of the time it had taken her. Helen had wanted everything to be perfect but she hadn't had a moment to relax and enjoy herself. It had all gone wrong from the start.

That stupid tart redhead was having a screaming fit after catching her scummy boyfriend sucking face with some other girl. As if that surprised anyone.

Someone had thrown up on the living room carpet. Thrown up, then just walked away. Decent student accommodation like this was gold dust. She didn't want to lose it. And Helen would be out of cups and mugs if people kept breaking them at this rate. Someone jolted her, spilling her drink.

"Have you seen Bekka?"

It was Darryl, another loser. Where were all the fit, buff men? Helen had to lean close to hear him above the thump of the music.

"Have you seen Bekka?"

Helen shook her head, shrugged. She had enough problems already. Bekka was a big girl. Maybe she'd found herself someone better than Darryl. Lucky bitch.

Whatever Bekka was doing it had to be more fun than this. The flats were rammed, people spilling into the halls, the garden and out onto the forecourt.

Darryl wandered off, squeezing between knots of people, a worried look on his face.

Half of these people she'd never seen in her life. If she ever found out who put the party on Facebook she'd kill them.

The neighbours had knocked twice to complain about the music. And some fuckwit who was a friend of Jerry's said he'd seen a police car cruise past. That's all she needed, the cops and the council turning up about noise.

And that fuckwit friend of Jerry's had just stood out there, waving at the police, big fat joint in his hand. Helen rolled her eyes at the thought. If uni students really were the brightest and the best the world was fucked.

Helen's wine spilled down her dress as someone yanked her shoulder. She turned, eyes blazing.

"What is your problem? Look what you've done."

"Helen, it's Bekka."

"What's the matter with her?"

"You'd better come."

The look on Darryl's face frightened Helen. She put down her wineglass and followed him, squeezing sideways through the crush.

It seemed to take them ages to reach the top of the stairs. They edged their way into the flat and down the hallway.

As soon as Darryl pushed open the bathroom door Helen felt sick. Bekka was sprawled across the bath mat like a rag doll, covered in vomit, skin a sickly blue white and glistening with cold sweat.

"Bekka!"

Helen knelt beside her flatmate, lifted her head. The stench was terrible.

"Bekka! Bekka!"

Her eyes were half closed and scary white, her eyeballs rolled up into her head. Helen shook her. A limp arm flopped on the mat. Helen turned.

"Darryl! For God's sake! Call an ambulance!"

CHAPTER 7

She attacked the burger as if she hadn't seen food in days. For a small girl Jessie certainly had a big appetite.

"You getting on ok here?" asked Danny.

Jessie, chewed, swallowed, nodded. "It's all right."

"You didn't say Jason was a footballer, famous."

"It was no biggie, didn't matter to us."

"That was a while ago."

"It still doesn't matter."

"Look, I've found a phone number."

Jessie lost interest in the food, looked up at Danny for the first time.

"He's running some DJ business. I haven't had time to check him out, I've got a lot on."

"Give me the number."

"Are you sure, Jessie?"

"Just, give me the number."

"Look, I'd like to check this guy out before you do anything but I'm really under the cosh right now. I'll give you the number, just to show I'm earning your money, but don't ring until I've had a chance to check, ok?"

Danny copied out the mobile number and tore a sheet from his notebook. Jessie snatched it from his hand.

"Just be patient, ok?" said Danny. "I've got to go away on a job but I'll come again as soon as I can. You ok here for a bit?"

Jessie stared at the piece of paper in her hand, didn't respond.

"Just be careful, Jessie, ok?"

"Yeah, whatever."

***

SURREY, THURSDAY MORNING

Danny was always wary of guns. He'd handled them, used them, knew what they could do. The first guy, the one with the cropped salt-and-pepper hair, was relaxed but watchful. Behind him, the younger one had a look-at-my-gun roll to his walk.

Salt-and-pepper adjusted the semi-automatic rifle across his chest. His pal ran a hand along the butt of his holstered pistol.

Danny sipped his lager as he watched the two policemen patrol the terminal. He didn't particularly fancy a beer at 6am. Then again, it wasn't every day you found a pub open at that hour. Had to be done.

Danny patted his pockets to check everything was where it should be. Passport, eticket, boarding card and a few Euros he had bought from the Post Office in Churchill Square zipped into his jacket. Ciggies and extra strong mints in the right-hand outside pocket, phone in the left.

He looked down at the small black bag, remembering the hefty packs he had lugged around in a previous life. Travelling light, cabin baggage only, was definitely the way to go.

Two pairs of boxers, two pairs of socks, spare T-shirt and jeans, tooth brush, paste, razor and blades, comb, phone charger, notebook, two pens and an Andy McNab paperback.

He'd covered everything he could think of. PPPPPP - Perfect Planning Prevents Piss Poor Performance, but it was always the thing you hadn't foreseen that tripped you up.

He'd shuffled through the snaking check-in queue behind two girls chattering with excitement about the many possibilities of their visit to Rome.

The press to get through security hadn't been too bad, apart from the usual hassle when the scanner gate lit up when it spotted his metal leg. He stood for a hand search under the curious gaze of his fellow passengers.

Then it was in among the crowds indulging in intensive retail therapy before their flights. What is it with airports and giant Toblerone?

The Red Lion was half full, puffy-eyed people sitting in sullen groups, hemmed in by luggage, overexcited children pulled out of bed too early.

Danny nursed his pint at a table by the big floor-to-ceiling window that gave the best view of Gatwick's runways.

Danny guessed the guy at the next table was probably a regular traveller. He looked more alert than most of the Red Lion's clientele and was tucking into the traditional English, chasing sausage, bacon, fried egg, baked beans, hash browns, mushroom and half a grilled tomato around his plate with urgent enthusiasm.

Danny looked back out of the window as a jet left the ground, its take-off shriek muted by the glass, and arrowed upwards, the morning light brilliant on its fuselage. Danny watched as it turned and began to climb away, flaps and wheels retracting, a haze of power spurting from its engines.

He sipped his lager thoughtfully. As least it cut the early morning taste in his mouth, the lingering acid of two cigarettes smoked on the trot before he entered the nicotine-free terminal building. He could do with another now.

With a little time to kill, Danny spread his paper on the table. That smarmy talent consultant was still appealing for fans to allow his client to heal in peace so she could complete her new album in time for Christmas. Counsellors were being brought in to help distraught fans still holding a candle-lit vigil outside the clinic where the singer was being treated.

The politician who had called a policewoman a "peasant" outside Parliament was fighting for his political career. He admitted having had a stressful day and exercising less than his usual courtesy but strenuously denied uttering the insult. He couldn't understand what all the fuss was about when they had a nation to govern.

Police were treating the discovery of a man's body on a beach at Canvey Island in the Thames Estuary as murder after he was found to have extensive burns on his lower body.

Some clothing manufacturer was set to become the first high-vis jacket millionaire. No surprises there.

Another Green on Blue in Helmand.

Danny looked up as Breakfast Guy rose from his table with a deep sigh of pleasure, picked up his briefcase and moved away.

As Danny watched him go his eye caught the flights board. His gate was open. He drained his pint, picked up his shoulder bag and headed for his aircraft.

***

Danny's memories of Amsterdam were hazy. He had only been there once before but the 48-hour trip was a hole in his memory. Pogo's stag weekend had been a boozy blur.

All Danny could recall was a series of crowded bars, narrow lanes of dimly-lit windows with scantily-clad girls of all shapes sizes and hues.

A visit to a club in the Red Light district had changed his view of bananas forever.

This trip wasn't likely to be quite so educational. It was a long shot, and an expensive long shot at that. Marion Carter's cash-up-front would easily cover his costs but it wouldn't do much for his profit margin.

She had insisted on being kept informed about his investigation but Danny had decided not to tell her about the trip. Wasn't sure why. Gut feeling.

And he had turned up no useful leads in Brighton, was running out of options. Danny had pressed her to contact the police but she still refused, didn't want family laundry aired in public, especially the stained kind.

It was all, he had to admit, pretty thin. A possible name for the artist from art dealer Antony with a vague pointer to Amsterdam had given Karol something to work with but he'd complained bitterly. Despite the griping he'd come up trumps.

Sean Collins had held three exhibitions, one in Manchester, one in London and one in Brighton. He'd sold a few pieces, several for four-figure sums, then dropped off the radar. The only clue was in his later work. He had given up nudes and concentrated on scenery. Seward had found the Amsterdam paintings in one of his catalogues and Karol had found more online, Dutch houses, canals, the odd windmill.

He ought to take something back for Karol, cheese, maybe, or clogs.

So, pretty thin but the best he had to go on which was why Danny found himself on a bike, cycling around Amsterdam to get the lay of the land.

It was one of those chunky sit-up-and-beg types, the kind delivery boys rode in old films and bread adverts. But instead of lads in cloth caps they were being ridden by tall girls with long hair and legs to match. They were all around him. Danny marvelled at the cardio-vascular health of the Dutch.

The traffic was another matter, like taking oncoming fire from three sides in a crazy swirl of cars, vans, trams and hundreds of bikes. The tramlines almost had him over his handlebars twice.

When the train from Schiphol reached Amsterdam Centraal Station Danny had walked down Damrak and checked out cheap rooms on the edge of the Red Light District. He hoped to get home that day but it paid to be prepared.

Hungry, he had stopped at Wok To Walk in Warmoesstraat and opted for the egg noodles, chicken and shrooms, garlic and pepper Saigon sauce. He found a bench near the Oude Kerk and ate enthusiastically from the carton while checking a city map.

Odd to think that sea level was somewhere above his head but the Dutch had been holding back the waters for centuries.

Once he'd hired the bike Danny cycled south before cutting across to the tree-lined square off Spui, following Karol's map that he had memorised.

Half way down Rokin the urgent clanging of a tram bell saved him from losing his other leg.

The square was edged with the city's tall, narrow houses and a number of bookshops.

Under a canopy of trees near the American Book Center he found clusters of art lovers browsing two lines of covered stalls. Danny walked round to recce the place.

Wares for sale included acrylic and watercolour paintings, ceramics and wood sculptures. Art was still a mystery to Danny. The closest he came was being able to sketch a half-decent map.

He zeroed in on two stalls selling paintings. As he studied them he quickly decided he preferred the naked girls to the ones that were just bright swirls of colour.

The man behind the first stall stepped forward, smiling as he stroked his carefully-trimmed goatee. Danny showed him the picture from Hedges's living room. He studied it but couldn't help.

The woman in the bright floral top on the second stall gave it a closer look, then shook her head. It was hard to tell, she said. Many artists painted such pictures for tourists. She suggested he try the market at Thorbeckeplein.

Danny set off eastwards, following the Singelgracht canal through the flower market. It had been an early start and he was still peckish, stopping in Rembrandtplein for a cone of chips and mayo. As he munch he wondered if the trip gave him the chance to call himself an international investigator on his website but decided that might be jumping the gun a bit.

Thorbeckeplein was a narrow, tree-shaded square that ran down from Rembrandtplein to the Herengracht.

Thijs Timmermans was Danny's idea of a typical Dutchman. He was tall, good looking, tanned, relaxed and friendly with a floppy fringe of light brown hair. He spoke English better than Danny did. He looked at the picture.

"So you know this guy, the artist?"

"Friend of a friend."

"I used to see him a lot. He came round here regularly but this place is more modern art. Your friend, he was painting city scenery. Some of the guys here looked down their nose but he makes a living."

"Do you have an address?"

Thijs looked doubtful. "I'm not sure. I don't like to give out a private address."

"It would be a big help."

"Are you buying?"

"Could well be."

"I don't want to lose the guy a sale," said Thijs. "Wait here a minute."

The Dutchman ducked back behind his stall and returned with a piece of paper.

"Here, it's near the Nieuwmarkt."

"Thanks, I'll find it."

"And say hello to him from Thijs," said the Dutchman as Danny swung onto the old bike and pedalled away.

***

BRIGHTON, THURSDAY MORNING

"Jas K talking, don't waste my time. It's precious."

"Hello?"

"Who is this?"

"Is that Jason?"

"Like I said, it's Jas K. What do you want?"

"Jason, it's Jessie."

"Jessie?... Hey, babe, long time. Howya doing?"

"I'm ok, I just wanted to call, say I'm sorry."

"Sorry? Yeah, well, things happen, babe. You know? It's good to hear your voice."

"Are you ok, Jason? Your voice, it sounds funny."

"I'm fine, babe, just, you know, emotional. It's been a while."

"Maybe we could... see each other."

"Yeah, sure, babe. Look, I've got another call but I've got your number. I'll get back to you."

"Are you sure you're ok, Jason?"

"Yeah, babe, yeah. It's just, like, a bit of a shock, you know?"

"Ok, call me then. Promise?"

"I promise, Jessie."

Jason Knight pressed end call on his iPhone and his face broke into a broad smile. He looked down at the white-blonde hair on the head bobbing up and down between his thighs.

"That's good, Princess. Oh, that feels *sooooo* good."

***

The Dutch liked their stairs steep and narrow to save space in a crowded city. Danny had run up four flights and hardly drawn breath. The guy who opened the door at the top looked as if he'd have to do the climb on his hands and knees.

He was tall but from the way his jeans hung you could tell his legs were like bread sticks. Dirty blond hair hung to his collar, clearly cut by a friend. The skin around his jaw and eyes was stretched into deep grooves. The voice was gravelly from booze, fags and medication.

"Yeah?"

"I'm a journalist. I..."

"Fuck off."

"I need to talk to you."

"You're no journalist."

"Look...?"

"You're nothing like the guy who ghosted my book, pissed and sweaty the whole time."

"It's about Marion."

He looked at Danny, thought for a moment, then swung the door wide.

"You'd better come in."

Danny followed Sean Collins into a small cluttered room. The walls were a mass of colour, paintings mounted edge to edge. Others were stacked against the walls. Dozens of squeezed paint tubes and bunches of brushes sticking up from jam jars full of murky water covered almost every flat surface. The place smelled of turps and dope.

The two men picked their way through the newspapers and food wrappers strewn across the floor and sat opposite each other in simple wooden chairs by a small table.

Collins picked up a thick roll-up from an overflowing ashtray. He ran the flame of a disposable lighter around the tip to get it going again, then sat back and studied Danny through watery red-rimmed eyes. "Marion, eh? Now there's a name from the past. What does she want?"

"Her husband's gone missing. She's very worried."

"Bill? Why she ever married that wanker I'll never know. You want a beer?"

Danny nodded. Collins shuffled through the debris and returned with two large tins of Amstel.

Collins took a long pull, sighed, wiped his hand across his thin lips, looked at Danny.

"It was all a long time ago. Why come to me now?"

"I'm just checking with people he knew."

"A different time, mate. A different bloody planet."

Danny pulled the crumpled photo of the portrait in Ron Hedges's living room from his pocket and slid it across the table.

"That one of yours?"

Collins nodded. "Yeah, haven't done anything like that in ages."

"It's Marion, isn't it?"

Collins nodded, drank again.

"Kit off," said Danny.

"You don't look the prudish type to me."

"So you painted her, Hedges put the painting up in his home and she married Bill. Quite a close little group."

"If you're thinking hippy commune, forget it. We were close, but we were a team, a bloody good one until the wheels came off. True, Marion and me, we had something special for a while. What is it they say about flames burning too hot? Then she vanished. Someone said she was in the club but if she was she never let on."

Danny looked around at the paintings, canal bridges, old Amsterdam houses, tall and narrow with their distinctive roofs, boats on the city's waterways. His eye was drawn to a small, cluttered shelf.

"You'd need a few toast soldiers to get that thing down you."

Collins followed his gaze. Saw the giant egg on its wooden plinth. His chuckle disintegrated into a wheezy laugh.

"Too right, a souvenir, ostrich. Don't know why I still keep the bloody thing given what happened."

"And what did happen?"

Collins took a long pull on the joint, held his breath, staring at the ceiling. Danny waited for long seconds until Collins wheezed out a long plume of creamy smoke.

"We were doing very nicely, making a good living. Then Jim comes up with this crazy idea for the 'big score'."

"Jim?"

"Jim Steele, or I should say the late Jim Steele. We must have been out of our bloody minds. We just sort of got caught up in it all, kept taking it a step further. Then it really looked possible. Then it turned to rat shit."

"What happened?"

"Africa happened. Namibia happened, diamonds. What did we know about fucking Africa? Way out of our league, way out of our neighbourhood. I mean, you don't mind travelling to where we're not known but that's a joke. And Steele chucking his weight around."

"Steele was the boss?"

"He thought he was. It got complicated, partly why it all went wrong."

"You got caught?"

"No, plane crash. Steele and some South African guy we'd hired were both killed. And they had the gear with them."

"So what did you do?"

"Legged it out of there as fast as we could. You do not want to see the inside of an African jail, trust me."

"And Bill was involved?"

Collins snorted. "Sort of, finances, accounts, cashflow. Steele did the planning, along with Ron Hedges. I did the logistics, cover, stuff like that."

"And you all made it out, apart from Steele and the other guy?"

"Couldn't get back to good old England fast enough. Soon as I arrived I was picked up on an old assault charge but I couldn't've been happier. Better than the alternative."

"And that's when you started painting."

"In prison, yes. It passed the time and I found I had a bit of a talent. When I came out some people put on an exhibition. Rich wankers who got a buzz from rubbing shoulders with villains. Posh cows in furs who get themselves wet thinking they're touching the dark side, saving a bit of rough from a life of crime, maybe getting themselves a tax break on the way. Still, it got me established and paid the bills."

"And you're still at it?"

"Sort of. Fashions change. Street art's big in Amsterdam but I'm too old for spray cans. That stuff would get you a clip round the ear when I was a kid. And I'm not big on modern art. I don't have the guts to stick my cat in formaldehyde and I'm pretty sure my Y-fronts wouldn't draw a crowd. Another beer?"

Danny nodded. Collins went to the fridge, came back with a can, passed it to Danny, paused, offered him the stub of his joint.

"You smoke?"

Danny shook his head.

"I do, sorts the bits the painkillers don't touch."

"Doesn't stop you painting."

Collins paused to fire up the last of his joint again, inhaled, disappeared in a lazy cloud of blue smoke. As it thinned he waved an arm at his art.

"This lot? Ye Olde Amsterdam, windmills, cutesie canals, the odd mouse on the stair, simple stuff for tourists, mainly Yanks. I make a crust. Some people are doing exciting things with watercolour. You ever heard of Allan Tazzyman?"

Danny shook his head.

"Yorkshireman, lives in Crete. Lashes himself to poles to paint storms, he's done some wonderful stuff with light on water, very hard in watercolours. Me, I'm beyond caring now, just want to make enough to keep me in rent, beer and blow till this bloody pancreas finishes me off.

"If you want to see some real art, something passionate, you should see the Van Gogh Museum while you're here. You know Van Gogh?"

"Sunflower guy, chopped his ear off."

"And they say the British education system is going downhill. His stuff, stabbing paint on, 3D passion poured onto canvas, that's really something."

"You mentioned a book."

Collins inhaled, exhaled and disappeared again behind a billowing blue cloud that glowed in the light from the window.

"Oh, yeah, they used to be big a few years back, you know, bad boy tells all, broken childhood and a life of crime. Publisher got this sweaty journalist to write it. Had to be careful. We didn't give too much away in case the law bought a copy but all the punters want is a bit of bad boy banter and a few slappings."

"Did you include much about Namibia?"

Collins shook his head.

"No, it wasn't something any of us wanted to remember."

"So you haven't heard anything of Bill Carter then?"

Collins shook his head, looked at his watch. He took a last drag on his joint, winced as his lip burned.

"Not for years. Look, I don't want to rush you but I'm meeting some potential clients. Couple rang this morning to say they wanted their portrait done. Don't get much work like that these days. Isn't young love wonderful."

"One last thing," said Danny, "You don't think there's any chance the Namibia business is connected with Bill's disappearance?"

"Nah, knowing Bill, he probably got himself lost walking home from Tesco. He never was the sharpest tool. God alone knows why she ever married him. Marion was always a girl with big appetites."

"She doesn't seem that way now."

"People change."

Danny wasn't sure they did.

***

Meatballs and beer, very tasty. Cafe Amsterdam was a cut above your usual airport catering. And a smoking room at the back as well. Danny knew he could get used to this.

As he ate he flicked through the book Collins had given him, Bad Boy – A Villain's Journey From The Slums To The Bailey, pausing to read a few paragraphs.

It wasn't helpful. The book told the story of a bright and talented lad who might have made something of himself if only he'd had the breaks. A passage about an armed robbery made it sound like a bit of fun. Danny doubted that's how the building society staff viewed it, cowering on the floor, ears ringing, covered in debris after a shotgun blast brought down half the ceiling.

He checked the departures indicator. Just time for a quick smoke before boarding.

***

BRIGHTON, THURSDAY

It could work out well. It could work out very well if he played it right. Boost the business and teach the bitch a lesson all at the same time.

He heard the toilet flush. Princess walked into the room, clawing her hair back into shape. She saw Jason stretched out on the bed, fell in beside him, hugged, kissed his shoulder.

"That was special, Jas, really special."

"You know me, Princess, the Clitoris King."

"Ripped and funny as well, you're just so talented, Jas."

"Ain't that the truth, Princess."

He moved and winced. "Fucking leg!"

"You want a line, Jas? Take the pain away?"

"Why not."

He watched her pad naked across the carpet. She was quality, seriously fit. Thick as shit but seriously fit. He liked it when she pulled her hair to one side. Then he could see his name in that big fancy lettering across the back of her neck.

Princess squatted down and began to slice a line of coke on the coffee table. She looked good like that, showed how small her waist was. You didn't get waists like that these days, too many fat birds.

He'd put a lot of time and effort into Princess. Best tits money can buy, none of that cheap leaky rubbish, proper realistic. Best teeth, too, all porcelain, lovely smile. All that in one tasty package and on top of that she could suck a golf ball through a garden hose.

But Jessie, whole different ballgame. She really was special. He'd have to give this one some serious thought.

CHAPTER 8

The flight back to Gatwick took less than an hour. Danny spent it reading more of Collins's book. It didn't help.

Africa was mentioned but it read like a bunch of mates on safari. A few hints were dropped, just to make it sound exciting, but dates, locations and what had actually happened were kept deliberately vague. The story painted Collins and his gang members as adventurers rather than thieves, all harmless fun really. It didn't help the case one bit. Danny wondered if Emma could get anything for the book on eBay.

With only his shoulder bag, Danny was off the aircraft and through immigration and customs quickly while others hung around the baggage carousel.

He took the monorail to the south terminal and headed for the escalator down to the railway platforms. Once on the train he called Marion to say he would bring her up to date tomorrow. He tried Jessie's phone but there was no reply.

He never noticed the two people who had also boarded the train at Gatwick watching him discreetly from the far end of the carriage.

***

Kate Van der Waals loved the walk to the daycare centre. It was quality time with Johanna before she caught the tram to her job at the Bureau Monumenten & Archeologie where she worked on the preservation of Amsterdam's cultural heritage.

They could talk, play a little together, just enjoy each other's company. Johanna was at the age when everything was interesting to her clear bright eyes. And the city looked so beautiful in autumn.

Today they were playing their letters and shapes game. Johanna had already spotted boat and bus. As they approached the little bridge Johanna ran to the iron rail by the canal. Kate called her back but Johanna was too absorbed by something she has seen.

She pointed a little finger at an object drifted out from under the bridge.

"Square."

Kate looked into the water. Johanna was right, a rectangular frame was bobbing by. It looked like some sort of canvas. Kate frowned, annoyed how some people spoiled the picturesque city with their rubbish.

Johanna squealed and pointed again. "X!"

Kate saw a collapsible wooden chair drifted after the frame. Now she looked again, the frame seemed to be some sort of canvas. Parts were darkened by colours smeared by the water.

"V, mummie! V!"

Kate was beginning to feel uncomfortable. The V shape Johanna was so excited about was clearly an easel.

"A 'T', mummie, it's a..."

As Johanna's voice trailed away Kate clamped her hand over her daughter's eyes. Johanna didn't resist. They stood together, startled into stillness, as Kate watched the body of a thin, blond man, legs together, arms outstretched, float slowly by amid an escort of dead leaves.

***

"Did she say where, Mrs Hudson?"

The woman, tall and solid with agitated hands, seemed irritated by Danny's questions. Probably fretting that he might bring trouble, lower the tone of her establishment.

Maybe it wasn't just him. Danny had the feeling that a lot of things irritated Mrs Hudson. God help the guest who was late down for breakfast

"No, as I told you, she just went out. She's entitled, isn't she? First time she's set foot outside my front door since you checked her in. I wish I had more guests like that, quiet as a mouse, hardly leaves her room."

"Doesn't eat either."

"Pardon?"

"Nothing, look, you're sure she didn't say where she was going?"

"I told you, no."

Danny handed the landlady his card.

"When she comes back, can you give me a call on this number?"

"I don't like prying into my guests' business."

"It's not prying, it's important."

The woman caught the tone in Danny's voice, paused.

"All right, I'll keep an eye open."

Danny stood on the doorstep of the B&B, thinking, as the door closed.

***

It looked fantastic, fanfuckingtastic, like something in a space ship. Mind you, it should, considering what it cost. Still, it was bought off a loan, not real money, so no stress there.

Jas K pushed a slider, turned some knobs, just playing. No point doing it for real unless there was money on the table.

And there could be a lot of money. Build the right rep and you could make a fortune, travel the world, private jets, star parties. Like it used to be.

Jas pushed back his headphones and swept his hand along the curved desk in front of him. Two Pioneer CDJ-2000 decks, and RMX-1000 remix station, an EFX-1000 effects box and a synthesiser, a Korg Kaossilator. That was a mouthful. Then there were his MIDI controllers and the MacBook Pro. Serious kit. The dog's.

The big room was empty and echoing, like some half-derelict warehouse. It looked a mess in full light. The blood red walls looked cheap and streaky with roller marks and bald patches.

The magic only happened when the lights went down, the music came, the punters packed in, and the effects, the lasers, smoke. Then it would be like being inside a beating heart. It's all in the presentation.

The Red Rooms, his club, would put Jas K back where he belonged, at the top. Only a few days to the big opening. Then he'd be killing it.

He looked up as a door opened. He watched the guy in the leather jacket cross the dance floor, the sound of his footsteps clacking back off the walls.

"Hey, Mitch. What's happening," said Jas. "Where's Paulie?"

"Just parking the motor. What do you need?"

"We need to sort this thing with Jessie."

"That skinny kid? Ok, Jas, if you say so."

"What's that supposed to mean?"

"Nothing, Boss, nothing. We were just wondering, like, what it was all about."

"What what's about?"

"Well, you know, she's just this skinny, moody kid, like. I mean, what's the big deal?"

"The big deal, Mitch, is that I want this done, and done proper."

"You knew her back in the day, right? You two've got history?

"That's right, Mitch, history. She's got talents, has Jessie. She could be really useful for my big opening if I play this right. And my special parties as well, especially the parties. But it's got to be smooth, know what I mean? Got to play it clever."

"Right, and you think she'll play ball?"

"Look, Mitch, she's a girl, right? Flash a little cash, say they look fit, tell them they've got a nice bum, and they'll purr like a pussy. Just relax, it'll be smooth."

"Right, boss."

Knight looked up as the club doors banged open again. His face snapped to an instant grin, arms spread wide as the line of girls sashayed across the dance floor towards him.

"Hey, my Pussy Posse. How are you girls doing?"

Princess took a step ahead of the pack, making the most of her expensive teeth, and the cleavage.

"We're good, Jason, really good."

"Ready for my big opening?"

"So ready, Jason," said Princess.

"You guys are just so useful. Useful, that's my word of the day."

He looked at Mitch who was eyeing the girls with a slack-jawed grin.

"And you can be really useful too, Mitch."

"Yeah, Boss? How's that?"

"You can stop mind-shagging my girls and do what you're paid to do."

"Ok, Boss."

***

There was a time when people would soil themselves at the mention of Big Eddie Archer's name. He had been a serious villain in his day with fingers in many pies, a vice-like grip on the tender parts of the city of Brighton and Hove.

Now he said he was retired, after a fashion, taking it easy after his wife Miriam died, spending time with his many grandchildren.

Danny had met him on a case a year or so back. Friendship would be too strong a word. With Eddie Archer, there was family and there was the rest. But Danny and Big Eddie had done each other favours in a time of danger. A reluctant respect had grown between them. Danny valued the man as a contact but he stayed wary. You don't tug your pet rattlesnake's tail.

Danny had run out to the Marina and back at first light. He tried to vary it, maintaining a steady pace most of the way, broken with bursts of fast walking and speed, racing passing cars. It kept things interesting, his own fartlek routine. There were few people about once the bad weather drove away the fair-weather runners.

Then he'd had a quick shower back at his flat, moaning softly to himself as the water surged over his back, rolling his shoulders as the scorching stream melted the knots in his muscles. Dried off and dressed, he'd jumped in the van.

***

PYECOMBE, WEST SUSSEX, THURSDAY
Danny braked to a slippery halt at the top of the muddy track. The smallholding didn't look like much. He climbed out and walked round a large shed into a yard.

"Fuck me, it's Sherlock."

Archer, dressed in body warmer, cords and wellies, stood in the doorway of a small cottage, grinning.

"I've just got breakfast on the go. Come on in."

Danny followed Archer inside.

"Wipe your feet, Danny. Don't want you treading pig muck in here."

Danny did as he was told. He knew Archer was proud of his pigs.

"How are the porkers?"

"Well, apart from the one in the frying pan there, very well. Beautiful animal, your Tamworth, Ferrari of the pig world."

Archer flipped extra rashers into the pan. Danny knew he'd had this place out at Pyecombe for quite a while. In addition to the pigs he kept a few goats and chickens and grew organic veg. It was a hobby, so he said, rhythm of life, restful now he was retired. Danny took it all with a pinch of salt.

Archer had once said his pigs needed a balanced diet of fibre, energy, protein, vitamins and minerals to thrive. Danny knew for a fact that some of those nutrients had been people whose last act on this Earth had been to rub Big Eddie Archer up the wrong way.

When the kettle boiled Archer poured water onto double tea bags in two big Seagulls mugs, then went back to chasing rashers around the frying pan.

"So," said Danny. "How's retirement?"

"Semi-retirement, son, semi."

"What have you been up to?"

"Bit of this, bit of that. Been keeping my head down since that Wolfram thing. But I've still got a few business interests in the city, if you know what I mean. Strictly legit now, of course. And I've taken up sea fishing."

"I used to fish," said Danny.

"I've got a boat down at the marina. You should come out with me sometime."

"Maybe I will."

Archer scooped the bacon from the pan onto buttered white bread, flipped slices on top and pressed down with a meaty hand. He brought them to the small kitchen table and sat down.

"Right, get yourself stuck into that."

Archer took a big bite of his sandwich, chewed vigorously, gave a groan of pleasure.

"Bloody marvellous. Don't let yours go cold."

He took another bite, studied Danny as he chewed.

"So, what brings the great detective out to the sticks?"

"Wanted a bit of advice."

"About what?"

"Armed robbery."

"Mugs' game. Back in the day you could make serious money very quickly. Now you've got all this CCTV, speed cams, GPS tracking, chemical dyes, bloody helicopters, it's a non-starter. The police even have a network on cameras that read your number plates. I mean, fair play, if you're a villain you take your chances. But you could still get clocked just for taking the wife's sister for a scenic run in the country. Civil liberties in this country are a joke."

They looked at each other. Archer held a straight face for as long as he could, then broke into a grin that showed gold fillings.

"What are you after, son?"

"I was interested in back then."

"Give us a second."

They ate their sandwiches, sipped their tea. When Archer was finished he sat back, looking thoughtful.

"It was pretty simple. Shotgun into the false ceiling, lots of noise and mess to get their attention, keep 'em docile. Be a brave man who had a go after that. Mind you, there were a few. North London was popular in my day. Plenty of banks and building societies. You were in and out and minutes from the M1, A1 and the North Circ. A fast car could get you miles away in minutes. Happy days. Now you can't take a dump without some jobsworth catching it on video."

"Where's the money now?" asked Danny.

"Different ball game. Now it's trafficking. Drugs, guns and hookers. Mainly eastern European, Turks and Albanians."

"Does the name Jim Steele mean anything?"

Archer laughed. "Yeah, I knew him. Tosser, ego as big as my knob. Why are you interested?"

"He did some job in Namibia. It might be connected to a missing persons I'm doing."

"Namibia? That Africa? Rings a bell. Some diamond thing. Way out of his league. That guy always did have ambitions his brain cells couldn't handle. It killed him, plane crash. You're asking for trouble once you step off home turf."

"Know anything about his crew?"

"Ooh, hang on, Danny. You're taking me back a bit now. Let me think. There was Ron Hedges, crafty fucker but a good head for a plan. Then there was Sean Collins, nasty temper, got into a few scrapes that way. I remember one guy, McCafferty, Andy McCafferty. He was with them back then but died soon after, car crash. I think."

"Anyone else?"

"No really, just the usual totty. You could call 'em that back then. Is this any help?"

Danny shrugged. "Not sure. The whole thing seems to be a bit hooky but the client's happy to pay so who am I to argue."

"That's the spirit, Danny boy."

"Anyway, I'd better make a move. Got a lot on."

"You'll get there, son. You've got skills. There's no flies on you, Sherlock. If there were, they'd be paying rent. Tell you what, take some of my home-grown veg with you. You'll taste the difference, trust me."

Archer pointed to a table against the far wall loaded with his organic crops. Danny looked across, saw something leaning in the corner.

"Thanks, very generous. What's the shotgun for?"

"Rats," said Big Eddie Archer. "You never know when one'll pop out of the woodwork."

***

As Danny let himself into his flat he was surprised to see Emma in the hall. She looked pale, wringing her hands. He held out a carrier bag.

"Picked up some free veg, organic. Looks good."

Emma ignored the bag, looked up at Danny, fingers worrying away at a piece of hard skin by a nail.

"You ok, Em?"

"Danny... it's your mum."

"Not another stroke?"

"No, she... Danny, she's dead."

"Oh."

"I tried your moby."

"Battery's dead."

"I called a funeral director, a woman. They should be here any minute."

"A woman? Mum'd like that."

"I'll make you a cup of tea. Shall I take the bag?"

"Yes, that would be good. Thanks, Em."

Emma took the carrier bag, went into the kitchen leaving Danny standing in the hall. He turned and looked at the door to his mother's room. It was open three inches.

He stepped inside. She was laying in the hospital bed, on her back, arms by her sides, mouth slightly open to reveal a ridge of bare gum. Even with the curtains drawn Danny could see her skin was yellowing as she went cold. The acid smell of old urine and disinfectant hung above the body like marsh mist.

He didn't hear Emma come up behind him.

"Here's your tea."

The doorbell rang.

"I'll get that, Danny. You drink your tea while it's hot."

CHAPTER 9

He didn't see her at first. The place wasn't crowded but she was tucked into a corner at the back, wearing a big woolly hat, head down, thumbs flying across the iPhone.

"Babe."

Jessie looked up, looked startled. "Hello, Jason."

He gestured around the room. "Why Starbucks? I could have come to your hotel."

"I just wanted some fresh air."

"You want anything?"

She indicated the hot chocolate in front of her. "No, I'm fine."

Jason sat down beside her, reached to touch her leg. "Looking good, babe."

"Don't, Jason."

"No, babe, I mean it. You're looking good, different but good. It's great to see you again, been a while."

"You look good too, Jason."

"Yeah, we're both looking good. I wasn't expecting your call."

"A lot's happened. I was under a lot of pressure. I just wanted to put things right, say sorry for the way I acted."

"That's big of you, babe. You hurt me, you know, really hurt me. I thought we had something really special."

"We did, Jason."

He reached out and touched her shoulder. She stiffened, then seemed to relax a little.

"Maybe we could again, eh, babe?"

"I don't... I..."

"Come on, babe. You said you were sorry. It's all in the past now. We could have a future."

"I don't want to rush anything."

"We don't need to rush, Jessie. Things are different now, got my own business. It's big. I'm going to be famous all over again, believe it."

"I do, Jason, but how..."

"Well, this music business, it's all about presentation, image. You'd be a big asset."

"An asset?"

"Don't say it like that babe. We'd be working together. I've got big prospects."

"I don't want to rush into anything, Jason. I want to take it gently."

"Ok, if you say so, babe. But the world out there's moving faster ever day. You jump on and hang on or chances pass you by, believe it."

Jessie started to get up.

"Where you going?"

"I've got to go."

"I'll come with you."

"No, I need some time to think."

"Don't think too long, Jessie. Big things are happening. You could be a part of that."

Jason watched the slight figure weave her way to the door. When she was gone he pulled out his mobile phone, found the record of her earlier call and saved the number to memory. Then he drank the hot chocolate she'd left.

***

The life was gone but the smells still lingered, thick creams for sore skin the texture of Weetabix, disinfectants, ammonia, the distinctive musty odour of old people and the sour smell of bowels relaxed.

He hadn't been there when she died but he knew how it would have been. He'd seen it enough times. The breathing growing fainter, hands and feet turning blue as the flow of oxygenated blood struggles to reach the extremities, perhaps a final flutter of the eyes, a last raspy breath and it's done. Perfectly normal.

He'd seen it before, young, fit guys maimed, the life leaking out of them. In combat, that was normal, too. Normal, but not natural. The chair creaked as Danny moved. It sounded loud in the stillness of the death room.

The last guy he'd seen had been in a stagnant ditch, horribly mangled, chest and legs, surrounded by bloody field dressings and bits of kit, the guys shouting his name, "Kenny, can you hear me?" "Kenny, stay with us, mate. Chopper's nearly here." Eyelids flickering like butterflies. Then he was gone.

No matter when it happens, bed or battlefield, you're on your own in the end. No matter how many friends you have, someone holding your hand. It's a single ticket for a one-way journey.

He turned at a noise. Emma stood in the doorway. There were people behind her.

"If you'd like a bit longer."

Danny stood up.

"No, let them get on with it. I'm going out."

"Do you want me to come with you?" asked Emma.

Danny shook his head. "No, I've got things to do, got a lot of work on."

"Danny! Not now! Give yourself a little time."

"I'll see you later, Em. And thanks."

***

Detective Inspector Eddie Aziz was trying hard to make sure he didn't spill his macchiato or drop his apple Danish. He'd already taken a bite and got crumbs on his suit.

Breakfast was absorbing so much of his attention he almost bumped into the woman with bed hair. When he saw her he stepped aside to let her pass.

Her face was pink, puffy and wet with tears. The man beside her had his arm around the woman's shoulder but she walked with the movement of a robot, barely aware of what was around her.

Aziz nudged open the swing door with his foot, careful with his coffee, and saw Myers as soon as he stepped inside.

"That the Michaels?"

Myers nodded. "Yes, Len and Martha."

"Poor bastards," said Aziz, testing the temperature of his macchiato.

"Yes," said Myers, "Bekka, Rebecca, was their only child."

"How did it go?"

"Pretty much as usual," said Myers. "Devoted daughter, sociable, talented, great academic record, made all the right noises when they gave her the drugs talk as a teenager."

"And the post mortem confirms it?"

"Yes, the formula's identical."

"What about the guy at Beachy Head? What was the name?"

"Hitch, Damian Hitch, a chemistry student. The PM showed no alcohol in his system, no narcotics."

"Must have been hell bent if he went over those cliffs stone cold sober."

"Maybe," said Myers. "But there's no sign he'd been anywhere near our mystery cocktail."

"So with Rebecca and the other two, that makes three victims then."

"Three so far," said Myers.

***

Danny didn't have much to tell Marion Carter. As he drove over to the Wilbury area of Hove he ran through the Amsterdam trip in his mind. All pretty thin, more doubts than data.

But the woman was paying for it all and he'd promised her an update. It was her call if she wanted to carry on. Danny wasn't going to take money on false pretences, false hopes.

As he walked up her front driveway he paused. The hair on the back of his neck prickled. He looked around, saw nothing odd, didn't know why. Mrs Carter's Blue Toyota Prius wasn't on the drive but that didn't mean anything.

Danny looked at the house. There was a light on upstairs but lots of people did that when they were out to deter burglars. Everything looked in its usual pristine suburban order.

He tried the bell, heard it chime somewhere inside. Nothing happened. He tried again. Same result. She might be out. The missing car said so.

The hair of Danny's neck was still prickling. He respected reactions like that, a kind of sniper radar he'd learned to trust.

He took a quick look back at the empty street. Shame to waste the petrol on a fruitless visit. He slipped down the side passage. It was dark and damp. Ridges of moss were growing through the cracks in the concrete. It struck Danny as odd. The rest of Marion Carter's place was barracks neat.

He stopped at the end, pressing himself against the wall as he peered into the garden. The only illumination came from the bedroom window of the house beyond the long garden which cast a faint silver light, throwing fuzzy shadows across the lawn. The nude rising from the fountain had a sort of ghostly glow. Danny slipped onto the patio, keeping his back against the wall.

It was then that Danny saw the broken glass scattered across the paving. As he took a step forward he saw the silver curve of a broken pane in the patio door.

As he stepped up to the door he saw someone had smashed the movement-sensor security light above, then broken the door glass by the handle. The key was still in the lock on the inside. Very careless.

Danny eased the door open, listened, opened it a little further. He squeezed inside and listened again. The house was quiet.

The sudden image of his brief career as a burglar came back into his mind. He'd been broke and drinking hard back then but that was no excuse. The judge certainly hadn't thought so.

Danny shook his head and concentrated. The house was still. No light, no sound, no smell.

He padded through the conservatory. Everything looked as obsessively tidy as it had on his last visit.

He moved deeper into the house, stopping every few paces to listen. Nothing. In the kitchen washing-up was stacked neatly on the draining board, tea towel hung to dry, everything where it should be.

He turned back and peered through the rear windows down the garden. Every blade of grass was in place.

Danny turned and surveyed the room. There was something odd about the house, more operating theatre than home. No pictures, no knickknacks, nothing personal, nothing quirky. A show home.

In the far corner was a desk. On a shelf just above it were small comic figurines of the same tubby character playing golf, darts and snooker. All in a dust-free immaculate row.

The paperwork on the desk was piled neatly in a stack of plastic trays. He picked up a handful, tilting them toward the faint light from the garden. Utility bills, credit card and bank statements, notification to shareholders of an annual meeting, a letter from the council about a neighbour's plan for a loft extension.

The desk had four drawers. Top left was full of stationery, paperclips, staples, Post-it notes, biros. Bottom left was empty apart from a few pills containers rolling around, diazepam, co-codamol, Imodium.

The top right drawer held a pile of ledgers. Danny flicked through what seemed to be scoring records for the chubby figurine's sports.

The drawer at the bottom right was stiffer than the others. As Danny gripped the handle he noticed the lock had been recently broken. The bare wood was still fresh where it had splintered.

The figurines and score cards indicated this was Bill Carter's desk. A locked drawer would be where he kept his secrets.

Inside, a tin cash box held twenty pounds in fivers and a scattering of change. Beneath it was a pub quiz book and a pile of Golf Monthly magazines.

Disappointed, Danny dug down. At the bottom of the drawer was a cardboard document wallet. He flicked it open and tilted the contents to the light. There were half a dozen computer printouts listing details of luxury holiday resorts around Siem Reap.

Danny had never heard of the place. As he sifted through the printouts something slipped from between the pages. It was another printout, folded small. He held it to the light.

Confirmation of a first class, one-way Malaysia Airlines flight from Heathrow to Phnom Penh with a stopover at Kuala Lumpur.

The named passenger was W Carter.

Danny studied the printout, memorising the detail, then he put everything back where he'd found it. As he turned to scan the room again his eyes lingered on the dark green tank and he moved for a closer look. Tiny fish of impossible colours and shapes swam round in circles, looking bored. Bubbles wriggled upwards from the shipwreck and treasure chest nestling in the gravel at the bottom.

When Danny's shadow fell across the tank the fish were at the glass in a flash. He tapped the glass and watched as they clustered round, trying to eat his finger. The house must have been empty for a while if they were hungry. How often do you feed tropic fish?

Then a thought occurred.

He went into the kitchen, searched the drawers until he found a claw hammer. Its handle was sheathed in rubber. He hefted it to check the weight, picked up a tea towel and returned to the extension.

Beside the tank was a box. Inside, neatly arranged, were containers of fish food, cleaning chemicals, and a fine-gauze net. He lifted the tank lid, set it gently crossways, and began scooping handfuls of shiny gravel into the tea towel. The fish went crazy.

When he had enough he allowed the excess water to soak into the towel before opening the extension glass door onto the patio.

He set the bulging tea towel down on the paving and swung the hammer. There was a satisfying crunch. He hit it three more times, careful to keep the noise to a minimum, then opened the towel. It was filled with sharp fragments of wet gravel.

"Diamonds do not look like that."

Instantly, Danny was on his feet, turning, hammer in hand.

CHAPTER 10

People always made such a fuss. They fussed about food and heating. They fussed about safety. They fussed about blood tests.

These people fussed so much they never had the time to enjoy the one life God had given them. It's not as if they fussed about anything important.

Nancy Hepworth remembered the hard times of the 1920s and 30s. She could still see herself and her mother looking up as plaster dust trickled through the floor boards above their heads as Hitler's bomb fell. But they hadn't fussed. They just brushed themselves down and got on with things. Always well turned out. Always properly fed. Fussing was just a waste of everyone's time. What was it they used to say? Keep calm and carry on. Sensible advice.

Granted, she had been lonely since Cecil passed but she wouldn't admit it. You just dealt with it and got on with things. She was perfectly capable of feeding herself, especially since Gavin had bought her that microwave thing. And she could still enjoy her passion for reading if she used the magnifying glass and sat under that special lamp Gavin had bought her.

The radio always seemed to be talking about electronic books these days but she had no time for modern fads. You couldn't beat turning the crisp pages of a properly bound hardback.

The trouble with young people is that they expected too much. They were frightened of losing something because they had never had the experience of having nothing. You had to take the good with the bad, that was what life was all about.

It was true that the hip hurt but that was hardly surprising. She was 92 years old. She could still dance the Big Apple if she really wanted to, still cut a rug if she did it gently, but you had to accept the passing of the years with good grace. It was the natural order of things.

Nancy eased herself up from the armchair, wobbling slightly as her bony legs took what little weight her thin frame still carried.

That dinner hadn't agreed with her at all. Some of them were quite flavoursome but she had never quite got used to the idea of heating up food in a box. If people enjoyed good home cooking there wouldn't be so many ailments in the world, she was certain of that.

A passing car drew Nancy's attention to the window. She shuffled carefully across the carpet, leaning on her stick, and pulled back the lace curtain.

No sign of the rain they had forecast. Why was it, with all their computers, they could never get it right? You can't rely on machines to do everything for you.

A big car pulled up on the driveway next door. A man emerged and moved quickly into the house. Nancy hardly knew her neighbours. The men rushed to work early in the morning, then rushed back late at night. Their wives rushed to school and then heaven only knew where. Rush, rush, rush, no way to live your life.

Nancy's old eyes narrowed when she thought she saw something strange in the swimming darkness before her. She squinted, tilted her head, trying to focus. She couldn't be sure. But better to be safe than sorry.

Nancy Hepworth shuffled back across the carpet and picked up the phone.

***

The woman was standing in the extension doorway to the kitchen. Danny, hammer in hand, studied her, angry that he had let himself be distracted and surprised.

She looked familiar. Options sped through his mind... a book... glass of white wine... Naomie the Bond girl.

"You were in the Bellerophon a few days back."

"Yes, Mr Lancaster, and we spoke on the telephone. I tried to hire you to find out some information. It is urgent but you were very busy."

"So you thought you'd find out for yourself."

"My name is Grace Nujoma, Mr Lancaster. I think we should go somewhere to talk."

"Bloody right," said Danny.

He indicated for her to go first through the broken back door and followed her along the side passage.

When they reached the end he tapped the woman's arm and signed for her to stop, peered round the gate and out along the driveway into the road. The street seemed quiet. As he took a step forward he saw something move, a curtain opposite.

Danny gripped Grace's arm. She resisted but tugged.

"What are you doing?"

"We've got to get a move on."

"What do you mean?"

Then they heard the siren.

***

Nancy Hepworth squinted round the net curtain. The street outside seemed very dark. It was no wonder people didn't feel safe. The council should do something. What did they do with all that money they charged?

She thought she saw shadows moving but it might just be a trick of the dull light, or perhaps her eyes. She had been reading rather a lot this evening and they were tired.

Then Nancy saw the reassuring sparkle. The patrol car streaking down the street, blue lights flashing off front windows, and came to a halt outside.

The two officers jumped out and walked up the empty driveway. Nancy watched as one studied the front of the house while the other made his way down the side passage with a torch.

Nancy was so absorbed by the excitement at No23 that she didn't notice a white van which pulled out from the kerb a little way up the road and drove slowly by.

***

They drove in silence. Danny just went the way the van was pointing. Grace Nujoma sat beside him, staring ahead at the darkness.

After a while Danny took his bearings, circled around, picked a pub he'd never been to before. He bought drinks, lager and white wine, and they retreated to a corner.

It was a barn of a place, the only other customers a large family gathered for some celebration at the far end. There were three or four generations, kids playing with toys on the floor, others running about.

A large group of women were talking loudly, breaking into frequent shrieking laughter. Two old men sat at the back nursing their pints and watching.

The younger women were dressed to kill. There was a steady trickle of guys going outside for a cigarette. On the small stage, a band was tuning up. "One... two. One...two."

"They seem to be enjoying themselves," said Grace.

"They do."

A glass shattered on the floor and a loud cheer went up.

"We'd better have our chat before the entertainment starts," said Danny.

"Very well, Mr Lancaster."

"Call me Danny. And you're Grace?"

"That is correct."

"OK, after you."

"It is a personal matter, Danny."

"Not so personal that you didn't try to hire me earlier."

"That is true. I do not know this country. It is my first visit. I thought I would need a guide."

"Guide to what?"

"I am trying to find some people. It is a question of lost property."

"And you think Marion Carter is somehow connected?"

"I don't know but I wanted to be sure."

"So you broke in. What got you interested in the Carters?"

"I believe they once knew a man named Jim Steele."

"Who was killed in a plane crash in Namibia?"

"Yes."

"And you would be from...?"

"Yes."

"Long way to come on a hunch."

"As I said, it is very important to me, a personal matter. I am here on behalf of a family that lost something very precious."

"Precious as in diamonds?"

"I guessed that was what you were looking for in the fish tank. Rough diamonds do not look as people imagine."

A wobbly electric guitar chord wanged around the room. Danny winced.

"We haven't got much time. You say you're looking for friends of Jim Steele. Do the names Ron Hedges and Sean Collins mean anything to you?"

"I have heard them."

"How about Bill Carter?"

Grace nodded.

"You say this is about diamonds but I thought the gang lost their haul in the crash."

"That is what the records say."

"But you don't believe it?"

"There is more to this case than a simple robbery."

They both turned at a large woman's raucous laugh. She was sitting, head forward, tearful eyes screwed shut, jaws locked open, shrieking. When she opened her eyes she saw Danny looking, ran her eyes up and down him, raised her glass, smiled.

A drum roll rattled around the room.

"Do you know that lady?" asked Grace.

"Never met her," said Danny. "Look, we're not going to get much peace and quiet here. Like I said, I've got a lot on at the moment but we seem to have interests in common so it makes sense to work together."

"I can pay you."

"We'll see about that. Do you have a mobile?"

"I bought one at the airport."

"Give me your number and I'll run you back to your hotel."

"And you will help?" asked Grace.

"We'll talk about it tomorrow."

After a noisy warm-up the band broke into Maggie May as Danny and Grace left the pub.

***

PORTSLADE, FRIDAY MORNING

She stood, one hand up high holding on to the open door, the other on her hip. Danny would have cracked some joke about teapots if it hadn't been for the look on her face.

"Hello, stranger."

"Hello, Cheryl."

They looked at each other.

"So can I come in?"

Cheryl stepped aside, swept her arm down the hallway. Danny wiped his boots on the mat, stepped inside and walked ahead of her to the kitchen.

"I suppose you want tea?"

"If it's not too much trouble."

As Cheryl filled the kettle Danny pulled his smokes from his pocket. He had the cigarette packet half way to his lips before he sensed his sister's disapproving eyes on him.

"In the garden if you're going to do that. It stinks the place out and turns the walls yellow. You should have given it up a long time ago."

Danny slipped his lighter into the packet and the pack back into his pocket.

"Ok, Sis, enough of a bollocking for one day, eh?"

He turned towards the back door but stopped when he saw movement in the hallway. Danny knew his face had set wide with shock but couldn't stop himself. This wasn't a poker face moment.

The legs seem to go on forever, muscles taughtened by the high-heeled shoes and tinged a faint orange with fake tan. The red dress stuck to her curves like cling film. The fake tan extended across the bare shoulders, fading slightly along the line of the dress's halter strap.

He knew his mouth was trying to move but words wouldn't form, no sound emerged.

"Hello, Dad."

"Hello, Hayley, you look … nice."

He heard a short laugh from Cheryl.

"Danny, meet your daughter. I've got to put the ironing away so I'll let you two get acquainted."

Neither of them looked as Cheryl swept up a big pile of clean laundry and walked out.

They stood still and silent for what seemed like a long time.

"You all right, Dad?"

"Me? Er, yes, fine. You?"

"Yeah, good. Haven't seen you for a while."

"No, been meaning to. I've been busy."

A quivering silence again. Danny was looking at the young woman in the tiny dress with the plunging cleavage. He was seeing a skinny kid chasing butterflies, squealing with the pure uncontaminated joy of a day on the beach. Big gap-tooth smile. Clear shining eyes. No fears. No bad memories.

No idea of what's ahead.

Then the young woman in the tiny dress was there again and it was Kathy, when they were first married, before the cancer came.

Danny felt his stomach spasm into a painful knot.

"Dad?"

He shook his head.

"Sorry, bit startled there. You're not a school?"

"I'm a bit late. There's a party tonight so I wanted to try this on. It's new."

"A party?"

As soon as Danny spoke the words he saw Hayley's face harden and regretted the tone.

"You don't like me going out like this?" She did a half-twirl.

"I just…"

"You think I'm a tart?"

"No, just dressed like one."

Danny saw Hayley's eyes were the same colour as her mother's as they flared with anger.

"I've already had the lecture from Auntie Cheryl. I know what I'm doing. I'm a big girl which you'd know if you ever bothered to visit."

Hayley snatched her handbag from the kitchen table and moved towards the door. Danny put his hand on her arm. She shrugged it off but slowed.

"Just give us a minute."

"I'm in a rush, the bus."

"You not changing?"

"I haven't time now."

"Look, Hayley, I'm not having a go, just want a chat."

He put his hands gently on her upper arms, held her away from him as he admired the flawless skin and tall, slender frame.

"You look good, Hayley, really good. It's just that I worry about you."

Her voice was softer now, buy wary.

"You've got a funny way of showing it."

"I just want you to be safe and happy."

His eyes ran down the dress, what there was of it, and back up to her face.

"And Cheryl's all right with this?"

"It's no big deal, Dad."

Danny forced a breath into his tightened chest, felt his shoulders drop.

"Well, you'll certainly pull the boys in that outfit."

She looked away, reddened very slightly.

"Just don't forget," said Danny. "You'll get noticed by the good-looking boys but you're also going to get the once-over from all the ugly guys, the fat ones, the pervs and the pensioners."

"DAD!"

"Just so you know, you look good, make the most of it. Just be happy and don't do anything you don't want to, don't take any crap. If anyone tries it on, knee them in the bollocks."

"DAD!"

Hayley looked up at her father. Her face softened. Then she stretched up, perched on the ridiculous heels, and pecked him on the cheek.

"I've got to go, my bus."

"Hang on a minute."

"Oh, *Daaad*."

The whining appeal rose and fell. Cheryl came back with an empty laundry basket.

"You still here, Danny? Wonders never cease. Must be a new world record."

Danny tipped his head back, screwed his eyes shut, pinched the bridge of his nose.

"I've got some news, didn't want to do it on the phone."

When he opened his eyes Danny could see he'd pricked the attention of his sister and his daughter. He looked at Hayley.

"It's Nan."

"What about her?" asked Cheryl.

"She died."

Cheryl pressed her face into her cupped hands. Hayley's crimson mouth collapsed into an ugly pucker. She lurched at Danny, reaching out. He folded his arms around her shoulders, held her tight as she fought for the breath to sob.

CHAPTER 11

BRIGHTON, FRIDAY

Hard to imagine what it would be like to lose every friend you had in a single day. Danny had lost mates, good mates, in combat. Remembered the feeling. The Shock. The Anger. The need to settle scores.

But everyone?

He'd been reluctant to take the book back to the library. Wanted to hang on to it. Had a last flick through in a comfy chair by the towering wall of dark glass that overlooked Jubilee Square before handing it in at the desk.

With the 100th anniversary of the First World War approaching he'd wanted to read up on it. The book on the Battle of the Somme had been hard work at times, 20,000 dead on the first day, 40,000 wounded. It did your head in.

And the Pals battalions, ordinary blokes recruited from the same town or the same job. Grew up together, worked together, joined up together, died together walking towards machineguns. Whole streets of widows and orphans.

It was different now, better training, better tactics, reconnaissance, communications, close air and artillery support. Even that didn't always work.

And it didn't make losing a mate any easier, one smiling face. But a hundred? It was just the sheer scale of it, the sheer numbers. Did really your head in.

To be fair, he could have kept the library book for a few more days. But, what with mum and everything, he wanted a bit of time alone, even if he was busy.

Pictures running through his mind, Danny wandered distracted down the wide grey pedestrian expanse of New Street. As he approached the Theatre Royal he glanced left at the Royal Pavilion and the statue of comedian Max Miller. He'd read some of the Cheeky Chappie's dodgy jokes in the library a while back. They made him smile. But not today.

As Danny waited for a gap in the North Street traffic he looked downhill towards the Old Steine. He'd visited the memorial there, 2,390 names from the first war. There was a plaque for the Old Contemptibles, the first British troops in action in France in 1914 against a much bigger German army.

Danny dodged through the traffic and cut through an alley into the Lanes. He passed a man with a long grey beard sitting in a doorway, ferocious concentration focussed on adding to the menageries of delicate origami animals spread out on the ground around his legs. The slightest of breezes tipped a yellow swan on its side.

Danny moved on, stepping it out, pausing once briefly outside The Druids, his dad had enjoyed a pint there, before walking on to Brighton Town Hall.

As he walked he recalled another memorial in The Steine, a Burma Star plaque, different war, same guys, vicious hand-to-hand fighting against the Japanese across a tennis court. The memorial bore the haunting Kohima Epitaph, 'When you go home, tell them of us and say, for their tomorrow, we gave our today'.

It was turning into a day of death, mum, the guys on the Somme and elsewhere.

The town hall was a grand old wedding cake of a building tucked away just behind the seafront off Prince Albert Street. Danny had a quick smoke before introducing himself at the register office reception on the ground floor.

He spent a few minutes in the over-hot waiting area before being invited into a small room by an assistant registrar with sinus problems.

Danny had found some furry old paperwork in a biscuit tin in his mother's room. He read out the relevant information as the woman filled in a draft death entry, full name, maiden name, date and place of death, occupation, name and occupation of husband, pension details.

It seemed unreal to Danny. Between nose blowings, the assistant registrar was soft spoken and sympathetic but he knew it was a sales pitch she trotted out umpteen times a day. She was just doing her job. But the frequent trumpeting into a tissue was getting on his nerves.

He checked a draft of the register entry, received a green form for the funeral director and a white one for the pension people, and paid for some death certificates.

So, now it's official.

Two minutes later Danny was relieved to be out in the crisp autumn air, away from the hothouse of the council office.

He stood and smoked, looking around. Nothing had changed. People still dashed about, traffic ground along, the world turned. It was as if mum had never existed.

As he walked away from the town hall Danny made a quick phone call. "Caffè Nero in 20 minutes ok with you? Yes... Prince Albert Street. See you there."

***

Jessie flushed, pulled the cubicle door closed behind her and crossed the tiled floor to wash her hands. She was angry, had come to the club to speak to Jason again, reassure herself, be certain. But he wasn't there, just two leering arseholes who said he'd catch her later on the front at Brighton Wheel, kept eyeing her up.

She was rinsing her hands when she heard the door open. Jessie didn't need to turn. A glance in the mirror told her there were five of them. Cleavage and fake tan. Dressed to party even if it was the middle of the day.

The one in the middle, the blonde with the long pink nails, stood three feet behind Jessie, hands on hips. The others took up station, two each side.

"What are you doing in here?" asked the blonde.

"Washing my hands."

"You can't be in here."

"Why?"

"It's the girls' toilets, for girls."

The others laughed.

The blonde reached to tug at Jessie's tam but she batted her hand away.

"Vicious little cow, aren't you? What's the matter? Got a bald patch or something?"

The blonde reached again. Jessie slapped her hand away.

"Oooh, vicious. You sure you're not a guy? Maybe I should get security. You might be a pervert eyeing the girls in here."

"I'm going," said Jessie.

She tried to move around the blonde but the others closed up. Jessie looked along the simpering wall of fashion and fake tan.

"Jas says he used to know you," said the blonde. Jessie nodded.

"What were you, like, his cleaning lady or something?"

"We knew each other a while ago," muttered Jessie.

"I can't hear you."

The blonde tried to prod Jessie in the stomach with a long nail. Jessie slapped her hand hard and the blonde snatched it back.

"Those are words you need to remember, 'A while ago'," said the blonde. "Like history, over, in the past. I can't think what Jas wanted a skinny little bitch like you for. Dental floss, maybe?"

The blonde reached forward, long nails trailing the front of Jessie's jacket. Jessie stepped back but the blonde stepped forward. Her fingers found Jessie's small breast through the thick material of her jacket, explored, closed, squeezed.

"Just checking," said the blonde with a smile. The other girls laughed.

The blonde started to turn, smile at the others. She reeled back with a yowl as Jessie's fist caught her in the mouth.

"You hit me!" hissed Princess.

She touched her face in shock and her eyes went wide when she saw her wet fingers.

"You bitch! I'm bleeding."

Princess hurled herself at Jessie who used the firm grip of her trainers on the tiled floor to pivot sideways. Princess lost her balance and began to totter off her heels, fell, reached out, grabbed Jessie's jacket, pulled her down.

They hit the floor in a grunting, panting heap. Princess, back to the floor, reached up. Her hands were claws, nails extended.

Jessie grabbed a shock of bleached blonde hair and banged Princess's head on the tiling. Arms were gripping Jessie's jacket now. She twisted to break their grip, wriggled free, slipped out between two of the girls.

Her friends helped Princess to her feet. She swayed on her heels, back of a hand to her bloody lips, staring venom at Jessie.

"Stay away from Jas or you're really going to regret it," hissed Princess, make-up running as her eyes watered.

Jessie spun round in the toilet doorway, stuck up a finger.

"Spin on this."

***

Danny bought two flat whites and joined Grace. She had picked a quiet table away from most of the other customers who were chatting, reading The Guardian, The Independent, or using the free wifi on their MacBooks.

"Sleep ok?"

"Yes, thank you. My hotel is very comfortable."

"So, what's Namibia like?"

"Have you been to Africa, Danny?"

"Kenya."

"As a soldier?"

"Training, yes."

"There have been too many soldiers in Africa. My father was SWAPO in the Border War."

Danny nodded.

"There has been much blood spilled. You English think ethnic cleansing is something that happened in Hitler's war. A hundred years ago, when my country was called German South West Africa, their soldiers slaughtered the Herero and Nama people and drove the survivors out into the Kalahari to die. It is a desert. It means 'thirst land ' in the Setswana language. The South Africans came to Namibia in your First World War to fight the Germans and later brought us apartheid. We did not own our own country until 1990."

"And what's it like now?"

"It is a beautiful place of deserts and mountains and nature."

"I like the sounds of that." He looked at his watch. "Anyway, niceties over, down to business. You want my help. I need to know what you know."

"I, too, am a private investigator."

"Who's your client?"

"That is confidential."

"Of course it is. Can you tell me something about them?"

"These people, Steele and the others, they took something from them, something very precious."

"Well, we are talking diamond thieves here."

"They were very well organised. They posed as a wildlife camera team making a documentary for the television. But it was all a front for volstruis."

"What's that?"

"It is a codename they gave to their robbery plan. In the Afrikaans language it means ostrich."

"Big bird that thinks it's invisible with it's head in a hole."

"I am sorry?"

"Never mind." Danny looked at his watch again. "From what you say, they were very organised, hiding in plain sight behind a cover story. You seem to know a lot about them."

"I have contacts. I spent a lot of time working on this."

"A hell of a long time," said Danny. "You said this diamond theft happened eight years ago. Why come here now?"

"A contact I know, a diamond merchant in Antwerp, told me someone had telephoned him. They wanted to sell."

"How do you know it's the same stones?"

"The man who called, he described one stone particular stone, the biggest in the haul. It is very distinctive. They call it the Demon's Eye."

"Did your man say anything about his mystery caller."

Grace shook her head.

"Not very much. But he left a telephone number. It was a Brighton number."

"Careless," said Danny.

"Fear and greed will do that to a guilty thief," said Grace.

"Ok, so we don't know where Bill Carter is and we don't know what's happened to Mrs Carter. She might have run off but she didn't strike me as the type."

"What do we do, Danny?"

"You keep your phone close. I'll ask around and see what I can dig up."

"That does not sound very positive."

"It's the best I can think of for now."

"That is not acceptable."

"Well, I'm sorry but it's the best I've got. As I said before, I didn't take on the job when you called because I've got a lot on already."

"It is urgent, Danny. Very urgent."

"Everybody's case is urgent. It's been eight years. A few more days won't make any difference."

"But this is the first strong lead I have had. Danny, please, I cannot wait another eight years."

"I'm doing the best I can," he snapped.

"Is everything all right? You seem distracted."

"My mum died yesterday."

Danny was startled he'd said it.

"I am so sorry. You should not be working now."

"No choice. Her problems are over now. I get paid by the living."

"Danny... I... I do not have much money. It is expensive here in England."

"Don't worry about that for now. We'll sort something out."

"You are a good man, Danny. I would value your advice."

"Well, the first piece is never surprise a man who's holding a claw hammer."

***

As soon as the door was open she was in his arms, her grip fierce. He could feel her shaking. Then she pulled away, looked up at him.

"Are you ok, Danny?"

"Fine."

"You look tired."

"I'm fine. Just came to see how you guys are doing."

"I've just brewed up. Come into the kitchen."

Danny's sister brought his tea to the table. He watched as she moved about, tidying things, straightening things, pulling the creases out of hanging tea towels.

"Cheryl, just leave it and sit."

She turned, gave him a weary smile.

"I just can't seem to settle. It's like a dream."

She brought her tea to the table and sat down.

"Did she... did she suffer... at the end?"

"No, it was quick. She wouldn't have known anything."

"We should have done more"

"Like what? She was as comfortable as we could make her. She stayed in her own home to the end, which is what she wanted. People die, Cheryl. Don't beat yourself up."

They looked at each other.

"How are the kids taking it?"

Cheryl shrugged.

"Wayne isn't too bad. He's younger, doesn't have the memories. Hayley's really upset. She grown-up for her age but kids these days don't seem to think people will ever die."

"Not a bad way to live till it happens," said Danny.

"But are you ok, Danny?"

"I'm fine."

"You're just saying that."

"No, she had a good run. She's not in pain or sitting in pee any more."

"You make it sound like a good thing."

"Had to happen sooner or later, Cheryl."

"So what will you do now?"

"I've got to get the arrangements sorted first. Emma fixed up the funeral director, a woman in Hove."

"Mum'd like that."

"I've sorted the paperwork and I'll arrange the funeral."

"Ok, Danny, and I'll do the food and drinks for after. You'll have to write a eulogy."

"A what?"

"You know, a tribute for the vicar to read at the service."

"Why me?"

"Well I can't string a sentence together."

"Ok, I'll sort it."

They both turned at a rumble of feet on the stairs. The kitchen door crashed open.

"Dad!"

Hayley rushed into the kitchen and threw her arms around Danny. She was a pretty kid but now her eyes were pink and puffy, her mouth distorted into a figure-of-eight stretched wide in a failed effort to let out the grief.

Danny hugged her, felt her narrow shoulders spasm with bursts of crying. The partygoer was gone. Hayley was a kid again. After long minutes she calmed down and pulled away.

"Are you all right, Dad?"

"I'm ok, Hayley. I'm fine."

"But you're in the flat all alone."

"Don't fret, I'll manage."

"I want to help."

"Don't worry, everything's in hand."

"But Dad..."

The words trailed away as she broke down again. Danny put an arm around her shoulder, looked across at his sister.

"Well, I'd better crack on."

***

Danny had a lot to do, paperwork for the funeral directors, sort the ceremony, tell people. Then there was Jessie, probably still texting away at her B&B.

He had told Grace he'd ask around about the Carters. It had sounded pretty thin when he'd said it. He knew it. She knew it.

There might be one line of inquiry about the Carters worth trying. He didn't hold out much hope but, then again, you never knew.

He took out his phone, scrolled through his contacts, dialled.

"Hey, Bob, yeah, it's Danny. Look, have you got a high-vis jacket I can borrow? No, Bob, you really don't want to know."

He ended the call. A lot to do but Danny felt suddenly weary, as if a plug had been pulled and he was leaking energy.

Someone in a hurry bumped his shoulder, glared as he swept past. What ever happened to politeness? Danny wandered on along the busy pavement. Two rough sleepers were playing chess in a doorway, blackened fingers emerged from the frayed cuffs of heavy overcoats to make their moves.

Danny's left leg hurt him. He could feel the movement of the prosthesis as he walked, chaffing the skin grafts. Odd, he never usually noticed.

***

It seemed to take a lifetime. Something so simple, something you never once gave a thought to, was now a major effort. She had been a wonderful dancer once. People had commented. Now, walking the length of her hallway could be like an Olympic event when her hip was playing up.

Nancy Hepworth leaned into her stick, slid a slippered foot along the carpet, took another shuffling step.

Through the bevelled glass of the front door she could see a yellow glow. She wasn't expecting anyone. It was probably a waste of her time but, even so, it was exercise. With the hip hurting, if she sat too long she seized up.

The yellow shape moved, someone rocking on the balls of their feet. Perhaps the visitor liked dancing too.

Nancy reached the front door and pulled the bolts. It was so much easier since Gavin had raised them so she didn't have to bend. She gripped the knob of the big door and shuffled a few steps back before peering round.

"Can I help you?"

"Parcel for Carter."

"I beg your pardon?"

He was wearing one of those ridiculous bright-coloured vests, a good looking young man with a lovely smile. He had one of those computer things in one hand, pointed over his shoulder with a pen he held in the other.

"Parcel for number 23 across the road. There's no reply so I was wondering if you could take it in?"

Nancy looked at the house opposite.

"I don't know the woman. I don't really know any of my neighbours."

"Not a problem," said the young man. "If you could sign for it I'll pop a card through their door to tell her where it is."

Nancy thought for a moment but the young man carried on.

"Lovely front garden you've got there. Must look really good in the summer. You do it yourself?"

"No, Gavin, my son, does it for me."

They both looked down when something made a chinking noise. Nancy saw her three pints of milk on the step. It was rather expensive but Barney, Harold and Trixie drank so much after they'd been out on their adventures.

"I'll take those through for you if you like."

Before Nancy could say anything the young man had scooped up the bottles and moved past her into the hallway.

She gripped her stick. Gavin had warned her about strangers calling. But he did seem a nice young man. Nancy pushed the door to and shuffled down the hall.

When she reached the kitchen the young man was putting the bottles in the fridge.

"No," said Nancy. "Don't put them there. My cats don't like their milk too cold. Just pop them on the top."

"No problem. Can I make you a cup of tea while I'm here?"

"Don't you have work to do?"

"A couple of minutes won't make any difference."

Nancy gave the young man a hesitant nod and watched as he put the kettle on, warmed the pot, measured out the leaves and lined up two cups.

"Mind if I join you?"

Feeling increasingly uneasy, Nancy shook her head. The man indicated she should sit at the kitchen table and she did as she was told. He put the tea in front of her.

"Do you know the people at No23? The Carters?"

Nancy shook her head.

"I don't really have much to do with my neighbours."

"I only ask because I've tried delivering before but they never seem to be in."

"Well," said Nancy. "I haven't seen him for a while. His wife was certainly about until a few days ago. I recognise her car but it wasn't parked on their drive last night."

"They must have a busy social life. Do they get many visitors?"

Nancy sipped her tea, looked up at the visitor. He had such nice manners, such a rarity these days. But he asked a lot of questions. And Gavin had warned her about strangers.

"Who did you say you worked for?"

"Delivery firm."

"What is the name of the company?"

"You wouldn't have heard of it."

Nancy took a firm grip on the handle of her walking stick.

"I don't think you're telling the truth."

The visitor looked at the expensive watch on his wrist.

"If that's the time, I'd better be going."

Nancy felt a shudder run through her as she pulled herself up faster than was wise. She surprised herself at how fast she walked the length of the hallway. The visitor was waiting in the doorway.

"One thing before I go. You shouldn't let people in without checking their ID first."

"You're not really a delivery man, are you?"

The visitor shrugged.

"I think you'd better go, young man."

Nancy looked up at him. A good-looking boy. Such a nice smile.

"Thank you for the tea. You make a very good cup of tea."

"No problem."

"And the Carters..." said Nancy Hepworth.

"Yes?" said the visitor.

"The only regular visitor is a young man. He drives a big silver car, the sort these so-called celebrities drive when you see them on the television news."

"Thank you, Mrs Hepworth. You take care of yourself."

Nancy stood in the doorway, watching as he walked towards his van, wondering how he knew her name. He was light on his feet, would have made a good dance partner.

As she pushed the door closed Nancy sighed, smiled.

***

As Danny walked down Nancy Hepworth's front path he was feeling pleased with himself. Dangerous if you let that carry you away but a little didn't hurt.

Half way to the van he had a sudden thought, weighed the risks, weighed the possible gains. Sod it, nothing ventured...

Glancing back to check Mrs Hepworth's curtains weren't twitching, he crossed the road and slipped down the side passage of Marion Carter's house. The moss-patched alley didn't seem quite so sinister in daylight.

The bin was stored at the back at the top of the garden. Danny opened it, fervently hoping it wouldn't involve too much digging. He didn't fancy having to climb in there.

Something old and fishy was lurking in the mouldering shadows. He found a garden cane on a flowerbed nearby and began to poke about.

Milk cartons, an empty baked bean tin, cardboard toilet roll tubes, face cleanser, coffee grounds, ready meal packaging, half a stale loaf. Pretty clear the Carters weren't big on recycling.

The fishy stench got stronger.

And then he found it. A wad of paperwork, some of it wet, all crumpled. Someone had made a bad job of tearing it up. Had to be something in there. He fished out the papers and pulled out an old newspaper stuffed down the side of the bin. At least that was dry. He bundled up his prize and shoved it in his pocket.

Danny felt chuffed. You needed a bit of expertise in this detecting job, and a bit of talent. But you also needed luck.

CHAPTER 12

She couldn't tear her eyes away. It really was like being hypnotised, the slow movement and changing perspective. It was like you could see the Earth turning.

Her art teacher had always said she was creative. It was the only good thing they ever put on her school report.

They dressed it up for the parents but she sort of knew what they meant. If she was standing in front of something, anything, she wanted to know what it looked like from the side, from the back, inside. Jessie leaned forward until her nosed touched the cold glass, watching.

"Fantastic up here, isn't it?" said Jas K. "I can see it from my balcony. I live over there."

Jas jerked a finger over his shoulder towards a gleaming white Art Deco-style apartment block across the road.

"It's named after some yank architect. Baby Spice used to have a place there. You should come over."

Jas turned back to look over Jessie's shoulder at the moving view.

"I come up most days, just to look around. You can see 25 miles on a clear day. Makes you feel like you're on top of the world."

He moved closer, reached up to put his hands on the wall above the window, forming a cage of arms that held her to the glass. Jessie could feel him close behind, his crotch pressing against her bottom. Was it just the movement of the capsule or was he bumping her?

"So," said a quiet voice close to her ear. "Are you going to give me what I need?"

Jessie felt his breath against her neck, tried to push closer to the glass.

"I don't know, Jason. I don't know."

"You came to find me, Jessie. You wanted to make up. You hurt me when you walked out, you know. Really hurt me."

"You were screwing that little slut. I walked in, or had you forgotten?"

"If wasn't like that, Jessie. You know it, I explained. I was under a lot of pressure. She was just a girl."

"Just a girl on all fours on our bed."

"It was nothing, babe. There was only ever you."

"Really?"

"Really. And now you're back we can be together. I've got plans, big plans. You can be part of that."

"Part of what?"

"You know what I need."

"I don't know, Jason. It's been... I was..."

"Let's not get distracted by details now, eh babe?"

"I don't know, Jason. I just don't know."

He gripped her arms, spun her round. Jessie flinched when she saw the look on Jason's face.

"Look, baby, you came back to me. You came to find me and make things better. You want to make it up to me. Got to, haven't you?"

Jessie tried to pull back but his grip on her upper arms was solid.

"Give me some time, Jason. Just a little time."

"Not too much, eh? I mean, I'm a patient guy." He stroked her hair. "You know that, Jessie. But things are moving. We've got to move with them. Right, babe?"

Jessie nodded. He turned her round to face the glass.

"You look at the view, babe. You look and you make up your mind soon."

***

The day was fading as Danny picked up a six-pack on his way to the beach. A guy in a duffle coat stopped him, asked for a light. So many people with a cigarette and no lighter. Piss poor planning. If I had a pound for every time...

He sat on the ridge of shingle just above the waterline. It wasn't comfy. It didn't matter. He rubbed at his left knee. The stump ached but it could have been worse. He should get it looked at when he could find the time.

The government had announced plans for specialist centres for wounded troops, prodded by Help For Heroes and BLESMA. From what he'd read in the paper, the nearest was Portsmouth. There was talk of bionic legs, powered by microprocessors, to help you climb stairs, kneel, even walk backwards. Top notch kit, cost a packet.

He was lucky he didn't need stuff like that. He'd got off lightly. Could have been wedding tackle or brain. He knew guys. And he'd kept his knee joint. Was just missing an ankle. That made a big difference to mobility. So he'd lost a leg, gained baggage which weighed more. But, really, it was just a scratch, a twisted sock.

Maybe he'd give Portsmouth a try but he wasn't getting his hopes up. A place like that needed the staff and the expertise. It needed people who took an interest, did their best for you, rather than griping about how you were stretching their NHS budget. He'd see.

Danny thought back to when the Taliban bullets had smashed his left leg.

His memory of that night was hazy. Might not even have been real. He'd been so out of it that the pictures in his head might well have been borrowed from Pogo's version, or Si's, when they talked about it afterwards.

He remembered a fantastic night sky, a rich black river carrying a cascade of swirling silver that sparkled and pulsed. The silver streaks were shooting stars. The coloured ones were tracer. The stinging on his face was dirt and grit thrown up by enemy rounds hitting the ground around him.

He thought he recalled shouting, urgent, and the rattle and tap of small arms. Then a voice close by.

"Jesus, look at the state of him."

"Can you hear me, mate?"

"Just stay with us, ok, Danny?"

Pain and confusion and darkness and screaming. Then someone stabbed him in the leg with a morphine autojet and the night collapsed in on top of him.

You can't remember pain, no one can. What you remember is the fear of pain, the indentations it punches into your brain. Angry and bitter at first, and afraid. Turned from athlete to cripple in a split second.

Civvies didn't understand violence. It's not glossy movie slomo. The speed of an explosion stuns you. A flash of violence can be over before you know what's happened, or why.

Memories fade or distort but something like that, it never changes. It's engraved into you for life like a burn or a tattoo. Like a stick of Brighton rock, the same message all the way through.

It wasn't surprising really. If you've had real fear, not an unpayable bill or a bollocking from the boss. If you'd been up close, too close, to panting, piss-yourself, shit-yourself fear, you can't help but be changed. You close in on yourself, pull up the drawbridge. Because you're always waiting for the next time.

Most people didn't understand, weren't interested. Most people think they're civilised, liberal, caring. But if a meteorite hit, took out comms, power, the internet, it would take just a few days before ordinary families were fighting to the death with sticks and bricks in Tesco's car park for rotting food in runny freezers. Horse would be a bloody luxury.

Even if you got a bit, how many could light a fire from twigs and leaves, build a bivvy to kip in after.

Fragile thing, civilisation.

Danny thought about life after the leg, the journey, waking up in hospital pincushioned with tubes, Headley Court, what seemed like an age walking on sticks, then the first wobbling steps.

He'd had moments of private terror in the dark since Headley Court. Sometimes he took his Afghan operational service medal from his sock drawer and sat staring at the silver disc with its red, blue and brown ribbon and clasp, Queen on the front, compass points and crowns on the back, his name engraved around the edge.

Other times Danny would hammer the walls, dark rage bubbling in a leftovers stew of Afghan, the baby Emma had lost, fear for the future, all sorts.

Sometimes he felt like trashing the flat just for the hell of it. Other times he jumped at the sound of a firework or a car backfiring. The sweating nightmares still crept up on him. He had a temper, everyone had. You just treated it like a big dog, kept it under constant control.

But the feelings bred a special awareness, alertness burned into your unconscious mind. Where people were, left or right, behind you. You watched movement, expression, mood, always anticipating, reading people, how they'll react. Even shopping in Churchill Square he couldn't stop himself checking the roofline and upper windows.

And even all that wasn't good enough. You had to be lucky too.

Sometimes he felt like screaming but couldn't be bothered. No point.

Some days, not often, it seemed simpler if he'd died out there, save himself a lot of aggro, save a lot of people the aggro.

Danny knew he would never settle, never be really at peace. It would all be prowling in the background until the day he died. Knowing that was the way it was made it somehow easier. Relax with a pint or two, enjoy time with friends, aware that it was lurking but ignoring it apart from the times when you really, really couldn't.

***

As Danny picked up another tin of beer and looked up, the horizon was a thin hammered seam between the blue-grey above and slightly darker blue-grey of the sea. The perfect sky was torn by a spear of cloud that shone brilliantly as it caught the last of the crisp autumn light peering over the western horizon.

Politicians talked a lot. Whatever happened to that guy who said not a round would be fired in Afghan? But a lot of blokes didn't get the support, physical or mental, they really needed. And all the time you knew a delegation of Taliban would one day be honoured guests in Parliament, following in the bloody footsteps of every other terrorist-turned-politician.

His day in the ditch was five or six years back now. Seemed like a lifetime. Danny missed the Army, the challenge, the mates. It was hard leaving an elite, well-oiled machine, being on your own. He tried to stick to the same principles, commitment, courage, discipline, integrity, loyalty, respect. It wasn't always easy.

Private investigation, his kind anyway, was a bit of a grey area. It was a case of use your own judgment, best guess, clearest option. And if it went tits-up you live with the consequences if you couldn't somehow duck out from under.

The flashing red pin prick of navigation lights marked the path of a helicopter following the coast. Danny always found the sound of choppers comforting.

He popped a ringpull and drank. There was a glow away to the south west where overcast blocked the setting sun. The last of the light leeched out of the honey cream facades of the tall Regency terraces along the front behind him.

Danny missed the magnetic clouds of starlings rippling over the girder ribs of the old West Pier.

He put the beer down, picked up his pad and pen. He'd never written anything in his life, apart from short reports for clients. They were factual, a chronology of events. How the hell did you write a eulogy? What can you say?

She was mum, says it all. Ordinary, nothing special, just mum. Kept things going after dad died. She'd take any job but wouldn't take any nonsense.

You read about benefit scroungers and the underclass but no one thinks about the people whose pride drives them through, no bonuses, no expenses, each day the same as the one before, and the one after.

No light at the end of the tunnel. Mum just ploughed on because that's what she did. Date-expired food brought from supermarkets at the end of the day, out to car boots sales in all weathers, looking for bargains.

Anyway, mum, the real one, was long gone. And not much left to show for a life lived, some Premium Bonds, a few bob in an old Post Office savings account, family snaps, a few clothes, two handbags, and one of those had a broken strap.

The husk in the hospital bed all that time was just the wreckage left by the disease that had eaten her mind, her personality. How many years was it?

It was so long since dementia had starting chipping away at Mum that Danny found it hard to remember the real woman. Just snatches of memory, like faded photos.

Neither a borrower nor a lender be. That was one of hers. Danny wrote it down on his pad.

The inshore lifeboat, moving fast from its station at the marina, buzzed a line of stitches in the leaden sea. There was always something sad about the close of day, the slow creep of darkness, endings and beginnings.

He finished the can, popped another, watched a couple of fishermen on the jetty to the west. As it grew colder the crowds thinned. Just a few joggers and dog walkers now, photographers pausing to snap the mangled birdcage of the old West Pier.

Away to his left he could hear the drumming of steel cables like Tibetan prayer bells on the masts of the dinghies at the sailing club.

A hunched figure bowed under the weight of a plastic rubbish sack shambled past, poking at the shingle with a stick. The guy looked across, muttered something, shuffled on.

Danny guessed he was heading off to kip in the arches by the pitch and putt. He didn't envy the guy. Danny had slept rough for a while, before he'd got himself sorted. Knew what it was like. Cold and dangerous. No wonder rough sleepers die 30 years or so before the national average. He'd read that in Jubilee Library.

Danny spent as much time there as he could spare, browsing, dipping randomly into stuff that looked interesting. Amazing what you came across. A world of information swirling around. It had passed him by for a long time. He had a lot of catching up to do.

A young couple walking their toddler steered the kid away from the man sitting with the beer cans round his feet.

Behind him, Danny could hear the town preparing to party, the first of the revellers drawn out by the darkness, packed taxis, a stretched white Hummer limo, a coach attracting driver's hoots as it tried to manoeuvre into a side street.

Maybe mum's death was the time for a new start. He'd only come to Brighton to look after her. Fair enough, he'd made some good friends and set up a business.

Danny smiled to himself. That had been a long and winding road, high hopes, that stupid Bogart office, accidents and injuries, women, good laughs, steep learning curve.

There was no denying Brighton was a weird place with its gender neutral public toilets. Every city has many faces but this one was different, a tart of a place, nose-in-the-air culture one minute, flashing knickers the next. As you worked your way down through her hazy addictions it was like peeling an onion. And it could make your eyes sting.

You could see two sides as you walked to the front down the side streets from Western Road. Regency buildings with their bowed fronts and porticos. But from the back it was peeling paint streaked by rusting fire escapes.

As a Londoner he'd been shocked that strangers actually made eye contact, talked to you. They were big on live and let live down here.

The place had a lot going for it, good pubs, the beach, the starlings, Jubilee Library and St Ann's Well Gardens.

A lot of stuff happened in Brighton. Something else he'd read in the library. Oldest aquarium, oldest cinema, first public railway in 1883, first commercial flight from Shoreham in 1911.

Abba had won Eurovision in 1974 at Brighton Dome and Bing Crosby gave his last public performance at the Brighton Centre in '77.

More Jedi lived in the city than anywhere else in the UK. Even the first blue film had been shot in Western Road, Woman Undressing. He'd seen some stills in a book.

But the place also had more than its fair share of nutters and weirdos. You never knew which of the mumblers were talking to their mobile and which ones weren't.

It was a regular contender for the title of Britain's drug death capital. Not so long ago it had seen the trunk murders, race track razor gangs lacing each other's faces with cut-throats, Mods and Rockers chucking deckchairs on bank holidays.

Now there were too many people desperate to pay for their next fix, too many kipping in doorways. A demo a day got a bit wearing. Traffic was bad enough anyway. And parts of the city ran with rivers of piss and vomit on Friday and Saturday nights.

Stay or go? Too tired to decide.

He looked down between his knees, picked up a handful of shingle, let it trickle through his fingers. The stones were cold and wet, mixed with shells and dark shreds of seaweed. It smelled of brine and decay.

Danny looked up as two seagulls squabbled over something dead at the water's edge. He'd read in the library that birds were descended from dinosaurs. Funny to think you'd got rellies of t-rex scoffing peanuts in the park.

He looked out at the blank, cold sea, reached for another beer but they were finished. He didn't remember drinking them all but the evidence was scattered on the shingle around his feet. Six more dead soldiers.

Danny dragged himself off the shingle, brushed his damp jeans and trudged up into town. As he walked he noticed a brittle, bird-like old lady, thinning white hair, bent back, osteo-clawed hands locked on the bar of tartan shopping trolley, tugging it as hard as she could to get home before darkness fell fully and the party people reclaimed the streets.

A chill wind was whipping up the last of the autumn leaves. As they spun through the aura of the street lights they looked like shooting stars.

***

Detective Inspector Eddie Aziz perched on the edge of Myers's desk, legs crossed, rocking gently as he thought.

"So this latest kid makes a total of four. This is shaping up to be a bad one. Do we have any indication where he did his shopping?"

Detective Sergeant Pauline Myers shook her head.

"No, drugs squad have spoken to the Argus and they're printing a warning. They've spread the word to the pubs and clubs but until the punters realise the danger that's as good as free advertising. No one thinks it'll ever happen to them."

"And they're sure it's the same stuff?"

"We're still waiting on the final toxicology but, yes, it's the same. It's distinctive, different and dangerous. Drug squad intelligence reckon it's someone new, outside the usual network of suppliers."

"God save us from entrepreneurs," said Aziz. He looked up as the door opened.

The woman was tall and slim with short red hair and geek chic glasses. Myers smiled as she walked towards them.

"This is DS Lizzie McIntosh," said Myers. "She's our liaison from drug squad."

"So what's new?" said Aziz.

McIntosh pushed her glasses up her nose, studied Aziz for a moment.

"Well, as you know, Operation Reduction is ongoing and it's making a dent in the city's drug trade. We're looking at two different types of dealer. One works in the night-time economy, clubbers, partygoers, weekenders looking for a high. The other preys on addicts. We think this new drug is coming from a new player and that they fall into the first group.

"There are four confirmed victims so far. We're trying to trace the source of the chemical components and we've circulated the usual warnings. We are keen to shut this down before it becomes an epidemic.

"All four deaths have been in Brighton but that doesn't mean the suppliers are local. People travel miles to party in the city. We can't rule out that it might be coming from outside the area but the feeling is that it's close."

"Why?" asked Aziz.

"It's only been available for a matter of weeks. The danger is that this is a test run, to see how it goes. If the suppliers get the demand they're hoping for this could spread like wildfire. London's only an hour from here by train. It could be across the country in a weekend. Basically, we're in a race to stop this before it is out of control. That's why it's important that everyone here makes maximum use of their contracts and local knowledge."

"Ok," said Aziz. "But how does this differ from all the other shit doing the rounds with the psychonauts?"

McIntosh pushed her glasses up her nose again.

"Use of traditional drugs, cannabis and cocaine, is falling but their place is being taken by designer drugs. One in four students at British universities have admitted taking legal highs. The EU drug monitoring agency is finding one new stimulant a week on average. The Home Office's Forensic Early Warning System identified 17 previously-unknown stimulants in just over a year. Some contain controlled substances so they're covered by the Misuses of Drugs Act. Others don't and they're often advertised as research chemicals, plant food or bath salts. One thing we do know about this one. It's called Amazon."

Aziz looked surprised.

"As in the Greek warrior? The women with one..."

He saw the warning look on the face of Myers and McIntosh and stopped himself from starting on mythical breasts. Instead, he coughed.

"Aspirin kills people," said Aziz. "How dangerous can this be?"

McIntosh looked from Aziz to Myers, touched her glasses.

"How long is a piece of string?" said McIntosh. "Someone, a chemical engineer or pharmacist, takes an illegal substance and modifies the chemical structure so it falls outside the law. It's easy to make mistakes and the user can never be sure what they're buying. It's trial and error and the buyer is the guinea pig."

***

Lance Corporal Dennis Hooper's brain felt as if it was wrapped in a hot, itchy blanket. Everything ached, joints, muscles, even skin. His stomach burned.

Something was happening but his mind couldn't grasp it. He felt a tap. No, more like a thump. On his shoulder. He swiped a hand in the general direction.

He was drifting away when he felt it again. The side of his head this time. Something wet. He muttered a curse, his voice hoarse, and swiped again.

Laughing, someone was laughing.

There had been a time when no one laughed at Lance Corporal Dennis Hooper, 16 years serving the Queen, Northern Ireland, Falklands. No one messed with Dennis Hooper. Now it was different. If you were sleeping rough you were invisible to most people, treated like shit by the rest. He couldn't even remember how he'd come to this, didn't much care anymore.

He felt another thump, between his shoulder blades this time. Suddenly he was angry but the roar emerged as a ragged croak. He pushed himself up, stiff muscles screaming, and looked around.

Faces, nasty little faces splitting with cold laughter. Hooper blinked to clear the gunk that filmed his eyes. Three, maybe four of them. Something pale flew past his head and he flinched. An egg? Someone was throwing eggs? More laughter.

"Oi, you lot, fuck off."

Dennis Hooper dragged himself into a sitting position. The nasty little faces were looking past him now, up the street, towards the tall man who had shouted.

"You gonna make us?" said the nastiest face.

The man kept coming.

"You touch me and I'll have you," said the nastiest face. "That's assault that is."

The nasty faces looked at each other, uncertain, aggregating their courage. The tall man kept coming. There was something about the way he walked, the way he carried himself, something scary.

Nasty Face took a step back, hesitated, checked behind to be sure the others were still there. The punch took him backwards, off his feet. The box flew in the air, eggs cracking down on the pavement. Blood poured from a broken nose.

He saw the shadow of one of the others step past him, then reel back yowling. Dec and Kev came forward together, clashed together as they were felled.

Trainers scratched on wet pavement, scrabbling to get away.

Nasty Face struggled to his feet. The pain was terrible. It hurt if he held it, bled if he didn't. He was hoiked upright by the collar of his jacket. The tall man was shouting at him again. Then he punched him. Then he shouted. The world was going mad.

The tall man shouted again, then punched him, and punched him, and punched him. Nasty Face could smell beer and cigarettes on his breath. The drunken old fart from the doorway was behind the tall man now, trying to pull him away.

The grip on Nasty Face's jacket loosened. He tore himself free and ran, stopped thirty feet away where the others had paused to watch, looked back, rocking on the balls of his feet, trying to ignore the pain and the mess it was making down the front of his Ben Sherman.

"Wanker!" yelled Nasty Face.

The egg smacked him on the forehead, splashing yolk and white across the blood on his face, dripping down onto his new shirt.

He tried to shout again but his mouth filled with cold, wet slime. He spluttered, spat, ran.

"Take it easy, mate," said Dennis Hooper as he looked up into the face of the tall angry man.

"You need an ambulance?" asked the tall man, beer on his breath. "My name's Danny, Danny Lancaster. Want me to take you somewhere?"

Dennis shook his head.

His watery eyes followed the crumpled ten pound note as the man took it from his jacket and slipped it into the breast pocket of the old soldier's filthy shirt.

"Ok then, take it easy, pal."

Dennis Hooper could see the man was weaving as he walked away.

***

"Your tea's ready!"

She stood in the hallway, gripping the steaming tray. She didn't know what had got into Benny. Chops! They could barely afford the electric and he wanted chops. They'd bickered about it for two days until she'd given in.

The front door was slightly open, made the draft even worse.

Chops! What was he thinking of? That said, they did smell good. Made a change from the usual, fish fingers, those thin leathery little burgers, sausages with bits in. Benny's horse meat jokes were wearing a bit thin.

Emma inhaled the rich meaty aroma, her nose chasing the rising steam. It was a real treat. And, God knows, they could do with one.

But it would be criminal to let them spoil. Why did Benny have to pick now to pop out to that wreck of a van he'd borrowed?

Emma looked down at the plate on the tray, drinking in the curls of meat, peas and beans to one side, a fluffy pile of mash to the other. She could see the thick gravy losing its gleam at the edges of the plate. Much longer and she'd have to stick it in that battered old microwave he'd brought home. She still didn't trust the electrics.

What was he playing at?

Well he could eat it anyway. No way was this going to waste.

She heard footsteps on the stairs, heavy and fast.

At last, they might sit down to their tea before it was stone cold.

The front door crashed wide, hitting the wall behind. Benny stood there, hair staring, eyes wide.

"Emma!"

"Benny."

He was frozen still but the heavy footsteps kept coming. Two big dark shapes filled the doorway behind Benny as he stood, panicked, mouth soundlessly opening and closing. A meaty hand appeared from the hallway, clamped on his shoulder.

"Benny, my son, you are nicked."

More footsteps. Another shape melded into the knot of men in the doorway.

"Cabling's in the back of the van, Sarge. Miles of it."

Emma couldn't look, couldn't speak. Tears blurred her vision as she looked down at the tray, watching the matt skin creeping across the surface of the dark gravy.

CHAPTER 13

SOMEWHERE IN WEST SUSSEX, SATURDAY MORNING
The boar was huge, more than 300lbs of testosterone-fuelled bacon on the hoof. It gouged the trunk of an ash tree with a gleaming tusk, exposing pale wood, coating the bark with its pheromone-laden saliva to marks his territory.

Then it stepped away and raised its head, sniffing the air, poor eyesight more than compensated for by its sharp sense of hearing and smell.

The boar rooted around, driving its long snout into the undergrowth, then moved on, dark bristled coat glistening with dew. It trotted along an overgrown path, swinging its big head.

When the boar heard the strange trilling sound it stopped, listened. The sound came again. It gave a loud snort of alarm.

The animal heard a rustling from behind. It turned its powerful shoulders. A clump of undergrowth was moving, a shape emerging. The boar watched, wary and alert, then turned away and trotted on.

Danny raked leaves out of his hair as he watched the boar walk away. It looked magnificent, roaming free, following its nature. His aching eyes followed it until the boar disappeared beyond a bend in the path. Then he looked around.

It was all a hazy memory. Somehow, God alone knew how, he had knocked up a rough bivvy from branches and dead leaves. As he moved, his foot tinked against an empty vodka bottle.

Now he remembered stopping at that corner shop offy, buying the bottle and some beers, running for the first bus he saw, arguing with the conductor.

He'd got off somewhere in the dark and walked and, somehow, pitched up here. He looked at the broken skin on his knuckles and remembered the old guy in the doorway, the kids throwing eggs.

He sucked in a lungful of the smells around him, damp earth, moisture on the leaves. There was birdsong, sharp and clear, and gossamer skeins of mist embracing the dark branches of the old trees.

It brought back memories, felt like home. Danny knew he could live, thrive and fight in this environment if his head wasn't thumping so hard.

On top of that, his scalp was crawling and it felt as if something had crapped in his mouth. The stump of his left leg hurt like hell.

A weird night, off the rails, way off. God alone knew how much he'd put away. Must have really ripped the arse out of it.

As he took a step Danny swayed, vision blurring, head thumping. He winced at the sound of his mind's foundations uprooting, tearing free of things familiar and trusted, wreckage drifting away. His face was a false wall, brain not connecting to the muscles of his eyes and mouth.

Teetering on the edge again. Time to take a step back.

Getting home for a shit, shave and shower was the first order of business. But he'd have to get there. Could be worse. For the old guy in the doorway, every night was like last night.

He remembered the sound that had disturbed the boar and rummaged in his pocket. Five missed calls. He couldn't be too far from civilisation if he was still getting a phone signal.

Danny gathered up his empty bottles and cans, put them in their carrier bag. The sky was overcast but the bright patch told him where the sun was.

He took a much-needed leak behind an old oak tree and started walking.

***

With overcast glowing faintly to the horizon, the view didn't get much clearer as the capsule rose. But it got a lot bigger.

Jason Knight stood with his arms wide against the window frame, drinking in the scenery. Despite the grey weather he could see little knots of people making their way up and down Brighton Pier.

Traffic along the front was getting heavy, little boxes shuffling along like racing beetles. To the west, beyond the wrecked pier, he could just make out Shoreham power station through the haze. To the east, he could see the marina with Roedean School perched on the hill above and the race course beyond that.

The city spread uphill as it sprawled inland. Beyond the cluster of building and the distinctive red bulk of St Bartholomew's Church was the crest of the South Down, a massive natural wall around the city.

"This is my kind of town."

"What, babe?"

Jason looked down at Princess, seated on a bench, absorbed by her iPhone.

"I said this is my kind of town, Princess."

"It's very high up here. Makes my tummy go funny."

"You always say that. And what's happened to your face?"

She replied with a dazzling white smile but couldn't stop her finger flying to the corner of her mouth where Jessie had smacked her lip against a tooth.

"Nothing, Jas, just a bit of a cold sore."

Jason flicked a smile back at her and pulled out his own iPhone.

"Mitch? Yes, it's me. Look, she's had long enough. You and Paulie, you go round to hers and help her make her mind up. Nothing physical, mind games, Mitch, mind games. That's how to play it, ok?" He cut the call, turned back to the view.

"What was that about?" asked Princess, head tilted.

"Business, babe."

"It's that skinny bitch, isn't it?"

"Like, I said, business. Nothing for you to worry yourself about."

He turned back to the panorama beyond the glass and smiled.

"One day soon, Princess, this is going to be my town."

"Sounds good, babe," said Princess, smiling hard.

The capsule was just passed its peak at 150 feet now, beginning its glide back down to the bottom again.

Jason had a thought, checked his watch, began to unzip.

He looked at Princess sitting on the bench seat.

"While you're down there, babe."

***

A 15-minute jog down a narrow track and Danny could see houses again. The movement felt like someone was hammering his head with a bat but he pressed on.

At a corner shop he bought a bottle of water and a Kitkat, then settled at the bus stop for a 40-minute wait for the Brighton service.

Back in the city he went to his flat, stripped and showered. He called Grace, arranged to meet, brushed the worst off his filthy clothes, dressed and was out again in less than twenty minutes.

An egg and bacon sandwich and a mug of tea was the best first aid for his dodgy head and stomach. The cafe was crowded so he bought a paper to pass the time until his order arrived.

The "peasant" politician was still hanging on but it seemed pretty clear his career couldn't last much longer.

A West Country vicar who had gone missing had been traced to a small hotel in Aberystwyth where he was sharing a double room with the wife of his parish council's chairman.

The fog in Danny's brain cleared instantly when he read that the burned body found in the Thames had been identified as a plumber from Basildon called Ronald Edward Hedges.

***

The guy in the high-vis waterproof jacket was tired and irritable. His shift had turned out to be long, busy and wet shift. Now the end of it was dragging, as if his watch was running slow.

He'd popped out for a quick ciggie. It was quiet over in the corner by the tall mesh fence. He liked it there. You could look out over the rooftops of Kemp Town on a clear day, see the English Channel sparkling. Fat chance now with mist and mizzle drifting in off the water.

And his dodgy colon was playing up again. If that wasn't bad enough, it was a racing certainty Mairead would still be banging on about her new bloody kitchen when he got home. Might have to stop off on the way back, just for a couple, before she got her bloody brochures out again.

The old banger of a Citroën over-revving its way up the ramp was the last straw. He charged at it, waving his arms.

The car swerved around him with a squeal of bald tyres and a wheeze of brakes. It came to a messy stop just beyond a parked police car and right across a line of ambulances, ignoring the double red lines on the scarred tarmac. All four doors burst open. Suddenly the guy in the waterproof jacket was surrounded by people, all talking at once.

"You can't park that thing here. It's a restricted zone. Emergency vehicles only. A £50 fine. Can't you read the signs?"

They hauled a limp shape from the rear seat of the Citroën, dropped it on the tarmac, picked it up again. The group began staggering like a sick crab toward the automatic doors.

"Emile, Emile is sick. Please, you must help us."

The guy in the jacket looked down and caught his first sight of what they were half carrying, half dragging. He was young, probably a student, face a fish-belly white, dark vomit down his T-shirt, a crust around his lips. The kid looked like a corpse.

"Ok, ok," said the guy in the jacket. "Get him inside. They'll take care of him."

As Emile's friends hauled him towards the automatic doors the guy in the high-vis jacket took a last look at their casualty.

He'd seen it all before, more times than he could remember. You didn't have to be a doctor to know that kid was dead as mutton. As the doors hissed open he shouted after them.

"When you lot have dropped him off, get this bloody car moved. This is A&E. Says so on the sign. It's a restricted zone, £50 fine. Parking for ambulances only."

***

When Grace reached at the cafe she looked slightly startled at Danny's sandwich and settled for tea and toast. Just as it arrived at their table Danny's phone rang.

"Hello... Who? Oh yes... Just now? Did they say what they wanted? Just... Just... look, try to stay calm. Yes, I know it's frightening. No, don't call the police. I'll be there straight away."

Grace was just finishing her first slice of toast as Danny got to his feet.

"We've got to go."

CHAPTER 14

The cab dropped them on the front by Regency Square. Danny pushed a tenner at the driver and was out and running. Grace followed.

When Danny reached the B&B he pounded on the front door. Nothing happened.

"Mrs Hudson, Mrs Hudson? It's Danny Lancaster. Open up."

He stepped back at the sound of scratching locks. The door opened a few inches until the chain went taut. A single blinking eye examined them, then the chain was released and the door opened.

Danny and Grace stepped into the hallway.

"Thank God you've come, Mr Lancaster. I don't know what happened. It was all so fast."

"Just calm down, Mrs Hudson, and tell me what happened."

It was clear the woman was in shock, blinking hard, restless hands fluttering.

"Take your time."

"This is a respectable bed and breakfast, Mr Lancaster. We've been rated by the council and the AA. Nothing like this has ever happened before."

"Mrs Hudson, tell me what happened."

"They were banging on the door, banging really hard. I went to answer as fast as I could but they just kept banging. When I opened the door they were shouting. They pushed their way in. They just kept shouting and shouting. I said I'd call the police and then they left."

"So they're gone," asked Danny.

"No, that's what frightened me. They're sitting in a car just down the road."

"Is Jessie in?"

The landlady nodded. "In her room."

"Ok, Mrs Hudson. I'm going to go outside now. Lock the door and wait for me to come back."

The woman nodded. As Danny walked down the hall he realised Grace was following him.

"You want to come too?"

"Yes."

"Fair enough."

He heard the bolts thud home as he trotted down the steps. As soon as he reached the pavement Danny had spotted the car, a dark blue BMW, cigarette smoke rising from its open windows. The driver had an Argus spread over the wheel. His passenger was looking round and locked eyes with Danny as soon as he saw him.

Danny made straight for the car. The passenger said something and the driver looked up from his paper.

They were less than twenty feet from the car now. When Danny kept on coming the BMW's doors opened. The driver was halfway out when Danny wrenched the door from him and slammed it, catching the guy's leg. As he slumped with a grunt Danny slammed again, the heavy door catching his head against the frame.

The man rolled out onto the road, moaning. He landed on all fours and one hand went for a pocket. Danny stamped on the man's other hand and his face hit the tarmac.

A thud made Danny turn. The passenger was out of the car but before he could help his chum Grace had grabbed his jacket, rolled him over her hip and slammed him onto the bonnet. He stood up unsteadily and went for Grace again but she grabbed his failing arm in a wrist lock.

He tried to fight her but she twisted her grip until he was keening in pain. She bent him steadily further until his knees buckled and he went down.

She looked across at Danny. He nodded.

The driver was half up now, leaning against the BMW for support, hand pressing against his bleeding head, hissing with pain. Danny leaned forward into his sight line.

"I'll say this once. You two piss off now and don't come back or I will lose my temper. Do you understand me?"

The driver didn't react.

Danny moved closer. The driver flinched.

"Are you deaf? Do you understand me?"

The man nodded.

Danny and Grace stepped onto the pavement and watched as the two men eased themselves into the BMW. As the car pulled away Danny saw the net curtains of the B&B fall back into place.

When the Beemer had turned the corner Danny and Grace walked back to Mrs Hudson's.

"Nice moves," said Danny. "Where did you learn that?"

"My father," said Grace.

***

"My, you are a pretty little thing, aren't you? First time I've seen you in daylight."

"Sorry to lumber you but this is a bit of an emergency."

"No problem, Danny, no problem at all. Was there a problem at the B&B?"

"Sort of."

Wanda glanced across at Bob who raised his eyebrows, looked confused. But Wanda, big smile of welcome, was rising to a challenge as she always did. She looked hard at Danny, his face and his clothes.

"You ok?"

"I'm fine."

Danny shepherded Jessie inside, Grace following close behind, until they formed a loose circle in the hallway.

"Right, introductions. Jessie you met at the Bellerophon. She's a client. Had a bit of bother at the B&B and I was hoping she could stay with you for a bit, just till I get things sorted."

"No, problem, Danny. We'd love to have her, wouldn't we, Bob?" said Wanda.

Bob nodded.

"And this is Grace," said Danny. "She's another client."

"Does she need a room too?"

"No, she's fine for now."

"Well," said Wanda, looking at the faces around her, "I'll put the kettle on."

***

Bob still looked confused when they settled in the living room. Wanda swept in with a tray of tea and Hobnobs.

Danny was standing by the doors to the garden, staring out down the lawn, thoughtful. Grace was sitting on the sofa with Jessie perched at the far end, looking around, uncertain, still in the same clothes, Rasta tam pulled down over her eyes, fiddling with her iPhone.

Grace studied her for a moment. "We haven't met."

"I'm no one," Jessie mumbled.

"Nobody is no one. I am Grace Nujoma. What is your name?"

"Jessie."

"It is a pleasure to meet you, Jessie."

They both looked up as Danny loomed over them.

"Any idea who those guys were?"

Jessie shook her head.

"I don't bet," said Danny. "But if I did, I'd reckon this has something to do with Jason."

Jessie shook her head violently.

"No, no, nothing like that."

"You got any other explanation?"

"He wouldn't do that. He was really kind. It was almost like it was before."

"You've seen him?"

"Yesterday."

"I should never have given you that bloody number, not before I'd checked him out."

Jessie looked up for the first time.

"I paid you to find him. Your job's done so it's none of your business."

"Shall I be mother?" asked Wanda.

***

It was late when Danny got home. Emma was going to say something as he walked in but her jaw dropped when she saw him.

"You ok, Em?"

"Danny, where have you been? What happened to you?"

"Nothing."

"Your jacket's filthy, you've got cuts on your face and your hand's been bleeding."

Danny realised he had showered when he'd got back that morning but thrown on the same clothes. It was only when he looked at the purple swelling across his knuckles that he knew how hard he'd hit the egg thrower. He shrugged.

"Busy day."

Emma patted the sofa beside her and he sat down.

"How are you feeling?" she asked.

"Fine."

"You don't look fine."

"Don't fuss."

"I'll make some tea."

"There's vodka in the fridge."

He could see she was about to argue, then changed her mind. When she brought the bottle she poured herself a small shot. Danny filled his glass.

"It's been a hell of a day, what with your mum and on top of that Benny's been nicked again."

"The usual?" Danny asked.

Emma gave a beaten shrug, nodded.

"The flat's so quiet now. I mean, she did make much noise, your mum. But it just doesn't seem real, does it?" said Emma.

"Real enough."

Emma watched Danny as he drank. He had the look that frightened her, dark distant eyes. When she followed his line of sight he was staring into the corner of the room, at the skirting.

"We can talk, if you want."

"What about?"

"Your mum, of course."

"It's been said."

"No it hasn't, not all of it. It's bad to bottle things up."

"Not you as well? Look, Em, mum wouldn't have lasted this long without you. We tried to do the best for her and you made it happen, kept her here in her flat until the end. It's what she wanted. She had a good run. She's out of it now, no more pain. End of."

"You don't have to play the hard man, Danny. Not with me."

She shivered when the dark eyes turned on her.

"I'm not playing, Em."

"I'm only trying to help."

"Look, Em, it's been a long day. I'm tired and I'm not in the mood for a home visit from Dear Deidre."

"You scare me, Danny. Sometimes, most of the time, you're Jack the Lad, life and soul of the party, a really warm, lovely guy. Other days you're like some sort of mental, the moods, the nightmares. And sometimes I think you don't really care about anything, least of all me. There's this whole part of you that's locked away."

"That makes me and Benny, then."

"You bastard!"

"You brought it up."

"It's not his fault. He was trying this time, really trying. He had a job, working the bins. It's hard."

"Especially if you're not used to it."

"What's that supposed to mean?"

"When was the last time Benny had a job that didn't involve trying not to leave fingerprints?"

"You can be a real shit sometimes, Danny. You really can. He's trying his best to make things work for us, we both are."

Danny started into the corner, shook his head.

"Let's just drop it, eh? This isn't going to get us anywhere."

"Danny, I worry about you. You're always getting hurt, getting thumped or shot at. Every time you come home there's a bit less of you. I don't want you to die."

He smiled but there was no warmth in it.

"That's the last thing I plan to do."

He refilled his glass and held the bottle out. Emma hesitated, her face was flushed. She was angry now. They glared at each other. Then she took her hand from the top of her glass.

"Just a small one."

Danny poured. She drank half of it in one swallow, tried to stifle a cough. A trickle escaped the corner of her lips. He went back to staring at the wall. Emma looked around the room.

"I'd better tidy up a bit before I go."

"Cheers."

She rounded on him, eyes red.

"Oh, so I'm useful when it suits you."

"For chrissake, Em, let it go."

Emma's mouth opened to speak but nothing came out. Her focus never left his face, drinking in every tiny detail, but holding his gaze was hard to the point of painful.

They glared at each other, breathing short, like desperate boxers looking for an opening in a bout that was dragging on beyond their stamina.

"Danny..."

Her tongue darted along her vodka-shiny lips. Danny's eyes flicked down to the brief coating of moisture before moving back up to her eyes. Her pupils looked huge.

She thought he looked like something coiled. A spring quivering at maximum tension. Or a snake wound tight to strike.

The colour in Emma's pale face was blooming pink now. Without taking his eyes from her face Danny could tell from the rise and fall of her T-shirt that her breathing has accelerated. Her hands gripped her thighs.

It punched the breath out of Emma when they clashed into each other. Danny gripped her hair, forcing their faces together, mouths mashing. Her fingers grabbing at his T-shirt.

They broke, gasping for air, and went at it again with increased ferocity. Emma's fingers scrabbled against the pressure in his jeans.

Danny tore her T-shirt as he ripped it upwards. Urgent hands were everywhere. They slid off the sofa onto the floor. The vodka bottle tipped, contents glugging onto the carpet.

When they parted for air a second time Emma lay on her back, kicked her legs up, yanked off her jeans and pants.

Danny stood, pulled his jeans down, the light catching the shaft of his leg. He tripped as he tried to wrench them over trainers, tugged, gave up.

Hobbled, he crawled to where she lay.

Emma gasped as Danny buried his face in juicy peach.

She rocked from side to side, teeth clenched, one hand beating a frantic time on the carpet.

But Danny couldn't wait. He rose up and mounted her in a single movement.

They rutted frantically, the friction of the carpet burning her buttocks and his elbows, sweat flying.

Emma's grunts as Danny pistoned into her turned into a rising yowl. She went rigid and silent. Mouth wide as her insides ignited and the full power of her orgasm burst.

Danny broke away.

Pulled her up.

Turned her.

Took her from behind against the sofa.

Grabbed a handful of her hair to pull her back harder against him.

Emma's head was up, back arched, grunting as she stared unseeing at the ceiling

Danny's other hand kneading her buttocks.

The sofa jerked on its casters.

He lasted, perhaps, two minutes.

Then she could tell he was close from his short, urgent strokes.

Then compressed breath hissing through his clenched teeth, his grip on her waist slackened.

***

Emma broke away, wiped herself with a tissue from a box on the table, saw red finger marks on her hips where he had held her.

She smiled as Danny fell onto his back on the floor, grinning. She lay down beside him and he put his arm around her, stroking her damp hair. Emma's fingertip traced the scars carved into his hard body.

"You're all sweaty."

"I should hope so," said Danny. "It'd be like dinner without gravy. Show's you're trying."

She slapped his arm.

"I'm lying in a wet patch."

Danny looked down the length of their entwined bodies. "It's the vodka."

***

BRIGHTON SEAFRONT, SUNDAY MORNING

Karol had moaned, a lot, but everyone needed a hobby. Danny knew it was a long shot when he asked but it had turned out to be surprisingly simple.

So now he was standing by the entrance to Burger King near the Sea Life Centre, watching the traffic. You didn't need to be a detective to spot the car, the screaming pink paintwork turned heads like a Mexican wave as it cruised down Madeira Drive.

Danny watched the blonde driver edge the BMW convertible hesitantly into a tight parking bay. She was touching up her lippy as he approached the car, saw him in her face mirror, looked up, smiling. He took in the perfect white teeth, anti-gravity breasts and orange tan.

"Oh, hello," she said.

"Hi," said Danny. "Nice car."

"Fantastic, isn't it," she said. "It's called Hawaiian Cerise. Jas had it done to match my nail colour."

Princess offered a hand to prove her point. Jason Knight, who had been busy on his mobile phone, looked up at Danny from the front passenger seat.

"What the fuck do you want?"

"A word."

"Fuck off."

"About Jessie."

Knight looked across at his girlfriend as she pouted into her hand mirror.

"Bit of business, Princess. You wait in the car."

"Oh, Jas, I was really looking forward to it."

"Tomorrow, eh."

Knight climbed out of the car and walked towards the wheel, gesturing for Danny to follow. Two girls, thick make-up, fake tan, maybe 14 or 15, edged nervously into Knight's path. One held out a marker pen. He signed the back of her hand. The other nervously lifted her top. Knight wrote his name with an elaborate flourish on the pale skin of her stomach, the girl giggling as the felt tip tickled. They ran away, clutching each other and squealing. Knight hadn't even looked at them. When he saw Danny watching him he shrugged.

"Skanks, eh? But you've got to build your audience."

They turned toward an insistent car horn. Princess was waving frantically from the BMW. Knight flipped a hand in her direction.

"I hate that bloody car, look a right wanker driving round."

"It's a bit loud," said Danny.

"Too right, but that's what she wanted, matches her nails."

"She said."

They boarded a capsule, felt a slight jolt as it move off, began to climb. Danny was surprised how small it was, how large the windows that gave wide-angle views across the city and the sea. As it rose higher he had the feeling of riding a chopper, door locked opening, low level, terrain-following.

He half-listened to the commentary by some comedian. Couldn't remember the name. The hotel where presidents and a napoleon stayed. Another that hosted Oscar Wilde.

Brighton stands on the 1,000-year-old fishing village of Brighthelmstone. King George IV built a tunnel from the Pavilion to his girlfriend's house, Brighton's first "dirty weekend".

Jason Knight studied Danny, jaws moving mechanically as they worried a stick of gum.

"Ok, so who the fuck are you and what do you want?"

"The names Danny Lancaster. I helped Jessie find you."

"Good Samaritan, eh? Very Christian of you. So what is it you want?"

"She's a kid, I just want to make sure she doesn't get hurt."

Knight laughed. "Are you for real? Who are you, her dad?"

"I'm serious. I reckon it was your thugs that had a pop outside the B&B."

"Me? You're winding me up. I'm a businessman, see, legitimate. Look, we had a thing a few years back, Jessie and me, real close. We're soul mates."

"And Princess?"

"What about her? Jessie walked away. We've both moved on. Now she's back but I reckon we can work things out. And I don't know about any thugs. Look, I don't know why I'm talking to you but let's get this clear. Do you know who I am?"

Danny looked out along the massive white lattice arm of the wheel, towards its hub, nodded.

"Back then, when we were together, I was a big name, an A-list celeb, invites to the top parties, minders beating off the paps. Drove a Lambo. And the babes, shit man, all the pussy you could ever want, begging for it so they can tell their skanky mates they've shagged someone famous."

Danny wondered how long it took the guy each day to trim the razor-edged lines of beard that followed his jaw. Where did he find the time? Knight didn't seem to notice the scrutiny.

"I was an elite athlete, a super star. And it was all wrecked in half a second by that cunt Harper. He should have been put in prison for that tackle. He ruined my life, took everything from me, everything. Made me a nothing. What was I supposed to do?

"The fucking pain, man, you wouldn't believe. Bone right out through the skin. Can you believe that? And it damaged the joint, got infected. Do you know what that does to a footballer's career? It still hurts like fuck. I couldn't even get laid. Babes go for a fit body. You wouldn't understand. And it slashed my earnings down to zero, smashed by dreams. It totally ruined my life."

Danny looked down at the pier reaching out into the water. At the far end, the 130-foot arm of the Scream ride swung like some giant cricketer limbering up.

"And?"

"The pressure, it split us up, me and Jessie. But I'm on my way up again now, a businessman. It's going to be big."

"And what do you do now?"

"I'm an entertainer, music mogul, a poet, a priest, a prophet, parties for the stars, big names. I'm building an audience. It's all about reinventing yourself, see, selling a personality. And I've got the chemistry. I'll get it all back, show them all, you'll see."

"So, you've got a good business and a girlfriend with a pink Beemer. What about Jessie?"

"Like I said, we can work things out."

"Not good enough, Jason."

Knight glared at Danny.

"Look, pal, it's a hard world. Jessie and me, you make your own decisions, make your own breaks. Sometimes people get hurt."

Knight turned, drinking in the expanding view as the capsule rose. Then he looked back at Danny, saw the look on his face. He pointed towards the specks of people on the promenade.

"Take a look down there and tell me you'd give a shit if one of them dots dropped dead. If I gave you a grand for every one that stopped moving, cash, tax free in your hand, you'd rip my fucking hand off."

Knight spread his arms to embrace the scene in front of them.

"I love this fucking town. It's my town."

"And Jessie?"

Knight leaned close, fanning Danny's face with breath of mint and garlic.

"Look, Mr Fanny Wankmeister or whatever your fucking name is, it's none of your business so keep your fucking nose out? Comprendez?"

Danny's gaze didn't waver. The guy was asking for a broken jaw but it was probably bad for business to chin your client's boyfriend. Not worth another skinned knuckle.

They rode the capsule in silence.

CHAPTER 15

Emma gave a hiss of exasperation as she went through the laundry basket. Danny's T-shirt and jeans were filthy, stained with dirt and crushed greenery. She scratched at a mark with a fingernail, wondering if it would ever come out.

There were specks of blood on the T-shirt as well. The washing machine was never going to clean all that up. She turned the pockets of his jeans inside out. Dark dirt and small twigs pattered onto the white top of the washing machine.

Emma reached up to the cupboard for the Vanish. It was like doing the laundry for a naughty schoolboy.

***

Danny knew it would be a waste of time, that he'd get an ear bashing, but it had to be done.

"You're getting careless with your clients, aren't you, Danny?"

"I just thought I should let you know."

"Very thoughtful. So your client, this Marion Carter, hired you to find hubby, then vanished."

Detective Sergeant Pauline Myers was at her world-weary best, thought Danny.

"That's right, house deserted, no sign of a struggle."

"Perhaps he popped home and they've run away together to rekindle their lost love."

"It's possible but I don't think so."

"Look, Danny, I'm up to my bloodshot eyeballs here. And the taxpayer doesn't fund Sussex police to clear up your little mishaps. Anyway, we can't do anything until she's officially reported missing. You want to make that report, Danny?"

"No."

"Then stop wasting my time and the taxpayers' money."

Danny hesitated, then jumped in before Myers cut the call.

"There's something else I wanted your advice on."

"Advice? Well, if you can't do the time, don't do the crime. Best I can offer."

"Words of wisdom, but I've got another client who's looking for a guy. I want to find out a bit more about him."

"Jee-zus! A misper? And you expect me to use police resources? Do you realise the shit storm I'd be in if I were caught helping a private investigator, and a dodgy one at that."

"It's not that, I found the guy, it's just there's something wrong about him."

"What's this, Danny, developing a copper's nose?"

"The client's just a kid. I think she might be digging herself into something."

"The answer is still no. What's the guy's name?"

"Jason Knight."

The line went quiet. Danny waited.

"Jason Knight, aka Jas K?"

"That's him."

"Used to be a footballer, rising star. What's he up to?"

"Reinventing himself as some sort of celebrity DJ. It's all about chemistry, so he tells me."

"Like I said, Danny, I can't help you. But you dig up anything interesting and I want to know straight away."

"Not really a fair exchange, Pauline."

"Who said life was fair?"

Detective Sergeant Pauline Myers cut the connection. Danny shrugged and slipped his phone back into his pocket.

***

Karol hadn't arrived when Danny reached the Bellerophon so he bought himself a lager and sat at their usual table.

It was quiet in the bar. Slate the pub dog asleep, Gareth the easyJet steward nursing a wine at the bar. Sudoku Wally poring over his puzzles, making the one Guinness last.

Danny looked around, drinking in the detail, remembering. He felt weary, his knuckles ached. His leg hurt.

Being busy was good, meant he was making a go of this detecting lark. But it wouldn't work if he didn't actually solve something.

Marion Carter had hired him, then vanished. Her house was deserted and there was no sign she'd been back. No idea how to find her or her husband. But there was more to that woman, Danny felt sure. More than one face. He'd already seen two of them, one in St Ann's Well gardens that first day, the other on Ron Hedges's living room wall.

And Hedges, floating in the Thames, badly burned. What was all that about?

Then he had Grace stashed in a B&B near the front. He was sure there was more to that story as well. You'd have to be pretty dedicated to follow someone halfway round the world on the wafer-thin information she claimed to have. There were connections here he wasn't seeing.

And no way to stop Jason Knight trashing Jessie's life for a second time. Danny had found the guy but he might just have dropped her in it by doing so. True, he wasn't her social worker or her dad. But she was just a kid. Someone had to take an interest.

The boss of the graphics firm, Mr Cunliffe, had been well pleased with the smudges of his sick list paraglider, Michael Onslow, touching down on Devil's Dyke. Perhaps a bit too pleased. Times were tough. Maybe the guy was trying to save on paying redundo.

Danny had done the rounds earlier, trying to keep on top of his cases.

Mrs Packham hadn't said a word, couldn't. When she opened the envelope, saw the photos of her husband's little car park tryst, she'd started crying, face a distorted purple, big sobs bubbling up from deep inside her, shaking her whole body.

Danny had made her tea. She'd left it to go cold. Every time he tried to speak she shook her head, unable to form words.

In the end, he'd left, walking down the hallway to the sound of her keening in pain, alone in her sparkling new kitchen, the wreckage of her life falling around her.

So, all things considered, not a good day. He sipped his pint as Karol walked over and handed him some computer printed sheets.

"Here is research you wanted. All afternoon it took me but, of course, I have nothing else to do with life."

"For Christ's sake, Karol, don't you start."

***

As he started the van his phone rang. When Danny answered it took him a second to recognise the name.

"Ah, Mr Seward, hello."

"Mr Lancaster, you may recall we met when you visited my gallery."

"Yes, I do."

"Well, there's been a bit of a development. I thought you might like to know."

"Sure."

"It's about Sean Collins. You were right, by the way. He was living in Amsterdam. There's been a sudden ripple of interest in his work."

"A ripple?"

"Certain people are re-examining his portfolio, reassessing the prices his pictures might command."

"Why's that then?"

"Oh, the usual reason why an artist's work is suddenly in demand."

"And that is?"

"He has died. Horribly, so I understand."

CHAPTER 16

Karol's research was bang on the money. The light was on in the apartment and occasionally he'd seen shadows passing across the recessed lighting in the lounge behind the balcony.

Different shadows, so they were probably both there.

Karol had dug up some details on Wikipedia. The place was named after the architect who built the Chrysler Building in New York. It was done in a modern interpretation of the Art Deco and Streamline Moderne styles, whatever they were. All in all, a nice billet.

Danny knew it was a long shot but with no leads to work on there was no point in sitting round like a lemon waiting for something to happen. You had to make your own luck.

And he did.

Thirty minutes later the gates to the underground car park rumbled open. A silver Audi A6 glided up the ramp, swung right along Marine Parade to the roundabout, then shot off westward with a roar.

Danny started after it, conscious of the van's aging gearbox grinding as he accelerated. The Transit was no match for the Audi but Danny had Brighton traffic on his side.

He followed it west along the front down Kings Road and into Kingsway. Traffic was fairly heavy and the road was lined with traffic cams. The Audi didn't have the chance to show what it could do.

Danny tucked the van in four vehicles behind the A6 as they cruised past Hove Lagoon with its wind-surfing lake and posh celebrity beach houses and on along the length of Shoreham Harbour basin, beyond the power station and into the outskirts of Shoreham-by-Sea.

He kept pace with the Audi along the High Street and followed it left at the roundabout onto Norfolk Bridge across the River Adur.

The tide was low and water birds foraged on the broad bands of green brown mudflats.

Once across the bridge Danny glanced right at the giant stone accordion that was Lancing College and was almost wrong-footed.

He had expected the Audi to tear off towards Portsmouth but as it cleared the bridge he saw its brake lights come on. The car slowed and swung off to the left.

Danny followed it through clusters of neat houses, hanging back as there was now nothing between them, until the Audi turned left again.

As Danny cruised past the junction he saw it pull up at the foot of a grassy embankment. He coasted to a halt in Beach Green, jumped out and sprinted back to the junction.

The driver was at the top of a flight of steps leading up from the car park to a path on top of the embankment that acted as a sea defence wall. Danny waited until the man was obscured by some trees, then ran across the car park and up the steps.

When he reached the top he saw his target step carefully onto a gangplank and board one of the houseboats sitting on the mudflats.

Apart from a few trees and shrubs along the path there was no cover. Danny didn't want to get too close until he knew what was happening.

So now he had more questions and still no answers. And the main one was, what was Jason Knight doing there? He didn't strike Danny as the boating type.

He was mulling this over, walking back down the steps, when he spotted another question that needed an answer. A vehicle he recognised was tucked away at the far end of the car park.

***

They sat in silence, the atmosphere thoughtful, leaden. Grace picked up her coffee, decided it was too hot, blew on it, put it down.

"This is very serious," she said, her voice low.

"That," said Danny, "is an understatement. Hedges is dead, burned and dumped in the Thames. Now Collins has been found floating down a canal. Are you sure there's nothing more you can tell me?"

Grace picked up her coffee, blew again, shook her head.

"The thing that bothers me, really bothers me, is that I saw someone following Marion Carter the day I met her. We had a bit of a scuffle at her house. Now Hedges and Carter are dead, and both of them just after I paid a visit. That can't be a coincidence."

"No," said Grace.

"And you can't shed any light?"

"Shed a light?"

"You can't think why? There isn't some little detail you forgot to mention?"

Grace sipped her flat white, shook her head. "No."

Danny picked up his coffee, took a slug, burned his mouth, drank anyway.

"The people in this case are dropping like flies and I haven't got a clue. And it looks like I'm leading the killers to their victims. That makes me angry."

"What will you do?"

Danny shrugged. "Still thinking."

"There is another problem, Danny."

"Another?"

"As I told you, I have very little money. The bed and breakfast is expensive. I don't think I will be able to stay much longer."

"You can't quit now."

"That is the last thing I would want to do but I cannot live on air, Danny."

He drank some of his coffee, cautious this time.

"I've got a room you could use."

Grace looked startled. "I don't think that would be a very good idea. It would not be proper."

"I'm going over to Bob and Wanda's to see how Jessie's doing. We could pick up your kit on the way. So you can walk away from the case after coming all this way or you can bunk down at mine till it's sorted. Up to you."

***

Cigarettes, green disposable lighter, three pound coins, blue biro, broken pencil, van keys, Hobnob, wine cork, minicab card, tea spoon, lucky dip lottery ticket, phone charger, gas bill, music CD, onyx Buddha, bubble pack of Neurofen.

Danny double checked he'd remembered it all, then grinned. Bang on the money.

"What are you up to?" asked Bob when he found Danny sitting on his living room floor with a tray between his knees.

"Memory training."

"Oh yeah, Kim's Game. I remember that from Scouts," said Bob.

"And now you know why, don't you? 'He wins his battles by making no mistakes'. Sun Tzu said that."

"Page 3 girl, was she?" asked Bob.

"Numpty. He was some ancient Chinese general. Came across him in the library."

"You and your books, Danny."

They grinned at each other. Things were looking up. He'd driven to Grace's B&B to pick up her kit, then stopped by Bob and Wanda's on the way to the flat to check on Jessie.

Unlinked pieces of his cases, Grace's and Jessie's, twirled around in his mind. But it felt good to take a step back, try to relax for a moment among friends.

Then they heard the scream.

Danny was first into the hall, followed closely by Bob. They almost collided with Wanda as she burst from the kitchen, drying her hand with a tea towel.

"What was that?" she asked.

"Upstairs," said Danny.

He was six steps up when the scream came again, then Jessie's brittle voice.

"It's them, outside."

He swung on his heel, jumped down, grabbed the golf club Wanda kept by the hat stand and threw open the front door.

There was a pause, a split second of recognition, then the two men came on.

Danny recognised the two comedians from the B&B. The one to his right, the driver, held a baseball bat. Eyes flicking between the two, Danny stepped clear of the porch to give himself room. Don't give them time. Attack. Hard and fast. He swung fast. The golf club smacked into the driver's head. The man gasped and pitched onto the lawn.

Danny reversed his swung, caught the second guy on the shoulder. He staggered sideways, was recovering his balance when Danny's second swipe caught his jaw.

As he toppled back onto the path the driver was struggling to his feet, holding the baseball bat high to protect his head.

He never saw the low swing that hit him between the legs. The guy went down again, vomiting onto the grass.

Danny stepped back, golf club raised for the next contender. The two men shuffled away on all fours until they reached the front gate, then helped each other up and set off at a painful trot for their BMW up the road.

As they disappeared behind a hedge Danny relaxed. He turned to find Grace in a fighting stance just behind him, Bob and Wanda peering out from the front door.

***

The bar of the Bellerophon was deserted which suited them perfectly. Bob and Wanda had been reluctant to leave the house but Danny had assured them it would be ok.

He put the drinks on the table and looked around. Bob looked worried. Wanda was angry. Grace was quiet and watchful. Jessie was playing with her phone. Karol looked around at them all and said nothing.

Danny sat down, took the top off his beer.

"So, what was all that about?"

"You tell us, Danny," said Wanda.

"It's bound to be one of your cases," said Bob.

"It is," said Danny. "Grace and I came across those two characters outside the B&B where Jessie was staying. That's why we moved her."

He looked at the top of her tam as she stared into her lap.

"Any ideas, Jessie?"

The tam shook a 'no'.

"And you're sure it's not Jason?"

Jessie looked up sharply. "No! He wouldn't do anything like that. Why would he? We're trying to mend something between us."

"Well those two gorillas work for someone. They found you at the B&B and they found you again at Bob and Wanda's."

"How can we be sure they won't come back to the house?" asked Bob.

Everyone looked surprised when Karol chipped in.

"You are safe at home because they are following Jessie."

"What?" said Danny, Bob and Wanda.

Karol reached out. "Can I see your phone?"

Jessie looked worried, held the iPhone protectively against her body.

"Give it to him," said Danny.

Reluctantly, Jessie handed it over. Karol stared intently at the screen as he flicked through menus. When he looked up his expression was weary. He handed the phone back. Jessie almost snatched it.

"You have a find friend tracking app running."

Jessie clutched the phone to her chest.

"I just wanted him to know where I was. It's like being close to each other."

"So," said Danny. "With this tracking thing active, anyone could get a GPS fix on where she was."

Karol nodded. Danny looked at Jessie.

"Lovely friends you've got."

***

Danny could feel the adrenalin starting to pulse. He was on the back foot, clueless in the combat zone, but things were happening, events were on the move. He could just feel it.

No way of knowing who was tracking Jessie's phone but it had to be something serious if those gorillas had been after her twice. And why Jason's sudden interest in boats?

On the back foot, reacting to events, not dictating them. The clever combatant does not allow the enemy's will to be imposed on him. Sun Tzu said that.

It was a good point. The guy was right. He was playing catch-up, nursemaiding Jessie instead of getting stuck into the case. But it was coming together, Danny could feel it. He just wished he could work out how.

As he approached the living room of his flat he heard a sniffling sound coming from his bedroom. He slowed and listened. A woman trying not to cry and failing, Grace.

She said something in a language Danny had never heard. He didn't understand the words but the tone of her voice told him everything.

Then a high-pitched voice. Same language. A question. Danny stepped into the room and heard the child's voice again, in English this time.

"Who is that man?"

Grace turned away from the laptop Karol had loaned her, wiping a hand across her eyes, sniffling.

"He is a friend."

A child's voice. "I don't like you being away, all alone."

"I am quite safe. And I will not be much longer." There was a catch in Grace's voice as she tripped over the last few words.

Danny could see the kid leaning closer to his webcam for a better view. Good looking lad, about eight or ten, took after his mother. Danny leaned into the shot and smiled.

"I'll take care of your mum."

"Thank you, sir," said the boy.

"Meme must go now," said Grace. "We can speak again tomorrow."

The boy seemed reluctant, hesitated as he tried to think of a reason to stay online, then blew a kiss. Grace blew one back and cut the Skype connection.

***

In the living room Danny walked to the coffee table and put down his beer and the bottle of white wine he'd picked from Tesco Express on the way back. His bedding was folded by the sofa. Grace's meagre luggage was in his bedroom. Jessie was curled up on a z-bed beside his mother's care bed. The health people hadn't been to collect it yet.

"Sorry about that," said Danny. "I didn't mean to listen in."

"I do not think you speak Oshiwambo, Danny. It is not a problem."

"That your lad?"

"Yes, his name is Daniel."

"Good name," said Danny. He glanced at the ring on her left hand.

"So you're married then?"

"I was, my husband died some years ago."

"I'm sorry, must be tough on your own."

"I manage. Are you married?"

"Was, she died."

"I am sorry. Do you have children?"

"Boy and a girl, they live with my sister."

They sipped their drinks.

"We should talk about the case," said Grace.

"Let's give it a rest for a bit, shall we?" said Danny. "There's a lot to think about but sometimes I find it's best to take some time off, let it bubble away in the background."

"It is urgent," said Grace. "I cannot stay here much longer. I have no money, and there's Daniel."

"So you're not enjoying your stay then?"

"I don't mean to be rude, Danny, but your country is cold, damp and it has no colour. I am missing blue sky, the green of the bush, the rich orange of the dunes."

"Colour's not all its missing but I guess we're used to it."

They drank again.

"And how are you feeling?" asked Grace.

"Feeling?"

"Since your mother died."

Danny shrugged. "Ok, I guess."

"You are one of these Englishmen with, what is the phrase... a stiff upper lip?"

Danny laughed it off but Grace carried on.

"You are like my father. You have been in battles. Parts of you are closed to those who were not there. But pretending that feelings are not there does not make them go away."

"I suppose you're right. There are times when I feel like screaming out loud."

"Why don't you."

"Can't be bothered. Wouldn't change anything."

"You must be gentle with yourself, Danny. There is a grieving process. You cannot ignore it."

"I'll tell you what does get me. You can't escape the paperwork even when you're dead. And I've got to write a eulogy. I wouldn't know where to start."

Danny looked at Grace, realised how still she was, watching and listening, realised how long he had been talking. She smiled.

"You are a strange man, Danny. Just tell her story, as you would tell a friend. What she achieved. What she believed. Do you have a pen and paper?"

***

BRIGHTON, MONDAY MORNING

He'd woken up with a thumping head and a pounding hard-on. God alone knew why. The headaches were back.

Danny was lying under an open sleeping bag on the sofa, thinking about last night. Grace was a good listener. Danny wasn't usually much of a talker but he'd seem to have waffled on for ages. He tried to recall if he'd said anything he shouldn't.

The door came open hard. Scratching his hair into place, he looked across.

"You opening a hostel?" said Emma

"It's complicated."

"It always is with you, Danny. There's a strange woman in your bed and some stroppy teenager camping in your mum's room."

"They're clients, two different cases. They were having trouble with accommodation."

"Well don't think I'm doing everyone's laundry. Now your mum's gone I'm not sure why I'm even here."

Danny hauled himself into a sitting position, scratching his chest through his T-shirt.

"I was thinking about that, Em. Look, I know you're short. Business isn't too bad at the moment. I thought, if you wanted to stay on, keep the place tidy, it would save me a job. And I'd pay you."

"You think I'm some charity case?"

" 'Course not, I just thought it would help, you know, in the circumstances."

"What circumstances?"

"No, I just thought..."

"You thought, did you? Well that makes a change."

"You said you and Benny were trying to make a go of things. He's going to be out of circulation for a while so, I just thought..."

"You thought you'd give me a few bob for scrubbing your floors?"

"Emma!"

"Or maybe you just want to keep me handy in case the rest of your harem want a day off their backs."

"For Chrissake, Emma."

"Don't try and sweet talk me, Danny."

"The offer stands, take it or leave it."

The living door slammed. Seconds later the front door did the same.

***

Danny knew he'd hammered the drink last night but it hadn't done him much good. Whenever the headaches came back the thoughts came with them. Demanding his attention, flitting just out of reach as he tried to force them back into their box, keep the lid screwed down. It was like herding cats.

Constant vigilance was hard wired into him. When it's saved your life it's a hard habit to break but that leashed energy made civvies uneasy. And it wore you down in time.

He'd heard of a guy kipping on his settee when his daughter crept up to surprise him. He blinded her with his fingers before he came awake.

He knew men done for wife beating, burglary, others rough sleeping. On the upside, the country had some top disabled athletes.

The brain was a powerful tool, powerful weapon. It can save you or destroy you, crush the weak like someone riding a big motorbike they can't handle.

Danny missed the thrill of combat, knew he was still chasing that adrenalin buzz. From what he'd read at Jubilee Library it had been the same for soldiers down the ages, Romans on Hadrian's Wall, the guys at Hastings, Waterloo, the Somme, all the same men, hard practical guys with mates, confident in their training, unit pride.

The only answer was to keep the lid screwed tight down, keep busy, exercise, drink, look for pleasure in small things, birdsong and sunsets.

No one understood so there was no point explaining. It was ok to have it in your mind so long as you didn't let it leak into your face.

And then there was Emma. What was up with that bloody woman? She was stony broke and stuck with that idiot husband Benny. The cleaning idea was a good one. You try to do the right thing and get your head bitten off. You just can't win.

Now Danny was running in the rain, trying to cure the headache and the hard-on. He liked the rain, it thinned the crowds, cleaned the city, freshened the air.

He pounded down the promenade along Madeira Drive, careful not to stray into the cycle path, quietly pleased with himself, good rhythm, good breathing. Despite the hangover.

He passed the Wheel and glanced up at the white facades marking the ends of Royal Crescent where Laurence Olivier once lived.

Keeping up a fast and regular pace he passed the Steve Ovett statue and the funfair, Victorian arches stretching along on his left.

As he circled the Black Rock Volks Railway station and headed back towards the city he could feel the stump of his left leg was hurting.

The skin graft had been chafing the cup of his prosthetic leg. He knew it would be raw when he got home, increased his speed.

The mizzle felt soft and cleansing on his skin until he was clear of the station. Then a sharp gust off the sea threw the rain at him, stinging. Hey ho.

A hundred yards ahead he saw a girl in a blue parka and short skirt. Not quite dressed for the weather, thought Danny.

As he drew nearer she looked over her shoulder at him, half turned. Danny's eyes flicked from her face to her crotch and back to her face. It reminded him of something he'd read in Jubilee Library, a response hard-wired into men's brains, something to do with checking dimensions, ratios.

The girl walked on, tugging at the back hem of her skirt. That was another of those weird animal things. How did she know he was behind her, looking? And why keep tugging the skirt? If she wasn't comfy in it, why wear it? A mystery. There wasn't anything in Jubilee Library about understanding women.

Suddenly Danny needed a jimmy. He dodged through the sparse traffic and into a public toilet opposite the Peter Pan Playground, wincing at the smell.

It was a relief as he drew lazy figures-of-eight on the stained porcelain. He didn't like having his back to the door. Never sat with his back to a room. Too vulnerable.

Standing there with his dick in his hand he felt like a butterfly pinned to a cork board. He looked up at the extensive and graphic graffiti spread across the wall. Lisa was a game girl, popular with the lads. If the graffiti was to be believed, so was Derrick.

Danny made a mental note to pick up a few bits and bobs on the way back. Before he could complete his mental shopping list he was a twitching heap on the wet tiles, hot urine spurting down his tracksuit trousers.

He'd never heard them coming, never felt the stun gun between his shoulder blades.

CHAPTER 17

Jessie sat on the floor in the smelly bedroom, back to the wall, legs drawn up. There was no light on, just the faint outline of the strange empty hospital bed. The place smelled of piss but she'd seen worse. The only illumination came from the screen of her iPhone as she checked Twitter.

follow me pleeeeeeez

Sometimes it overwhelmed her, all these people she'd never met baring their hearts and souls to the world. Everyone trying to get noticed.

OH MY GODDDDDD YOU ARE INCREDUBLE

At times it felt good to know there were other people out there. But sometimes it was frightening to peer into these unknown lives. So intense.

Luv you so much <3

Jessie's nose itched. She rubbed it with the back of her hand and kept scrolling. So much pain. So much desperation.

PLEES COME BACK I MISS YOU SO SO MUCH

Sometimes the waves of need sucked you dry. All that intensity scattering out into cyberspace, passionate, obsessive, anonymous.

I H8 U !!!!

Jessie wondered who they were, what their days were like, what music they like, where they had fun, whether they had a job, if they hated it. Her fingers flicked until the tweets accelerated into a blur.

I WOULD DI IF IT MADE U WELL xxxxxxxxxxxxxxxxxxxxxx

She squeezed her eyes tight shut to stop the tears, smacked away the wet tracks on her cheeks, turned off the phone, sat in the dark.

***

You fucking idiot. You total *fucking* idiot. How did you get yourself into this? Take your eye off the ball for a split-second, one split-second, and you're in the shit. You total fucking idiot.

Danny knew railing at himself was pointless. But it kept him busy, kept him angry. Better that than concentrate on what was happening beyond the stale-smelling hood that scratched his face.

There was a strap across his chest. His hands were bound behind him, against the small of his back. His feet were held by something broad, another strap of some kind. He could barely move but shifting his shoulders produced a creaking noise, could be a plank beneath him. His head was higher than his feet. He couldn't be sure what was coming but, whatever it was, it wasn't good.

Footsteps. Light footsteps, whispering. Trainers on a concrete floor? There was a chill in the air. The place felt musty, damp.

And quiet. He thought he could just hear the rumble of traffic but it was very faint, masked by the thumping in his ears that was his heart beating.

"Hope, that's the worst bit of it."

A voice. Male. Young. Posh-sounding. Confident.

"Hope's the worst because there isn't any."

He was close now. Danny was sure of it. Then a big hand dug beneath him, tested the plastic ties that held his wrists. The guy moved to test the bonds on his ankles. Danny pushed down hard on the balls of his feet and tried to arch his legs as far off the plank as he could. It wasn't much.

"Right, that looks ok," said the voice. "I'm told you're ex-army. Para, isn't it? Signed up for all the values, right? What is it, commitment, courage, discipline, something like that. Integrity, loyalty, respect. Sounds very noble but it's not going to do you a bit of good. Like I said, there's no way out. And no one can resist what you're about to experience. So there's no hope, no hope at all. You might want to think about that before we get started. Could save us all a lot of time and trouble."

A door clicked shut.

***

Jas K hated paperwork, lots of words on lots of sheets, all jumbled up with numbers. The whole thing was a right pain but it had to be done, and done right.

Some people had ambition, ideas. Others read paperwork. Jas K massaged his scalp in the hope it would boost his concentration, lips moving as he read.

He looked up, irritated, when the door nagged open.

"Hey, Boss, how's it going?"

Jas K forced a smile. "It's going very well, Mitch. It's going brilliant."

Jas took a closer look.

"Jesus, you look a state. That guy must have given you a right pasting."

"He caught us by surprise, wouldn't have stood a chance if Paulie and I had been ready for him."

Jas laughed.

"Well, either way, the message has been sent."

"You want me for anything?" asked Mitch, wincing at his bruises, keen to change the subject.

"You got that booze stashed out back?"

"Yup, Paulie's just shifting the last of it now. Are we going to be ready on time?"

"I, Mitch, I will be ready. And it is going to be fanfuckingtastic."

"Should be," said Mitch, "the money it's costing." He flinched at the look on Jas's face.

"What do you know about the money, Mitch?"

"Nothing, Boss, nothing. It's just that, like, well it must be expensive, something like this, stands to reason."

"Let me worry about the money," said Jas. "You just stick to shifting boxes. But you're right. It's going to be something else."

"Lots of girls?" asked Mitch hopefully.

Jas's face cracked into a grin.

"Girls, celebrities, the lot. We'll have them queuing from here to Worthing."

"Who've you got, Boss?"

Jas looked at Mitch, thoughtful.

"Still waiting on some confirmations. You know what these people are like but when they find out how big this opening night is going to be they'll be paying me for the publicity."

"How about Michelle Keegan, Helen Flanagan?" asked Mitch. "They're fit. You got them coming?"

"Wind your tongue in, Mitch, you're dribbling." said Jas.

Sometimes he regretted hiring Mitch and Paulie. Sure, the lights were on but there wasn't anyone home very often. Still, he didn't need them for their brains. They were there for the heavy lifting. And they were good at that. Usually.

"Mitch, we are going to have everyone on opening night, and I mean everyone. TOWIE, EastEnders, a couple off X Factor. I've got some Page Three girls sorted and maybe a few from the Olympics, the proper sports, not the wheelchair ones. I'm working on Fatboy Slim, Norman, watsisname. He only lives up the road. No distance. I want class, Mitch. I want quality. We'll have lasers, flame and smoke machines, crowd-walking zorbs. They'll be fighting to get into the VIP room. No liggers, no losers. It'll be epic."

Mitch nodded, mouthing the word "epic".

"And then we have the icing on the cake, my star prize."

"You sure about that, Boss? I mean..."

"Mitch, you just stick to shifting boxes and let me get on with this fucking paperwork."

***

Danny tried pulling his wrists apart until his muscles quivered. He dropped back against the board, rolling his shoulders to ease the pain. No prospect there.

He tried moving his legs. Flexing his feet as the strap was tightened had bought him a few millimetres. He could work with that.

The door opened.

"Sorry to keep you waiting."

It was the young confident guy again. But there was a shuffle of shoes. More than one of them. Danny tried to stay relaxed, conserve his energy. It was hard work.

He felt a waft of breath across his masked face. Cigarettes. And something else. Mint, maybe gum.

"No second thoughts then?"

A pause.

"Sure? Ok, let's get cracking then."

The faint light through the hood disappeared as a towel went over his face. He'd guessed what they were going to do but knowing didn't make it any better.

His back arched at the first splash, ripping as much air into his lungs as he could squeeze. The hood tightened against his face. It kept on coming. Water softly glug-glugging from a plastic container. Soaking the towel. Running into his eyes, nose, mouth.

His heart was hammering as panic rose on the endless tide of water. He could hear it splashing into a bucket under his head. An endless flood hunting relentlessly for ways to break into his face, into his body. He wrenched against the straps but barely moved.

Everything in Danny's life, every memory, event, thought, action, it all vanished. Nothing else mattered but breathing, tasting air, feeling your chest fill.

But his screaming lungs wouldn't fill because water blocked his nose and mouth. How many minutes? How many hours? Panic started to nibble at his mind like a bushfire in undergrowth.

He knew the technique. Knew the psychology. Knew he wasn't really drowning. But the autopilot parts of his brain did not and they couldn't be persuaded.

Danny felt sick. Tried to turn his head. Didn't want to choke on puke if it happened. The weight on his chest was unbearable. He gagged, swallowed water, gagged again. Tried to clear his mouth and nose but more water flooded in. He could feel his airway closing in spasms.

Danny wanted to scream but couldn't spare the air. Tried to distract himself, calm down. He remembered something he'd read, something at the library. T something... T O something... toca, that was it, toca, Spanish water torture, used by the Inquisition. Bastards!

The water trickled to a stop. He winced at the leak light as the sodden towel was lifted from his hood.

"Not bad, sixteen seconds. Not bad at all. But we only washed your face that time. Tell us what we need to know and it'll all stop."

Danny tried to speak. Choked as water trickled down his throat, coughed, tried again.

"What, so you can shoot me."

"Well, obviously," said the voice. "But it's a lot less distressing than this, don't you think? So, where are Marion and Bill Carter?"

"How... how... how the hell should I know?"

"Come on, Danny. You're taking the piss. You're ex-military. Marion hired you as a minder. So she must want something minding. We want to know where it is?"

"I'm not a minder. I don't know anything."

"Danny, Danny, Danny, you know how this works, right? It's not a Hollywood movie. You don't wriggle free, overpower the evil henchmen and walk away. That's fantasy and you know it. You can end up half-drowned, shot and dumped in a ditch. Or you can be shot and dumped in a ditch. Your choice."

"Fuck off."

"So I'm really going to have to get my trainers wet? Oh Danny."

Everything went black as the towel was placed over the hood again. Danny started breathing hard, pumping oxygen into his blood while he had the chance. Hypoxia, that was what they called it. He'd been on a course. Too little air to the brain. Carbon dioxide built up, made you confused and panicky.

Danny wanted to puke again but he fought it. Water filled his nose. He struggled to hold his breath, stop his throat opening to suck in the precious air. He spluttered, breathed, took in air and water. Felt the water trickle down towards his lungs. The plastic bonds bit into his wrists as he thrashed. And the water kept coming.

"Where have you stashed the Carters?"

Splash.

"Where are the Carters?"

Splash.

"Where's the stuff they're hiding?"

Splash.

"What did they tell you to do?"

Splash.

"When are you meeting them?"

Splash.

Danny tried to shout something but all he could do was gargle.

Then the towel was gone again.

"Have to say, Danny, whatever they're paying you, they're getting their money's worth. Look, you're not a stupid guy. And bullets cost money. So what we're going to do is give you a few minutes to think about it, a chance to assess your position. If you co-operate, maybe we'll talk about your future. If not, well, I'm just glad this place doesn't have a water meter."

Danny gargled, tried to spit, lay wet and panting as he listened to two lots of footsteps leave the room. A mobile phone beeped a text message alert. The door was open and the noise echoed. Danny listened.

"He wants me now."

"Immediately?" said the quiet voice.

"You know what he's like. Now is now. I'll be back as soon as I can. There's a Red Bull in the bag if you're thirsty."

The room went quiet. Danny heard the faint sound of suction. Kissing? Couldn't be.

"But what about Lancaster?" said the quiet voice.

"Just keep an eye on him till I get back. He's not going anywhere. I don't think he's going to be much use anyway. If you get bored, shoot him, kill him dead."

Danny heard the door clicked shut.

CHAPTER 18

It was a bit like being God. A lot like being God, really. You take something and reshape it at the molecular level, create something new, part of you, in your own image.

That was powerful. Damian was a fool. He fretted, he worried. Creativity strangled by some stupid idea of conscience and ethics. Then he'd gone a step further and upset the others.

It was no wonder he'd run away. Clive wondered what he was doing now. Shut up in his bedroom back home with his parents, probably. Surfing porn. Sulking.

Maybe he'd run off somewhere, skulking in some tatty B&B where no one knew him, too embarrassed to meet anyone he knew and admit he'd failed.

Still, Damian's loss. Clive could cope on his own. Always knew he could. He'd been carrying Damian really, only invited him along because they'd been friends. Big mistake, that was. He was too soft for his own good. But not any more. People weren't worth the trouble. The guys who taunted him. The girls who sneered. People were a waste of time. From now on he'd stick to molecules. They were reliable, predictable. They could be controlled, did what you wanted.

Clive chuckled to himself. Mind you, you had to keep control. If you were God to the molecules you had to keep them in line. Get careless and you were sitting on a great big bomb.

***

Danny tried to calm his breathing but his mind was racing on a road to nowhere. These people were not mucking about. He could be dead in the next ten minutes. Even if he wanted to cooperate it wouldn't do any good. He didn't know enough about the Carters to make it worth them keeping him alive.

As his breathing settled he coughed hard to clear his throat but that just started a savage burst of hacking that made his bonds cut deeper as he thrashed.

He slumped back on the plank, sweating. He guessed the hot wet sensation round his wrists was probably blood.

Danny weighed his options. There weren't any. You don't get to pick the battlefield you die on but he'd never reckoned it would be some smelly garage.

Still, being about to die is a poor excuse for giving up. Utrinque Paratus, paras were ready for everything.

He arched his back but the chest strap was solid. He couldn't raise his spine two inches off the plank.

Paras didn't surrender. He ran the words through his mind again and again like a mantra. Danny flexed the ties around his wrists. The pain was intense but they didn't budge.

If you're going to die like a dog you might as well go down fighting like one.

He tried to move his ankles. The strap ran over the tongues of his trainers which padded his feet slightly. He pushed downward along the plank. Nothing.

He tried again and felt a slight movement.

Rippling his body like a slug in a hurry he tried moving his left leg down, into the arch of the strap. His foot moved. Maybe just a millimetre but it moved.

He paused, panting, did it again, trying to twist his left hip upward, his leg down towards the strap. Another slight shift.

Danny drew in a series of big breaths, concentrating on his body and the pressure points that held it. He tried for a third time, channelling all the mad angry energy he could muster into a last hopeless charge.

His left foot moved down deeper into the strap which scraped across the tongue of his trainer. It caught for a second on the knot in the laces, then moved again.

He breathed, pushed again, hard, face purple, breath hissing between gritted teeth. Danny pushed again and pushed again and pushed again.

The strap slipped suddenly above his trainers, against the shin of his right leg and the slim metal shaft of his left one.

Danny twisted his left foot until it was pointing away from him. Then he hooked the heel of his trainer on the plank and pulled, drawing his leg up, gradually loosening the grip of the strap.

His trainer dropped onto the floor with a flop. Danny jerked upward at the sudden freedom and the plank nearly went over.

He paused for breath, then decided not to waste the time. He wriggled his right foot free and flexed both legs to get the blood moving.

***

Maths is bollocks. He had never been good at it, right from the start. He'd always sat at the back of the classroom in school. They'd had a right laugh back there, more fun than all those shit numbers.

Miss Feiner had tried to help him but he wasn't interested. Extra classes after school? Fuck that. He wanted to be outside, playing football.

But Miss Feiner didn't give up easy. She kept nagging, kept pushing. You can do it. It's not that hard. Just try it in easy stages. She'd kept on at him right up until he squeezed her tit. The look on her face. That sorted it. Exclusion. Then he could kick a ball till he dropped.

So maths was a mystery. But you didn't need to be some clever bastard to understand the figures in front of him. And Brighton was rich pickings, a fertile hunting ground. People went crazy for drugs in this town. Drugs to Brighton was like golf to those posh places where bankers lived.

It was like the Amazon in Brighton. He'd done it in geography before they chucked him out for fighting, that big river, a massive, rich, constant flow of nutrients.

Jason Knight poured himself a triple measure from the bottle of Crystal Head vodka on the table beside him, sipped it neat.

Numbers were crap but they proved stuff. And he wasn't stupid. He'd checked. A third of people in Brighton had used illegal drugs. A third. He'd come across it in some do-gooding government report. A third! Ok, weed was still big. So was coke and speed. They reckoned there were a couple of thousands heroin addicts in the city. Everyone from kids to crumblies, they were all at it, all jonesing for that buzz that made all the aggro go away, make your weekend sparkle.

So the market was big, big and fertile. But you'd have to be a mug to flog the usual stuff.

Chemistry, that was the answer. Take the illegal stuff, the psychoactive gear that would get you nicked under the Misuse of Drugs Act, get some geek in to give it a makeover so it looked different and bingo! Same buzz, same profit but totally legal. Fucking a-mazing.

So, brew up a kilo of crystals a week. Cut that to make eight kilo of product. Knock it out at a fiver a gram, maybe seventy quid an ounce to special customers. That worked out at...

He pulled out his iPhone, opened the calculator, jabbed uncertainly at the buttons. Gibberish. He tried again. More gibberish.

He shook the phone in frustration, tried a third time. Knock it out at a bargain fiver a gram, a thousand grams in a key, one key of crystal cut to make eight.

Jason Knight sat back, staring at the calculator, drumming his fingers on the glass skull vodka bottle.

He whistled. Forty grand a week.

***

It was an improvement but his chances were still wafer thin. If he tried to get down, the plank would come off the trestle with him and the noise would bring them running.

But the guy with the confident voice had said he was going out. If he moved now there might only be one of them. His position still looked hopeless but it wasn't going to get any better if he hung around.

Danny forced himself to relax and breathe. No sound came from beyond the door he'd heard close. He breathed again, sucking in big lungfuls, holding them, then going for the long exhale.

No way of picking a good time to go so it might as well be now.

He braced himself and rocked the plank. As it gathered momentum he threw himself to the left, felt it teeter, then slip off the trestles with a crash.

Danny cracked his head on wet concrete when he hit the floor, the plank on top of him. He scrabbled for a footing, his one trainer squeaking on the wet floor.

When he struggled into a squat position, the plank sloping up like a ramp over his shoulders, he hauled himself upright.

Disorientated, he listened and instantly heard the handle of the door turning. He waited, panting, hunched low, until he heard a gasp. Then he launched himself backwards as hard as his thighs could pump.

Danny and the plank shot towards the door. He skidded on the floor but kept powering backwards, grunted when they hit something. The door hinges squeaked as the plank cannoned into it. Then he had something soft and moving pinned between the plank and the wall.

He pulled away and rammed the object again, using all his weight and muscle, heard a grunt. He pulled away and slammed into his target again.

There was a crack and a moan. Something sagged down between the wall and the plank.

Danny stopped still, braced, listening. Nothing happened. He breathed out hard, collapsing his lungs, and pulled himself downward. The strap clung to his chest, pulled up his T-shirt, snagged at his chin. Then he was through it and down.

He crouched, pushing his arms down behind him to the floor, then stepping carefully over his linked wrists, right foot, then left, to bring his bound hands to his front.

He clawed the mask from his face, wincing as pain danced around the stump of his left leg.

The body slumped on the floor in a pool of water was small and dressed all in black. It looked like a kid. No time to think about that now.

He listened, couldn't hear anything outside. When he peered round the door it was into a featureless concrete corridor yellowed by the dim light of lamps in caged mounts. Underground car park maybe.

At the end it opened into a large bare space, the concrete floor covered in scared green paint.

Yellow and black steel posts protecting concrete pillars. Odds and ends were stored haphazardly against the far wall, plastic crates, big panes of glass, cardboard boxes.

The place smelled of damp and fumes. Pools of oily water quivered at the vibration from humming machinery, an aircon plant maybe.

Danny studied the area under its harsh lights but nothing moved, guessed it was the service area for a block of flats or offices. The guard kiosk was empty.

He stepped out and ran as best he could, paused to listen, then ran again. He turned left, saw a ramp up to daylight, ran harder, burst out into grey daylight and a thin drizzle falling.

Danny tilted his face to the freshening rain as he walked on, left, then right. When he felt he was clear he stopped at a junction and sawed through the plastic ties on the corner of the brickwork.

As the strands frayed and snapped Danny saw the plastic was embedded in his wrist. He gripped a severed strand in his teeth and peeled it out of the raw flesh.

When the pain had eased a little he set off down the road at a sloppy trot.

***

Clive blew out his cigarette smoke, the last of it propelled by a series of small coughs. He adjusted the cigarette between his fingers. It didn't feel right. He'd just have to keep practicing.

He didn't smoke much, didn't like it much. But he was sure it was good for his image. Now, leaning on the rail, looking out over the mud towards the sea, it felt a little better. He looked like a rebel. They wouldn't laugh at him now, not if they knew.

The cigarette was half finished. Clive let it drop onto the mud, watched the tiny red spot at its tip fight a losing battle as the white stick wicked up the water.

The mud stank. The others complained. But not Clive. He loved it, loved the eggy smell of methane. Chemicals, you just had to love them.

This stuff was big. The operation was small at the moment but the potential was big, really big. And the responsibility. You had to be a scientist and an artist in one. And it took some nerve as well. The whole thing was one ginormous bomb. The smallest mistake, tiniest miscalculation and, bang, half of Sussex goes up in a mushroom cloud.

You'd got ovens, vase heaters, distillers and solvent traps. There were half a dozen volatile substances, ethanol, toluene, acetone. And the process needed total attention to detail. No wandering away to play games on your phone. Total attention.

The chemicals were highly flammable. Some gave off explosive vapours. If any of the potassium mirror glasses broke the solvents would dry on the mirrors, burn with the water in the air, explode the vapours above. Liquid nitrogen was great to stabilise the reactions but you could seriously burn yourself, or someone else. The acids and alkalis could make your hair curl, literally. The whole place would be a death trap if it wasn't for his skill.

He had taken a simple chemical formulation and changed it, improved it, made it all his own. Clive couldn't understand why anyone would want to mess with their brain. It was the best part of your body. But lots of people did want to and he was the man who could help.

He had created Amazon. No one else, him, Clive, the one they'd laughed at. The chemical formula was a thing of beauty, a series of symmetrical links. If he was any good at drawing it would win the Turner Prize.

So the others were wrong, all wrong. He could see why they thought he was some sort of nerd. Clive had to admit the glasses didn't help but he just couldn't get on with contacts. And the weight wasn't his fault. It was in his genes, so his mum said. He was just big-boned.

The others thought he was just some clumsy geek but they were so, so wrong.

He was the creator of Amazon, bringer of pleasure, bringer of death, a rebel.

CHAPTER 19

His whole body ached and his lungs felt raw but he just kept walking. At first he didn't know where he was. When he did he stuck to side roads where he could.

Danny dug his hands into the pockets of his track suit trousers to hide the wrists. He tugged down the legs to conceal the bare prosthetic foot. But no one took any notice of the tattered, shambling man. In Brighton they were used to it.

Two bits of good news. He'd left his mobile at home when he went running so the waterboarders had no chance of gaining information from that. And his flat keys were still in his pocket.

He let himself in and picked up a packet of cigarettes from the hall table. He leaned again the wall, slid down until his chin rested on his knees, lit a cigarette and smoked it as he stared into the gloom.

When the smoke cleared, the smell of sweat and damp of the garage wafted to his nose. Danny walked into the bathroom, stripped, stepped into the shower, gripping the safety rail as he discarded his leg.

When the water hit his head and streamed down his face he was suddenly gasping for breath, choking. Wet hands scrabbled for the tap, turned it off.

He stood for a while, gripping the rail, face upward, breathing. After a few minutes he stepped out and ran his wrists under the cold tap in the basin. Then, wedging himself between the basin and the wall, he bathed the sore stump of his left leg. Finally, he washed himself down with a scratchy sponge. It would have to do.

***

Danny was sitting on the sofa smoking another cigarette when Grace got back. She walked into the living room holding a shopping bag, glanced at him and looked away for a second before her head snapped back.

"Danny! What happened!"

Danny looked at her with a weary smile.

"Rough day at the office."

"Don't make jokes, Danny. Look at your wrists. What happened?"

"Would you believe I got jumped in a gents' toilet?"

"It's not funny."

"You're telling me."

"The wounds must be cleaned."

"There's a first aid kit in the cupboard under the sink."

Grace brought the kit and a bowl of water. Gently, she began cleaning the cut marks around his wrists, teasing patches of grit and dirt clear of the wounds with a soft cloth.

"Tell me what happened, Danny."

"Someone came at me from behind. I woke up in some underground room and they asked me questions."

"What questions?"

"Doesn't matter. They didn't get the answers."

He winced as Grace drew what looked like a piece of gravel from the deep groove in his right wrist.

"This is becoming dangerous, Danny."

"It was dangerous from the start, Grace. You knew that."

"We should call the police."

"And tell them what? I don't know what happened and, like I said, I was there. They'll want to know everything, who you are, why you're here. Then they'll write up a report and shove it in a file somewhere."

"Oh my God!"

They both turned to see Jessie, hands pressed to her shocked face, staring at Danny from the doorway.

"Danny, what happened to you?"

"What you might call first contact, nothing to worry about."

"That looks really bad. Does it hurt?"

Danny looked at Jessie and smiled.

"You know what they say, pain is just weakness leaving the body."

Grace looked closely into his eyes.

"Are you feeling all right, Danny? I think you are talking rubbish."

"I'm fine, fine. And we don't have time to faff about. We've got things to do. Opportunities multiply as they are seized, an old Chinese general said that."

He pulled himself off the sofa with a grunt.

"Come on, Grace, let's get weaving."

He picked up his jacket.

"Lock the door behind us, Jessie."

***

RIVER ADUR, SHOREHAM-BY-SEA, WEST SUSSEX

Roger Benjamin was worrying away at a patch of wet leaves stuck to the decking when his back twinged again.

He shot upright to relieve the pressure and that's when he saw them. They made a striking couple. The guy was pretty untidy, perhaps it was some new street chic fashion that had passed him by, the lived-in look. But there was something about the way he carried himself that made you pay attention. His girlfriend was very striking. She walked erect, head high, with the bearing of an athlete. People-watching was one of Roger's favourite pastimes.

The man turned and saw Roger looking at them, he smiled.

"Nice taking a walk by the water, isn't it?" said Roger.

"Yes," said the man. "These old boats look really interesting."

Roger stretched his back, leaning on the broom for support.

"It's a fabulous place to live. Alison and I, Alison's my wife, we wouldn't live anywhere else. Once you've tried a houseboat it spoils you for dry land. We all pitch in and look after each other. There's a book club, pub night, that sort of thing. We have quite a little community going here."

"Some of these boats look as if they've got a bit of history," said the man.

"Certainly have. Most of them have seen better days. It's an endless battle to keep them ship-shape and liveable. You'll get rats inside if the wood of the hull splits. Eventually they just give up the ghost and collapse. But there are advantages, fresh air, bird watching, that first cup of coffee in the morning with the sun on the estuary. And you don't need planning permission for houseboats. If you want a new window you just get your tool box out, put it where you like. You can't beat it."

"Is that an old warship?" asked the man, pointing.

Roger turned to see what he was looking at.

"Ah, well spotted. That one really has been through the wars. It's an old MTB, a motor torpedo boat. It's a Fairmile D, one of the biggest they built in an effort to rival the German e-boats. They used to call them dog boats."

"You know your stuff," said the visitor.

"Made a bit of a study of it, looked up a few things up on the internet. That one served in the Norwegian navy during the war, sailing across the North Sea to attack shipping in Scandinavia. Sank quite a few, had a few close shaves."

"Funny to think of her seeing out her days here," said the visitor.

"Well, she's still working, in a sense. A noble retirement, you might call it. A bunch of lads are renting her at the moment. They keep themselves to themselves. Well, at that age they've got better things to do than our pub nights."

"Fascinating," said the visitor. "Thanks for that."

"My pleasure," said Roger.

The couple strolled on, pausing to point at some of the houseboats. The place was a living museum of nautical history, ex-navy, barges and some that looked like garden sheds with hulls. Some were fresh painted, others crumbling as they rotted. A few had been reduced to a wooden ribcage sticking up out of the mud.

Most had fences running along the path with mail boxes and neat gardens behind, flower and vegetable patches.

Roger Benjamin watched the couple walk on down the path arm in arm, wondered what the man had done to his wrists to get those nasty cuts.

"Your tea's brewed," called Alison from the doorway of the deckhouse.

"Nearly there, dear."

As she padded out in her slippers she saw him bend over the broom again with a grunt.

"Haven't you finished yet?"

"Nearly, I was just chatting to that couple over there. He was asking about the Fairmile."

"You and your maritime history, Roger. I bet you didn't mention that bloody dog."

***

The only other people in the terrace garden of the Bridge Inn were two smokers huddled in a corner for a quick gasp before they returned indoors to their drinks.

As the chilly haze from the river crept around her, Grace pulled her coat tight, shivered, folded her arms across her chest.

She turned at a sound behind her and saw Danny negotiating the steps with a pint of lager and a glass of white wine. He sat in the chair beside her, both facing out over the Adur as the last of the dusk feeding birds left the mudbanks. Danny rubbed his knee, could feel the damp.

"What do you reckon?" asked Danny.

"I don't know."

"Big old wooden boat, tucked out of the way, a bunch of lads who keep themselves to themselves. We need a closer look."

"You kissed me."

"Cover."

"Pardon?"

"There were guys on the deck of the Fairmile. Might have been Jessie's unwelcome visitors, I couldn't be sure. The light was going. But Knight visited the boat so he must know them."

"I was... shocked."

"If I offended you, I'm sorry. It seemed the best way to hide our faces as we walked by."

"I understand your reason. I was... surprised."

"The guys on the back deck, did you see what they were wearing?"

"Coats."

"Heavy coats, bit warm for that."

"It is definitely not warm. This is a cold, damp country."

"It's not that cold. They're carrying."

"Carrying?"

"Armed."

"You mean weapons?"

"Oh yes."

They sipped their drinks, Grace studying Danny, trying not to be noticed.

"Are you all right, Danny? After what happened."

"Me? I'm fine. Bit tired but fine."

"You are sure?"

"I don't have time to feel sorry for myself. It was nothing. Forget it."

Danny sipped his pint, looked out across the misty river to the houseboats on the opposite side, the faint grey shapes clustered like piglets suckling against the embankment.

***

Bob Lovejoy moved to the full-length mirror, considered the reflection looking back at him. He turned to one side, then the other, face puckered with indecision.

It was nice to have the house to themselves again, back to a bit of peace and quiet. Danny was a great bloke but trouble followed him around like a bad smell. It wasn't the first time they'd got dragged into one of his detecting cases.

You helped your mates out, that was a given, but it could get hairy. Bob was enjoying his semi-retirement from the building trade and all for the quiet life at home with his wonderful Wanda.

He studied his image in the mirror again. After an anxious analysis he dropped it back in the drawer, picked another at random, held it up, looked at the reflection.

Why did this always have to be so complicated? What was supposed to be a happy time, a celebration, turned into a nightmare.

He turned to one side again, then the other. The whole business was a mystery to him but you had to get it right. The thought of getting it wrong did not bear thinking about.

"Not your colour, really."

Bob spun round, stood making fish mouths, saw Wanda in the doorway, that wicked smile of her face.

"I... I..."

"Probably not your size either, Bob. You're probably more of a c-cup."

He realised he was still holding the red bra up to his chest and dropped it as if it burned.

"I... I..."

"Up to you, Bob. Whatever you're comfortable in. But when you've finished playing in my underwear drawer your tea's going cold."

***

When they got back to the flat they were both quiet and thoughtful. Grace poured wine and settled in the living room. Danny tapped on Jessie's door.

She was sitting on the floor, back against the wall, legs stretched out. The same dowdy clothes and that bloody Rasta tam. He dropped down beside her.

"You ok?"

She nodded.

"You eaten?"

Jessie nodded again.

"What?"

The fingers were still flying across the iPhone keypad.

"Biscuit."

"You won't keep a sparrow alive on that. We'll order a takeaway."

Jessie didn't respond. Chewed thumbnails flew across the iPhone's tiny keyboard in a flamenco blur.

"Who you talking to?"

"Friends."

"You are a popular girl. Have you told your parents you're here?"

"No."

"Don't you think you should?"

"Dad's gone."

"Your mum?"

"She's busy."

"Mates?"

"Not any more."

"So it's just your friends on the phone?"

Jessie shrugged.

"You'd probably have a few mates if you just put that bloody thing down for a minute and talked to people face to face."

He saw her hesitate. There was a judder across her shoulders as if she was fighting something. Danny knew the feeling.

What happened next took him by surprise. She dropped the phone in her lap, leaned towards him with startling speed. Her arms went round his neck, grip fierce, pressing her lips to his.

Danny was so shocked that Jessie had forced her tongue into his mouth before he could react.

He reached behind, prised her hands from his neck, lifted her arms away.

"*Whoa, whoa, whoa*, what's all that about?"

Jessie sprang back as if she had been burned. Her pinched face was ghost white.

"I thought... I... I thought that's what you wanted."

"Well you thought wrong. Whatever gave you that idea?"

"I don't... I don't know. It's..." She began tearing up. "It's just... I'm not used to people being nice to me."

Danny leaned back against the cool of the wall, breathless and speechless. He watched as tiny silver tears picked their way down her pale cheeks. Jessie swiped roughly at them, angry they might be noticed.

"I just... I... I just don't want to be alone."

"No one does," said Danny. "Look, put that bloody phone away, come on through to the living room and I'll order that takeaway. You all right with Indian?"

***

Jas was watching Princess polishing her nails when his mobile rang. He looked at the number, pulled a face, thumb hovering over the 'answer' button.

"Who is it, babes?" asked Princess.

"Never mind," said Jas as his thumb jabbed down.

"Yeah, it's me. How's it going? oh, right... ok... right... you what!... Why? Why now?... Look, I can't... I've got things happening. I just can't... ok... all right... look, I said all right, ok?... yes... yes... Just one question. Why? Why now?... ok, ok, ok... I'll get it sorted. Yes, I said I'd sort it... all right... yeah, you too."

Jas cut the call, threw himself back against the sofa.

"Was it about that skinny bitch again?"

"No."

"Who was it, babes?" asked Princess.

"Never mind," said Jas.

CHAPTER 20

He thought he had over-ordered but they'd done it some serious damage. The tray on the floor held a buckled tower block of empty foil containers. An oily film on the plates was slowly losing its gloss sheen.

Grace looked across at Danny. The TV was on, sound turned down, but he was looking beyond that, into the empty corner of the room. Regularly, she saw him lift his lager can and sip. But his eyes never left their target.

"Danny?"

No response.

"Danny?"

He blinked, looked at her.

"Sorry, I was miles away."

"Thinking about the case?"

"Always."

"It seems very complicated."

"Wouldn't be any fun if it was easy."

"I do not mean it as a criticism, Danny, but our progress is very slow."

"Don't rub it in."

"Sorry?"

"Never mind, I was just thinking about that ransom note, the one Marion Carter gave me the day we met. Something's bothering me."

Grace saw a sudden light in Danny's eyes and sat forward in her seat.

"What is it?"

Danny dashed into the kitchen, came back with a newspaper package. He opened it and spread the contents on the table beside the ransom note. The paperwork from the Carters' bin was still damp. Danny spread out the ragged fragments and began assembling them like a jigsaw puzzle.

He mixed and matched the torn scraps, lifting pieces to squint at sections where the type had smeared, the ink had run. One sheet was a phone bill. The second a council tax bill. The third a supermarket delivery note and there were more.

After twenty minutes he was getting frustrated.

"Is this helpful?" asked Grace.

Danny shook his head.

"Useless."

He sat forward, head in his hands, looking down at the table, eyes flicking between the ransom note and the debris from the bin. Then he saw something. His finger stabbed down.

"There!"

Danny picked up the newspaper the bills had been wrapped in, peeling the pages apart. They were full of holes.

He flipped a page, checking the other side, picked up the ransom note and held it beside the newspaper. A hole matched one ragged-edged section from the ransom note.

"It's the newspaper, the one from Mrs Carter's bin. Some of it's whole words and some of it's letters cut up to make words. It's a mix of curly type, what do you call it, serif, and some of the straight stuff."

He tipped the note to show Grace the reverse of one section. It read 'YOUR PAGE, YOUR VOICE."

"See that? It's page ten, readers' letters."

He folded over another section. The visible type read 'gus.co.uk/news'.

"That's at the top on a lot of pages, it's their website."

Danny turned more pages of the paper, found the words he was looking for, checked the reverse. After finding four words cut from the paper for the ransom note and checking the print on the back he was convinced.

"That's it then. The ransom note was made up from words cut from headlines in Tuesday's Argus."

"Is this important, Danny?" asked Grace.

"I brought Tuesday's Argus. It's the same paper. They match."

"I don't understand."

"Marion Carter said she got the note the day before I saw her, Monday. But these papers, mine and the one from the bin, are from the same day, Tuesday."

"Perhaps she was confused."

"Doesn't strike me as the confused type. And why was the cut paper in her own rubbish bin?"

"The kidnapper could have put it there when they delivered the note."

Danny shook his head.

"Can't see it. Why take the whole paper along to the drop. It's not as if you're going to be cutting and sticking a ransom note in a car parked near the victim's house."

"So what are you saying?"

"I'm saying that this note came from close to home. Question is, why?"

They fell into a thoughtful silence. Grace leaned forward to reach her wine, careful not to wake Jessie. When the strange thin girl began to mutter in her sleep, Grace stroked the long dark hair on the head resting in her lap. It brought her a calmness she had not felt since arriving in England. It felt good to comfort a child.

Danny watched the gentle, stroking motion of Grace's hand and smiled.

"I'd better put her to bed. The poor kid's cream crackered."

Grace looked puzzled.

"She's very tired," said Danny.

"I thought my English was quite good," said Grace. "But I cannot understand much of what you say."

"You're not alone," said Danny as he started to rise from his chair.

"No," said Grace. "I will do it."

With a single delicate motion she swept the sleeping Jessie up in her arms and rose from the sofa.

"Don't take too long," said Danny. "We've got stuff to think about."

***

Despite his Luddite attitude to new technology, Danny had managed to find Shoreham-by-Sea on Google Maps, with Grace's help. He was pretty impressed. It gave a good overview of the town and the boats and helped him fix keys points in his mind.

"You are proposing we board the boat?" asked Grace.

"Yup."

"It will be dangerous, especially if the men we saw do have guns."

"Oh, they have guns all right."

"And this does not bother you?"

"It's not the guns that are the problem. It's the people holding them. But if whatever's on the boat is worth risking a five-stretch for possession of firearms it has to be something serious."

"I understand. But why do you think this is important to do?"

"I'm pretty sure the guards we saw were Jessie's visitors, Tweedledum and Tweedledee. And we know Jason Knight has visited the boat."

"But how does this help my inquiry about Carter, Hedges and Collins? I cannot waste time, Danny."

"I told you that when I went there I saw Knight park his Audi by the sea wall?"

"Yes."

"He parked it not far from a blue Toyota Prius, Marion Carter's Prius."

"You did not tell me."

"Nothing like a bit of drama to zip up a briefing."

Danny grinned. Grace looked cross for a moment, thought he looked tired, smiled.

"I approve of your plan. But how do we get past armed guards."

"Don't worry, we'll sort that."

Danny sipped his lager, topped up Grace's white wine.

"And when will this happen?" she asked.

He looked at his watch.

"We'll go tomorrow night."

"Not now?"

He looked at her and was surprised by the intense look in her eyes, bright and sharply focussed.

"It's too late. Just relax and enjoy your wine. We've got 24 hours to kill. It'll happen soon enough."

"What are you suggesting?"

"Me? Nothing."

"Danny, I am in a strange country, a long way from home, and I miss my son. I think you would like to take advantage of that."

"No. I mean, you're easy to talk to. It's the detective thing. We're both used to setting people at their ease, digging a bit deeper. And you helped me with that eulogy thing. But... no."

"I think you are forgetting something, Danny."

"What's that?"

"I am a detective too. I read signs, read people. That is what I am trained to do."

"So what are you reading?"

"That you are curious about me. That you want to make love with me."

"Your training was pretty thorough."

"You are a strange man, Danny. A good man but also a strange man. But you make me afraid."

"Me? Why?"

"I have not... since my husband..."

"Oh, I see."

"You are an attractive man. You keep yourself fit. But I think this would be a mistake."

"Not all mistakes are bad."

He watched her thinking, weighing up the pros and cons. It seemed to take for ever. And it felt like the longest six seconds of Danny's life as he saw her come off the sofa, kneel by his chair, stretch up and kiss him lightly on the mouth, like the brush of a butterfly's wing. He tasted wine and spices, turmeric, cardamom and nutmeg from the takeaway.

When they broke her voice was a whisper.

"We must have condoms."

"Sorted. There are half a dozen in the bedroom."

"I hope you live up to your promises, Danny."

"Utrinque paratus."

Grace looked puzzled.

***

BRIGHTON, TUESDAY MORNING

Grace was still sleeping when Danny woke and slipped out of his bed. His throat felt sore and his eyes were gummy. As he padded into the kitchen he knocked Grace's open bag from the back of a chair.

Too many fags, too much booze. While the kettle boiled he stood by the kitchen window, pondering. It was still half dark but showed signs of brightening into a good day. Maybe he should go for a run. Mustn't let the fitness slide.

He found the last box of tea bags in the cupboard and brewed up, two mugs, two bags apiece. He put bread under the grill and found a near-empty pot of marmalade next to where the tea bags had been. As the golden smell of toast wafted around him he stood thoughtfully by the sink.

Things were looking up. He was finding out new information all the time. His cases, all of them, were gathering pace.

Danny felt a twinge of excitement. The bursting point, where all the facts, good, bad and irrelevant, came pouring out, was close at hand. He could just feel it.

He had things to do today, and tonight they'd find out why Jason Knight visited a houseboat in Shoreham. And why Marion Carter's Prius was parked nearby.

***

Grace was in that luxurious zone between waking and sleeping as Danny carried the dented tin tray into the bedroom. She stretched and smiled, raising herself up against the bunched pillows.

"You made breakfast for me?"

"All part of the Danny Lancaster experience."

Grace reached up, touched his face.

"You are a strange man, Danny."

"So you keep saying."

He put the tray on the dressing table and carried the tea and toast to the bedside table, perching on the edge of the mattress.

Grace studied him without embarrassment, hard ridges of muscle, hard ridges of scar tissue. The tattoo on his arm. She traced the outline with a feather-light touch of her fingertip.

"What is this?"

"Pegasus, the winged horse."

"And the rider with the spear?"

"Off to kill a monster."

"And the words?"

"Latin, utrinque paratus, ready for anything."

Grace giggled.

"It is from your army time?"

Danny nodded.

"You miss that," asked Grace.

"Yes, I miss the blokes, miss the buzz. But life moves on."

Grace picked up a mug of tea, blew on it, sipped.

"I hope the tea's not too strong. Sugar's on the side there. You ok with that?"

"Yes."

"I buttered the toast and there's marmalade, thick cut. It's a meal in itself. I can't stick that jelly stuff."

"That is wonderful."

"You ok?"

"I am very good, Danny. This is not the tea I am used to but it tastes very nice."

"Good, don't let your toast go cold."

Grace lifted the mug to sip, then stopped, holding it with both hands close to her mouth.

"Thank you, Danny."

"What for?"

"For last night."

"Well, I wouldn't exactly say I was doing you a favour."

"No, I mean... for making it... natural."

"Natural?"

"Since my husband was killed I have been alone. I wanted... a friend but the thought frightened me. I am not afraid now."

She laughed nervously, a flash of perfect teeth.

"But it hurts where you bit my bottom."

"Sorry, got carried away."

"You have a lot of energy for a crippled man."

"Crippled? Bit harsh. Anyway, when you're lying down, who needs legs?"

Danny ran a wandering finger around the smooth skin of her shoulder, marvelling at its silky blue blackness in the dim early morning light from the window.

"Last night was a first for me too."

He felt Grace stiffen, looked up into her narrowed eyes.

"What do you mean by that?"

His finger traced figures-of-eight around the ebony skin of her arm.

"You know, sleeping with you."

CHAPTER 21

As soon as Bob heard Wanda coming he tried to stuff the Sunday colour supplement under a cushion. It was hidden when she walked into the lounge but him patting down the upholstery couldn't look anything but suspicious.

"This is about the birthday present, isn't it?"

"Well..." muttered Bob.

"Why do men always get this so wrong? Look, Bob, women love frillies, they really do. But they wear them for themselves, to feel sexy."

"I just thought..."

"Yes, Bob, I know you did. I don't mind a bit of dressing up. You remember our Wonder Woman evening after we got back from holiday?"

"The lasso of truth..."

"That's right. I don't mind for special occasions but there's a difference. I want to feel slinky walking around Tesco, not end up looking like a hooker drumming up trade."

"So it's back to the drawing board then?"

"Yes, Bob. It is."

"Any clues?"

"No, Bob, you have to work this one out for yourself."

***

Grace's eyes were hard now, her grip on his arm solid and urgent.

"What did you mean by that? Why did you say that?"

"Say what?"

"You know what you said, Danny. That I was a first for you."

"Well, it's true."

"Well what did you mean?"

"You know perfectly well. You might as well admit it."

"I..." her eyes flicked to the half-open bedroom door. "Have you been spying on me?"

"Not spying, no. I didn't have a clue, to be honest, although your story's been bothering me."

"You looked in my bag?"

"I bumped into it when I was getting a brew on. It was open, hard to ignore."

"I was going to tell you."

"Oh yes? When?"

Grace was looking down into her tea mug, her face angry, and something else.

"Look," said Danny. "We need to talk. Finish your breakfast. I have a feeling we'll be burning more calories today, and not lying down this time. I'll be in the living room."

As he moved towards the door Grace looked up.

"Danny, I am sorry."

"Don't be. Like I said, I've racked up another first. Never been to bed with a copper before."

***

They sat in silence on opposite sides of the coffee table. Danny had brewed up again but Grace's mug stood untouched.

"In your own time."

"I don't know where to start."

"Try the beginning."

"Danny... what I told you, most of it is true. I was involved in this case but as a police officer, not a private detective. I work for Nampol's Protected Resources Unit in Swakopmund. The unit is responsible for the protection of wildlife and game but also for natural resources."

"Which would include diamonds?"

Grace nodded. "Do you know anything about diamonds?"

Danny shrugged. "They're a girl's best friend. Apart from that, no, not really."

"Very well, I will explain a little. Diamonds are formed by great heat and pressure between 140 and 190 kilometres beneath the earth. They can take more than three billion years to form and are brought to the surface by movements of the earth such as volcanoes. They are named after the Greek word 'adamas' which means unbreakable."

Danny twirled his mug between his fingers. It squeaked against the table top.

"Very dramatic, I can begin to see the attraction."

"Diamonds in Namibia were carried down the Orange River into the Atlantic Ocean and spread northward along the coast by the currents. When the Germans colonised my country in 1885 they built the town of Luderitz on the coast.

"When they built a railway inland they found diamonds near what is now the deserted town of Kolsmankop. In those days people could crawl on their hands and knees to gather diamonds from the ground. Today it is more complicated. As the land deposits are exploited exploration is moving under the sea, where there are deposits in the gravel beds.

"The biggest rough diamond ever found was at Cullinan, which is in South Africa. It weighed more than 3,000 carats and was cut and polished into many smaller stones. Two of them are in your royal crown jewels."

Danny nodded thoughtfully. Grace continued.

"The industry in Namibia can mine two million carats a year, that is 400 kilograms of diamonds. We are the eight largest gem diamond producer in the world. It is an important part of my country's economy. So you can understand, Danny, why we do not like people taking what is not theirs to take."

He twirled his mug again, weighing what he had been told.

"I'm not an expert on international police procedure," said Danny. "But it still looks a bit odd to me, you being here on your own on a shoestring budget. Is that how your people usually do these things?"

"No, I am here on holidays. I am working alone... unofficially."

"Well, that shows real commitment. Why do it?"

"The unit pursued investigations for many months but we made no progress. The case is still open but it has been eight years now. It is not active."

"So you decided to carry it on yourself?"

"Yes."

"Why?"

"For personal reasons."

"And they are?"

"Personal. Look, Danny, everything else I told you was true."

"Ok, putting that aside for a minute, tell me what happened."

"These criminals represented themselves as filmmakers, making documentaries about our wildlife. At first we thought them very professional, very thorough, until we understood their real purpose.

"They had all the necessary permissions. It was considered good for our tourism, for our economy and the image of our country. It is a very beautiful place but not many people know about it. The world heard about Namibia six years ago when an American actress came to have her baby. But mostly we are forgotten. These people, this gang, they used a ship, a research vessel. And they had an aeroplane and 4x4 vehicles.

"Sounds like a small army."

"As you say. They were very thorough, filming the Jackass penguin colony and the fur seals near Diaz point, Benguela dolphin, the wild desert horses at Garub. All of these places are close to the Sperrgebiet, the forbidden zone, where diamond mining is carried out.

"Criminals are drawn to diamonds, Danny, and we are always fighting them but they are clever. They are dangerous and devious people. Some shoot packets of diamonds over security fences with catapults or make the bottom of their shoes sticky. Others eat them to smuggle. Workers are often X-rayed but this cannot be done too often as it becomes dangerous to the workers' health.

"Slowly we became aware of a pattern. Small amounts were disappearing but with diamonds there are no small amounts. Mine workers were being paid or threatened to work as couriers. The circumstances, coincidences, made us think the filmmakers were responsible. An officer of my unit was sent to work inside."

"Undercover?" asked Danny.

"Yes."

"What did he find?"

"Our undercover officer discovered they had a code name for their crimes, the plan they called Volstruis."

"Ostrich."

"As you say. The last theft they planned, the one they called a 'big score', they codenamed Kaapse Kobra, Cape Cobra, a big, fast strike. Our undercover officer was to make a delivery, a large one, and my unit would meet the aeroplane when it landed."

"Did he succeed?"

"Yes, but we found what was left of his body on a beach."

***

SPERRGEBIET, NAMIBIA, EIGHT YEARS AGO

Fantastic rock formations glittering under silver starlight shimmered through the night vision goggles. Steele looked at his watch, lit another cigarette, continued his sweep.

"He's late."

De Ruyter stretched in the front passenger seat of the Toyota Land Cruiser.

"Relax, man. He'll be here. This is Africa. You can't run something like this with a stopwatch."

Steele wound down the driver's window and threw out his cigarette stub. A thick haze of cigarette smoke slid lazily out of the gap into the night.

The terrain around them was a moonscape glowing silver under the light of a sky sparkling with billions of stars, horizon to horizon.

Steele knew people paid good money to see scenery like this but tonight it made him uneasy. Too far from home. Too far out of his comfort zone.

De Ruyter reached down into the footwell and pulled up a thermos.

"You want coffee?"

Steele shook his head, adjusted the straps of his goggles and began to scan the empty wasteland again. Nothing moved. He reached for his cigarettes on the dashboard.

"You'll get cancer, man," said De Ruyter, that annoying tone of mocking contempt in his voice again.

Steele didn't really want another cigarette. His mouth was acid from chain smoking. But they helped to mask the sour smell of De Ruyter's body.

He hated the man, wished he'd never hired him. But De Ruyter had the skills.

"It's three hours to sunrise," said Steele. "I wish he'd get a move on."

The passenger seat creaked again as De Ruyter flexed to get comfortable.

"Look, man, the plan's set. There's nothing we can do now. You hired me to do a job. There's no need for talk. There's too much talking in the world, not enough doing."

He twisted towards the door, resting his head in the vee between the metal and the seat headrest, closed his eyes.

Steele scanned the landscape ahead of them. His neck was starting to ache. He hated De Ruyter for being so relaxed. Just now he hated this bloody country. Just wanted to be back home, with the kids. He missed the kids.

His hand went to the breast pocket where he kept the picture but his fingers halted, pressed against the fabric. De Ruyter would come out with another of his cracks if he started mooning over family photos. Stay calm. Stay focussed. It'll be over soon.

Steele continued to probe the wilderness. His eyes hurt. He tensed as a faint sound reached him, sat forward in his seat, then realised it was the buzz of De Ruyter snoring.

Just as Steele cursed silently, the man farted. The stench mingled with the smell of sweat and cigarettes. Steele wished he had a mint or some gum. He fiddled with the straps of his goggles and began watching again.

Time seemed to have stopped. There was no noise. Nothing moved. The heat of the day had given way to the creeping chill of night. The Milky Way was brilliant, stretching across the sky like a cascade of diamonds, punctuated by denser clusters of cold white light. As the minutes ticked silently by Steele realised he could see the star shadow of the rocks moving ever so slowly as the earth turned. As if the boulders strewn across the desert were trying to creep up on them. He shuddered.

"There!"

De Ruyter moved beside him. Steele nudged him with an elbow.

"I can see something. Over to the left. Something moving."

De Ruyter hauled himself into a sitting position and the two men watched as a speck of movement zigzagged towards them through the frozen, prehistoric terrain.

"It him?" De Ruyter asked.

"Who the hell else is it going to be?" snapped Steele.

De Ruyter drew a knife from a sheath on his belt. It was huge, over a foot long with a curved tip and serrated teeth along the top.

"You can never be too careful in this business." He began to tap the point on the dashboard.

The man was only a couple of hundred yards away now. From the light of the stars they could see him staggering, weaving from side to side, momentum battling exhaustion to carry him forward. De Ruyter opened his door.

"We'd better greet our guest."

The man had seen the Land Cruiser now and that seemed to focus his last reserves of energy. Steele and De Ruyter were standing beside the vehicle when he reached them, collapsing on the ground, fighting for breath.

"Good trip?" asked De Ruyter.

Steele handed the man a bottle of mineral water. He nodded his thanks, gulped until he choked, then poured the rest over his head.

"You got it?" asked Steele.

The man's head jerked a yes. They stood watching him, torn trousers, no shirt, panting on all fours, trying to punch out some words. Steele turned to De Ruyter.

"What's he saying?"

"Shit pills."

The man's drooping head nodded. Steele took him by the arms and hauled him to his feet. Then the man saw the black PVC body bag stretched out on the ground. His eyes flared wide.

"What is that for?"

De Ruyter smiled reassuringly.

"We've got to catch a plane, can't afford to get messy."

"Give me the shit pills."

"The Citramag? Sure."

De Ruyter looked at Steele. Their eyes met, the signal that passed between them too tiny for the wheezing man to spot in the dark.

Steele hesitated. "The Citramag, right."

The man was still panting hard. He bent forward, hands braced on his knees, trying to fight his breathing back to normal.

When he hauled himself upright Steele shot him twice in the head. He dropped like water.

De Ruyter stepped astride the body. The man's wide white eyes seemed bright in the darkness. De Ruyter tapped the body with his boot.

"Nice job, for a moment there I thought you might fuck it up."

Steele turned, dropped the revolver onto the front seat.

"Let's just get on with it."

De Ruyter slipped a black plastic bag over the shattered head, gripped the dead man's legs and dragged him into the open body bag. As he hefted the big knife in his hand, De Ruyter looked up and grinned.

"You don't have to stay for this if you can't handle it."

Steele said nothing, lit a cigarette, looked away.

De Ruyter grunted as he drove the knife deep into the dead man's belly. The wound made a sucking noise as he sawed upwards.

Steele tasted salt in his mouth as the serrations began biting through ribs. As he walked round the Land Cruiser and climbed into the driver's seat he heard De Ruyter laugh.

He sucked hard on the cigarette, wishing he had a radio or something to stick in his ears, wishing he was at home with the kids.

In the silence of the wilderness it was impossible to blot out the noise of the serrated blade snuffling through cartilage and bone, punctuated by De Ruyter's grunts.

Then a series of snaps, like twigs being broken. He heard De Ruyter spit, then a thick squelch as something heavy and wet dropped to the ground. Air bubbled from tubing. Body fluids oozed with a phlegmy sucking sound.

Steele's breathing quickened. He tried to force the salt wash back down his throat. Tried to focus on the kids, then pushed their image sharply away. He didn't want thoughts of them mashed up with what was going on beside the Land Cruiser.

"Jesus, what has this bastard been eating?"

De Ruyter spat again, then grunted. Something runny spattered into the dirt. It seemed to go on for ever. Steele was almost in a trance when he heard the voice.

"You can come out now, and bring some water."

De Ruyter was stripping off his bloody shirt. He bent and rammed it through the open section at the top of the body bag's zip. Steele saw steam escaping through the gap. The smell made him gag. De Ruyter took the water, rinsed his bloody forearms, grinned.

"It's done. Give me a hand here."

They dragged the body bag to the rear of the Land Cruiser and manhandled it into a heavy duty camera equipment case. De Ruyter stamped the gutted corpse down, slammed the lid and snapped the catches.

When the case was loaded they climbed back into the Land Cruiser. De Ruyter pushed his head back against the rest and blew a long, low whistle through his teeth.

"You enjoyed that," said Steele.

De Ruyter shrugged. "Just a job. Just another lump of bush meat. But the guy did his job. Hell of a journey through the Sperrgebiet. You have to admit, he had guts."

Steele could still hear him chuckling as they headed west along the B4, the dusty deserted highway to the coast. He drove as fast as the surface would allow, maybe a bit faster.

De Ruyter stared out of the passenger window. As the sky in the east began to lighten, colours trickled back into the monotone miles of stone desert.

***

WALVIS BAY, NAMIBIA, EIGHT YEARS AGO
It was a joke, a farce. She knew the two guys were watching, and others beyond them. The two men were less than ten feet apart. Yet each pretended he wasn't looking, fiddled with unimportant things, not concentrating.

She was lying on a white towel which highlighted her tan. It wasn't shop-bought or a careful holiday tan. It was a deep rich red-brown gained from spending hours outdoors.

The bikini bottoms were tiny, not worn to cover her but to draw the eyes to what wasn't covered. She stretched out on the towel. The movement made her large breasts jiggle.

Both men blinked in sync. When she was still, one of the men picked up a clipboard, then put it down. The other spat noisily out of the door.

Their attention locked on the woman again when she raised the plastic bottle to arm's length above her. Fat gobs of creamy liquid spattered across her breasts. She lay for a moment as the cream began to warm, thin, and trickle, then began to spread it.

The men watched her breasts quiver and squeeze under the woman's circular massage movement. When the cream was gone and her skin glistened she poured more into her hands and began to massage her thighs. As she drove her fingers hard against taught muscle her mouth opened, her tongue traced her lips.

Neither of the men was breathing when the door behind them rattled open.

"What is it?"

"Message, Kaapse Kobra, they're taking off."

The radio operator handed over the message slip and leaned forward for a better view of the forward deck.

One of the men turned suddenly, scowled.

"Get on with your work."

***

At Luderitz Airport, Steele and De Ruyter pulled up close to the aircraft, an Aero Commander 690. Someone called a greeting as they manhandled the big case into the back of the fuselage. Steele called back and the man laughed.

Nothing out of the ordinary. Just another normal day. All part of the plan. They left the Land Cruiser in their usual parking bay.

Steele stepped clear of the aircraft and had a cigarette while De Ruyter removed the covers and tie downs, checked the fuel and oil, ran an eye over the fuselage to be sure it was clean and tested the control surfaces.

As the 690 climbed into the sparkling morning air Steele looked across De Ruyter to Penguin Island, Seal Island and the Bogenfels rock arch stretching out into the sea to the west.

They headed north over Boot Bay and cut between Ichaboe Island and Douglas Point, across the curling neck of land that was Hottentotspunt and back to the coast at Hottentot Bay.

As the red hemisphere of the rising sun broke free of the eastern horizon, spears of brilliant light bathed the savage terrain, chasing shadows, soaking a rich ochre colour into the desert.

The country fascinated Steele. The place was scorching hot but dry, no humidity, no mosquitoes. Watching the changing light paint a palate of rich colour over the landscape gave him a strange feeling of peace he'd never felt before.

The wildlife fascinated him, right down to the fogbasker beetles that stuck their bums in the air to drink the water that condensed on their shells from the sea fog. He had watched gemsbok, with their distinctive black markings and spear-like horns, trekking the wilderness. He'd walked the dunes, stretched out on them to make sand angels, looked up at a black sky splashed by a brilliant rivers of silver, Mars, Venus, Orion, Alpha Centauri and the Southern Cross, glittering puffs of cloud that were distant galaxies. The air clean and clear. Namibia was like visiting another planet.

As the aircraft clawed northward he looked down at the abandoned diamond camps of the Charlottenfelder and could see the sun-dried remains of ox wagons and A-frame wooden bungalows.

Further, the wreck of the Eduard Bohlen, driven ashore in 1909, now stood 200 yards from the waterline, moulded into the landscape by relentless blowing sand.

The strengthening sun explored the dunes, liquid light pouring like mercury down the slopes and folds to make then shine a brilliant golden orange.

Steele was stunned by the awesome desolation. Hard to believe such beauty existed after the horrors of the night time.

As they cruised the length of Conception Bay, Steele saw the specs of black-backed jackals scavenging the seal colonies dotted along the waterline. Once, he was sure he spotted the dark bulk of whales below the flecked green of the sea.

Steele was jerked back to reality by the pilot's elbow.

"Time to say goodbye to our passenger," said De Ruyter.

***

Grace paused, looking down at the table, deep in thought. She picked up her mug, sipped the tea, didn't seem to notice it was stone cold.

"Our PRU team was waiting at Walvis Bay airport but the aeroplane crashed south of the town. It hit a bird. By the time we realised what had happened their vehicles had raced from the port and reached the crash. We found tracks in the dunes. They had boarded their ship and left. They went north, into the fog, to Angola, and disappeared."

"And the diamonds."

"The aeroplane had exploded and burned. It was so badly damaged we think they must have carried explosives of some kind. The debris was scattered over a big area. We found some diamonds but not everything that the courier carried from the mine."

Danny steepled his fingers thoughtfully. "And no trace in eight years?"

"They were cunning and they had money to pay for their escape and the silence of those who helped them."

"How much do you really know about them?"

"All of them were given immigration documents when they applied to make their films in Namibia. Much of the information was false."

"But you know who they were?"

"Their leader was Mr Steele. Mr Hedges was responsible for their organisation, their planning, of the filming and the thefts. Mr Collins was their cameraman, their camouflage. They had many crates and boxes of equipment. As I said, they seemed very professional. And Mr Carter was their accountant."

"And that was all of them?"

"No, there were some others, drivers and people to carry their equipment. Afterwards we thought that some tourists who were there at the time might have been part of their gang."

"So you don't know exactly who they were?"

"No."

"And they all disappeared?"

"Yes."

"Until your Antwerp diamond contact got in touch."

"Yes."

"And your bosses didn't want to follow that up?"

"The information came from a source of mine that I had developed during the original investigation. There was nothing definite apart from the Brighton telephone number that was left. My superior said he would need more information."

"But you decided to come here off your own bat?"

"My bat?"

"Alone."

"Yes. I was sure that my contact's description of the biggest diamond he was being offered was the Demon's Eye. They had given it a name because of its unusual shape."

"So you decided to spend your life savings and come over here alone to find it?"

"Yes."

"I don't believe you."

"Danny..."

"You've lied to me already. You pitch up here, try to hire some wally to do your legwork. You're carrying cop ID but say you're working alone. You told me yourself the gang had money to buy people off. For all I know you could have come here to collect your cut."

"Danny, no..."

"There's no way I can check your story."

Grace picked up her bag, took out her police ID and laid it on the table. Then she dug into the bag for something else. She placed a small photo beside her badge and slid it towards him. The photo was faded and cracked, one corner bent. Danny could see a younger Grace, Daniel as a toddler and a tall smiling man.

"What's that then?"

"The undercover police officer was Nelson Nujoma, Daniel's father, my husband."

CHAPTER 22

The woman was seriously fit. He'd already seen her up close and naked but it was out running that he could really appreciate her athleticism.

There was power and economy in the way she moved, matched with a fluid lightness. Grace by name, grace by nature. Her face was a mask of concentration and determination. She was not a woman to be beaten. Danny smiled as he recalled their earlier conversation.

"Do you run, Danny?"

"From what?"

"Run for exercise?"

"It's been known."

They set a brisk pace along the front, out toward the marina, ignoring the cold and the chilly gusts off the sea. His aches and pains fizzed and crackled as he moved but Danny could feel the potent mix of blood and oxygen purging and renewing muscles, rebooting brain cells.

He circled the Black Rock Volks Railway station and Grace followed. They started back towards the city. He glanced at Brighton Wheel near the Palace Pier. Maths wasn't his strong point but he did a quick mental calculation, wondering if anyone had joined the one-thirtieth-of-a-mile-high club yet.

As they powered along Danny snatched glances at Grace running beside him. A picture in a handbag didn't really prove anything. It still wasn't anything he could check.

But the look on her face when she told him, there was no doubting that.

While he lived, Nelson Nujoma had been a very lucky man.

***

Danny and Grace stopped off to pick up some beers and a bottle of white wine. Back at the flat Danny knocked on Jessie's door and listened. No response. He tapped again, ear to the wood, heard nothing.

"Jessie?"

He tapped again.

"Jessie?"

Danny pushed the door open and peered in. It was dark. All he could see was the z-bed lit by the hall light behind him. He sniffed. The room still smelled stale. He wondered if it would ever clear.

He stepped inside, picked up the iPhone from the z-bed. Ok, it was nosy but, hey, you're a detective and there's something about this kid.

Smartphones were a foreign country to Danny. His made mobile calls and texts, took the odd small grainy picture. He couldn't begin to understand how so many people spent their waking day glued to a phone. As he peered at the big screen it lit up.

love you Can I be your friend ????

He didn't really know what he was seeing on the screen but it looked like gibberish, a perfect storm of emotions swirling in a torrent of hormones.

ur the nisest person ever xxxx

Danny had seen some of Hayley's texts once, by accident, sort of. Kids had a whole new language of their own, a whole new code. He scrolled.

DIE BITCH !!!

He blinked at that one. Danny had read about girls, kids, sending naked pictures to boys at school, sometimes pressured to do it. He didn't think Hayley would do that, hoped she wouldn't. It worried him but the idea of raising the subject made him wince. He scrolled again.

Letz haave babies together!!!!!!

"You're spying on me!"

Danny turned to see Jessie in the door, dressed in her usual tam and baggy jeans, a towel in her hand.

"No, I just came to say..."

"You were spying!"

She snatched the phone from his hand, threw it on the bed.

"Take it easy."

"You're just like all the rest." Jessie threw the towel, dropped on the bed and lay there, bouncing. When the springs were still she drew herself up against the wall, arms locked around her knees, glowering.

"Ok," said Danny. He crouched on the floor, to eye level. "I'm sorry."

"Bastard!"

"Look, I said I'm sorry. But you have to admit, you're a bit of a mystery. And I am a detective, after all."

Having avoided his sightline, Jessie turned to look at him, eyes narrowing.

"You're my client. I have a sort of... responsibility."

"For me?"

"Yes."

"So what did you want to know?"

"Oh, you know, basic chit-chat stuff. Where are you from?"

"I'm a Sanddancer."

"A what?"

"A Sanddancer, from South Shields."

"A Geordie, then? A long way from home."

Jessie nodded.

"And?"

"And what?"

"What about your family? They all still up there?"

"My mum's there, and my kid brother. All my family's from Shields. Well, Granda was from Yemen, wherever that is, but he was a proper Geordie. Never met dad. Mum's always working, my brother's always in trouble."

"Why'd you leave?"

"Came south for work."

"What do you do?"

Jessie shrugged. "Stuff."

"You miss home?"

"It's beautiful there, where the Tyne meets the sea. I miss walking in the dunes, and the cliff top path, The Leas, down to Marsden Grotto and Souter Lighthouse, going down Wapping Street and watching the ferries go by to Ijmuden. I always wondered where it was, what it was like."

Danny could see the distant look in Jessie's eyes as she walked herself back through her recent childhood.

"It used to be all mining and shipbuilding round there. That's gone now. The walking's good," she said. "Fills you're time when you're broke. If we had some money we'd go to the pleasure park or the chippies and curry houses in Ocean Road, maybe go to Kirkpatrick's or Glitterball, that's a club. I miss watching the soaps with mum, sitting together on the settee eating baked beans."

"We've got baked beans down south."

"It's not the same."

"What about stottie?"

"Now you're taking the piss."

"Ok, sorry about your phone. I've no idea what it was all about anyway."

***

Danny took a shower while Grace tried her hand at making good strong Army tea. Standing under the pounding power jet was easier than before but several times he gagged when the water surged over his nose and mouth.

When he was done he made way for Grace and towelled himself dry in the bathroom as he watched the water cascade over her sweaty glistening body.

When she wiped the soap from her eyes and saw him looking she swiped the shower curtain closed. Danny was about to make a suggestion when he heard his phone trilling.

***

Cheryl was hysterical. She started gabbling as soon as Danny answered but her words tripped over themselves. Danny couldn't understand what she was talking about.

"Cheryl, Cheryl, calm down. What's the matter?"

When his sister began to talk she had to keep stopping to suck in breaths between sobs.

"Danny... Danny... it's Hayley."

"What's happened?"

"She's disappeared. She went to see her friend Sasha but I called her mum. They were never expecting her. She was due back three hours ago. She's not answering her phone. Danny..."

"All right, Cheryl, calm down."

"I can't calm down, Hayley's missing."

"Did she say anything?"

"No, not really... well... yes. She's been really upset about mum. Wayne's younger, he didn't know her so well. But it's really upset Hayley. And she was worried about you."

"Me?"

"Kept saying you were all alone in the flat... where mum died. About how you never got emotional, how there was no one there to look after you."

"That's daft."

"Maybe to you, Danny. But she's a kid and she's had a shock and she's upset."

"What do you want me to do?"

"I've called the police. I just want you to stay at the flat in case she turns up there. Don't go dashing off on one of your jobs. Just be there in case she turns up, please."

"Ok, ok, no problem."

***

Bob was hunched over the laptop, pecking uncertainly at the keyboard with two fingers, concentrating so hard his lips were moving.

He never heard Wanda in her fluffy slippers.

"Not ogling porn, I hope?"

Bob slammed the laptop lid, winced as his thumb caught.

"No, no, just browsing."

"Are you sure, Bob? You're looking shifty, and a bit pink."

"No, no, I was..."

Wanda burst out laughing.

"It's my birthday again, isn't it?"

Bob nodded solemnly.

"How can one man make a career out of choosing one silly present?"

"I wanted to get you something special."

"I don't need anything, Bob. If I did, I'd pick it up myself. Remember the salad bowl."

"Well, yes, I thought it looked great."

"It did, but it's not really a birthday present, is it. Bob?"

"Ok, no. What about a scenic flight. They do them from Shoreham. You can see all of Brighton and the Downs."

Wanda shook her head.

"How about a spa weekend? You'd like that."

"Nope, I like the skin I'm in and I'm quite relaxed already."

"Jewellery?"

"No."

"Shoes?"

"Nope."

"Wanda, give me a clue, please."

"I'm having too much fun."

"Wanda, please, you know what'll happen otherwise."

She nodded. "You'll buy something hideous and I'll have to take it back."

Bob nodded. She moved closer, put a hand on his shoulder, tilted his chin up to look at her.

"I have a wicked plan."

Bob wasn't sure where this was going, didn't react.

"I need you to plant a seed."

"Seed? What sort of seed?"

"I need to give it some thought first. Then you plant the seed and I'll nurture it."

"And that's all you want for your birthday?"

"Oh yes." Wanda was grinning her grin now. "Just a bit of fun. But that'll be more than enough."

***

Danny was finishing some washing up. Grace was drying, stacking plates in a cupboard, cutlery in the drawer, when the door bell chimed.

"I'll get it."

As soon as Danny opened the door she was in his arms, crying, the impact so hard it carried him back two paces.

"Hayley, thank God you're safe. What are you doing here? Cheryl's going mad."

"I can't stop thinking about Nan."

Danny held her tighter.

"I know. It's a shock. But she hadn't been well for a long time. She's not in pain any more."

"But Dad..."

"Shhhh... Look, I'd better ring Cheryl. She's really worried."

"You mean angry."

"That too."

"She's treating mc like a kid."

"Don't forget, Nan was her mum too. She's upset."

"So am I. And so are you. And you're all alone."

Hayley pulled away, looking past Danny's shoulder.

"Who's she?"

Danny turned to see Grace in the kitchen doorway.

"Don't be so bloody rude, Hayley."

Grace smiled. "I am a friend of your father. He is helping me."

"He's always helping strangers."

Danny gripped his daughter's shoulders.

"Look, come on in, get your breath back and calm down. I'll sort us something to eat."

"Not hungry."

"Well try. It'll give you an excuse to stay a bit once I've rung Cheryl. Then I'll drive you home."

"Can't I stay with you?"

"It's a bit crowded around here at the moment."

Danny reached to his mother's bedroom door and banged twice.

"Jessie, what do you want to eat?"

Hayley glared at the closed door, then at her father, said nothing. She let herself be guided reluctantly into the living room. Danny fetched his daughter a Sprite from the fridge and stepped out into the hall. Hayley took a tentative sip from the can and looked up as Grace walked in.

She could hear her father in the hall, voice muffled on his mobile, as he calmed his sister and told her the news. Then she heard him shout "Jessie, come on," and he was back.

"Auntie Cheryl's not happy. She's had the police out looking for you. Anyway, I've calmed her down and she's ok if you stay an hour or so. I said your mobile was flat. Give her a bell when you've had your drink."

Danny indicated Hayley's can of Sprite.

"You might want a glass for that."

Grace passed one from the sideboard. Hayley stood up, reached for it, began to pour. Then her fingers sprang open. The glass dropped, clipped the table, spun, sprayed fizz across the carpet. Hayley screamed.

"OH...MY...GOD. OhmygodOhmygodOhmygod."

CHAPTER 23

Splayed fingers were pressed to Hayley's mouth. Eyes like saucers, she was gasping for breath.

"Hayley!" said Danny. "What's the matter with you? Look at the mess you made."

He looked behind him at Jessie standing in the doorway, tam pulled down over her eyes, phone in her hand.

"OhmygodOhmygod," Hayley, white-faced, tears in her eyes, looked close to fainting.

"For Chrissake, Hayley. What's the matter. Get a grip."

"But Dad... But Dad... it's..."

"It's what?"

"Scheri, Dad. It's Scheri."

"Who?"

"It's Scheri, Dad. Only the biggest music star, like, ever."

"Hayley, she's a client. Her name's Jessie, Jessie Shafto."

"I know that, I know that. She's just so fantastic. I know everything about her. Jessie's her real name. Scheri's her music name."

Danny looked at the skinny, scruffy girl, strands of chestnut hair coiling down from under the big tam. Something rang a vague bell. Think... think. He recalled something in the paper, some teeny pop star in rehab.

He looked at Jessie who gazed sheepishly back.

"You?"

She nodded.

"I must be a really crap detective."

***

They sat around the coffee table, hunched forward like a conspiracy. Danny nursed a can of Sprite, rolling it around between his fingers.

"So, if I've got this straight, you did a runner and this manager guy put out the rehab story when he couldn't find you."

"Yes," said Jessie.

"And you wanted time out to find Jason?"

"Yes."

"And he knows who you are?"

"Yes."

"Which would explain why his chums are so keen to get their hands on you."

"No! I said before. Jason wouldn't do that."

"He's trying to set himself up as some music guru, opening his new club. That's tonight, isn't it? Don't you think his career would make a bit of a leap with you fronting things up?"

"He wouldn't. He just wouldn't. I know him."

"I wonder."

"Besides," said Jessie. "If you were right, if he just wanted me for the opening, he's left it too late so that can't be his reason, can it?"

Danny shrugged, looked across at Grace. She had been listening quietly. He didn't know how much of this had made sense to her but she smiled at him. Hayley moved closer to Jessie.

"Can I take a photo?"

Jessie hesitated, then nodded.

Hayley scrunched up next to her on the sofa, threw an arm round Jessie's shoulder. They leaned together, cheek to cheek, pulling faces, as Hayley reached out with her phone.

"What are you doing?" asked Danny.

"Oh Dad, taking photos. What does it look like."

"From the front?"

Hayley looked confused, then suddenly realised what her father meant.

"Duh! It got a camera on the front and the back. Takes pictures or you can use it as a mirror. there's an app."

"App?"

"Just a thing that makes it work. Uses the camera so you can check yourself."

A picture flashed into his mind, one that had puzzled him. Marion Carter at the bottom of Montpelier Road, tilting her head at her phone, using the mirror app. She knew she was being followed. He rubbed his tired eyes.

"Look, this is going to take a bit of thinking about," said Danny. "And we can't do that on an empty stomach. Who's for Chinese?"

He looked across at Grace.

"You ok with Chinese?"

"I have never tried one."

"Well come along, see what you fancy. I'll run Hayley home and we can pick up a takeaway on the way back."

"Oh, Dad."

"Don't start 'oh dadding' me. Auntie Cheryl's chewed my ear off once this evening and I've already bought you an hour."

"Oh, Dad."

"She could stay here with me."

Everyone turned towards Jessie.

"Why not?" said Jessie. We can sit and talk, play music."

Danny looked at the breathless ecstasy on Hayley's face.

"Ok, I'll ring Cheryl again. This might take a while."

***

To be fair to Cheryl, she had a lot on her plate. With her husband gone and Hayley and Wayne plus her own to kids to look after she had her work cut out.

That said, there were times when she could be difficult just for the sake of it, or so it seemed to Danny.

All right, she didn't think the detecting lark was a real job. All right, she thought he should spend more time with his kids. But he was doing his best. No point in banging on about it.

The phone call had been short and fraught. It was made harder for Danny because he couldn't mention that he wasn't the only attraction at the flat for Hayley.

Cheryl had insisted she come home straight away. Danny had only persuaded with the argument that if she spent a little time with him she might not go dashing off again.

Reluctantly, very reluctantly, Cheryl had agreed.

Grace had seemed quite excited as she read the menu. All in all, it seemed like an excuse to celebrate so Danny had over ordered, chicken curries, pancake rolls, some spare ribs, seaweed and plenty of rice, plain and vegetable fried.

It was more than they could get through in an evening but he could always have the leftovers cold or refry them. No point wasting anything.

He was feeling good. It wasn't every day you got to spend an evening at home with an African copper, an international singing sensation and your daughter.

When they got back he saw the door of the flat was half open.

CHAPTER 24

It looked as if a bomb had hit the place. The chain had been ripped out and one of the hinges was bent and dragging.

"Hayley!"

The hall table has been tipped over and the contents of its drawers strewn along the passage. The door to Danny's mum's bedroom had a size 12 footprint punched into the centre where someone had kicked it open.

"Hayley!"

Glazed shards of an old vase were scattered on the hall carpet. You could see the mark on the wallpaper where it had ricocheted before shattering. His mum's NHS kit, commode, zimmer, bath seat, had been stacked by the front door to give Jessie some space while it awaited collection. It was strewn along the hall like crash wreckage.

"Hayley!"

Danny and Grace searched the rooms at a rush. When Grace came out of the kitchen she found him in the living room, staring down at the upturned coffee table.

"Danny?"

He looked up, eyes burning.

"Jas's heavies, got to be."

"Can you be sure?"

"Who else can it be? He wanted Jessie. And he wanted me to back off. Has to be. I'll have that bastard."

"I will come with you."

"No, you'd better stay here."

Grace saw the look on his face, in his eyes, like unstable explosive waiting for a jolt.

"No," said Grace.

"Ok, let's move."

She followed Danny into the hall but he turned into the kitchen. She was puzzled until she saw him wrapping his biggest kitchen knife in a tea towel.

"What are you doing? You cannot take that."

"I can. And if Jas bloody Knight has laid a hand on Hayley I'll cut his fucking balls off."

Grace saw his eyes, how he was struggling for control, knew this was Danny's war face.

She felt a prickle of fear. It was useless to argue. She followed as he pulled the van keys from his pocket and headed for the front door.

***

Traffic was backing up in surrounding streets. They heard the noise long before they saw the cause. As Danny and grace rounded the corner they stopped to take in the chaos.

The road was blocked with people, milling groups trying to jockey for position. The queue behind the roped-off lane was bulging off the pavement.

Half a dozen bouncers formed a suited wall of muscle across the entrance to The Red Rooms, their Security Industry Authority cards strapped to their biceps. Most were trying to hold back the crowd while two of them checked ID and picked those who would get inside.

A thin line of police officers tried to clear the road by carving a path across the front of the club. Two van-loads of reinforcements arrived as Danny and Grace watched.

Scattered cheering broke out as someone famous arrived. A slender arm tipped with long red nails waved over the bobbing heads before the figure was hustled to the front and in the main doors.

Someone at the front started shouting. A space appeared around the guy as the crowd pushed back. He was clutching his girlfriend's arm, swearing as he waved a tattooed arm at the security men.

When he charged the steps one bouncer gripped the guy's raised arm, pushed it down, turned him and propelled him back into the crowd. Someone cheered. The girlfriend stomped away on five-inch heels.

"How will we get in?" asked Grace, wide-eyed at the free-for-all in front of them. Danny looked at his watch, impatience engraved across his face.

"We can't muck about," said Danny. "A frontal assault's a non-starter so we'll take them in the rear. If there's no joy there it'll have to be the front."

"But how, Danny?"

"We've got to find Hayley, and fast. I'll ram raid the bloody place if I have to. Let's move."

***

They turned away, pausing to watch a stretch limo, its windows outlined with blue lights, try to edge its way through the jam.

Danny had a pretty good grasp of Brighton's street plan built up through jogging, minicabbing and curiosity.

He guided Grace in a wide circle that brought them to a road between the club and the sea. A narrow lane ran off to one side. It was lined with garages and big wheeled rubbish bins. A pile of leaking carrier bags began to move and they watched as a rat sprinted across the alley and under a door. Grace looked at Danny, pulled a face.

"What do we do now?"

"We wait."

They pressed against a damp brick wall to escape the stiff breeze blowing from the sea. A mist drifted with it, the haze chilling them as it coated their jackets and formed haloes around the street lights. The sound of sirens rose and fell along the main road.

Danny seemed to be looking at his watch every twenty seconds. He was on his fourth cigarette and Grace was huddled deep in her coat, shivering, when they heard bolts.

They pressed themselves back against the shadow of the brickwork and waited. It came again, the sound of grating, then a thud. About half way down the alley on the other side. Then a creaking. A fire door ground open.

"Thank Christ for that," said a young guy who burst out into the bracing air, arms waving above his head.

"It's freezing," said the girl in the tiny dress who tottered after him.

Danny and Grace watched as three more people came out. Four formed a huddle in the lee of the door, taking long pulls on their cigarettes to cut their time out in the cold. Long plumes of smoke curled up into the mist off the sea.

The fifth reveller zigzagged across the alley, made a strangling sound, them vomited over the carrier bags. His friends cheered. The puker doubled over, bracing himself against a bin, as the second wave hit him. They cheered again.

Danny touched Grace's arm and nodded towards the open fire door. They crossed the alley, hugging the wall while the clubbers formed a semi-circle around their friend.

"You all right, Paul?" asked one of the girls.

One of the guys broke away from the group, opened his fly, drew lazy Ss across a pile of rubbish sacks as he relieved himself in a cloud of steam.

Danny and Grace were by the open exit now.

One of the guys jabbed puking Paul in the back with a finger.

"He's just a big wuss."

Danny slid round the door. Grace followed, clipped it with her shoe.

"What was that?" said the girl, hugging herself for warmth.

"Probably just a rat," said the guy.

"A rat!" the girl squealed. "Come on, let's get back inside."

"Ok," said the guy, turning to Paul. "Come on, wuss."

***

Afterwards was always the best bit. They'd talked about it, agreed. The lovemaking was necessary and wonderful but the glow afterwards, sticky and relaxed, warm and snuggled, that was the best bit. They were never closer than in those precious moments as the sweat dried and the heart rate settled.

They were stretched out, heads tilted together on the pillow so they touched, as if the contact might express more than they could say in words.

"JJ?"

"Yes, Vic?"

"Do you think he can do it this time? Really do it?"

Vic felt a slight shrug as JJ mulled the question. It wasn't a problem. His big body so close was reassuring.

"Well," said JJ. "He's been working on it long enough. It's important to him, the biggest thing in his life. Nothing else matters."

"Nothing, JJ?"

"Well, of course, there's us. That goes without saying. But resolving this is the thing that drives him. It focuses all his energy, keeps him going. So, yes, I think he'll finally get what he wants this time."

"And what about Lancaster. I really fucked up there."

JJ leaned across, kissed Vic's forehead, tasted salt.

"Can't be helped. No one's perfect, Vic. Mistakes happen."

"But he was angry, really angry. I don't like it when he's like that."

"He's got a lot on his mind, Vic. It'll blow over. Don't beat yourself up."

"And afterwards, JJ? What about afterwards?"

The mattress shifted as JJ leaned across again. Vic felt the calming pressure of lips.

"There isn't an afterwards. You and me, Vic. And Dad. The three of us, there'll always be us, Vic, always us."

***

As soon as he entered the dark corridor beyond the fire exit Danny could feel the noise. It pulsed in his ears and trembled up from the floor through his feet.

Multi-coloured lights ebbed at the end of the passageway. Danny waved Grace forward and set off at a trot.

They burst into the club's main lounge. The place was dark but splashed with a kaleidoscope of moving colours. Lasers raked the ceiling and jets of smoke and flame formed a palisade around the DJ. Danny squinted through the glare around the stage, saw Jason Knight.

He was bouncing up and down, big headphones over his ears, one hand of the deck, the other punching the air.

Before they'd got in Danny had worried he'd stand out but everyone was too busy enjoying themselves. The place was rammed with people.

His urgent eyes swept the room, a sea of smiling sweaty faces, fit girls wearing very little, more than he could count, a forest of arms waving like sea grass, light and noise and vibration. His eardrums hurt. The base line pounded up through his feet into his guts.

Grace looked across at Danny, wincing as the music throbbed. The sound was too loud for them to speak. She asked the question with her eyes. He half raised a hand, wait.

Then Jas was shouting above the roar.

"Ok, Brighton, now we've warmed up a little on this opening night of The Red Rooms, I want you to give it up bigstyle for our first guest tonight, the talented, the fantastic, DJ *THURUBAD!!!*"

Danny saw a pale, thin guy with a whispy goatee standing next to Jason behind his console of decks and equipment. Jason high-fived the guy then, clapping his hands high over his head, jigged his way off the stage.

Once down the steps he headed towards a corner. Danny saw a door that blended into the wall. He indicated it to Grace with a glance and they began squeezing their way through the dense leaping crowds. Danny had the door half open when a shadow loomed beside him.

"Oi, that's private."

The guy loomed over him like a toppling Victorian wardrobe. Danny pushed on into the small hallway behind the door. The bouncer came too, pressing against him, waiting for the space to get a grip.

Behind the door was a small hall leading to a flight of steps. As the bouncer made his move he suddenly stopped, a look of panic flashing in his eyes.

"See that?" said Danny.

The guy looked down at the kitchen knife pressed against his guts. The moment he did Danny punched him hard. The bouncer's head hit the wall and he crumpled with a rasping sigh.

Grace came through the door, closing it behind her. She looked down at the beefy body on the floor, then looked at Danny.

"Come on."

He led her up the steep narrow stairs at a run. When they reached a small landing they turned left. Another security guy was peering towards the stairs at the sound of fast steps just audible against the thunder of music outside.

When he saw the two intruders he came for them. Danny dodged sideways, grabbed the lapel of the guy's suit, crouched low and turned, took the guy's momentum on his hip and over his shoulder.

The bouncer, six six if he was an inch, hit the landing hard. It punched half the breath out of him. Danny's boot punched out the other half.

He turned to Grace. She thought his eyes were wild. Then he swung back and hit the door with his boot, just by the handle.

As it burst open they both heard a squeal. Jason Knight was standing behind a large desk. In each hand he held a wad of banknotes, each as thick as a telephone directory, secured with broad elastic bands.

"You can't be in here. Why are you in here?"

The wads of wonga dropped from his startled fingers.

"Where are they?"

"Who?"

Danny drew the kitchen knife again, the steel glinted silver in the light from the anglepoise on Knight's desk.

"Don't mess me around, Jason."

"No, I mean who... I mean I don't..."

"I won't say it again. Tell me where Hayley and Jessie are or I am going to fillet you like the bottom-feeding mackerel you are."

Danny took a step forward. Knight adopted an exaggerated fighting stance, clenched fists raised.

"I'm warning you, I know krav maga."

"Who's he play for then?" said Danny but his eyes weren't laughing as his boot caught the edge of the desk. It crashed over. The lamp went out with a crack. A half-empty can of Diet Coke just missed Knight, bursting across the wall behind him in a spurt of bronze foam, spraying his shirt.

Danny had Knight by the collar, brushed the knife down the side of his neck, lifted it to show the first trace of blood. Knight's tensed arms dropped.

"Please... look... please..."

"Look at me, Jason."

Danny gripped his chin, forced his head around until their faces were ten inches apart.

"Nobody, *nobody*, touches my daughter. And nobody touches Jessie when she's in my care. Do you understand me? If you don't tell me in the next three seconds I am going to open you up from dick to tit."

Jason's mouth flapped like a goldfish. He made mewling noises. When the tip of Danny's kitchen knife pricked the skin just above his penis he started whimpering.

"There's a houseboat..."

The knife snagged his trousers, began to cut.

"If you're lying to me..."

"No, they're at my houseboat... in Shoreham."

"With those two bell ends you had chasing Jessie?"

"Ah, yah, Mitch and Paulie, they're minding them with a couple of other guys."

"If they've been hurt..."

"No... No... No... They're fine, honest."

"You sure?"

"On my life... Honest... Really... Honestly."

Danny released his grip on the man's shirt. Jason stumbled, clipped the side of the swivel chair beside him, toppled sideways, hit the floor on all fours, weeping.

"You'd better be right," said Danny. "If you're winding me up I will find you. You'd better believe that."

Knight forced himself to look at Danny, met his eyes, looked away.

"What about the money?" he asked. It was a whisper.

"What?" said Danny.

"The money? What about the money?"

Danny looked at the piles of cash on the desk, crumpled notes all arranged with the Queen facing the same way. Then he looked down at Knight. It didn't need words. He glanced over at Grace.

"We'd better move."

She nodded.

Danny turned towards the door, then paused as Knight pulled himself to his feet. Panic lit up across the DJ's face again.

"Why?" asked Danny.

"W...w... why what?"

"Why take Hayley and Jessie? Hayley's nothing to you and Jessie would have been no good for your shindig downstairs if she wasn't willing. So why?"

"A fav... a favour."

"For who?"

"I can't... I didn't..."

Danny moved towards Knight, saw him flinch away just as Grace gripped his arm.

"We don't have time, Danny. Think of Hayley."

Danny shook himself free, threw the kitchen knife. The tip embedded itself in Knight's desk, the vibrating blade strobing under the overhead strip light.

"One last thing," said Danny. "Don't even think of warning the boat. If they're expecting us I will come back and we will have a very serious conversation that you will not enjoy. Understand?"

Knight nodded.

"Understand?"

"Yes," whispered Knight.

Suddenly Danny was aware of Grace moving round him. Knight recoiled, throwing up his hands, fingers spread, in a spasm of panic.

"No... please... not the face... not the face."

Danny was really impressed with the punch she threw.

DJ Thurubad had the crowd going wild as Danny and Grace slipped out through the fire exit.

CHAPTER 25

It was soft drinks at the Bridge Inn this time. Danny and Grace were tucked away in the corner of the garden patio, wrapped up warm.

Tendrils of the ebbing tide explored channels in the bare mud. The houseboats opposite and the houses beyond were a patchwork of lit windows.

To their right, traffic was steady over Norfolk Bridge and the road westward. Downstream, they could see the old river footbridge which was closed while a replacement was built.

Danny was aware of Grace shivering, huddled in her coat. He was anxious to move, constantly checking his watch, glancing across at the MTB moored on the other bank. But it would be a mistake to go off half-cocked. You only got one chance. Failure did not bear thinking about.

They shared a burger and chips and another round of soft drinks. Keep the calories and the fluids up, he had told her. He was aware of Grace watching him but his cold hard eyes never left the houseboat across the river for long.

"Are you all right, Danny?"

He looked across at the MTB again.

"I'm fine. Don't fuss."

"It is very cold. How long must we wait?"

"If I had my way we'd be over there now, trust me. I'd like nothing more than to go crashing in there and sort those bastards out. But we need to succeed. We'll know the moment. Nip inside for a warm if you want."

He pointed. A dim yellow light had come on aboard the Fairmile. Even in the dark they could make it out clearly, its sheer size dwarfing the smaller boats that flanked it.

Danny looked around the terrace, checking they were alone. When he was satisfied they weren't watched he drew the small pair of binoculars he kept in the van from under his jacket and scanned the opposite bank of the Adur.

He could make out the distinctive raked lines of the Fairmile and the shark's mouth painted on its bows. Danny blessed Karol's laptop skills as he ran through the information the grumpy Polish chippie had unearthed, grateful he'd done it after their earlier recce so he had to it hand now.

More than 200 Fairmile Ds has been built to combat the German high-speed e-boats. Known as Dog Boats, the Fairmiles were armed with six-pounder guns or torpedo tubes plus cannon, machineguns and depth charges. Weighing more than 100 tons and 115 feet long, they carried a crew of 21 and could make more than 30mph.

The one he was looking at, with its iron-hard mahogany hull and plywood decking, had been built by P K Harris of Appledore in Devon. It had spent its war with the Royal Norwegian Navy, based at Lerwick in the Shetlands, prowling the coast of Norway for targets, battling the weather and the enemy.

Karol had punched up the layout of the interior for Danny. It was a warren of little rooms crammed together, no space wasted. Problem was, as the neighbour had said on their recce, you didn't need planning permission for houseboats. Bang a window or a door anywhere you fancy. Danny had a clear mental picture of what the inside would have been like in the Fairmile's Shetland days. There was no way to know what they were facing now.

"Eyes on," said Danny.

"What is it?" asked Grace.

"Movement, bunch of guys, three of them, just appeared on the path. Must have come up from the car park on the other side. They're carrying something."

"Can you see what it is?"

"Not clearly, two long packages, could be canoes."

Danny watched the men enter the Fairmile. He passed the glasses to Grace. She tracked the length of the opposite embankment, then back again, focussing on the big houseboat.

"So, three guys arrive and Knight said Tweedledum and Tweedledee were already there," said Danny. "That makes five, five that we know of, anyway. And some are armed."

Grace handed the binos back.

"You must have a plan?"

"Oh yes. When we stopped on the way over I did a bit of shopping."

"And you are confident?"

"Yes."

***

Detective Sergeant Pauline Myers was staring without seeing, face crunched in deep thought as she ran through the details again.

"It's scary when you think about it, really scary."

"What is?" said Lizzie McIntosh.

"The way these guys operate. For the amount you reckon they're producing, they could be set up in someone's back bedroom, a tiny operation hidden away. The chemicals can be lethal but they're in such small amounts they won't cause a blip in the records of legitimate suppliers. It's like looking for a needle in a haystack."

"I thought this was supposed to be a relaxing drink," said McIntosh. "Do you ever let it go?"

Myers thought about that for a moment, then shook her head.

"No, never. If you're going to get anywhere in this job you can't afford to, especially if you're a woman. It's the same for you, isn't it?"

McIntosh shrugged.

"I guess. Maybe I just don't have your ambition."

Myers took a swig from the wine bottle, passed it back to McIntosh.

"It's not just about ambition. I don't like puzzles, don't like surprises. We know the what. We know the how. It's the who and the where. It's like an itch I can't scratch."

"You can get too wound up in a case, Pauline, lose your focus. You need to take a step back."

"Not while people are dying." She took the bottle from McIntosh, had another swig.

"Something's niggling at me, something I missed, something someone said."

Myers raised the bottle again but it stopped in mid air.

"What's the matter?" asked McIntosh.

"Danny!"

"Who?"

"Danny Lancaster, he's an ex-soldier, fancies himself as some sort of cowboy private detective. I've had a few dealings with him."

"What about him?"

"He called me a couple of days ago, try to cadge a favour. Wanted some help with a misper, some girl looking for her lost love. I told him where to get off but it's something he said about the missing boyfriend, something about chemistry."

"Sounds a bit thin."

"Maybe, but we've got nothing else. It's worth checking."

Myers made to move but McIntosh put a hand on her arm.

"You can't check it now."

"Why?"

McIntosh laughed.

"Because it's the middle of the night."

Myers looked at her watch, smiled.

"You're right. Where did the time go?"

"If you think it's worth it we'll check it out first thing in the morning."

"Ok, till then I suppose I'll just have to do some of that relaxing you keep talking about, try to cure that itch."

Myers put the wine bottle on the bedside table. When she yanked the duvet off Lizzie McIntosh's naked body she gasped.

Then Myers began to circle her tongue around the soft, taut skin just below the drugs squad detective sergeant's navel.

***

The pale concrete of the embankment path was overgrown. The overhead lighting was weak with black patches where bushes sprawled. Wisps of mist spiralled from the mud. The air smelled eggy.

Danny walked lightly, keeping to the shadows. Passing one boat he heard the muffled noises of a television. Music drifted from another. Danny recognised Rihanna's Diamonds, smiled to himself in the darkness. It felt good to be doing something at last. A little further on someone was strumming a guitar, fluffed a chord, started again.

The Fairmile was just beyond a slight bend in the path. Danny hung back, watching. He could make out two shapes sitting against a makeshift wooden structure at the stern near a gangplank made of old armour plate from the boat's bridge housing.

It was too dark to see faces but by the way they moved he was pretty sure it was the two comedians who'd turned up at the B&B and at Bob and Wanda's, Mitch and Paulie. They weren't the sharpest tools but they might have guns. Stupid people and firearms were never a good mix.

Danny checked his watch again, Couldn't hang around too long or people would get suspicious. Then he felt the phone vibrate in his jacket pocket. It was the signal. He set off down the path.

The two guys ignored him until they heard the gangplank gate creak open.

"Private property, mate. You can't come in here."

Danny stayed by the gate, letting them come to him, out of the lee of the boat's superstructure. It was a short distance but they seemed reluctant to move out into the cold sea breeze. Sloppy and careless, like before. Danny had depended on it.

They were only a few feet away when one stopped, looked startled.

"You!"

The guy's hand went inside his jacket. Danny stood watching him, hands in pockets. Posing no threat, drawing him forward. The plan was a bit ambitious but the best he could think of in the time. If it failed, the only thing left was to rush the guy, rip his lungs out before he had the chance to pull whatever was under his jacket. All that mattered was reaching Hayley. The gangplank groaned as the nearest guy stepped on it. Mitch or Paulie? Didn't matter.

"Stay perfectly still," said Danny in a calm, clear voice.

They hesitated. It was the wrong thing to do but Danny was banking on it. You could almost hear the brain cells grinding together. They looked at each other for reassurance, then started to move forward again.

"I wouldn't," said Danny, pointing.

They gasped in unison when they saw the spots of red light dancing around their chests.

"Don't speak. Don't move. Don't even cough or my friends over there will cure it with a dose of 7.62mil Night Nurse. Do you understand mc?"

Their heads bobbed, very, very slightly.

"Ok, take the hardware out carefully and lay them on the deck."

Each produced a handgun from inside his jacket, pinching the butt between finger and thumb, holding the weapons away from them as if they smelled bad. When the guns were on the deck Danny told the men to step back and face the wooden wall.

He scooped up the pistols, Sig Sauer P228s, compact 9mils with 13-round magazines, nice piece of kit. Danny pocketed one, checked and cocked the other. Then he stepped up close behind the two men and secured their wrists with cable ties. One of the men grunted as the plastic bit. Danny wasn't feeling sympathetic.

He turned towards the embankment path and waved. Then he herded the men into the rickety wooden shed, bound their feet and covered their mouths with gaffer tape. He taped over the ties to secure them and warned what would happen if either of them made any noise or tried to get outside. Then he patted them down and found four more loaded magazines. These guys were serious.

When he slipped back out onto the deck Grace was there.

"That was very clever."

He grinned in the dark. "Not all weapons are guns."

Grace looked again at the laser pens in her hand before slipping them in her pocket. Danny took out the second Sig.

"You know how to use one of these?"

Grace removed the magazine, cleared the chamber, checked the mechanism, reloaded and cocked the weapon.

"Fair enough, ok, follow me, keep low, keep quiet and keep close."

His rubber-soled boots were silent on the wooden deck as he made his way forward along the port side, signing to Grace to take the starboard.

The sliding door into the bridge was open. They peered in, listened. Nothing but the weary creaking of ancient woodwork as it shifted on the mud beneath it.

Danny jerked his head and they moved onto the foredeck. A thick wooden pole stood at an angle where the Fairmile's forward gun had once been mounted.

Danny eased up a hatch cover and peered down into the pool of dark below, watching and listening. He carried a Maglite in his pocket but didn't want to use it unless he had to. When he was happy, he tested the step, edging down slowly. Grace followed.

The forward mess deck was large and cluttered. A single lamp in the corner threw out a weak yellow light. Two Acrow props supported the sagging deck above their heads.

The far end was a cluttered of collapsible beds and sleeping bags. The cabin had the sour cheesy smell of a men's locker room.

Windsurf boards, sails, wetsuits and two canoes were stacked against one wall. There was a sofa, chairs and a dining table covered with newspaper and magazines. Danny checked the two tiny compartments forward of the mess deck that had once been the crew toilet and washroom.

They both crouched low, listening. To the rear was a narrow corridor with, if the plans Danny had studied were correct, the commanding officer's cabin and wireless room on the left. Danny and Grace crept forward. On the right was the officer's wardroom and a galley fitted with a rickety hob sitting on two LPG gas bottles. The size of the wardroom created a dog-leg in the passage.

When they reached the dog-leg they leaned round the bend to look ahead. Light leaked beneath a door at the far end that had been cut through a bulkhead to what had once been the forward fuel tank compartment.

They could hear a faint humming and what might have been a buzz of conversation.

Danny and Grace looked at each other, weighing up their next move. When the door began to creak open their weapons snapped up to the aim. He saw a man's shoulder in the widening streak of light.

Then Danny had a split-second impression of scrabbling claws, the light catching yellow fangs. He threw up his left arm and a lightning burst of pain blitzed through muscle and blood vessels.

CHAPTER 26

Teeth like a row of steak knives filleting into Danny's forearm. He crashed backwards under the animal's weight, screaming in pain and terror.

He curled into a ball to protect his face and nuts, horribly aware of the great weight dragging at his arm, staring into mad red eyes and yellow teeth inches from his head.

Flames of pain were crisping the edges of his brain but he beat down the urge to screw his eyes shut, too much happening.

The man's shoulder was through the door now. And a shotgun.

The dog was shaking its head, tearing Danny's flesh. As he heaved the dog onto his chest it felt as if the bone of his arm was bending under the strain, its weight pressing him down, his mind shrivelling with the pain.

The shotgun blast was deafening, the flash dazzling. Danny felt the dog spasm and go slack, dead weight. Danny heard Grace fire two quick pistol shots and the man in the doorway was gone.

The dog's head lolled, tongue long and loose, eyes bulging, breath rattling. It looked like some horror puppet head set on 25 pounds of glistening mincemeat.

Danny keened through clenched teeth as he used his other hand to force open the jaws. Fangs sliding from flesh drawing skeins of thick bloody spittle. As he rolled away Grace leaned down and shot the dog once in the head.

Danny lay on his back panting as he replayed what was probably the worst four seconds of his life. Grace moved silently to the open door, peering in, pistol raised. She glanced back.

"Are you all right?"

Danny started to laugh but the movement made him wince. Once he'd struggled to his feet he hobbled to the open door, dripping blood as he went. Shotgun man was lying on his back, Grace's two 9mils in his chest. Nice grouping, thought Danny through the fog of pain.

The massive copper petrol tanks had been ripped out when the boat and been decommissioned, along with all military and valuable fittings. Now the walls were lined with metal benches. Cardboard boxes labelled with symbols were stacked beneath.

Two steps away was another door cut through into what had been the engine room. More metal benches covered with chemistry equipment filled the space once occupied by four massive 12-cylinder Packard engines.

On the packed benches were a series of racks holding round glass bottles. He could see an oven and a fridge. There was a lot of other fearsome looking equipment Danny didn't recognise but you didn't need to be Stephen Hawking to work out it was something dodgy.

In the far corner a chubby kid in a lab coat was clutching at the wall and jibbering.

Grace secured the techie with a cable tie and led Danny back into the crew room. She rummaged around, clearly unimpressed with the dirt and disorganisation.

She found a couple of tea towels but they were too filthy to be bandages so she washed Danny's wounds with water, then vodka from a half empty bottle on the table, wrapped them in a plastic Tesco bag and bound them with the tea towels over the top.

"How are you feeling?"

"Pity it didn't go for the leg."

***

When Danny tried to stand, the room started spinning. His body was shaking on waves of adrenalin. He grabbed a chair to steady himself.

"You should rest."

"No time. Can you smell something?"

Grace shook her head. Danny shrugged.

They went back to the chemistry lab. It was hot and the strange smell seemed to grow stronger.

Lab Coat was still in the corner, jabbering. Suddenly Grace raised her hand for silence. They stood, listening. A faint scratching sound was coming from beyond the lab.

Danny waved them forward and they followed opposite walls to the far end. Another door had been cut through the rear of the engine space. Danny knew it led to the seamen's mess and petty officer's cabin. They eased it open and stepped through.

Danny opened the first door while Grace covered. It was a store room filled with untidy piles of cardboard boxes. The second room held more boxes.

They both turned towards a sound, the faintest thumping. Danny knew the only room left was the steering gear compartment. He took a step back but Grace laid a hand on his arm, shook her head. He moved to one side. She stood back in the narrow corridor, raised her leg and slammed her foot against the door by the lock. It burst open.

The smell made them wince. Then they spotted movement in the gloom. A small figure exploded from the room, grabbed Danny.

"Dad! Dad!"

"Hayley?"

He prised her away, bent to face her.

"You ok?"

Red-faced and crying, Hayley couldn't form the words to speak, just clung to her father. Grace ducked into the room and helped someone else to totter out, Jessie.

"They came for us just after you left," said Jessie, her voice hoarse. "They put us in there and tied us up. Hayley had just got her wrists free when we heard the noise. Was that shooting? Dad, what happened to your arm?"

Then Hayley saw the Sig in his hand and her eyes widened.

"I was so scared. What's going on, Dad?"

"Questions later. Let's get out of here."

"There's someone else in there," said Jessie.

Grace went back inside, raking the gloom of room with Danny's torch. He heard someone whimpering.

"Rats, I hate rats."

With the pistol tucked in her belt, Grace half-carried, half-dragged Bill Carter into the passageway. His clothes were torn, eyes wide and vacant. A dry crust outlined his lips. And he stank.

"I HATE fucking rats. HATE them."

Danny and Grace looked at each other.

"We'd better get moving before anyone else turns up."

They all stiffened at a roaring sound. Suddenly the air bloomed hot around them as gas from the leaking LPG tank ignited.

The first bullet missed Danny's head by two inches.

***

It was always the way. Just when you'd decided you were in for a quiet night it all kicked off. Echo 02 pulled out onto Old Shoreham Road and swung right.

White Watch Manager Ken King checked the time, glanced across at the sprawling cemetery opposite. The ragged rows of tombs always concentrated the mind on the way to a shout. After 17 years with East Sussex Fire And Rescue Service. King still got that rush of excitement when the alarm sounded at Hove fire station in English Close.

The report said West Sussex FRS were committed to a major house fire in Arundel. Their call on the direct line to East Sussex FRS control at Eastbourne had reported a ship on fire in Shoreham Harbour. That opened up a world of possibilities.

Traffic was light. King glanced across the cab, smiling to himself at the calm concentration on Kate's face as she sat behind the big wheel of Echo 02, Hove station's extended rescue pump. She accelerated the 11-tonne Volvo tender with its two-ton cargo of water steadily up to 50mph, making the most of the straight clear road. Whiskey 02, Hove station's water tender, followed close behind.

Echo 02 crossed a junction, Kate braking gently as the crew scanned to right and left. Once, clear, they surged forward. Two hundred yards further on, Kate braked and slowed Echo 02 slightly into the roundabout and on down Upper Shoreham Road, sounding the klaxon to warn a dawdling Saab that hadn't spotted their lights and sirens. King looked at his watch again. One minute fifty seconds gone. First response should be on scene in three minutes.

When they reached the junction with Old Shoreham Road Echo 02 swung left towards the town centre. King could see a column of glowing smoke rising beyond the river.

***

Despite the pain searing his arm Danny spun and returned fire, down the passageway, through the smoke, into the laboratory, the crack of rounds deafening in the cramped corridor.

He saw movement across the far door into the main cabin and fired again. Grace pushed the girls back into the stinking compartment, out of the line of fire. Carter bellowed when they landed on top of him.

As Danny ejected an empty magazine to reload, Grace opened fire. Rounds thudded into the woodwork, spraying splinters. Someone in the laboratory shouted in pain.

For as long as they could maintain a cone of steady fire down the passageway and across the lab they were safe. It wasn't a long-term solution. The smoke was thickening, the air getting hotter.

Danny waved for Grace to check behind them. She returned in seconds. There was a small ladder in the steering gear compartment but the deck hatch at the top was padlocked.

He hauled Hayley and the others away from the door, leaned in, fired twice at the padlock. They heard the rattle and clatter of a chain slipping free.

"Go!"

Danny pushed Hayley back into the compartment, towards the ladder, then Jessie, then Carter. They were clumsy, frightened and stumbling, but he pushed them as hard as he could to get them clear while Grace laid down covering fire. Carter was the last of the hostages on the ladder. Looking up, Danny saw him staring intently down at each step me took.

Then something scuttled past the bottom of the ladder. Carter screeched. Danny saw him release his grip and winced as the man's jaw cracked onto a rung, snapping his head back. He fell, smacking his head against the wall before deflating into a limp heap at Danny's feet.

Danny heard Grace's ejected magazine hit the floor and turned towards the lab. Another movement. He leaned out of the cramped compartment, fired two shots, then two more.

The bangs was deafening, eardrums near bursting as the sound waves cracked back off the woodwork.

A bubble of heat washed over them. Then the lab was lit by brilliant orange flame. Danny saw the tea towel on his arm start to smoulder, felt the plastic bag shrivel onto his skin. Someone was screaming.

"Carter's down," yelled Danny. "Get him out."

Grace nodded and ducked into the tiny compartment. He saw her try to lift Carter but the slack body was dead weight.

Danny stood, half in and half out of the door, glancing back down the passage, ready to put a round through anyone who came through the flames.

"You go," he shouted to Grace. "I'll pass him up."

A shape shimmered through the flames. Danny fired twice, counting his rounds. When he ducked back into the compartment Grace was out on the deck and leaning down through the hatch, reaching. Danny stuck the pistol in his belt, gripped Carter's jacket with his right hand. Teeth grinding with the pain, he jerked Carter's limp body to his feet and shoved him up the ladder until Grace could grasp his shoulders.

Danny saw the unconscious man's feet sway up through the hatch. He took a last look along the passageway. Flames were boiling towards him, moving faster, growing. He kicked the bulwark door shut and began to climb.

As his head and shoulders cleared the hatch dense acid smoke boiled up past him. Thick tendrils like snakes chased him as they sought the sucking draft.

When Danny reached the rear deck he was coughing hard, the jerk of each spasm shooting pains along his savaged arm.

He had just stepped clear of the hatch when an explosion in the lab sent a pulse of fire down the passageway. It smashed through the bulkhead door and surged up the steps, blasting out of the hatch three feet from Danny and up into the night, taking his eyebrows with it.

CHAPTER 27

Flames were leaping out of the bridge door and windows, giving an evil glow to the thick smoke that shrouded the Fairmile.

Coughing hard, Danny waved the others towards the gangplank. As Grace began to shepherd them off the boat, dragging Bill Carter, he ducked into the shed and cut the tapes and ties on his two prisoners.

When he reached the path Danny saw that Grace and the others had made it down the steps beyond the embankment and into the car park.

The centre section of the Fairmile was a mass of fire now with flames shooting thirty feet into the air. He sprinted to the next boat, through the gate, hammered on the door.

"Fire!" The door was opened by a confused guy struggling with a dressing gown cord. Danny waved towards the Fairmile, then ran to the first boat on the opposite side to raise the alarm.

When he'd roused the immediate neighbours he looked across towards Norfolk Bridge at the sound of sirens. Then slid down the embankment into the car park.

***

Bill Carter wasn't a big guy but his limp body weighed a ton. Danny and Grace carried him between them into the flat and dumped him on the floor in the corner of the living room.

"You know where the first aid kit is."

Grace brought the kit, towels and water and began working on Carter.

Danny sat on the sofa, arms resting on his thighs, head low, puffing a cigarette, trying to ignore the pulsing pain in his arm.

Ten minutes later Grace was standing beside him, wiping her hands.

"He's still unconscious. He may have a concussion and, perhaps, a broken jaw."

"Can you sort him out? He's not seeing a hospital till we're done with him."

"He will be in pain when he wakes but I think he will live."

"That's all he has to do," said Danny wearily.

"I must change the dressing on your arm," said Grace.

"Later," said Danny. He looked at the others.

"No," said Grace, "We must do it now so there is no infection."

"Ok," said Danny, "But not here."

She followed him into his bedroom. Danny sat on his bed as Grace peeled off his shirt. It was then that she saw the blood on his side, a cluster of punctures where the shotgun blast had missed the dog.

She washed the wounds, teasing out pellets of shot with a pair of tweezers. When Grace was satisfied, she peeled the dressing from his arm, examined the chewed flesh and began to clean the teeth lacerations gently with a cloth, rinsing it into a bowl of warm water that soon turned bloody.

"Do you have a sewing kit?" asked Grace.

Danny gave a theatrical wince.

"Kitchen drawers, second from the left."

The kit was only a pocket travelling pack for fixing lost buttons but it would have to do. Grace cleaned a needle in boiling water and sterilised it with vodka. When she returned he sat quietly, teeth clenched, staring at the blank wall. Eventually he spoke.

"You're very good. You've done this before."

She leaned back, studied his hard body, its scars, the tattoo.

"And you have done this before. You have been in many fights."

Danny forced his mouth through the pain into a weak smile.

"You should see the other guys."

***

As they walked back into the living room Jessie came in with a tray of teas. She handed him a hot mug. Danny smiled his thanks.

Hayley looked at her father, eyes red raw. She tried to speak but started crying again. Jessie put an arm around her. Danny thought she looked surprisingly calm.

"So what happened?" asked Danny.

"About 20 minutes after you left there was a knock," said Jessie. "A guy said they had a parcel. We ignored it. He kept asking then, bang, the door flies open."

"Go on."

"We tried to fight them off, chucked stuff. But they weren't going to give up. I thought they were perverts or something but when they pulled out guns there was nothing we could do. They just grabbed us and took us out to a van."

"No, you did well. At least you're both in one piece."

Danny looked across at Grace, rubbed tired eyes, half hoping the pressure might reach into his brain and kickstart a bright idea.

"I'm thinking out loud here. Bear with me. Jason owns the Fairmile, he admitted it this evening. We turn up later and find some kind of chemical lab. Jason's set himself up as some sort of clubbing king. Drugs and music, makes sense."

"He wouldn't," said Jessie.

Danny was tired and in pain. His flat had been trashed and he could feel the pressure of the Sig in his pocket. People had probably died tonight.

"Look, Jessie, I know young love is a wonderful thing but face facts. Maybe you had something going with the guy a few years back but now the only thing Jason loves is money, that and himself."

"No!"

"Drop it!" He sipped his tea, burned his lip. A bit more pain didn't matter.

"Thing is," said Danny, glancing at the crumpled form in the corner of the living room. "Why was Bill Carter on the boat? And when we visited the first time, why was Marion Carter's Prius parked there?"

***

SHOREHAM, WEDNESDAY MORNING

Detective Inspector Eddie Aziz wafted his hand in front of his mouth, pulling a face and puffing to clear his nose.

"This place stinks."

The crime scene manager in the overall chanced a small smile at Detective Sergeant Pauline Myers. Then he looked at his clipboard. Myers knew him by sight, knew his name was Cunningham. Seemed to know his stuff.

"If only we could preserve this as a training exercise," said Cunningham. "This scene has everything."

"Everything?" queried Myers.

Aziz and Myers, dressed in paper suits, masks and gloves, had signed in with the scene guard. Now they stood on the narrow path looking down past Cunningham to the wrecked houseboat. The cramped space, cut off by crime scene tape, was crowded with uniformed and plain clothes police, fire fighters, crime scene staff and, at the far end, the coroner's officer.

All that was left of the houseboat were the ribs of the hull, blackened and smoking as they curved up from the keel, and a section of deck astern of the bridge structure. It looked like the ribcage of an incinerated dinosaur.

Cunningham looked as if he was enjoying himself. The man clearly liked a challenge.

"It's quite a party. The East Sussex FRS maritime team are here from Newhaven and we have a lifeboat on the river as safety boat. It took a while before we could get started because the FRS had to make the scene safe. What's left is pretty unstable and we've had to lay stepping plates around it. Part of what you can smell is methane from the mud around the boat."

Cunningham indicated the wreck over his shoulder.

"The foredeck was destroyed when the LPG gas bottle connected to the stove vented. It acts like a flame thrower. With the fore and after hatches open the boat turned into a wind tunnel, very nasty. The wooden frame is mostly mahogany. It's tough but never stood a chance against the combined effects of the LPG bottle plus a whole palate of interesting chemicals."

"What chemicals?" asked Myers.

"Well, it's early days, we're still collecting residues. But we're found packaging with labels that indicate ethanol, diethylethane, toluene and acetone among other things."

"So, a drugs lab?"

Cunningham nodded.

"The one we're looking for?"

"Too early to say but if I was a betting man, which I'm not, I'd say you're on to a racing certainty here."

"You said this would make a training exercise," said Aziz. "What else have you got?"

"Where to start," said Cunningham. "The whole scene is unstable. The fire gutted most of the hull, leaving us," he waved behind him.

"With just the ribs of the frame and a few stern compartments. We're lucky there are no high tides due but as the water rises it might well carry away any evidence on the mud near the scene or anything that's fallen around the keel."

All three turned to look at the wreckage again. Then Cunningham continued.

"The fire was very intense, hence our victim."

Cunningham pointed a pen down from the embankment into the blackened mess below them. When Aziz and Myers looked hard they could just make out a crispy black oval shape about the size of a sports bag. As they looked closer they could see shrivelled arms and legs. The dead man looked as if he was riding a horse.

"You'll see," said Cunningham, "Our man is in the equestrian position, knees up, arms flexed. Obviously, it's down to the post mortem to decide but it's my guess he was alive during the fire."

Someone called up to them. All three looked down the embankment again. Cunningham stepped to the edge of the path.

A masked and overalled SOCO working near the body was pointing up at marks on a wooden bulkhead frame as a crime scene photographer took pictures.

"What is it?" called Cunningham.

"Bullet holes."

Aziz and Myers looked at each other.

***

None of them had a good night. Exhausted, they slept where they dropped. It was early when they breakfasted on tea and toast, sat round the TV watching live coverage of a smoke haze drifting across the Adur estuary, the blue sparklers of fire engines in the background.

"They don't tell you much," said Jessie.

Danny shook his head. "Fire brigade's still damping down. They won't know anything until fire investigation and forensics get at it."

"And what will they find?" asked Hayley.

"A chemical lab for sure," said Danny.

"And bodies?" said Jessie.

Danny shrugged.

A snotty snuffling drew everyone's attention to the makeshift bed in the corner. Carter's crusty eyelids were twitching. Grace knelt beside her patient, raising his head so he could sip some water. This seemed to give him strength so she eased him up, propping him against the wall with pillows.

They all watched as his eyes flickered open and he tried to make sense of his surroundings. Grace brought him tea. Filthy, black-nailed fingers locked round his mug. He sipped and swore when the hot liquid burned his cracked lips.

Slowly, the light of memory rekindled in his bloodshot eyes.

"Fucking rats. I hate fucking rats."

"Mind your language, kids present," said Danny.

Carter looked across, blinking.

"Who the fuck are you?"

"I won't warn you again. You started all this."

"Me, what?" said Carter, uncomfortable at the sudden attention.

"You're the key."

"Me?"

"Yes, you. When you went walkabout your wife hired me to find you."

"Bitch."

"Where were you?" asked Danny.

"Nice little B&B in Eastbourne, stayed there as a kid. Got a bit fed up after a few days and went home for a change of clothes. They jumped me as soon as I opened the door."

"Who?"

"Dunno, didn't see."

"So why did you run? What was all that about a lottery win?"

"That? Just bullshit, first excuse I could think of. Marion and me, we'd made a bit of a life for ourselves down here on the coast, kept ourselves private. Then I find out she's been contacting Ron Hedges and, well, I panicked."

"So you'd been hiding yourself from the rest of your Namibia lot?"

"You know about that?"

Danny looked at Grace, nodded. "Volstruis, Kaapse Kobra, the lot."

"If that bitch..." Carter muttered.

"Shut up and listen," said Danny. "We're not doing relationship counselling here. This is serious. Where are the diamonds?"

"Wouldn't you like to know?"

"Yes I would, and now."

"What makes you so sure I've got them?"

"Steele, Hedges and Collins are dead. Your wife seems very keen to find you. You're the only one who could have them."

"Go to hell."

"Look, Carter, it's been a long night. Each of the flats here has a mesh cage in the basement for storing stuff. Hardly ever used. It's dark, really damp, full of creepy crawlies, rats as well, probably. If you don't tell me what I want to know I am going to stick you in bug heaven till Christmas."

Real fear flared in Bill Carter's eyes.

"I hate fucking rats."

"You said, and mind your language in front of the kids."

Danny could see Carter was shaking now, rings of ripples on his tea. Fatigue, shock and fear of what was to come grinding him down.

"I... I can't."

"You can, Carter. You have to. You don't have any friends left and, the way things stand, we're the nicest enemies you've got."

"Ron and Sean are dead?"

"Yup, both of them, and just after I'd visited."

"Who...?"

"I have no idea but it wasn't the houseboat mob."

"I... I've... It's... that bitch."

"Look, forget this bitch business. If you want out of this alive and in one piece you've got to help us. Where are the diamonds?"

Carter had avoided looking at Danny. Now their eyes met, briefly. Carter's flicked away.

"How much do you know?"

"Bugger all, really," said Danny. "It's pretty clear some of the haul didn't go up with the aircraft. And you're the guy who called the dealer in Antwerp. Used your home phone. That was really stupid. But the diamonds have got to be here somewhere."

Carter tried to laugh but failed.

"And I get to walk away?"

"If you co-operate."

"It's been a long time, like a lifetime. You get into a habit of secrecy."

"Just tell us."

Carter shrugged, put his mug on the table.

"They're at my place."

"Your house?"

Carter nodded.

"I checked the fish tank."

Carter managed a laugh this time.

"The sunken ship? The treasure chest? My little joke."

"Hysterical, so where are they?"

"Fountain, in the garden."

Danny pulled the Sig from his pocket. Carter recoiled into the cushions, relaxed a little when he saw Danny begin to strip the weapon. Grace took her cue and did the same.

"Dad! The gun, they kill people, like those kids in America. They're dangerous."

Danny looked up at his daughter, tear-streaked and dirty, and smiled.

"Not half as dangerous as trying to explain last night to my sister."

No one laughed.

CHAPTER 28

It seemed an odd thing to do, stand around watching someone on the phone. But after the events of last night they somehow felt the need to stick together.

"Hi, Skids?" said Danny. "Oh, Richard, yes, and good morning to you too. In bed? Yes, it is early. I know, sorry. Should have guessed you guys would be asleep. Oh, you were in bed but awake, OK, can I speak to Skids? I need a favour..."

When Danny had finished he hung up and turned to see the others still watching him. He ruffled Hayley's greasy hair.

"Skidmarks will be here in 20 minutes. He's a good guy. He'll see you safe home."

"Can't I stay with you, Dad?"

Danny shook his head.

"Pleeeese?"

"I've got things to do. I want you safe back home with Cheryl, out of harm's way." He looked at Jessie. "You too."

"You won't forget about today, Dad, will you?"

"No, Hayley."

"Midday."

"I'll be there."

"It's important."

"I know that. I'll just get this sorted then I'll be over straight away."

***

Danny had to admit it was a brilliant idea, and simple, like all the best plans. The ornate fountain, with some half-naked Greek goddess losing her robe as she rose from among the rocks, was surrounded by a circular pool.

The bottom of the pool was covered with multi-coloured stones that would have sparkled in the sunlight of a bright day.

Danny scooped them all out onto a bath towel spread on the grass. It was hard going with his injured arm and Jessie pitched in to help. As they worked, Hayley sorted the bright coloured stones and flipped them into a bucket. As the pile of the towel grew dowdy, Grace began to examine them closely.

When all of the big stones were out of the fountain Danny trawled the bottom with the fine net from the fish tank indoors. Grace and Bill Carter were kneeling on the grass head to head as they compared each possibility in turn.

When they were finished, Danny ran his finger through a small pile of irregular-shaped silver-grey stones.

"Doesn't look like much," said Danny. "A few peas, most of them are the size of rice."

"But they are worth many, many thousands of dollars," said Grace.

"Unbelievable," said Danny.

"And there is this," said Grace, opening her hand.

Danny leaned closer. It was an oval stone, about the size of pigeon's egg, with a slight indentation that escaped the light that touched its outer curves.

"The Demon's Eye," said Danny.

"Oh, thank God you're all right."

Everyone turned.

***

Emma leaned across the settee to reach the remote control and turned up the sound. Benny didn't like her watching the news but he wasn't here.

The guy was standing on a towpath, hair scratched flat, eyes tired, face pale from lack of sleep. His right arm was tight around the shoulders of a woman who had clearly been crying.

"I'm talking to eyewitnesses Roger and Alison Benjamin who live on a houseboat close to the seat of last major night's fire. Mr Benjamin, can you tell us exactly what happened?"

A microphone peeked into the corner of the shot.

"Well, it all happened so quickly. We were just sitting watching the television when someone started banging on a front door, really banging. I answered it and all he said was to get out fast.

"I didn't know what he was talking about. You know, it could have been one of those distraction burglaries you hear about. Then I saw the flames. The fire was massive, and there were explosions. It was like one of those Bruce Willis films.

"There was a lot of smoke. If that chap hadn't sounded the alarm I don't know what might have happened. We got away as fast as we could. Then the emergency services arrived and we spent the night in the school hall. They haven't let us back yet so we don't know the extent of the damage."

Alison Benjamin began to cry quietly. Her husband tightened his grip around her shoulders. The camera moved to the reporter, perfect blonde hair, razor-edged lipstick and a heavy coat against the wind off the sea.

"Police have so far refused to comment on reports that there are a number of bodies in the burned wreckage of the houseboat, a former navy ship. Forensic teams are now working in the debris and, because of the extent of the fire and reports of explosions, bomb squad and anti-terrorist officers are on the scene. A police spokesman said a statement on the cause is expected later today."

The news bulletin cut to an advert for payday loans. Emma stared at the screen without seeing it for a moment, then looked at her watch. Nearly time to go.

***

Marion Carter was standing on the path by the side of the house, dressed in a long coat, boots and carrying a large leather bag.

"Mr Lancaster, you found Bill. But what are you doing in my garden?"

She walked towards them, looking hard at each in turn.

"I've been out of my mind with worry. I went away to visit friends. Why didn't you call me?"

Danny watched her coming, weighing the options.

Bill Carter climbed to his feet. He seemed unsteady, shaking.

"You bitch..."

"Bill, what's the matter? You look terrible? Where have you been?"

Marion Carter looked at the fountain and the stones on the towel.

"What's going on? Why are you emptying the fountain?"

"You know bloody well why," Carter snarled.

Marion Carter threw back her head, let out a harsh laugh.

"The fountain, that bloody fountain. I've searched every inch of this house more times than I can remember and all the time they were sitting in your precious bloody fountain."

"You knew they were here?" Bill Carter seemed startled.

"Knew? Of course I knew. Who else could it be? It was you and Sean at the crash site. If Sean had pocketed the stones it would have been obvious. He wouldn't just disappear, keep it quiet. It would've been all tarts, champagne and speed boats. It had to be Bill, timid, nervous little Bill."

"All these years..." Bill Carter was stumbling over his words. "Seven years and that was all you wanted. I thought..."

"You married him," said Danny. "And stuck with him all that time just to find the diamonds?"

"Only way I could stay close. There could be a lot of reasons to let that beery old bastard hump me twice a month for seven years but a million in uncut diamonds is better than most."

She laughed again.

"Men! You really are clueless. Wankers! Women have sold their fannies since the world started turning. Do you think pretty girls really get off on sleeping with rich old gits? Better than working behind a building society counter. Fluttering eye lashes and a tight fanny are as good as oil, gold, platinum, even diamonds. Cash in the bank. It's an asset, like playing the piano or building bridges. It's the only real asset you're born with. I've got no time for these soppy tarts who hand it out for free on a Friday when the pubs chuck out."

She looked at Danny.

"What are you? 30? 35? You're a kid. The tough stuff's still to come. You still think it's all about love. Let me tell you, that rubs off on your hands like wet paint. The harder you rub the faster it vanishes. Then you're left with what's underneath and it's not always pretty. Jim, Ron, Sean, they got hard-ons just thinking about how clever they were, how they organised everything. But their best ideas came from seeds I'd planted in their stupid, knob-obsessed brains. It was all my idea. And it would've worked if they hadn't fucked it up. Those are *my* diamonds.

"When Bill came out with that stupid lottery story, and the move to Thailand, I knew something was up. He never was any good at planning, couldn't organise his balls in his own Y-fronts.

"And I knew someone was following me, at the park and back here. I didn't know who, still don't. Maybe I was getting lazy. Seven years is a long time. I knew I had to move things along. I was going to cut Ron in for a share if he helped but then, well, things got out of hand.

"I thought a few days with the rats might loosen Bill up. And I hired you for window dressing, Danny, in case anyone started asking questions. But you were a bit too keen so I thought grabbing your girl might get you back under control. Shame it didn't work out."

"So what happens now?" asked Danny quietly.

Carter's face was dark as he struggled for words. He stumbled, took two steps, clutched his chest, fell to the grass.

Danny thought the strain had been too much. The guy had keeled over. He winced at the pain from his wounds as he bent by the still body. It was only when Danny was crouched by Bill Carter's side that he saw the sticky dark blood.

CHAPTER 29

"We are here today to mourn the passing of Elizabeth May Lancaster but also to celebrate her life. Known as Betty to her many friends, she was born in North London and did well at school, winning awards for her handwriting.

"She passed her Eleven Plus and, at the age of 16, Betty started work at the Barratt sweet factory in Wood Green. It was here she met her future husband, George. They honeymooned in Southend-on-Sea before returning to Edmonton to make their life together.

"Their union was blessed with a daughter, Cheryl, and later they celebrated the birth of their son, Danny.

"Cheryl tells me of a strict but loving childhood in which Betty would insist on a clean plate at every meal and offered helpful words of advice to set them on their paths in life, do unto others, neither a borrower nor a lender.

"After the sad death of her husband, Betty moved to Brighton where the couple had enjoyed many outings in their younger days.

"Betty loved being by the sea, enjoying a special treat of fish and chips on the Palace Pier and long walks, exploring the city on foot and making best use of her free bus pass to venture further along the coast to resorts such as Worthing, Hastings and Eastbourne.

"Our sister Betty had a keen eye for a bargain and was well known in the family for visiting the many car boot sales and jumble sales in the area for that special purchase.

"The birth of her four grandchildren brought new purpose to her later life and Betty could always be relied upon to volunteer for the peeling of the Christmas Brussels sprouts.

"The family faced new challenges when Betty contracted a debilitating illness tragically early in life. Her years of illness were born with inspirational courage aided by the love and care of her daughter Cheryl, son Danny and local nursing services who fulfilled Betty's last wish to spend her final days in the Brighton flat she loved so much.

"She was a respectable and hard-working woman who devoted herself to her family, stubborn when the moment demanded it, caring when her children suffered from the pitfalls of life, be they skinned knees or broken dreams.

"Betty enjoyed her life to the full and will leave a large gap in the lives of those she leaves behind."

The vicar looked up from his notes at the eight people before him, bunched close in the front pew of the empty chapel.

Andrea, the district nurse, sat at one end. At the opposite end of the pew Emma looked angry. Cheryl's two children were hunched, nervous and sullen. Wayne was staring down at his shoes, trying very hard not to look at the wreath-topped coffin between the curtains.

Hayley was shaken by spasms of crying, Jessie beside her, extending a thin consoling arm around Hayley's shoulders. At the centre, Cheryl sat motionless, her face dark with rage.

The vicar looked along the line and forced a small consoling smile.

"Let us pray."

***

Danny felt the pressure of the Sig in his pocket but it might have been a million miles away for all the use it was.

There were two of them. One tall and built, the other tiny. Both with hoodies pulled up, only mouths and the tips of noses visible. They stood apart giving each other space to move and a clear field of fire. The only other key element in Danny's split-second evaluation was the Glock 9mms that each carried. Fitted with silencers.

He recognised the big guy as the one who had followed Marion Carter that first day, the one he'd fought with in Marion's side passage. Danny was fairly sure he'd slammed the smaller one against a wall with a plank.

Marion Carter was still screaming. "My husband, my husband, he's hurt."

The small intruder waved the group away from the sprawled Bill Carter and stepped closer, looked down, shot him twice in the head. The noise just a compressed hiss.

Marion Carter opened her mouth but no sound came out. The intruder waved the gun again.

"Inside."

They moved into the conservatory slowly, in single file, Marion cringing away from the guns. Danny moved carefully, nursing his bandaged arm, taking care the shape of the Sig didn't show through his clothes

His eyes never stop soaking up the scene. Grace was watchful without catching their eyes.

As they shuffled about in the conservatory the big guy positioned himself in the far corner. He had a clear view of his captives plus the door to the kitchen on his left and the garden door to his right.

"Vic," he called the smaller one without taking his eyes off the prisoners.

"JJ?"

"Get the stones. I'll hold them here."

Vic's tiny frame skipped out of the door and across the lawn. With the hood up, the shape looked more like one of Santa's elves than a killer.

"What are you doing..." but Danny didn't get the chance to finish.

"Shut up," said JJ.

They all turned when they heard a strange electric whining sound. It rose and fell, growing steadily louder.

"Jesus Christ!"

The powered wheelchair rolled into the doorway, came to a halt. A gloved hand tilted the tiny control stick. The chair rotated through ninety degrees, inched forward, stopped.

"No, Marion," said the man in the wheelchair as he adjusted the big black patch over his left eye. "Not Jesus Christ. I don't walk on water. I don't walk anywhere after what you did."

"Jim?"

"Don't look so surprised. You must have guessed." He turned to JJ. "You got the stones?"

"Yes, Dad."

"Excellent, excellent, give them to me."

JJ threw the bag of diamonds. Jim Steele reached up and caught it, hefted it in his hand, savouring the feel of them through the material. His one eye looked strangely large, always moving, sucking in detail like a black hole.

"Doesn't seem like much for all that trouble, all that pain."

"Jim Steele?" said Danny. "From the plane crash?" They ignored him.

"We thought you were dead," said Marion Carter.

"I very nearly was, no thanks to you."

"Bill and Sean got you out of the crash, back to the boat." There was urgency in Marion Carter's voice, playing for time. "They blew up the plane. No one ever knew how many were on board."

"And then you panicked," said Steele. "If you'd gone to South Africa, I could have got medical attention, might have stood a chance. But you lot just wanted to get away so you went north, to Angola, dumped me and vanished."

"We... we did what we could, Jim."

"Which was fuck all but save your own skins. It took me months, months in that shithole of a hospital, before I was able to travel. By then it was too late. You cost me my legs, my whole life, for this!"

He held up the diamond bag in a clenched fist. Then he threw them.

"Take care of these, son."

JJ caught the bag and slipped it into his hoodie pocket.

"They're your kids?" asked Marion.

"I broke my back, not my dick. But these two were young'uns back then. Since I made it home they're been my legs and a lot more. This is my lad JJ, Jim Junior."

The big guy gave a brief, reluctant nod.

"And this is my beautiful and talented daughter Victoria. Good kids, the pair of them. Do what their dad tells them. Eh JJ? Eh Vic? And it worked. Because I'm here, aren't I?"

The smaller gunman swept the hood from her head to reveal short bobbed hennaed hair and sharp green eyes. Danny knew she was the one he'd struck with the plank, could see bruises around one eye and down the side of her face. The one he'd heard kissing the other waterboarder.

"A really close family, aren't you?" said Danny.

Jim Steele smiled, nodded slowly. JJ and Vic both turned sharply, looked hard at Danny.

"Dad," said JJ. "We need to get moving."

"All right, son. I've waited a long time for this."

"And now we know who you all are I'm guessing we're not coming with you."

"You always were a sharp one, Marion. You and me, we could have run rings round the others. Could have walked away rich. But it's too late now so, yes, you're right. The only ones leaving this room are me, JJ, Vic and the stones."

"Dad!"

"When I'm ready, JJ!"

"So you're going to shoot us here?" said Marion.

"Yes," said Steele.

"In that case, can I have my bag? A girl wants to look her best, even on a slab."

Steele gave a cold chuckle. "You always were a looker, Marion. And you made it work for you, I'll say that." Steele laughed again, a sound like rocks grating. "Give it to her, JJ."

"What you need, Gran?" asked JJ. "Heart pills, panty liners?"

"JJ, give her the bag."

"Shall I check it, Dad?"

"What? You think she's going to stick you with her nail file? Just give her the bag, son, and let's get going. No speeches. I've had my say."

Danny was the first to move when the shot was fired.

CHAPTER 30

It was pretty bloody obvious the district nurse couldn't wait to get away. She expressed her condolences once again and practically sprinted across the car park to her Nissan Micra.

Woodvale Crematorium didn't seem part of the city. It sat in a wooded valley rich with shrubs, lawns, rockeries and flower beds that might raise the mourning spirits with a display of colour in spring or summer. Now the foliage was dying into winter and what remained was a rich green, sodden with rain.

Dark clouds moved fast across a lumpy grey sky, spitting rain. Cheryl and Emma stayed close to the shelter of the chapel wall, pulling hard on their cigarettes, casting side glances at the thin girl who had come back with Hayley in a minicab from Danny's just as they were leaving for the service. Hayley had been babbling about some famous singer. Made no sense.

The kid looked weird but they'd been too focussed on the funeral to find out more. Hayley had been out all night despite Danny's promises. Both kids looked like they'd been dragged through a hedge. Cheryl and Emma wanted answers. But that would come later.

"Come here, you'll get soaked walking about out there," said Cheryl, her voice harsh and cracking.

Wayne took no notice, carried on kicking the toe of his trainer against the ground.

They stood in a semi-circle, Cheryl, Emma, Hayley, Jessie, not speaking, staring down at the rain drops pitting the pools on the dark tarmac.

When the silence started to stretch it was Cheryl who broke it.

"How's Benny?"

Emma stiffened, started to form a word, gave a little shake of her head. Both women lifted their lipstick-stained cigarettes to their mouths. They smoked in silence. Then Emma spoke.

"How could he?"

***

JJ yelped and looked at his bloody right bicep where Marion's round had hit. As she pulled the pistol clear of her bag he saw the smoking hole in the designer leather.

Victoria Steele turned her Glock on Marion.

A window shattered. It was fear fire, panic, banging blindly away for self-preservation, startled, comfort in noise and action.

Grace drew her Sig and fired over Danny as he wrestled his pistol free through the blinding pain of his arm.

Wood splinters hissed. Hot cartridge cases tinkled across the Italian tiling.

Steele reversed his wheelchair from the doorway, out of sight. As the whine of his motor faded, bullets punched a row of craters in the tiling as Marion tried to hit him through the kitchen wall.

A light fitting exploded with a crack and hiss.

JJ fired wildly, blasting plaster from the ceiling. Vic used the shock and awe to change magazines. Then JJ's pistol clicked on empty. He fumbled with a fresh magazine, changed his mind, ducked out of the kitchen door after his father, clutching his arm.

Vic, crouched and determined, fired around the room to cover them.

A bullet went through the fish tank. A spout like someone peeing arced from the cracked glass. Then there was a groan and the tank burst.

Vic saw JJ was gone and followed, stepped backwards, still firing into the room.

Five seconds of chaos.

By the time Danny had his pistol in his hand it was quiet. Apart from the ringing in his ears.

He heard the crash of the front door. He and Grace held their weapons trained on the kitchen doorway to the hall. Danny nodded his head and they moved up to either side of it. Danny slipped out as Grace covered him. He was back in seconds.

"All clear."

Grace was crouching over Marion who lay on her back on the floor, legs at a clumsy angle. Thick strands of black blood were exploring the grouting grooves in the tiling, curling into the spilled fish tank water.

Grace had opened Marion's blouse. There was an ugly bullet wound in her chest and another in her left shoulder. A third round had carved a glistening groove in her temple. Grace looked up at Danny and gave the tiniest shake of her head.

Marion started to laugh but it mutated into a gurgle.

"That bad, is it? That bad, eh?"

She coughed, then her face twisted with the pain it brought. Grace pressed tea towels to Marion's chest and shoulder to stop the bleeding and she cried out.

"Jesus God, that hurts."

"I'll call an ambulance," said Danny.

"Don't bother," Marion wheezed. "They'll patch me up for a prison sentence. I'd rather die on my Italian tiling. It cost me enough."

She tried to laugh and the pain brought her shoulders up off the floor. The spit round her mouth was a frothing pink now. She looked at Danny, blinking to focus.

"You're a bright lad... Worked it all out... didn't you? You're better than you think... If I was younger..."

Danny crouched low, his mouth six inches from her ear.

"You're not going to make it, Marion."

"Don't you think I..." another coughing fit and a thin keening through clenched teeth. "... know that?"

The skin of Marion Carter's face was puckered with pain but the eyes were fierce. She folded up in another spasm of coughing. Blood welled up through the tea towel Grace was pressing to Marion's chest.

"Jesus, that hurts."

Danny could see Marion was burning the last of her energy. Only willpower was keeping her talking. Nearby, a dying betta splendens flapped, gauzy powder-blue fins whipping a blood pool into strawberry milkshake.

Her voice a rasp now. Danny didn't know where she found the strength. Her hand trembled its way to his collar and gripped, pulling him closer. As her muscles clenched the blood oozed from her chest wound. Her speech came on a series of grunts now. They made her wince, flecking Danny's shirt with pink droplets.

"I might look rough as fuck to a kid like you but, believe me, I was bloody good once. Maybe if you and I had..."

She tried to laugh. Blood bubbled.

"It was my idea... my plan... my team... my diamonds. They were my diamonds."

Danny shook her shoulder.

"Simon..." said Marion.

"Who's Simon?"

"My beautiful Simon. I want my beautiful boy... Simon."

- 261 -

"Who's Simon?"

She looked at Danny again, eyes fierce. When her lips parted her teeth were outlined in bright red blood. As Grace pulled Marion's blouse open wider to get a better grip on the dressings, Danny saw something glisten. Nestled against the lace of her bra was a pendant on a long chain. He'd seen it before, in the portrait over Ron Hedges's fireplace. It wasn't a snake. It was a gold letter S.

"The diamonds," said Danny. "What's Steele going to do with them? Where's he going?"

"It was my plan, mine all the time. I shagged them all to keep them in line... you know... to find the alpha male. And I did... It was me."

The light faded from Marion Carter's eyes. Her grip on Danny's collar went slack. The arm fell away. The hand splashed into a pool of blood, spattering a shipwreck and a plastic treasure chest.

***

Cheryl shook her head, looked at her watch, sucked on the cigarette until the tip burned bright.

"Wayne, I won't tell you again."

He carried on kicking. The two women stared out at the engorged greenery, ignoring Hayley who stood beside them, trying to suppress the sobs that made her shoulders heave. She wiped her nose with a soggy tissue but all it did was smear her face. Jessie put a hesitant arm around her damp shoulders.

"Bastard," said Cheryl.

Hayley tried to refold the tissue but it just dragged strands of silver mucus from her runny nose. Both women tried to ignore the maddening metronome thump of Wayne's trainer beating against the tarmac.

"Where's that bloody cab got to?" said Cheryl.

"How could he?" said Emma, shaking her head. "How could he?"

"His own mum's funeral," said Cheryl. "Bastard!"

***

It was a real effort to keep himself from flooring the accelerator but the last thing they needed was to trigger police traffic cameras or get pulled over.

The pain in his arm pulsed with waves of fire but he was too angry, too hyped to notice. He pulled out to overtake a Ford Focus, accelerated, pulled back into the stream of traffic. Keep it smooth, anonymous.

Danny's eyes were on the road but he was aware of Grace's regular glances across the cab of the van. Eventually she spoke.

"So what do we do now?"

Danny slowed as a bus indicated and began pulling over to a stop.

"They're not getting away, that's for sure."

"But how can we stop them? Where are they going?"

"I don't know but I know a man who does."

"Who?"

"Knight, he's up to his shaved armpits in this."

"Do we go there now?"

"We can't storm into his flat. There's security and we don't want to attract attention. We need a chat with him somewhere quiet."

"And you have a plan?"

"Oh yes."

***

Paulie's brows were knitted in concentration. He hated doing this. Wasn't his job. It was embarrassing. But there was no arguing with Jas, specially when he was in one of his moods. He had the right hump. Paulie had never seen him in a mood like today's.

Paulie looked down at his wire basket. Two Jose Cuervo tequilas, Two Smirnoff Red, Two Havana Club, he liked a rum once in a while, and a case of Bud. And he'd remember the Pringles selection, sour cream and onion, prawn, Thai sweet chilli and a curry one.

Shopping, running errands, it really was an embarrassment. His job was security, personal bodyguard. That was the deal. Popping round the shops was out of order.

Sometimes he wished he still had the job as a personal trainer. He'd liked that. Piece of piss, spend the day impressing the girls, flexing your abs, pecs and quads. And you could use the equipment for free. He'd still be doing it if it hadn't been for that little shit of an estate agent. Thought he was really something, kept taking the piss in that voice of his. Paulie had tried, he'd really tried, specially after the deputy manager had taken him aside, given him a warning.

But the estate agent had kept at it, pick, pick, pick with the sarky remarks, trying to make his stuck-up mates laugh at Paulie's expense. He knew he had a temper on him. Caitlin was always complaining about it, right up to the day she walked out.

But that estate agent just kept pushing. The little shit was asking for a twatting and he got one. What else was he supposed to do?

He looked down at the basket again, thought that was it. He was sure that was it. Still, it paid to check. If he cocked it up again Jas would go off on another one.

As Paulie turned the corner at the end of Aisle Two he stopped in his tracks, mouth open. He stood, startled to a standstill, for a second or so until the family-size tin of baked beans hit him hard on the bridge of his nose. He tottered back into a display of jars, heard the sound of smashing around his feet.

He was still stunned, dragging his feet, as he was hustled out of the supermarket. Paulie tried to concentrate, understand what was happening to him. But all he could hear was the bing-bong of the supermarket PA.

"Rajesh, Aisle Two, please. Broken glass and spillage."

CHAPTER 31

Staring at it didn't make it go any faster. The green light just kept winking. He had a rotten headache, his jaw hurt like fuck and that bloody green light just kept winking.

That black bitch would never have chinned him if she hadn't caught him by surprise.

"Come on, come on."

He reached across the desk, popped more painkillers from a blister pack and washed them down from the can of flat Diet Coke beside his keyboard.

"Bitch."

The green light was still blinking.

"Come on, this is taking for ever."

The pain just kept nagging. No one did that to him, no one. If he wasn't a gent he'd have decked her. He heard the front door go just as the green light stopped winking. He snatched the USB drive from its slot and slammed in another. The blinking started again. Jason Knight saw his minder stumble into the room as he was pushed hard from behind.

"Paulie?"

His aching jaw dropped when Danny and Grace followed the minder into the room. Danny looked around at Knight's apartment. The large living room was all white leather sofas, glass-topped chrome-leg tables, big flat-screen. Pretty much what he'd expected.

"Why are you... What are you..."

"Where's Jim Steele," said Danny.

"Look, you can't just charge in here and..."

His eyes bulged when Danny pulled out the Sig. Jason took a step back and Danny moved towards the desk.

"Where's Steele?"

"I... look... I..."

Danny raised the pistol. Knight took another step back, found himself pressed against the tall windows that gave him panoramic views over the Palace Pier and the Wheel. Danny cocked the pistol. Jason pushed back against the wall as if the pressure might make it open and let him out.

As Danny took a step forward he saw a dark stain blossom across the front of Knight's designer jeans. It opened out like a diseased flower, growing and spreading down his left leg.

"I don't... I can't..."

Danny heard Grace gasp behind him as he pointed the pistol at the wet leg. Knight let out a sob.

"Talk to me, Jason, or you'll be trying to DJ with no kneecaps."

"Marion's said... Marion wouldn't..."

"Marion Carter's dead," said Danny.

Knight's face turned a sickly yellow. His breath leaked out of him in a long whine as he sank down the wall into a wet ball on the carpet.

"No!"

They watched as Knight, arms wrapped round his drawn-up knees, began to rock, keening through clenched teeth.

"I'm not going to say this again. Where's Steele?"

"Marion's dead?"

Danny looked at the rocking, sobbing bundle on the floor. Grace was shocked. Paulie, sitting quietly out of trouble on the sofa nursing his nose, was disgusted.

"She bankrolled the club?" asked Danny.

Knight nodded.

"And the lab on the houseboat?"

Knight's head moved again.

"So you've lost a business partner. Not interested. Just tell me where Steele is."

"Marion... she..."

Danny grabbed Knight's shirt. Buttons popped as he hoiked him to his feet, ignoring the pain in his arm, slammed Knight back against the glass wall. Tears were streaming down his face.

"I don't have time for this. Where is Jim Steele?"

"He's taken the van." Danny and Grace turned to look at Paulie.

"Jas's van," said the minder. "The one we use to shift the music gear. His kids turned up just before I went out. They said we could have it back in a couple of hours."

Danny looked down at Knight.

"This true?"

Knight's head bobbed.

"Ok," said Danny. "He's going to want to get the diamonds as far away as possible. The guy's in a wheelchair so what are his options?"

"Gatwick Airport?" said Grace.

Danny shook his head.

"Too public. You'd need to request help."

"Newhaven?" This was Paulie.

"Possible, but still public... I know, Shoreham, private aircraft, slip away, minimum of fuss."

Danny rolled the idea around.

"He'd like the idea. He's got a track record with planes. The wheel comes full circle. It's got to be Shoreham."

He glanced at Paulie, still sitting on the sofa looking weary at his prospects.

"Why did Steele come here? Why ask Knight for transport?"

Paulie shrugged.

"Why did Knight grab Jessie? It was too late for the club opening and she wouldn't have been any use anyway if she wasn't willing."

Paulie gave a half laugh.

"It wasn't Jessie we were after. It was your kid."

"Hayley?"

"Mrs Carter's idea. She said she hired you for a bit of window dressing, to look keen in case anyone asked, but you were getting too close. She wanted you warned off."

Danny puffed out his cheeks, shook his head.

"Jeez."

He pocketed the Sig.

"Ok, how long ago were Steele's kids here?"

The minder looked at his watch.

"Not sure, less than an hour."

"Come on, Grace. We need to move."

Paulie looked up.

"What about me?"

"If I were you I'd clear off and keep going."

Paulie jerked his head towards Knight.

"And him?"

Knight cringed as Danny stepped closer. A whimper escaped twisted lips. Danny grabbed the man's shirt. Buttons ripped.

"Don't even think of trying to warn Steele. Remember what I said before."

Knight's head jerked.

"I can't hear you."

"Yes... yes... I remember."

As Danny glanced down he saw thin links of gold snaking down Knight's bare chest. Swinging at the end was a golden letter S. Simon.

Danny shook his head.

"Families, eh?"

***

The pain in Danny's arm was coming back with a vengeance now. The alcohol and painkillers were wearing off. The dressing was starting to leak.

Grace drove the van, pushing as hard as she could along the coast road westward without attracting attention of tripping a speed cam.

As they crossed Norfolk Bridge Danny looked left and saw fire appliances still damping down the charred remains of the Fairmile. It was hard to be sure at that distance but it didn't look like there was much left. She had burned down to the mud. He hoped the neighbouring boats had been saved.

Grace checked their route and Danny indicated they should go right at Saltings Roundabout.

Beyond the cluster of houses they passed under the railway line into Shoreham Airport and down Cecil Pashley Way. One road in, one out.

***

Danny, nursing the Sig in his lap, pointed out a space to Grace in the car park opposite the airport's art deco terminal building. When she switched off it seemed unnaturally quiet.

They sat together, listening to the tick of the engine cooling, running their eyes over the vehicles parked around them.

"What do we do now?" asked Grace.

Danny shook his head. "Blowed if I know. I can't see Jason's van. Even if we're right about them flying out we don't know when. We're winging it here."

"We could ask about aircraft movements."

"Worth a try."

He slipped the pistol in his pocket as they stepped out of the van. Danny eased himself down gently to avoid bumping his arm. While Grace bought a pay-and-display parking ticket, Danny walked towards the row of flag poles on the central green, pausing to look at a war memorial made from an aircraft propeller.

Beyond it, another memorial marked the death of a display pilot killed flying a Hurricane at the airport's annual airshow.

When Grace joined him on the neatly-clipped grass they looked around. On their right was the airport's museum and to the left of that stood Terminal 3, a single-storey building of corrugated blue-grey. Through the gap between the terminal and the main building they could see aircraft and a slice of the airfield. Danny jerked his head in that direction, Grace nodded and they set off.

Public access extended as far as the airfield's apron which was screened off with a metal crowd barrier that extended to the airside of Terminal 3. Beyond the terminal were hangars and workshops. Light aircraft were parked on the grass beyond the apron.

Danny and Grace looked around.

"Not much happening," said Danny. He looked at Grace, saw the fear of failure in her face.

"I hope this is not a wild goose chase."

Both heads turned at the urgent whine of engines powering up.

"Hear that?"

Grace nodded.

"Worth a look."

They moved to the railing, leaned over to get a clear view away to their right. The engine noise grew louder, eased off, then rose again. A twin-engine Cessna nosed out of a hangar and swung onto the tarmac. It came to a halt, rocking gently against its wheel brakes.

As they watched, a dark-coloured van moved slowly away from one of the buildings. Something looked odd, missing. It took Danny a moment to realise it didn't seem to have a driver. If it did, it was a very small one.

"Come on."

As Danny swung a leg over the barrier someone in a high-vis jacket shouted from somewhere behind him. Danny waved the Sig in the air. The man put up his hands, backed away, turned, ran.

The vehicle slewed to a stop on the airfield side of the aircraft as the Cessna's engines rose to a roar, its turning propellers discs of silver.

An empty wheelchair tumbled from the open side door of the van, hit the tarmac, rolled over. Vic Steele dropped from the driver's door. She saw Danny and Grace immediately, crouched, fired.

Exposed in the open, they hit the ground and rolled. Danny's arm was on fire. He heard his teeth creak as he ground them together at the impact.

A round hit the tarmac and spun away, then another. A third panged into the barrier.

CHAPTER 32

They were flat on the ground, no cover. Danny looked over his prone shoulder. The outlines of air traffic control staff peered from the control tower on top of the terminal building.

Beyond the main building he spotted an aircraft refuelling point with a yellow and white tanker parked on the grass nearby. Not an environment for gunfire.

When he looked back towards the Cessna, Vic Steele had the wheelchair upright and was half pulling, half dragging her father out of the van.

A hand came from the cockpit window. JJ Steele shot wildly, bullets kicking spurts from the tarmac, firing so fast Danny couldn't count the rounds.

He tapped Grace's arm and indicated, rolled to his feet. Together they printed toward Terminal 3 and rounded the corner just as three shots thunked into the corrugated metal.

Customers in the main terminal's restaurant terrace stared open-mouthed. A woman picked up her lunch plate and ran inside. A man grabbed his pint and followed. Others dodged under their tables. Somewhere, people were shouting.

Vic Steele was leaning her light body hard against the wheelchair now, trying to improve the steady speed of its motor, pushing it towards the long nose of the aircraft and round to the passenger door in the far side,

Danny and Grace crouched in the cover of the corner, weighing the risks of firing towards a fully fuelled aircraft, the risks of drawing fire that hit bystanders.

"Got to be done."

Grace pulled a face, cupped a hand to her ear to indicate she couldn't hear him above the roar of the Cessna.

Danny chopped a hand toward the big square tarmac apron and the grass beyond, indicated a curve, tapped his shoulder and hers. She understood, adjusted her grip on the Sig, nodded.

"Come on."

Then Danny pushed himself up, ignoring the pain, using one arm, and started forward. They ran, crouched low, vaulted the barrier, stumbled, rebalanced and ran.

Heads low, they heard the crack of shots but didn't see where they hit. They crossed the tarmac, toward the grass, The firing continued, two weapons now.

Danny and Grace hit the ground and rolled. There was no cover, nothing, everything cleared under the Foreign Object Debris regulations for aircraft safety.

A cluster of aircraft were parked behind them, on the grass at the far side of the apron, but they were at extreme pistol range. Better than drawing fire onto lunchtime drinkers and tanks of avgas.

Vic, Jim Steele and the wheelchair were by the nose of the aircraft when she paused, turned and fired again, paired shots, three times. Danny and Grace rolled apart, rounds whining off the tarmac. Danny cried out in pain, tears blurring his vision for a second, as his weight came down on his chewed arm.

As Vic Steele turned back to the wheelchair her father stood suddenly on rubber legs, hauling himself up, fingers splayed wide for support against the long rounded nose of the Cessna, punching the sky above his head, diamond bag gripped in his fist, eyes alight, laughing like a maniac.

Then his unsteady weight shifted. His grip slipped on the glossy surface of the aircraft's skin. He started to totter. As Steele began to drop clumsily back into the wheelchair Danny saw what was going to happen. A split second later he heard Grace gasp and knew she'd seen it. Steele collapsed into the wheelchair. It began to roll under the impact.

Then Vic Steele saw it too. Began to scream.

"No! No! No! No! *Noooooooooo!*"

The 80-pound aluminium Hartzell propeller blades of the starboard engine spun like giant swords, their tips moving at 300mph, spinning at 1,200rpm, each tip passing through the same space twenty times in a second.

Steele's head vanished in a pink vortex. Lumps of flesh and brain, hair and wet tubes spun into the air, spattered across the tarmac. A severed arm arced high overhead, turning lazy circles.

Vic Steele was still screaming, the noise rising above the roar of the engines. She lunged towards her father, disappeared into a haze of pink minced meat and offal, butchered by a thousand slashes.

Danny and Grace couldn't tear their eyes from Vic's head as they followed its trajectory over the aircraft's starboard wing.

The whole world stopped apart from the whirling propeller blades which drove blood and lumps of flesh along the rough tarmac.

Stunned and still, Danny and Grace could just hear an animal screaming above the roar of engines.

"No! No! No! No! No! No! No! No! No! No! No!"

The hand came through the cockpit window again, firing. Danny and Grace rose to a crouch, took careful aim. Their rounds punched through the bloody Perspex four inches apart. The arm jerked. The gun slipped from its fingers, clattered against the fuselage. The arm went limp and sagged.

Danny struggled to his feet without taking his eyes from the glistening, marbled meat draped over the wheelchair below the spinning prop.

"Fuck me," said Danny.

"As you say," said Grace.

They stood, eyes locked on the carnage, for long seconds until Danny broke away.

"We've got to get moving. You tidy up. I'll be a second."

Grace began collecting their spent bullet casings. With CCTV and a live audience it probably wouldn't make much difference but it was worth a try.

Danny jogged towards a line of parked aircraft, skirting the lacerated remains of Jim and Vic Steele. The bloodied meat was steaming in the cold air. Jim Steele's severed arm didn't want to let go of the diamond bag. Danny had to use both hands to prise the fingers apart. His arm hurt like hell.

As he turned back he saw Grace standing close to the mangled bodies. She raised her pistol, fired a shot into what was left of Jim, a second into Vic. She bent to collect the spent cases.

They ran back to the van, Danny glancing at his watch. One road in, one road out. They were on Norfolk Bridge when they saw the blue lights coming. Danny could hear Grace sobbing quietly as she drove.

CHAPTER 33

Danny pushed the door of his flat closed with his foot, his attention taken up with the fourteen missed calls on his mobile, all from Cheryl. Not good.

Grace had wanted a walk, needed some fresh air, time to think. And she had some phone calls to make. He'd dropped her by the West Pier.

When he walked into the living room Danny knew Emma had been drinking, her eyes red and intense, make-up smudged. She looked up at him from under heavy eyelids, tumbler in hand, weighing him up.

"Don't talk. Don't say anything, Danny. Don't even try. We sat there, me Cheryl, the kids. The district nurse made the effort to turn up. Even Hayley's new best friend came along. There is no excuse, no excuse on this earth to justify missing your own mother's funeral. And look at the state of this place. The door's smashed. There's blood on the carpet, bandages in the swing bin. It's just... I just don't..."

Emma pressed a hand to her forehead and closed her eyes.

"The kids, Danny, the kids just couldn't stop crying. The whole thing, it was just a total bloody nightmare."

She looked up at him and seemed to focus.

"And look at you. You look terrible. What happened to your eyebrows? And you're bleeding... your arm."

"Long story."

***

BRIGHTON, TWO DAYS LATER
As Danny walked silently down the thickly-carpeted corridor the bouncer, beefy arms folded in front of him, stepped into his path.

"I'm expected."

The bouncer looked him up and down, didn't seem to believe it. Danny jerked his head towards the door. The bouncer knocked. Danny smiled as it was opened by a cracking brunette wearing a Bluetooth earpiece and carrying an iPad.

"You are?"

"Danny Lancaster."

She checked her tablet.

"Oh yes, follow me."

Danny walked into the hotel suite. It seemed vast, expensively furnished with tall windows looking out over the beach and sea. A dozen busy people were milling around.

The greeter gave a two-fingered wave to attract the attention of a short, tubby guy in an expensive shiny suit. He excused himself from the group he was talking to and walked over, weighing up Danny as he came. He looked a question to the greeter.

"This is Danny Lancaster, Herbie."

The guy's face broke into an instant smile. He stuck out a chubby hand, shook Danny's. The grip was light, the fingers soft.

"Lancaster, right, the detective guy. Herbie Fielder, talent consultant, great to meet you. You take a latte?"

Fielder gave a little flick of his head and the greeter went off in search of coffee. Fielder took Danny's elbow and guided him to a quiet corner of the room.

"It's crazy here today," he said. "Scheri's story is a sensation. She's giving an interview next door as we speak. Timing's perfect to start the buzz for her next album. She'll be along in a minute."

The greeter brought their coffees. The two men stood looking at each other. Fielder, apparently conscious of the height difference, was bouncing on the balls of his feet.

"Got to say, I owe you big time, Danny. Is it all right if I call you Danny? When Scheri went missing it took years off my life, I can tell you. The old ticker won't take that kind of strain these days. I thought kidnap, I thought accident. Maybe worse. We had our people looking everywhere. I haven't slept since I don't know when."

Danny sipped his coffee. Too milky but, hey, it was free.

"You may not appreciate this, Danny, but that little girl is unique, a genuine raw talent. Thousands of kids, thousands, try to get on Gonna Be A Star. The ratings are huge. That show, it's a meat grinder, I can tell you. They take kids from the asshole of nowhere and throw their dreams on the barbecue. Only the strongest survive heat that intense. And that's our Scheri."

Danny nodded, sipped.

"Did you know she worked part-time in a supermarket? Only one in her family with a job. And she wrote the lyrics to her first songs on torn up packaging because she couldn't afford the paper.

"That show, wow, it attracts egomaniacs, losers, delusional people. The judging can be cruel. So can the audience, believe me. Kids can crack, cry, throw microphones, get angry. But it's a gateway to a whole new life if you have what it takes. And Scheri has that in spades."

Danny nodded again.

"Did you know she didn't tell anyone back home? Just packed a bag and headed south. Didn't want to raise expectations. Even created a name for herself, Scheri. A fresh start. A new beginning.

"But our girl made it, made it through the auditions, through the talent tests, made it all the way. After all the tension and the tears, when our girl took the stage for the final she was so scared she almost wet her pants. But as the lights went down, those 4,000 people in the audience just vanished, poof. The judges vanished. For three minutes there was nothing in that big hall but Scheri, the microphone and emotion, raw emotion that poured freely from her heart and touched everyone there. And the people saw that. They gasped when that big voice tore out of that little girl. And they loved her for it. Everyone on their feet, clapping and cheering. That's why she won. That's why she's going to be a global star.

"Her records sales were sensational. Her concerts sold out. Then she went away but you brought her back to us, brought her safe to the world again. And that experience has re-energised her. She's come home to us with a new perspective, new ideas. And that, Danny, is why we're rushing out her new single, to make the most of Scheri's rebirth as an international singing star.

"So I owe you a big, big debt, Danny Lancaster. Scheri's fans all over the world owe you that same debt."

The greeter was hovering, waving two fingers to attract Fielder's attention. Danny put his cup down, leaned closer.

"I'm not bothered if she can hold a tune, Herbie. She's a kid, a human being, not a performing seal. You take good care of her or I may have to call again."

"Danny!"

Both men looked across the big room. Jessie was waving from a doorway on the far side. Danny almost didn't recognise her. The tam was gone. Thick swirls of auburn hair cascaded over her shoulders. Designer jeans and a famine relief T-shirt had replaced the baggy, raggy clothes she'd worn before.

She ran across the room, weaving between her startled staff. Danny just had time to lift his injured arm out of the way before she threw herself at him.

Heads turned as Jessie clung to Danny, squealing. She grabbed his hand and led him through the press of people into a large and luxurious bedroom, perched on the massive mattress and pulled him down beside her.

When she eased her grip he pulled her to arms length, looked into her face.

"You ok now?" He indicated the busy room next door with a sweep of his head. "You know, with all that?"

Jessie grinned. "I'm alreet," playing up the accent.

She laughed, tossed her hair. Perfect white teeth flashed. Danny thought he must be a crap detective if he'd managed to miss this energetic, bright, beautiful young woman hidden beneath a few grungy cast-offs.

"It was stupid, what I did. I know. But I've given it a lot of thought over the last few days. A while back I just knew the estate and the dunes. Then you walk out on that stage knowing everything you ever wanted is decided in the next few minutes. Everyone wants it, your one chance rise above the wanabees, meet the people who make things happen. You walk out into the lights and you walk back a hero or rubbish. Just those few minutes change your life, you're flying. And suddenly it's like the whole world knows you.

"People treat you different. People who wouldn't give you a second glance suddenly want to be your best friend. You're always being watched, judged. And you life's not your own any more. You're trying to sleep in planes and cars, different hotel every night, photoshoots, TV, radio, crazy busy, no time alone. It got on top of me. I felt, I dunno, lost, out of my depth. It all happened so fast.

"I started thinking back to when it started, when I won on the show. I couldn't believe it at first. It was like a fairytale, like being a princess, people bringing you clothes, doing your hair, your make-up, fixing your drinks.

"Then I started to feel the pressure, so many people depending on me, not wanting to let me mam down after all she'd done. It was..."

Danny saw Jessie's big chocolate eyes start to shine. He squeezed her hand. She forced a sob into a smile.

"Then I thought of Jason, right from back at the start. I remember thinking, what, me and this famous footballer? Taking me out to fancy places, all those photographers outside. But he seemed to know what he was doing. I thought I was in love. I felt safe. Does that sound daft?"

Danny shook his head, squeezed her hand again.

"So when it all got a bit too much I just headed down here. I thought Jason could sort it all out, that I could feel safe again. And you know the rest of it."

"You came through it ok," said Danny. "That's all that matters."

Jessie nodded.

"I came to Brighton looking for a hero. And I found one."

"Sounds like a line from a bad song," said Danny.

She leaned forward, kissed his cheek. Danny felt her cool lips. She pulled back, flustered.

"I'm fine now," said Jessie. "The album's doing really well. The tour starts soon. The money is just daft. I'm just going to focus on singing."

They looked across as the bedroom door sighed open. Danny saw a woman leaning in, small and thin with hoop earrings and a fierce perm. The look in her eyes was intense as they studied Danny.

Jessie looked at her and grinned.

"Mam, this is Danny."

"Our Jessie tells me you've been taking care of her."

"Yes," said Danny.

"You did a good job, pet." She walked over, patted Danny on his good arm and her face relaxed into a smile. She turned back to her daughter, pinched her cheek and squeezed.

"And now I've got my little cherry pie back, haven't I, pet?"

Jessie's face coloured with embarrassment.

"Mum!"

"I meant to ask about that."

"The name?" said Jessie.

Danny nodded.

"Cherry, it's my middle name. I just respelled it a bit."

Jessie's mum turned to indicate a waiter in a white jacket manoeuvring a wheeled trolley through the bedroom door. It carried a large white plate covered with a silver dome.

Jessie's mum touched her daughter's shoulder to get her attention.

"It's your baked beans, pet."

***

GATWICK AIRPORT, THREE DAYS LATER

Neither of them seemed to have much to say so they didn't. They had coffee but drank it mostly in silence. The few efforts at conversation fizzled out. Danny looked up at the board.

"Better get going."

Grace nodded, picked up her hand luggage. They walked towards security.

"So you fly to Frankfurt?"

Grace nodded.

"Yes, then I take the Air Namibia flight from there to Windhoek."

"Sounds exotic"

"It sounds like home," said Grace.

"What will happen when you get back?"

Grace shrugged. "I do not know. There are rules I have broken but the case has been resolved."

"Know the feeling," said Danny.

"I have submitted a report of what happened here and the diamonds have been returned to my country by courier from the high commission in London."

"All neat and tidy," said Danny.

They walked on in silence to the security lanes. At the barrier Danny turned to Grace, looked at her, shrugged.

"They fuck you up, your mum and dad."

Grace slapped his arm.

"Danny, why are you using bad words?"

"Not me, an English poet, guy called Larkin. Read it in the library."

"I did not know your poets wrote like that."

"He has a point. I've met some dysfunctional families but this bunch, Jesus. Steele stole his kids' youth to get his revenge. It's like one of those Shakespeare plays, you know, tragic but sort of inevitable."

Grace nodded thoughtfully.

"And we still do not know who Jason's father is."

"No," said Danny. "Could have been any one them or none of them."

"Are you going to pursue Jason?"

"Nah, with an ego like his and a chip the size of a football he'll get his comeuppance sooner rather than later."

"And your children, Danny? What about them?"

Danny's face contorted thoughtfully.

"You might have a point there."

She patted his arm.

"All you can do is your best, Danny. All I want to do is return to Daniel."

"One thing puzzles me."

"Oh, what is that?"

"At the airfield, you shot them both, even though they were mincemeat."

Grace closed her eyes for a moment, held her breath, thinking.

"I am not proud of it, not now. But then it seemed necessary, for all the pain. One bullet for Nelson, one for Daniel."

Danny looked down, thoughtful, then nodded, looked up again.

"Got your passport and boarding card?"

Grace patted her pocket.

"No sharp objects or liquids in your hand luggage?"

"No."

"How about solid objects?"

Grace looked puzzled. She felt Danny's hand touch hers. Something pressed against her palm. She gripped it instinctively and looked down.

"The Demon's Eye."

"Slipped out of Steele's bag. Can't say I wasn't tempted to hang on to it but bling doesn't really suit me."

"Bling?"

"Never mind, I just thought if it was going home you should be the one to take it."

Grace moved closer, kissed him on the cheek.

"Thank you, Danny."

"And say hello to Daniel from me."

They kept eye contact as Grace moved to the security booth, showed her flight documents. She gave a little wave, then joined the scanner queues. Danny stayed, watching her liquid walk as she moved away from him until Grace vanished into the crowd.

CHAPTER 34

BRIGHTON, FOUR DAYS LATER

Danny looked up from his paper as the street door of the Bellerophon opened and smiled when he saw who it was.

"Detective Pauline, always good to see my favourite Peeler."

"Funny, Danny, very funny."

Detective Sergeant Pauline Myers sat down opposite Danny and put her shoulder bag on the floor between her feet.

"Drink?" said Danny.

"Mineral water, I'm working," said Myers. "You drink too much."

Danny sipped his pint, grinned. "It's like medieval times round here. You know what the tap water tastes like so it has to be beer."

"This isn't a social call. What happened to your arm?"

"Home improvements. Putting up a shelf. Screwdriver slipped."

"And the wrists?"

"My Fifty Shades theme evening got a bit out of hand."

Myers sighed.

"Oh, right, and your friend?"

"What friend?"

"The one you drove to Gatwick."

"Gatwick? Oh, that was just a minicab job for Skidmarks, helping him out on a busy day."

"You are so full of bullshit, Danny. You should go into politics."

"What's all this about?"

"A very good question. Since you've been in Brighton you and your investigation business have done a fair bit. Which is why I'm here to give you a warning."

"From who?"

Myers pointed her index finger towards the ceiling.

"How high?"

"All the way up."

"So it's serious, then?"

"Stop joking, Danny. You've been sailing close to the wind, running risks, not just this latest thing but ever since you set up your dodgy business. It's only because you've had some spectacular results that you've got away with it so far."

"You're saying I've handed you people you couldn't nick yourself."

"It's not funny, Danny. This isn't the Wild West or some Guy Ritchie film. You leave a trail of bodies wherever you go. Not good for the crime figures. It frightens the taxpayers and that upsets the bigwigs. There are rules these days, thousands of the bloody things. And you're embarrassing the people who administer them. Take a holiday, let things cool down."

"A holiday?"

"A gap year, a pilgrimage, whatever. Just go away and be someone else's problem for while."

"So, you help the good guys and this is the thanks you get."

"Danny, I told you. This isn't a joke."

"But it's not kosher is it, not official."

Myers shrugged. "Doesn't matter. Piss them off enough and they'll find a reason to take your front door off its hinges just before dawn. That's what I'm saying. They could make life difficult for you if they wanted, vehicle checks, breath tests every time you get behind the wheel, stop and search when you pop out for a paper. Danny, listen to me, all we need is reasonable suspicion. And suspicion is your middle name."

Danny swirled his half glass of Kronenbourg, watching the bubbles as if they might predict the future.

"Well, Pauline, I appreciate the heads-up."

"Look, Danny, I see a lot of shit in this job, unbelievable shit, what one human being will do to another, scum. You can't let it get to you but sometimes it does. Don't you dare think I'm getting soft but sometimes, in bed in the dark, it's a comfort to know there are a few people out there who try to do the right thing, live their life with a good heart."

"How many have you had?"

"Fuck off, Danny. Forget it. Bad day at the office. Just remember what I said. Piss off till things cool down or there'll be trouble."

"Now that's the Detective Pauline I know. I'll give it some thought."

"Good, I'll have a proper drink now. I bloody need it."

***

BRIGHTON, SIX DAYS LATER

The herring gulls were excited, swooping and screaming in an ever-tightening swirl, eager to be the first to the prize. They were in for a disappointment.

Danny looked up at the grey overcast, watching the birds' black-tipped wings slicing the drizzle that bathed his face, cool and clean.

Only a few hardy revellers had braved the Palace Pier. The rides and stalls were almost deserted although he'd seen a few kids in the amusement arcade and a handful of drinkers sheltering in Horatio's Bar.

They stood in a secluded spot at the very tip of the pier behind the Waltzer and the Crazy Mouse. No one else about. No one watching. The white paint of the salt-crusted Victorian railings was peeling badly and scored along the top with overlapping graffiti and brief declarations of love. The more devoted had clamped love locks to the lacy ironwork below.

They stared out to sea at row after row of grey green waves rolling in. A sudden gust of wind slammed into them. One of the kids, taken by surprise, took a step back. Danny spat over the side.

"Dad!" barked Hayley.

"Just checking the wind."

"That's horrible."

Danny looked down at the restless water.

"Trust me, there's a lot worse down there."

They felt the rumbling vibration of the rides through the wooden decking beneath their feet. Danny glanced down. The planking was old, its edges rounded by wind and rain. Through the gaps he could see dark water churning between the cast iron pilings. The sound of kids screaming as a ride reached its peak was carried to them of the buffeting wind.

"Should you say something?" asked Cheryl.

Danny shook his head.

"It's all been said."

He finished his cigarette and ground it out on the decking. No fire risk on a day like this. They shuffled closer to the railing, Cheryl at the centre, her two kids to one side, Hayley and Wayne on the other. Emma had her arm around Hayley's shoulder.

"Ok, let's get this done."

Danny gripped the container, screwed off the lid. The gull chorus rose to a crescendo as the thin stream of silver-grey ash arced over the railing. They all watched as it was whipped into a faint mist and vanished before they saw it hit the sea.

"Bye, Mum," said Danny.

The gulls screamed their disappointment.

They stood in a sodden semi-circle, watching, as if something might happen. It didn't. Danny could hear the kids' trainers scuffling restless on the wet deck behind him. Then Cheryl's voice.

"Come on, kids. Let's give your dad a minute."

They began to walk slowly back down the pier, braced against the wind that was trying to push them faster.

Danny looked around, east towards the dark spine of the marina, west towards the slender tower of Shoreham power station. He glanced over his shoulder. He was alone. His hand tested the solid weight in his pocket, thinking as he bounced the object in cradled fingers.

It felt strange, reminded him of something, a film. Dickie Attenborough as that psycho gangster, showdown on the pier, maybe even this exact spot, a pistol plopping into the water.

He took it out and flicked it through the railing. The dark L-shape of Grace's Sig Sauer spun like a boomerang until the restless water swallowed it.

Danny's hand closed around the matching shape of the second Sig in his other pocket as he weighed the options, weighed the risks. A solitary seagull, wing tip feathers making tiny adjustments to ride the wind, floated ten feet in front of him, watching.

By the time he caught up with the others they were beyond the Horror Hotel and standing, undecided, by the Dolphin Derby. Wayne had wanted a go. Cheryl had said it wasn't the time.

As Danny approached through the smell of candyfloss and frying he could see their hair plastered flat in rats tails. Dark patches showed on their coats where the wet had soaked the material.

He slipped an arm around Hayley and Wayne.

"Ok, who's for fish and chips?"

***

He dropped the others home in the van but Emma came back with him to the flat, put the kettle on.

Danny felt strangely weary which was odd as he hadn't really done that much. The arm still hurt like hell. Emma brought the tea and sat beside him on the sofa.

"You want half a Kitkat with that? I found it in one of your pockets."

Danny nodded, didn't speak.

"You ok?"

"Fine," said Danny. They sat in silence for a moment.

"Danny?"

"Yes?"

"I've been thinking, you know, about what you said. I was upset, what with your mum, and Benny. If you still want me to do your cleaning and whatever, well, I'd be happy too."

"Fine," said Danny.

When he didn't offer anything else she plumped up a cushion and stood up.

"Might as well make myself useful while I'm here then."

"Ok," said Danny. He smiled, reached out.

"No, Danny. Not like that. Not now. There's laundry."

"Suit yourself."

He turned on the TV. Some afternoon quiz show. Name No1 hits of the 1980s. Danny closed an eye as he concentrated. Two Tribes, Vienna – no, that only reached No2 - Lady In Red, that Band Aid charity thing. He leaned closer to the screen, playing tunes in his head.

***

In the kitchen, Emma started going through an untidy pile of crumpled clothes. It wasn't even worth trying to get the blood out of that shirt. There was too much and it was dried. And she'd found what looked like teeth marks. Lord alone knew what he'd been up to.

Emma turned the pockets of his grubby jeans inside out. A cascade of silver-grey dust and tiny pebbles rained onto the top of the washing machine.

It really was like doing laundry for a naughty schoolboy thought Emma as she swept the mess into the pedal bin.

CHAPTER 35

BRIGHTON, A WEEK LATER

It was going to be a long day for Marie Morgan. She'd been up early to eBay a few more bits and bobs and make some more of her jewellery. The matching earrings and pendants were looking good. She'd sold a few.

And her delivery had been late. The driver was very apologetic, traffic and a loading problem back at the depot, he'd said.

Still, she was on her round now and she could make up a little time. Some of her 90 deliveries were multiple drops to the same address. That saved time and it paid well too, 90p up to £1.70 per item.

Christmas seemed to start earlier every year. You could tell just by the increase in parcels, all shapes and sizes from Amazon and the big stores as people shopped early.

Sometimes it was hard. It was certainly never easy. Marie's old Volvo estate was feeling the strain. The gearbox was getting temperamental after all the stop-start driving and the rear suspension was creaking after she'd pushed her luck a few times overloading.

Sometimes, alone in the evening with a glass of wine, she cried. She liked the courier work, getting around and meeting people, but her degree, a 2-1 in art and design, was a fat lot of use and the loans that paid for it were helping even less.

But she and Zach were doing OK. They are happy together, just the two of them.

There had been no reply at her last drop so Marie had popped the package in a recycling box and dropped a card through the letterbox.

She was halfway down the drive, checking the next delivery on the screen of her hand-held terminal, when something made her look up suddenly.

***

It was chilly with the roof down but this was a day for the wind in your hair, a day of celebration.

Normally Jason Knight hated driving Princess's Beemer. Just the colour made him puke but, as she was always telling everyone, it matched her nails. He preferred motoring in the Audi. That was one cool machine.

But today it didn't matter. What were a few little irritations when you'd smashed it bigtime? Jas had to admit, if only to himself, it had been a close call at times.

When that psycho Lancaster and his bitch had left the Van Alen apartment he'd gathered what he needed and legged it. He left Paulie, sacked him. The guy was a loser, bigtime.

His jaw still hurt like hell, bitch. But it could have been worse, a whole lot worse.

Hiding up at Princess's till the heat died down was inspired. Crap sound system and the bathroom looked like some kind of chemical factory but it had been the smart play. Let things cool. He'd really really thought he was going to get dropped in the shit. They had been some serious players. But he'd ducked and weaved his way through, feinted and scored.

He took a quick glance over his shoulder at the holdall on the back seat, the takings and the formula. They had been some serious opposition, major players. But a bit of fancy footwork and the brains behind them and he'd cracked it. He'd got the money and the know-how to set up anywhere he fancied. Maybe they'd give Ibiza a go. Get a tan. And more. He might change his name too, just to be sure. Pick something classy, something proper showbiz, not his real name, that was for sure. No one was going to party to a DJ called Simon.

He grinned across at Princess.

"Looking good, babe."

"Looking good, Jas."

He turned up the music and put his foot down, pounding the beat on the steering wheel, laughing. Who's the daddy, eh? Went up against all those big bastards and came out on top. A player, I'm a total winner. I should get that tattooed, yeah, maybe in Chinese writing like Beckham. Got the dosh. Got the girl. Got the respect.

He looked across at Princess again. Fit as a butcher's dog. She'd entertained three of the lads at that important promo gig, important to get that right, nothing like a Sunday roast to get the punters taste buds going. Takes it up the arse like a trooper. Princess was a real asset to his business.

And it was an asset he'd invested in, bigtime. Top-of-the-range tits. And top dental work, porcelain, smile that would give a monk a hard-on.

Needed to splash the cash for his image, got to look good, got to look the business.

Just glancing across at the curve of her cleavage was making him hard. Success was making him hard. Jas K unbuckled his belt, dragged his trousers down to his thighs.

"Get busy, Princess."

She looked across, smiled, went to work. Trooper.

Jas pressed the accelerator, driving with one hand, the other cupping Princess's head, urging her to take it deeper.

"That's it, baby. That's it Princess."

He looked up at the sky and roared.

"You lucky bastard, Jas boy. You lucky, lucky bastard."

***

You should get extra for this, time and a half or some special payment. It wasn't part of his job description. He'd have to have a word with the union bloke.

You cave in to something like this and the floodgates are open. They'd be running you ragged in no time, and all on the same rate of pay. It was taking liberties, taking the piss.

Ok, he'd do it this once, just for a quiet life. He didn't need any more trouble right. It was only a bit of cabling, scrap ends really. Everyone banged on about how important it was to go green. All he'd been doing was a bit of recycling. Trouble was, he wasn't sure the court would see it that way, not with his form. With the hearing coming up he'd have to have words with his brief, work on the story a bit.

And Emma, well Emma, that wasn't going to be easy. She'd been in a foul mood since he'd been pulled. Never even got a chance to eat his lamb chops. Bastards!

She'd barely spoken to him but he could understand. She wouldn't be looking forward to him going away again. He'd have to patch things up before the hearing, just in case. But it'd work out. Get a takeaway and some videos in. Get a few drinks down her. She'd be right as rain.

Muttering under his breath, Benny Driscoll hefted the bolt cutters and lined the jaws up on the chain. Weighed a ton. He could get a back injury doing this. And the compo for that would be way more than time and a half or a special payment. That would serve them right, stupid bastards.

He squeezed the handles of the bolt cutters. Nothing happened. Still muttering, Benny squeezed again. The blades sliced through the chain with a sigh.

He looked at the bright cut metal, turned the red padlock over between his fingers. He remembered the message from the time he'd first found it – 'Jessie luvs Jason xxx' with a heart carved around it.

Stupid sods. Why couldn't they just get on with it like normal people and stop making his life a misery.

Benny threw the padlock and chain into his wheeled bin and trundled off along the waterfront.

***

"ZACH!!!"

A spasm of horror twisted Marie Morgan's guts as she saw the car slam into the rear of her Volvo estate.

Parcels stacked on the tailgate scattered over the road. Glass shattered. Metal crunched. The Volvo was shunted along the kerbside, nudged to the halt against the back of a parked van. A hubcap rolled drunkenly away.

"ZACH!!!"

Marie dropped her terminal and ran, heart pounding her ribs as she wrenched open the Volvo's front passenger door.

CHAPTER 36

The high pitched laugh was like music. Big brown eyes looked up at Marie Morgan above a wet, gummy smile. Zach squealed with delight and clapped his chubby hands. Marie snapped open the straps on his child seat and scooped him up, crushed him to her chest.

"Zach, oh thank God, thank God."

Zach threw his head back and laughed as Marie stepped away from the Volvo. She looked beyond the mangled tailgate to the other car, some sort of flashy convertible, a horrible pink.

Marie was about to vent her rage on the driver when she saw him.

The man sat still in the driving seat, eyes terror wide, staring ahead, bloody hands held out in front of him, fingers splayed.

As Marie looked on, bouncing the gurgling Zach in her arms, a woman rose into view behind the cracked windscreen. She had blood around her lips and down her chin. Her mouth was open in a silent scream. She seemed to be choking on something.

***

BRIGHTON, THREE WEEKS LATER

Deep under the duvet, Hayley checked the time on her mobile again. She couldn't believe the thing was really working. This was taking for ever.

Auntie Cheryl had caught her once already, seen the glow under the door. Lights out early on a school night. Now Hayley was under the duvet, earphones in, waiting.

The seconds of the digital clock seemed to be dragging themselves through the minutes as Hayley rocked back and forth, sick with excitement.

Then the hour clicked over, midnight.

The connection was slow but she wasn't surprised. There must be millions and millions of people doing the same.

She watched the download bar creep and twitch as the file struggled with a busy website and the dampening effect of the duvet on Auntie Cheryl's wifi.

Then it was done. Hayley felt sick. Her ears were ringing, heart pounding as she adjusted the headphone and hit 'play', felt her head fill with the music, tried to mouth the words so she could memorise them.

> Looking for something lost
> Don't care the line is crossed
> No matter what the cost
> And you came,
> Hero
>
> Crying through a mist
> Vodka shots, pissed
> Blade on my wrist
> And you were there,
> Hero
>
> Lost in a mist of pain,
> Didn't even know my name...

When the track finished tears trickled down Hayley's cheeks. She played it again, concentrating hard to remember the words.

Scheri's new single was, like, just the most amazing thing ever.

***

Danny had never worried about his knob. He'd read somewhere that some men spent their whole lives sweating over whether the family jewels were up to scratch.

Danny had never worried. It did the business, looked ok, no complaints so far. But this was different. Sometimes you got yourself into situations. Agreed to things without thinking it through.

Once you realised, if you could get yourself out, you did. If you'd dug yourself in too deep all you could do was bite the bullet and wait it out, see it through.

He couldn't move his head, just flicked his eyes sideways. His false leg was propped in the corner. It looked lonely. He wished he could reach for it but he couldn't.

He sipped the shallowest of breaths. To get through this he had to remain immobile. The secret of camouflage, absolute stillness. The slightest movement catches the eye. Suddenly he wondered what mum would think. Laugh, probably.

He sipped another breath. The room was silent apart from the sound of scratching and a ticking wall clock. It seemed to be five minutes fast. At least the place was warm.

The skinny guy with the wild hair and wire-rimmed glasses look very intense, very serious.

The plump woman with the chunky amber necklace bothered Danny more. She had a weird half-smile made more noticeable by her crimson lipstick.

The rest of them he couldn't see, hadn't had time to form a judgment. He was aware of uncertain eyes flicking back and forth, some drawn to the red raw scars on his arm and round his wrists, others to the faded mauves of older wounds and the smiley face of a skin flap below his left knee. So, no option, just wait it out.

The clock ticked. Close by, paper rustled.

"That's brilliant, Danny. Can we try another pose now?"

The tension left the room as people shuffled and stretched. More paper rustled.

He looked across at Wanda, charcoal stick between her fingers, wild mane of bubbling red hair bright above the pale white of the big white art pad on her easel. Her face split into a wicked teethy grin.

"Cheer up, Danny. This is my birthday present. And you're getting ten pounds an hour."

Danny couldn't stop himself laughing.

The woman with the crimson half-smile couldn't stop herself watching his penis jiggle.

END

ROUGH DIAMOND

THE AUTHOR

Bill Todd is a journalist and award-winning travel writer who has visited more than 40 countries from Arctic Finland to the deserts of Namibia.

He enjoys Greece, maps, genealogy, military history, strong cheese and good beer. Bill is married with a daughter and lives in Brighton and London.

The Wreck Of The Margherita, Death Squad and Rough Diamond are the first three Danny Lancaster stories. The fourth, Rock Hard, will be published Winter 2013.

NAMIBIA

Namibia is spectacular, a vast, beautiful empty place that deserves to be more widely appreciated. It was a German colony in 1884 until they were pushed out by the South Africans in 1915 in a little-know campaign of the First World War.

Namibia became an independent republic in 1990. Etosha national park in the north offers the classic safari experience of lion, elephant and rhino while the Namib Desert is the world's oldest.

Its sand sea is a vast stretch of dunes up to a thousand feet high and twenty miles long. The colours and the silence truly take your breath away.

THE FAIRMILE D AND COASTAL FORCES

The houseboat featured in Rough Diamond is based on MTB 618, a Fairmile D "Dog Boat" that saw out its days at Shoreham after an active wartime career.

Coastal Forces are among the many unsung heroes of World War Two. MTB 618 was crewed by men of the Royal Norwegian Navy and operated from Lerwick in Scotland, battling treacherous seas and a brutal enemy to attack shipping in Scandinavian waters and ferry men and supplies.

The crew of MTB 345 were captured. After interrogation by the Gestapo they were tied to depth charges and dropped into a fjord near Bergen.

For more about these small frail boats and their brave crews, visit www.coastal-forces.org.uk

ROUGH DIAMOND

THANKS

Rough Diamond is a work of fiction but I have tried to make it as real and as accurate as possible. Please excuse any tweaks of fact to keep the story moving.

The characters are creations of the imagination. Any errors or omissions are mine but I could not have written the third Danny Lancaster novel without the help of many people who contributed their time, enthusiasm and knowledge.

On land and sea, I would particularly like to thank Keith Ring QFSM, former Brighton borough commander of East Sussex Fire And Rescue Service; Paul Metcalfe, RNLI operations manager for Eastbourne Lifeboat Station; Ross Hardy, director of the Beachy Head Chaplaincy Team; Physiotherapist Paul Brown for guidance on sports injuries; Peter Ritchley of Headley Court; Andy Merricks of Skerritts, Hove, for his detailed local knowledge; James Howson for his chemistry insights; the people at southshields-sanddancers.co.uk; Angela Reed of the Shields Gazette; Małgorzata Kosidowska; Paul Moreton; and Stuart Higgins.

In the air, I'd like to thank Janie Lubbe of Scenic Air charters, Namibia; Christelle du Toit and Tamsyn Kintscher of Sossusvlei Lodge & Conference Centre and Desert camp, and pilots Stefano Uys of Desert Air, Namibia, and Dewald Visser; Paulus Homateni Nakawa of Air Namibia; and Shoreham RAFA Airshow press officer John Periam.

Not forgetting Fran, Zoe, Antony and John Gaule for their help and patience and Paul Thorogood for his keen eye and enthusiasm. Additional thanks to Zoe and Mike for the cover artwork and Steve and Charlotte of stevehampshirephotography.com.

Thanks, too, to the many others who have given their time, expertise and experiences, you know who you are.

And not forgetting the city of Brighton and Hove for being such a varied and exciting backdrop for Danny's investigations.

I also offer my gratitude and respect to John David, Frederick and Neville. They shall not grow old.

Bill Todd, Brighton, 2013

Danny Lancaster will return for his fourth investigation in
ROCK HARD
- published Winter 2013. Here's a taste:

The heat was murder but that wasn't the worst of it. There were the bodies. They'd seen them from the road, knew what had happened. They knew it was pointless but had to check, had to cover themselves.

Javier had bumped the minivan onto a dusty patch by the side of the road. Joaquin climbed out and scanned the beach through binoculars. The rest of them stayed in the vehicle, making the most of the aircon.

It didn't last. Joaquin waved them out and they all clambered into the searing sun. The Englishman winced. Even with shades on the brightness made his head hurt.

They started down a narrow sandy track. The Englishman hung back, reluctant, lighting a Marlboro before he followed the others.

The path wound down a sand dune pocked with tufts of coarse grass like an old man's chin. It wasn't much of a challenge but the Englishman still stumbled, the toes of his trainers clipping embedded rocks. His sweat-sodden T-shirt stuck to his body like clingfilm. At least it was quiet and there was no traffic.

When the slight breeze dropped away completely it was quiet and still. He could hear himself wheezing.

He clawed his wet T-shirt away from his beer gut, tripped again, kept his eyes on the track. It saved him having to look forward toward the waterline.

They were spread out around the little cove, a dozen or fifteen of them, sprawled and limp, arms waving with the water like a bored chorus line. Fit young men, women, kids, a baby.

Scattered around them was the wreckage, what there was of it. A few broken planks, an oar, some plastic sheeting, drinks cans, a load of plastic mineral water bottles.

The others were walking the line of bodies, kicking one here and there to be sure. The Englishman hung back. What was the point? He shouldn't be even here. Fucked up again. He could just hear The Ex's voice screaming at him.

When he glanced up he wished he hadn't. Joaquin was waving him over. Slowly, dragging his feet, the Englishman walked up to him.

"This make you sick?"

Joaquin grinned. The Englishman heard sniggering behind him, said nothing. What was the point? He knew what had happened. They all knew. Just one of the risks of the business. Unfortunate but there you go. No big deal. They'd paid up front.

They'd handed over more money than they'd ever seen in their lives and set off. Desperate people heading for hope in a belt of bright light on a hostile shore. So near and yet so far.

They weren't sailors, many had never seen sea, never heard of currents and tides.

It could have been anything. One person panics, kicks off, then they're swamped, all in the drink, non-swimmers splashing for their lives in the darkness. Or it's all ticking along nicely when a cliff of ship's bow powers out of the night, flooding them, smashing the boat, sucking them under where the gigantic copper alloy propellers made them into mincemeat.

The Englishman tried not to look at Joaquin. His eyes went down to the body at his feet.

What was he? 12? 13? The eyes rolled up behind half-closed lids made the kid look like some sort of zombie. The skin was blue black but the age, the build, he could be Jackie.

The Englishman could hear The Ex shouting again. Wondered how Jackie was getting along with his mum and a new dad. A fucking estate agent, for chrissake. What was it? Darren? Darryl? Gelled hair and greasy personality to match.

He hoped Jackie was ok, really hoped. He had footballer's legs, skill, potential, should be out kicking a ball, getting into a big of bother. That boy would be a magnet for the girls when he was a bit older.

The Englishman wished he could be there to see it but it was too late now. He'd fucked that up big style. He slapped his bicep as an insect landed. The sun was making the big angry mosquito bites all down his legs itch like hell.

Joaquin grabbed his arm, squeezed. The Englishman broke the grip, shook him off.

"This make you sick, English?"

The Englishman looked down again. The boy's knock-off Man United shirt was sun faded. It was a No3 shirt, Patrice Evra. Is that what the boy had dreamed of? The shirt was torn under one arm. Kids playing? Heavy tackle, maybe?

Big black flies were flickering around the boy's eyes, lips and nostrils. The Englishman waved a flip-flopped foot at them. They scattered, then immediately started to settle again.

"What's the point of this? We know what happened. Why hang about?"

Joaquin's laugh triggered the sniggering again. The Englishman wiped trickling beads of sweat from his forehead with the back of his hand, wiped it on his shorts, turned, started for the path.

They were calling out now, taking the piss. He didn't stop, didn't look back. When he reached the minivan he pulled open the door, sat on the step, lit a cigarette.

Looking down he saw one of the others rummaging through a backpack. Another pulled bangles from a dead woman's wrist.

He could feel his heart pounding, the beat thumping in his ears. Fucking heat, fucking flies, his whole life was one fucking big dog's breakfast.

Then the Englishman had an idea. He pulled his mobile from the pocket of his shorts, began to scroll through contacts. The others were starting up the path.

He found the number, looked at it on the little screen. As he lifted the phone to his ear someone grabbed his wrist. The Englishman looked up into Javier's dark suspicious eyes.

"What are you doing, English?"

"Phoning a friend." He shook of the restraining hand, pressed dial.

The pause seemed to last for ages. Then the phone began to ring. When he looked up, Javier was at the front of the vehicle, whispering to Joaquin. Both men looked back towards the Englishman.

The phone kept ringing. The others were dawdling up the path now, casting curious glances.

The phone kept ringing.

Javier said something else to Joaquin. The boss nodded, then they both looked back at him again.

The phone clicked. "This is the Vodafone voicemail service for...."

Bloody voicemail!

"...hang up or press the hash key for more options..."

The voice sounded almost reassuring as he sat amid the heat and flies that were the wreckage of his life.

The Englishman was startled when the recorder kicked in with a beep.

"Oh... hi... yes. Hey, Danny boy. It's me... Pogo."

Find out more at www.billtodd.co.uk